Books by Sierra Cartwright

Mastered

With This Collar
On His Terms
Over the Line
In His Cuffs
For the Sub
In the Den

Bonds

Crave
Claim
Command

The Donovan Dynasty

Bind
Brand
Boss

Master Class

Initiation
Enticement

Impulse

Shockwave

Homecoming

Unbound Surrender

The Donovan Dynasty

BOSS

SIERRA CARTWRIGHT

Boss

ISBN # 978-1-78430-874-2

©Copyright Sierra Cartwright 2017

Cover Art by Posh Gosh ©Copyright 2017

Interior text design by Claire Siemaszkiewicz

Totally Bound Publishing

Published in 2017 by Totally Bound Publishing, Newland House, The Point, Weaver Road, Lincoln, LN6 3QN, United Kingdom.

Printed and bound in Great Britain by Clays Ltd, St Ives plc
1

BOSS

Dedication

For so many new friends, especially those from the Wicked Wine Run group. Your friendship is very much appreciated. Barbara—you're the glue.

Andi Joy—you're a ray of sunshine! April Nichols Wilson, thanks for going above and beyond on my research questions!

Katherine Deane, thank you for the running insight. Sandi Klemencic Fusser, in you I have definitely found my 'people'.

Cassandra Caress, you're so damn inspiring and fun. And of course, there's never a book deadline without BAB. Yeah, I waited for you.

Readers, I love to hear from you and interact with you. You're my daily inspiration. Please, keep reaching out.

PROLOGUE

"Is that Kelsey Lane?"

Startled, Nathan Donovan glanced up from his phone screen and looked over at his older brother, Connor. "Yeah. I just got her file."

"On a Saturday night?" Connor raised his eyebrows. "At Grandfather's centennial celebration? Better not let him see you working."

Nathan had snuck off to a corner of the big fucking tent where he'd hoped he wouldn't be disturbed. Since there were nearly a thousand guests in attendance, he should have known better than to think he could work instead of socializing and not get caught.

"Anything interesting?" Connor asked, after a glance around.

Realizing his brother wasn't going away, Nathan turned off the screen and dropped the phone back into his pocket. "She has a master's degree. Been with Newman Inland Marine around six years, including internships. Loyal. Trusted. Exemplary record. Promotions faster than expected."

Connor nodded, as if the information wasn't a surprise.

"What do you know about her?" Nathan asked.

"Not much. Her name crossed my desk a couple of days ago. A recruiter was searching talent for BHI."

Connor's wife owned BHI, and Connor had a seat on the board of directors. As CEO, Lara counted on Connor's support and opinions. "Interesting," Nathan said. As their businesses grew, these types of conflicts were inevitable. Unwelcome, but inevitable. He knew that BHI had interests in shipping and logistics, but since they were ground-and-air based, they were at best minor competition. "What capacity are we talking about here?"

"Oil and gas."

"Interesting."

"We don't have to pursue her."

Nathan refused to stand between her and success with another company. And if her skill set would benefit BHI, they deserved the chance to woo her. "You're welcome to go after her."

Connor no longer seemed to be listening, and Nathan followed his brother's gaze. His wife Lara was talking to a tall cowboy who leaned toward her. Too close, if the sudden scowl on Connor's face was anything to judge by.

"Excuse me," Connor said, jaw set. Without waiting for a response, Connor strode toward his wife.

Thankfully, that left Nathan alone again.

He took out his phone and returned to the information on Kelsey. *Info?* If he was honest with himself, he would admit he wasn't only interested in her biography. He wanted to look at her picture.

Her smile appeared a bit forced, as if she were impatient with the photographer. Even that didn't detract from the beauty of her hazel eyes, the fullness of her lips or the sight of her long, dark hair.

Everything about her appealed to him.

If the acquisition went through, the gorgeous Kelsey Lane would be his assistant.

That was incentive to work longer and harder.

A couple whose names he couldn't remember stopped to chat. Hiding his annoyance, he put his phone away and shook the man's hand.

It took a full five minutes before their attention wandered and they excused themselves.

He wondered how many more times he would be required to smile before making an escape. Unbelievably, people were still arriving. Some were even in limos, which was supremely impractical on a ranch, not just because of the dirt roads but also the distance from a major town.

Straddling the line between irritation and impatience, he glanced at his watch. Not that it was a watch, even though it told time with the accuracy of an atomic clock. The unit was more like a mini-computer. It never needed recharging since it was powered by his body's movements. Barring that, light reenergized it. The Julien Bonds-created masterpiece wasn't just intuitive, it often anticipated Nathan's actions.

The unit vibrated. In response, he swiped his finger across the sapphire-glass surface. A tiny hologram of his sister-in-law Sofia appeared. Beneath her, in script that advanced forward as he read each word, Sofia said, *"It's not yet eight o'clock, Nathan. You're expected to stay at least two more hours. As a reminder, please ask your mother to dance. And oh, Connor just told me to lock you out of the Wi-Fi until eleven p.m., even at the guest house, so even if you run away, you won't be able to get online. He says it's for your own good."*

What the fuck? He went to swipe away the image, but she started speaking again. *"You might as well relax, have something to drink and enjoy yourself. Bye-bye!"* With a cheery little annoying wave, her image vanished.

He groaned.

Everyone apparently knew he'd rather be anywhere but here. *Fucking parties. Waste of time. Even bigger waste of money.*

He ran his finger along the inside of his shirt collar. Even though it was October, it was hotter than hell at the family's Running Wind Ranch in South Texas.

If it had been his choice, he'd have stayed in Houston to work on the Newman Inland Marine deal. It was getting close to crunch time. He was sleeping fewer and fewer hours, fueled by the challenges and opportunities. It was heady stuff. To him, it was like a drug. And he was all but shaking with the need for his fix.

As if on cue to save him, a server passed by, bearing a variety of wines all from locally grown grapes.

"Don't mind if I do." He snagged a glass of something red.

"Glad we didn't burn the ranch house down?"

At the words, he turned to see his sister, Erin. "It's not too late, is it?" he asked.

"Stop it, you cheapskate. This is fun."

"Fun?" Maybe to some people it was.

"Sofia did a hell of a job."

Even he had to admit that, despite the exorbitant cost. He'd secretly scoffed at her idea of erecting tents on the grounds. He'd even wondered aloud if the whole thing were a circus.

But the inside didn't resemble a tent. The thing was massive, had windows, tables, a dance floor, French doors and, blessedly, air conditioning. She'd even managed to get the Matthew Martin band to interrupt a nationwide tour to provide entertainment. It was world-class, from covers to their own top-ten hits, ballads to country swing, and they'd even managed a few obligatory line dances. Not bad for a band that had won country music's most prestigious award three out of the last five years.

"Granddaddy says this will be good for business."

"Not sure how that's possible when we're locked out of the Wi-Fi."

"For Christ's sake, Nathan. You won't die without your phone. Have you always been such a bore? I used to enjoy hanging out with you." She frowned. "At least I think I did. Maybe my mind is playing tricks on me."

Sometime during the evening, she'd ditched her shoes. Her hair was piled on top of her head and she'd woven some small white flowers through the strands.

She'd chosen an interesting outfit, a short leather skirt and a black corset. *Of course.* "Dressed to spite me?"

"Please." She rolled her eyes. "Get it through your thick skull. Not everything is about you."

This was an old argument. He and Erin saw financials differently. She insisted he was overly cautious, to the point of being out of step and stuffy. He didn't mind the accusation. When his father had died, Connor had inherited a company headed toward disaster. Nathan had seen how close the Donovans were to losing the hard-fought legacy that had been handed down through the generations. When he'd been appointed CFO, he'd vowed to be a good steward so that future Donovans would have something to be proud of.

Erin preferred to live for the moment, determined to do what good she could for the world. She was a dreamer. He was a planner. And when she'd approached him to invest in her friend's corset store, he'd refused.

Undaunted, she'd used money from her own trust fund to help her friend.

"So, do you like it?" she asked, interrupting his musings.

"Like what?"

"The outfit." She spun. "I'm modeling it."

"You're what?"

"Helping visibility of the shop by showing how versatile the piece is. It can be worn anywhere, even a fancy event. Corsets are not just for the bedroom."

"They should be." Or a BDSM club, which was where he preferred them. He loved lacing a submissive into one, cinching it tight so he could enjoy looking at her cleavage.

Erin smacked his arm.

"And the necklace…? Are you also modeling it?"

"Oh, this?" She touched the exquisite—and if he didn't miss his guess, fucking expensive—teardrop pendant. "No. This was retail therapy."

"Was there a reason you dropped money on an extravagant piece of jewelry?" She'd inherited a treasure trove full of stuff from their great-grandmother. Surely she could have just reset some of those stones.

"I bought it right after Connor's wedding reception," she answered vaguely.

Before he could ask anything else, she took a sip of wine. "This is good," she said approvingly before taking a second, longer drink. "So, why didn't you bring a date? That would have helped."

He regarded her. "To this command performance?"

She shrugged. "I know what you mean."

Since all of the family members had arrived Friday and planned to stay until Sunday, he'd nixed the idea of bringing a woman he barely knew to meet the family, endure endless questions and share his space.

There was little room in his life for a relationship, and he was fine with that. He adored the subs at Deviation, the city's intriguing new BDSM club. An occasional visit satisfied his primal needs. And after a few hours, he went home, even more focused on business. Scenes didn't just soothe his savageness, they energized him.

Glass in hand, he walked over to where his half-brother Cade stood talking to his mother, Stormy.

Although Nathan was a little surprised she'd accepted the invitation, he was pleased to see her. To his knowledge, it was the first Donovan event she'd ever attended.

"Stormy." He shook her hand.

"Nathan. Always a pleasure."

The woman was tall, willowy and dressed exactly the way he'd expected. Convention be damned. Her slim-cut jeans were tucked inside boots she'd likely hand-tooled herself. Her white T-shirt was form-fitting, and she wore a brown leather vest over it. She had a quick smile, a firm grip and a direct gaze. He could see why his father, Jeffrey, had fallen in love with her, even though he had been expected to marry Nathan's mother.

The Running Wind Ranch wouldn't have been what it was without Stormy's guidance. And Cade, the oldest Donovan brother, did a damn fine job of running the ranch. It had been Stormy who'd fought for her illegitimate son's inheritance and who'd instilled a love of the land in his soul. Though Nathan had little interest in that part of the business, Cade's intelligence and hard work had made it a financial success. And that, Nathan appreciated.

"Well, look who's here," Cade interrupted with a long, slow whistle.

Nathan glanced over his shoulder and saw Julien Bonds just inside the French doors. "I didn't know he was expected." A group of people moved in around him, blocking him from general view and the always-prying eye of cell phone cameras.

"Connor insisted on sending Bonds an invite," Cade replied. "No one really thought he'd show, but Sofia reserved a guest house for him, just in case. I imagine he took a helicopter from Houston." He shrugged. "I still want to see his prissy ass on a horse."

"I'll give him lessons," Stormy volunteered.

She'd spent years wrangling and was an accomplished horsewoman. If Nathan remembered correctly, she'd been the one who had taught his father to ride. That was probably the summer they'd fallen in love. "I want to ask him about a few of the watch's features," Nathan said.

"Watch? You have a Bonds watch?" Cade demanded.

Nathan flashed his wrist.

"Fuck," Cade said. "How the hell did you rate?"

"I indicated an interest in investing. He turned me down. Says he won't go public and let some board of directors interfere with his creative ideas." The man was on track to having one of the largest privately held firms on the planet. "As a consolation prize, he sent it to me for beta testing."

"And?"

"It's astounding. But…"

"But?"

"Quirky."

Cade frowned.

"Plays theme music when it's turned on. And the hologram—"

"It has a hologram?"

"Of Bonds himself. Greets you personally and suggests ways for you to improve your life." The ego was astounding. Last week, Bonds had recommended Nathan go to bed

13

slightly earlier and sleep longer, saying his life expectancy would increase if he enjoyed more REM sleep. Bonds had added that Nathan would be twice as effective if he slept twenty percent longer, which was a good investment of his time, according to the genius.

After that, Nathan had taken the fucking thing off almost every night when he got home from the office. Problem was, it was so useful that he missed it. "Who's that with him?"

"Meredith Wolsey." Cade took a drink of beer. "Heard he brought her to Connor's reception."

"What? Bonds was there?"

Cade nodded. "They stayed on the patio. Only a handful of people saw them. I wasn't one of them, either. I heard about it from Sofia."

"Sneaky bastard."

Erin, a determined frown buried between her eyebrows, descended on their small group. "Dance with me." Erin grabbed Nathan's wrist and dragged him toward the front of the tent.

"I was just going to say hello to Julien and Meredith. Go with me? It's been a long time since you've seen him, hasn't it? Not since that night in—"

"Nathan, please," she said.

"Can't it wait?" He scowled.

Generally Erin was a great hostess, and he'd bet she'd chatted with everyone in attendance. But the way she pleaded and looked at him, eyes beseeching, he had no choice. She'd always been a pest, the little sister who could get her big brothers to do almost anything she wanted. After the death of their father, something that had devastated her and sent her to her room for weeks, she'd become even more indulged.

Cade shrugged as if to say *better you than me*.

"Now. Excuse us," she said to Stormy and Cade.

Nathan put down his wine, and she was already tugging on him. "Stop dragging me," he told her.

Her grip was desperate and her nails were digging into him. Despite the fact that he hated to dance, he went with her.

"Lead on," he said.

On the floor, to the beat of the music, he led her into a two-step. "What's the panic?"

"No panic." She gave him a huge, sunny smile.

If he hadn't noticed the way she glanced to the back of the room, at Julien and Meredith and their sudden mob of people, he might have believed she just wanted to dance. After all, she'd put her four-inch heels back on.

She lapsed into silence, and he let her, since that suited him, as well.

At the end of the number, she thanked him then excused herself before heading toward their mother, who was seated at a table with a few of her friends and his aunt, Kathryn... as far away from Stormy as possible.

When he reached Julien and Meredith, the enthusiastic greeting party had thinned, and they were standing with Cade.

Cade introduced Nathan to Meredith, an attorney he'd hired from a prestigious firm in Northern California. Julien's hand rested on the small of her back, which Nathan recognized as a move of easy intimacy. To his eye, they were much more than professional associates. And since he suspected Bonds at least dabbled in BDSM, there might be some possessiveness there too.

They made a striking couple—Bonds with his tight, slim-fitting jeans, dress shirt, leather jacket, narrow tie and trademark hideous tennis shoes, and Meredith with her open-back black gown. As dark-haired as he was, she was his blonde counterpart. A recent celebrity magazine had called them the newest power couple.

"What do you think of my masterpiece?" Julien asked as they shook hands.

"It's..." How did he tell the creator what he thought of the watch?

15

"You love it, don't you? I still have a few things to work out with the hologram."

"About that—"

"The tone of my voice isn't quite right when I give the daily update." He shook his head. "My engineers haven't done the synthesizing correctly."

"It's supposed to do that?" he asked incredulously. "Tell me I need more sleep?"

Julien scowled. "Of course it is. That's why people will buy it."

"I see." He actually thought some people wanted him to boss them around? Nathan wondered whether the man was certifiable or a genius.

"Overall?" Julien persisted.

"It's fucking indispensable."

Julien's mercurial frown vanished and a slow smile spread across his mouth. "Indispensable," he repeated. "Yes." Then he touched the screen of his own device. His image popped up. "Use the word indispensable in the marketing materials."

Julien's image bowed toward him. "Yes, genius."

The voice, the tone, was dead on.

Obviously the engineers had heard that term plenty.

Julien brushed the sapphire-glass surface and the hologram vanished. "Where were we? I wanted to congratulate the Colonel."

Cade pointed out the table.

Before walking away, Julien said, "I'll upload the latest software update to you next week."

"You mean I need to download it?"

"No. It will happen automatically."

"How intrusive is this thing?"

"Check your heart rate when you see a beautiful woman and ask me then." Julien nodded politely before walking away.

"I think he wants to rule the world," Sofia said, joining them. "I caught the end bit."

16

"Rule it?" Nathan asked. "Dominate it is more like it."

Cade shrugged.

The band segued into an up-tempo song and announced yet another line dance.

"Show me how it's done, Mr. Donovan," Sofia said. "The only reason I accepted this job was to see you line dance. Remember?"

Proving how besotted he was, Cade tipped his hat. "Anything for my lady."

With that, as if there were no one else on the planet but the two of them, they headed toward the dance floor.

Nathan resumed his favorite position, an arm propped on one of the bar-height conversation tables.

A tall brunette wearing a sequined dress so tight it should have been impossible for her to move sashayed past him. She caught his eye and smiled. Everything about her was perfect — hair, makeup, shape.

She stopped long enough to accept a glass of wine and to look back at him, being sure he noted her interest.

Rather than engage, he checked his watch. And his heart rate.

Clearly Julien was wrong about the watch. It didn't show any reaction to the bombshell who was telegraphing her availability.

He looked back up to note that she'd moved on to someone considerably more appreciative.

Which left him free to peruse his own thoughts. There was little Nathan enjoyed more than the strategy. Except the chase.

1

Juggling two venti mochas with extra whipped cream, her electronic card key, a purse and a bag stuffed with her workout gear, Kelsey Lane exited the elevator and strode toward the set of double doors at the end of the hallway. Since it wasn't even seven o'clock, she had almost the whole building to herself, something she liked, especially on Monday mornings.

This early, if she drove, she typically didn't have to fight traffic on Houston's busy roads. If she rode the train, she could always find a seat. Regardless, she liked to get a jump on the week, organizing and preparing before the phone started to ring.

The lights were on in the office, so she tested the handle, hoping the cleaning crew was still there and that the suite was unlocked. Thankfully it was. "Good morning!" she called out so she didn't startle anyone.

With her foot, she shoved the door closed behind her.

She moved through to her desk and put down the drinks and keys before dropping her purse and bag on the carpeted floor. Then she turned to open the blinds so that she could see the upcoming sunrise reflect off the nearby skyscrapers. This had to be one of the biggest perks of her job. A spectacular view of Houston, from forty stories up.

As she turned, she noticed a potted yellow hibiscus in the corner. It hadn't been there when she'd left on Friday evening. While it was beautiful, it wasn't something that Samuel Newman would have brought in.

"Hello."

Startled by the very masculine, very sexy bass that

sounded nothing like her boss's voice, Kelsey glanced up.

A man she'd never seen before filled the doorway and she sucked in a panicked gasp. His shoulders were unbelievably wide. He had on a white long-sleeved shirt with turned-back cuffs. A light gray tie was loosely knotted around his neck, and he stood with arms folded across his chest and a slight frown on his face.

Fear and uncertainty slammed her pulse into overdrive. "Can I help you?" She reached toward her phone so she could alert security about an intruder, though how anyone could have gotten past the guards in the lobby puzzled her.

"You're Kelsey Lane. And I promise you, you don't need to call for help."

Kelsey scowled. "You seem to have me at a disadvantage. Mr…"

"Donovan. Nathan Donovan."

She exhaled in a rush and moved her hand away from the phone. Of course. Though she'd never met any of the Donovan brothers, she knew their reputation. Cool. Fearless. Calculating.

Nathan, if she remembered correctly from the numerous articles she'd read in Houston's weekly business newspaper, was the youngest son. He reportedly had an uncanny eye for numbers, for investments. As the financial brain behind the family dynasty, he'd ruthlessly acquired business after business, streamlined them, sold some of them off and made others operate on thin margins, exhausting the remaining employees while terminating the rest. But one thing they all had in common after he was finished with them was profitability.

"I see you've heard of me."

"Who hasn't?" she returned. He was rumored to be outwardly friendly in a way that disguised his true Machiavellian personality. He wasn't a man to be underestimated. But the bigger question was, what the hell was he doing in Samuel Newman's office before seven o'clock in the morning?

"Was any of it good?" he asked.

"Any of…?"

"The things you've heard about me."

He looked at her through shockingly green eyes, and his gaze was so intense that she had to resist the impulse to squirm. His voice was a rich, deep baritone. Though she imagined his words were meant to keep things light and invite conversation, ribbons of unease gripped her stomach.

Rather than answer directly, she hedged, "Is Mr. Newman in there?" She leaned her head to the side, but she was unable to see past Nathan's body and into the office beyond.

Nathan scowled. "I assumed you'd be expecting me."

A moment earlier he'd seemed at ease, welcoming. But now he looked ferocious. His jaw was locked and he took a step into the room, narrowing the distance between them.

"He didn't call you? Contact you in any way?"

She shook her head.

He cursed, low and vicious, making her wince.

"Newman was supposed to tell you," he said.

"Tell me what?" Her legs no longer seemed able to support her and she sat on the edge of the polished desk.

"He no longer works here."

"But…" She grabbed for her purse and dug out her cell phone. This simply wasn't possible. "What do you mean he doesn't work here? It's his company." Newman Inland Marine had been battling some legal and financial issues, but nothing insurmountable. Or so she'd thought. She'd stayed late on Friday going over some paperwork, and she'd told her boss she had no plans over the weekend and that he should feel free to call her if he needed help with anything.

He'd looked at her over the rims of his glasses and given a tight smile before sending her on her way. When she'd said goodbye, he'd given no hint that anything unusual was happening.

She keyed in her phone's passcode then checked the display. There were no messages or missed calls.

Literally and figuratively, Nathan stood there, larger than life, giving her space to sort through things at her own speed.

"I'm afraid I'm confused." She didn't want to call Nathan a liar, but...

"Ask him." He tilted his head, indicating her phone.

After nodding, she dialed the number. She reached Mr. Newman's voice mail.

The recording was so loud she knew Nathan could hear the tinny echo. She left a brief message then followed it with a text. Not that Samuel would respond to that. He preferred to speak to people. More than once he'd said that texting and messaging were ridiculously impersonal, and he would never do business that way. He was proud of Newman Inland Marine for the way it treated its customers. Incoming calls were answered by real people, not a voice-mail system.

Which made his current behavior all the more puzzling.

"You should have been among the first people told."

She put the phone on her desk. "Until I hear otherwise, Mr. Donovan, I'm afraid my loyalties are to Mr. Newman. And I'd ask you to stay out of his office."

He gave a curt nod. "While you wait for him to call back, why not look at the sign on the door?"

After scowling at him, she pushed off the desk and walked toward the double doors. With every step, she was aware of Nathan Donovan watching her, studying her.

In the hallway, she looked at the brass plaques on the wall.

Breath rushed out of her lungs.

When she'd left on Friday evening, the wording on the top one had said *Newman Inland Marine*. It now read *Donovan Logistics*.

The second plaque—the one that had been engraved with her boss's name—had been replaced with one that bore Nathan's. The metal gleamed, new and promising.

Unable to help herself, she traced the capital *D* with a

shaking finger.

Now what?

Everything Nathan had said appeared to be true. No matter how powerful they were, Donovan Worldwide would not have been allowed to come into the office building over the weekend, replace signage and access the executive office suite. It evidently meant nothing that Mr. Newman hadn't spoken with her. And that shocked her. She was supposed to be his greatest confidante, privy to all the things that went on in the company. What else didn't she know?

She pulled back her shoulders from their dejected slump. She had no choice but to face her future. But that didn't mean she had to like it.

"Satisfied?" he asked.

He stood in the middle of the space—her space— arms folded over his massive chest. With his legs spread shoulder-width apart, he looked imposing, commanding, comfortable. As if he owned the entire freaking place. Which he appeared to.

"I'm perplexed," she admitted. Sidestepping him, she hurried toward her desk, her shoes silent on the plush carpeting. Until now, she hadn't noticed how small the area was. In her stiletto heels, not a lot of men had the ability to make her feel small. But with Nathan and his massive, more than six-foot-tall body in the center of the room, things seemed dwarfed.

Because she was a little uncomfortable, she sat in the custom, ergonomically designed chair behind her desk and reached for her coffee.

Then, because he stood in front of her and towered over her, she wished she hadn't. "Do you mind explaining things to me?" she asked.

"Why don't we go into my office?"

Her first instinct was to reply that it wasn't his. The next was to say she'd rather stay here. Then curiosity trumped both thoughts.

Coffee in hand, Kelsey grabbed her cell phone and followed him.

The sight of the office made her gasp. In just two days it had been transformed.

Gone were all the framed snapshots of Samuel's friends and family. The oversize picture of him and the governor of Texas shaking hands and grinning was nowhere in sight.

And that was only the beginning of the changes.

Shelf after shelf of knickknacks and memorabilia had been removed. On Friday, every key moment in Samuel's life had been memorialized in some way, from newspaper clippings to trophies, certificates to awards.

And now… The bookcases had been ripped out. The cozy, inviting leather guest chairs facing the desk had vanished. A pair of low-slung, modernistic ones were wedged against a far wall, clearly not inviting visitors to linger.

The blinds had been replaced by a privacy screen, and a minimalistic terrarium filled with cacti sat on the window ledge. Somehow, even the scent of cigar smoke had been obliterated.

The homey green walls had been covered in a no-nonsense steel-gray paint. And the words Donovan Logistics had been stenciled on the wall in bold, black lettering.

Every trace of Samuel Newman and his caring, effervescent personality had vanished.

Nathan pulled over a chair for her. "Please. Have a seat."

She remained standing. That didn't stop him from sinking into a space-age-looking chair, crafted of steel and covered in a breathable mesh fabric. His desk and matching credenza dominated the room. And that was the only word for it. Dominated. The pieces were massive. Nathan had dual, oversize flat screen monitors, all bearing the Bonds Electronics logo. His cell phone was propped on a phone stand so he didn't even have to glance down at it when it rang.

This looked like a place from which Nathan Donovan could rule an empire.

He leaned back, silent, waiting for her decision.

Eventually, she sat. The chair wasn't as uncomfortable as it looked.

She noticed the pile of manila folders on his desk. The top one was open, and she glanced at it. Her personnel record.

Her pulse skidded to a standstill. Until now, she'd only been concerned about Samuel. But she realized Nathan probably intended to replace her, as well. Of course, her résumé wasn't up to date. She'd invested years into her current job, building the company and relationships. If she were honest, she'd probably sacrificed too much in terms of her personal life as well.

"There have already been a lot of changes," he said when she met his resolute gaze. "And Samuel impressed on Donovan Worldwide how important you will be to the success of the takeover."

He hadn't said merger. Which meant things weren't friendly. She exhaled.

"If you'd like to continue your employment, Ms. Lane, you're my new assistant."

"Your..." Kelsey wasn't often at a loss for words, so she took a drink of her mocha to buy some time. "Mr. Newman is more than a boss to me. He's a mentor. I interned here during my undergrad studies, and he hired me after I received my master's degree. I owe him a great deal."

"And you can repay it by staying on, at least temporarily."

She crossed her legs then recrossed them in the opposite direction. "I can't make any promises until after I talk to Mr. Newman."

"Of course."

Her mind raced. If she didn't know what had happened, it was likely that no one did. She had only another forty-five minutes until the rest of the employees began arriving.

"Why don't you try him again?"

It wasn't like Mr. Newman to ignore her calls. Then again, everything in the last ten minutes had been surreal. She dialed his number. This time, it rang.

Just when she was certain she would get his voice mail, he answered.

"Kelsey." His voice sounded weakened, dejected.

She knew without hearing anything else that everything Nathan had told her was true. The reality she'd been trying to deny crashed into her.

Unable to have the conversation with Nathan watching her, she returned to her desk and slumped into her chair.

"I'm a coward," he told her.

A coward?

"I meant to call you yesterday. But…" He let out a ragged breath. "Forgive me."

Betrayal and confusion rocked her. How could he do this? Not just to her, but to the entire company, hundreds of people.

"I need your help."

She squeezed her eyes shut. In no way was she prepared for this.

"Kelsey…"

Her business instincts kicked in, and she shoved aside her personal feelings. "Is there—was there—a plan to tell the company?"

"It was supposed to be different…" He paused. "I was going to come in and meet with the top management and introduce Nathan. We were going to go to the docks so he could meet the people formally. He's been out there before, a couple of weekends ago."

"Okay. And what's the new strategy?"

She heard jostling and a woman's voice. Then, "Kelsey?"

"Mrs. Newman?"

"We're at the hospital, dear."

Kelsey's jaw went slack.

"It's his heart."

Before Kelsey could utter a word, Holly went on, "The doctors say he'll be fine. But…"

Damn it.

"The company needs you."

Over the last few years, Kelsey had talked to Mr. Newman many times, stressing the need for a succession plan. She'd encouraged him to groom senior managers to take over, or solicit from the outside. He'd been stubborn. He was going to live forever, and there was plenty of time.

Now, she blinked back a sudden burst of tears. There was no more time. Newman Inland Marine had a new owner, and the stress had devastated Samuel.

In the background, she could hear Samuel and Holly whispering, overlaying the hiss and beep of what had to be hospital machinery.

"Samuel wants me to tell you he's counting on you. He wants Donovan to succeed." Holly's voice was taut with emotion, maybe frustration, perhaps anger and certainly some fear.

"May I visit him?"

Holly gave the name of one of Houston's most renowned hospitals then added, "Not today, dear. Perhaps tomorrow. He needs some rest. But, Kelsey? He'll get better faster if he knows he can count on you. He's worried about the employees, as I'm sure you understand."

She gave a tight nod, even though Holly couldn't see her. "You can count on me." After a few pleasantries— platitudes, mostly—she ended the call.

Kelsey put her phone down and gave a shaky exhalation, composing herself. When she looked up, she saw Nathan standing there. "How long have you been there?" And how had he moved so silently?

"Long enough." He pulled up a chair.

The juxtaposition startled her. A few minutes ago, he'd been behind his desk, in control. Now, he sat in front of her, leaning forward, hands steepled, a concerned frown burrowed between his eyebrows. He seemed somewhat less formidable and, because of it, more dangerous.

"Heart attack?" he asked.

"Mrs. Newman didn't exactly say." Knowing Samuel, it could be the stress of turning over the business to someone as ruthless as Donovan. She wasn't sure what had led to it, but she knew it had to have killed him a little bit on the inside. The knowledge angered her, made her pissed off at Donovan.

Since that wouldn't help anything, she took a breath to steady her emotions. "The prognosis is good, apparently."

"Glad to hear that."

"Are you?" she challenged. Perhaps it wasn't wise to antagonize him, but he was the only outlet for her frustration. Indeed, he appeared to be the reason for it.

Nathan sat back in his chair. The concern was replaced by a flash of annoyance, flitting through his eyes with the heat of a brushfire. "For someone who wasn't part of the negotiations, knows nothing about me or my relationship to Newman, that's out of line."

"Are you calling me ignorant?"

"Uninformed," he countered. "And I will certainly educate you as we go along."

The resounding finality in his voice sent a shock up her spine. This man's reputation appeared well-earned. He was controlled, relentless.

"You're the backbone of this company, Ms. Lane," he went on.

She shook her head. "Mr. Newman is."

"Was. In his own words, you were his most trusted advisor. No one else but you knows who everyone is, how they fit, what their value to the company is. If the company is to survive, let alone grow and thrive, it will need your assistance."

"That's a lot of responsibility for an executive assistant."

"You're a hell of a lot more than an executive assistant, and you know it. According to your file, and what Newman said, you're the equivalent of a senior manager or VP. You've got a master's in—what is it called—Global Energy Management?"

He *was* informed.

"I'd hazard a guess that you know as much about the

business as anyone here." He checked his watch, an odd-looking contraption. It was more than a timepiece, she realized.

"We've got about forty minutes until the office workday officially starts," he said. "Some of the managers will start to arrive soon. Rumors will start. The press will find out. We need to get ahead of this." He raked a hand through his hair.

It was at that moment that she saw him as a fallible human. He'd counted on Samuel notifying people. He hadn't shown up this morning planning to handle this alone.

"Are you in, Ms. Lane?" he asked, voice tight. "Will you offer me your loyalty?"

"That's a hell of a request, Mr. Donovan."

"It's more than that," Nathan countered, keeping his voice even. "It's a demand. I only surround myself with people I can trust implicitly." Even though he'd seen pictures, read her employment file, knew about her ambitions, heard how intelligent and indispensable she was from Newman, Kelsey Lane was nothing like Nathan had expected.

He'd arrived slightly after five this morning, and later he'd vaguely heard her enter the suite. The way she'd shouted good morning had penetrated the haze he'd been in since he'd started reading through the biographies of all key personnel, from tugboat captains to the CFO, memorizing names and accomplishments, envisioning each person's role in the success of the company. It wasn't just the cheeriness in her voice that had gotten to him, it was her tone. It was a bit lower than he had expected, containing a sexy rasp that made him think of anything but business.

The first sight of her when he'd stood in the doorway had momentarily taken him aback. Her hair drifted over her shoulders and teased the middle of her back. In the photographs he'd seen, she'd probably been wearing it up.

She was also considerably taller than he'd anticipated. Her business suit was professional, her slim-fitted skirt finishing a couple of inches above her knee. Her white silk blouse clung to her torso, and her jacket had obviously been tailored.

Nothing about the ensemble was inappropriate, except in his thoughts. She wore stockings that he'd mentally replaced with fishnets.

In his mind, he'd traded in her heeled pumps for stiletto sandals before he'd shaken his head to clear the vivid image.

Then she'd tipped back her head and met his gaze, and he'd been captivated by her eyes. They were more hazel than green, beneath dark, well-sculptured eyebrows.

The absolute most fascinating—and dangerous—thing about this woman was the sexual attraction that walloped him.

Even though he was often surrounded by beautiful women, both at work and at Deviation, it had been a long time—years, perhaps—since he'd had this sort of reaction. And it intrigued him. Kelsey didn't seem to intimidate easily, was fiercely loyal and, according to Newman, innately intelligent about how the business operated. Nathan respected that. Brains, beauty and no interest in him? He was done for.

His watch vibrated in a way it never had before. Annoyed and curious, he glanced at it.

He saw a hovering pink heart icon. As he watched, it beat even faster.

Fuck.

Had Bonds been serious? The thing could tell when he was attracted to a woman? The damn thing had lines on it when he was working out. How was it possible the watch knew the difference between exercising and lust?

No mistake, though. Lust was a powerful, precise word. And he felt it for this woman. He couldn't help but picture her on her knees, looking up at him, hazel eyes full of anticipation and trust, and maybe highlighted by a dizzying brush of trepidation.

Determinedly, he shoved aside the thought and pulled

his shirtsleeve over the watch's surface. He continued to remain silent while she sorted through her response, though he guessed what it would be.

She'd brought two coffees with her this morning, which meant she'd thought of Newman on her way in. Nathan was betting that her genuine concern for others would trump her antagonism toward him.

He merely had to wait for her to reach the same, inevitable conclusion.

"Let me be as clear in return," she said finally, looking across at him. "I can't and won't blindly offer you my loyalty. That's not something I give away. It has to be earned." She brought up her chin a fraction of an inch. "It's an extension of respect."

"Well said," he acknowledged.

"Until I know more about you and your ethics, I won't give it to you." Her voice had dropped and he could hear the emotion — nervousness as well as conviction — mixed in. She was testing him as surely as he was testing her. "If you can't accept that, Mr. Donovan, then I'm afraid I'll have to offer my resignation."

"Do you always speak your mind, Ms. Lane?"

"I figured you were a man who appreciated knowing what I'm really thinking. And the truth is, I'm still sitting here because the Newmans asked me to. Not because of you. Because of them and our employees. I think it's highly inappropriate that I came in to find a new name plaque on the wall and everything removed from his office. Samuel Newman is beloved here. By everyone, not just me," she returned.

"So I've heard." And that wasn't necessarily a good thing. Newman Inland Marine often appeared on yearly lists of the best companies to work for in Houston. He knew the man was regarded as a saint, benevolent in ways CEOs weren't renowned for. But it had come at a cost. Newman accepted excuses when he shouldn't, forgave mistakes that should have cost a person their job, allowed employees to be paid for working fewer hours than they reported. And finally, he'd sheltered the tugboat skipper who had been involved in a costly accident.

Truth was, Newman had approached Donovan Worldwide. It had been a desperate move to protect his company's future. The man had already paid out tens of thousands because of the accident. Findings from an investigation were scheduled to be released within a month, and Newman was smart enough to surmise the results might damage the company's reputation.

"The fact that they are now working for one of the Donovan companies will not be received well by most," she said.

He clenched his jaw, but then, realizing it, forced himself to relax.

"And for Mr. Newman's sake, I will help you today. He said he planned to meet with senior staff to introduce you. I understand you were also going to visit the docks."

Setting aside everything she'd said in order to concentrate on business, he filled her in on the details. "Newman was supposed to have arrived by seven. He would have introduced you to me. Then we would have asked the most senior management team to join us in the boardroom at eight."

"Tight timeline." She glanced at a wall clock. "But doable. Did he give you a list of names?"

"It should have been in my email by Saturday noon."

"But it wasn't?"

"That's why I was going through HR files."

She reached beneath her desk to power up her computer.

"He had further suggested we have a company-wide meeting early this afternoon."

"We'll stick with that plan. What was the message?"

"He was retiring."

Her eyes narrowed. "You expected people to believe that?"

"I beg your pardon?"

She picked up her coffee and sipped from it. He couldn't help but notice she hadn't offered him the other cup. And he refused to ask for it. Truth was, he could do with a shot of coffee, badly enough to consider hiring Thompson away from his big brother, Connor. This deal had been in the works for a few weeks, which meant it had moved shockingly fast. Due diligence took him months, even a year.

But branching into logistics was a natural extension for Donovan Worldwide. As it was, their shipments were handled by a brokerage firm. Most of the time that worked well. But if they could broker for others, there was money to be made, and Nathan had been looking at opportunities for a long time.

Starting their own logistics business was always a possibility, but the potential to scoop up a company that was in a perilous condition had galvanized him and the team.

That had meant, however, that he'd operated on less than four hours sleep a night for at least the past several weeks.

"Mr. Newman has always been honest with the company. Transparency is one of our core values."

"So everyone knows that the tugboat captain had a previous accident?"

She opened her mouth. Before she spoke, she closed it again. "He was exhausted. Had a newborn baby at home."

"And?"

Unflinchingly she met his gaze and asked, "Are you always a cold-hearted bastard, Mr. Donovan?"

The words hung between them, a challenge more than a question. Any other employee would be fired for insubordination, and he suspected she knew that. But because he needed her, and because of the genuine note of emotion in her voice, he held on to the edges of his fraying temper. "You don't protect one person at the potential risk of the entire company, Ms. Lane. Perhaps you didn't learn that in business school?"

"Not everything is so clear in life. Have you ever given anyone a second chance?"

"When someone in accounting has an arithmetic error? Sure. But when the risk is this high? Not ever." He paused momentarily to be certain she understood his position. "When his wife gave birth, Seward could have applied for a leave of absence. There are provisions for that. Paid leave, even. Instead, he took medication to stay awake. His history will come out during the investigation. And because Samuel protected him—and continues to do so—the company could be held liable."

Her shoulders slumped.

"The potential fines may still cripple the company. Seward should have been fired after the first incident. The company has a zero-tolerance policy for drugs and alcohol. Showing leniency sets a bad precedent. As my first act as CEO, I am terminating him. You can let HR know, or I will. Which do you prefer?"

Her hand shook as she put the cup back on her desk.

He saw her eyes narrow, barely disguising the anger in them.

"I'll do it." She nudged her chin up.

"Donovan is taking a risk here. A big fucking one, Ms. Lane."

"Don't expect me or our employees to appreciate that," she replied infuriatingly. "Painting Mr. Newman as a villain, or inept, will only make you look bad."

She was right about that. "So what is your recommendation?" he asked.

"We'll say that Mr. Newman realized he had some health issues and wanted to spend more time with his family. You have been working behind the scenes at an effortless transition. The timing had to be ramped up."

He nodded.

"You're stepping up to help him out. We'll do our best to make you look good. Like a hero." She gave a half shrug, as if that weren't possible. Then without giving him the opportunity to respond, she continued, "At this morning's meeting, we'll announce the date of Mr. Newman's official retirement party." She nodded and began scribbling notes on a pad. "We'll host a company-wide event, a barbecue or something, for Mr. Newman as soon as he's able."

"We're watching the budget."

"Employee turnover will cost you much more than a party," she countered. "I'd suggest you don't rob people of the opportunity to say goodbye and pay their respects. Many people have spent their careers here. Unheard of in today's business environment. Like it or not, you will be the target of their anger."

He didn't want to be swayed. After Connor's wedding and the centennial celebration, he'd had enough events to last him for the next decade. All he wanted was an evening at Deviation to recharge. On the other hand, he recognized she had a point. "Very well."

She nodded. "You'll need to present him with some sort of token of appreciation. A plaque, award…" She tapped her pen. "Something. And it will be a good time to distribute corporate goodies. T-shirts, duffel bags, lanyards, the like."

"Budget, Ms. Lane," he said.

"Don't be a penny-pinching miser, Mr. Donovan."

This woman… In all his years in business, he'd never worked with anyone who challenged his authority as much as she did. "Do you often have frivolous gatherings?"

"You mean morale boosters?" she corrected, undaunted. "Yes. Twice a year for the entire company. With pizza parties for each profitable quarter."

"You're serious."

"Each team has discretionary spending for that that purpose too. Teambuilding."

He sighed. At least he saw areas to cut spending going forward. "Is that something you arrange?"

"No. I generally hire it out."

"Good. My sister-in-law's company, Encore Events, will handle it." At least he'd have some form of control that way. "Sofia Donovan. Call her once you've come up with a date. She'll be in my contacts. And add it to my calendar."

"You've given me access?"

He tapped his watch. The annoying hologram of Julien Bonds popped up. Nathan swiped it away.

"What the heck is that?"

"A product I'm beta testing," he replied without looking up.

"Was that Julien Bonds? How did he do that?" she went on without waiting for a reply to her first question.

"Some sort of electronic wizardry. If it weren't so irritating, this would be the most useful tool I've ever worked with." Since he'd already entered her name and company email address, granting her permission to his files and calendar took only two taps on an icon.

A message scrawled across the screen.

Would you like to add a picture of Ms. Lane? For yes, upload now, or tap button to take a photo. Or we can find a picture of her on social media. That could be interesting.

How the hell did Julien's program do that? Freaky as hell.

Nathan tapped a button, tilted the watch toward her and said, "Smile for the camera."

She didn't.

Nathan took the picture anyway.

With her mouth set in a stern line and a slight furrow between her brows, she was quite appealing.

Upload complete.

He glanced at the picture and the beating heart returned to float above the screen. Irritated, he swiped it away then glowered when it moved to the upper right hand corner rather than vanishing as he wanted.

Would you like to notify Ms. Lane of her accessibility, Mr. Donovan?

"Yes," he replied.

Message sent.

Her phone dinged. Good to know that her work email went to her phone.

"You can talk to that thing?" she asked.

"It's intuitive enough that it interacts however you want." Except for the damn glitchy heart-rate monitor.

She glanced at her phone. "My email address has already been changed to Donovan Logistics," she said, sounding incredulous.

"Handled yesterday." Or sometime early this morning. After Friday evening, everything was blurred.

"You move fast."

Over the hands he'd pressed together, he regarded her. "It may seem that way to you. And I'm sorry for that. But it's been in the works for quite some time."

She sat back, as if the air had left her lungs.

"As a rule, in business, I seize good opportunities, but I'm never reckless. I'm methodical, ensuring everything is in order." He tapped his index fingers together. "The timeline was accelerated because Samuel was hoping a change in ownership would allow him the opportunity to defer or decrease fines and penalties. If you'd look at it objectively, you might realize it was a hell of a good decision. And that I'm not the bastard you called me."

"*That*, Mr. Donovan, remains to be seen."

2

"There's a limit to how much I'll tolerate, Ms. Lane. Even from you. *Especially* from you. Are we clear?"

A chill raced down her spine. The way he looked at her, with his stern green eyes focused narrowly on her, made her squirm. No man had ever gotten to her this way before. She didn't like overbearing men. In fact, she did everything possible to get away from them. So this—whatever it was that she experienced with Nathan Donovan—disoriented her. Disturbed her. Left her shaken. Made her want to test him to find out his limits. It was crazy, exciting, scary.

"As I've mentioned, this will all go much better with your support. But I do have people at Donovan Worldwide who I can bring over as an assistant on a temporary basis," he continued. "As for the actual mechanics of this job, I'm willing to bet that, for the right price, I can hire Ted Ramirez."

The name of one of the VPs from North Star Marine startled her, though it shouldn't. Donovan clearly knew the industry and had studied it. North Star was Newman's largest competitor, and no doubt Nathan was correct. Ted Ramirez was ambitious. Ingratiating himself with the Donovans would be a perfect play.

Nathan's voice was relentless, his gaze uncompromising, as he finished, "This discussion is over. You either work for me—with me—or I will happily accept your resignation. I'll see you get a decent severance package."

The threatening tick in his jaw warned her not to push him.

Being fired from this job wouldn't look good on her

résumé. Even if she said she was terminated during the transition, she doubted Donovan would give her a good letter of recommendation. Her choice was no choice. She owed it to the employees, as well as the Newmans, to work with Donovan.

Her entire life, she'd stood up to powerful males...her father and grandfather who had rigid expectations about a woman's role. After her mother's death when she was thirteen, Kelsey had instinctively rebelled against what she saw as oppression.

Even though she'd cared for her younger sister while her father was at the office, Kelsey had diligently fought for scholarships and worked her way through college.

Ironically, Kelsey had chosen to work in a male-dominated industry. Still, nothing in her experience had prepared her to deal with a man like Nathan Donovan.

"I'm waiting."

Pretending her heart wasn't racing, she nodded. "Understood, Mr. Donovan. But I'm not apologizing for anything I've said."

"Noted."

She realized he hadn't agreed with her, only that he'd heard what she said.

"So a truce?" he asked.

From her perspective, it was an uneasy one. After several more seconds, she managed to tear her gaze away from his.

Purposefully ignoring the Donovan Logistics logo that was bouncing across her screen, she moved her mouse to wake up the computer.

After entering her password, she opened a few documents, including an organizational chart. She printed it off and handed it to him.

He glanced at it, put it down then grabbed a pen. "Who needs to be at this morning's meeting?"

She blocked out the image of him, the rakishly long hair and strong jawline that she would find appealing in any other man, and determinedly read off names. He put checkmarks next to them with precise, quick strokes.

"Give me the name of someone who's a maven."

She tipped her head to one side. "I'm not sure what you mean."

"Every company has someone. A person who seems to know everyone and their personal business. Always knows what's going on. Keeper of information."

"A gossip?" she asked.

He shrugged. "But one who people generally like."

"Martha Leone. She's the receptionist for the HR department." Kelsey nodded, understanding where he was going. More and more, she recognized how astute he was.

He scanned the organizational chart.

"She's not on there, but maybe she should be. Martha's been with Mr. Newman since the beginning. In fact, she held this job before I did. When she was ready to retire, we created a position for her with less demanding hours. Martha's the grandmotherly type, and she knows everyone's secrets." Including one or two of Kelsey's own. "Martha gets invited to baby showers and weddings."

"I'll make sure I spend a few minutes with her."

"We should also bring in a few people via video. I'll arrange for it. What time?"

He looked at the watch that she was sure most of the people on the planet coveted.

"I'd like to stick with my original schedule. Eight o'clock?"

It would take a small miracle. Fortunately, having worked for Mr. Newman full-time for four years with a couple more summers where she interned, Kelsey specialized in miracles. "I'll get out a group text and give the IT department a heads-up."

He nodded brusquely before standing. "This isn't the way I'd imagined this morning happening," he said.

"Me either." She'd expected Mr. Newman to arrive, walk into the office suite with a smile, point at the coffee cup and ask, "Is that for me? You're an angel, Kelsey." Instead, he was in the hospital, he'd lost his business, and now she worked for Donovan Logistics and had to call Nathan *boss*.

He extended his hand. "Welcome to Donovan Logistics, Ms. Lane."

She couldn't force herself to respond in kind. But she did stand and accept his hand. Then she wished she hadn't. His grip was sure and strong. She realized how much he towered over her. She was tall, and the heels she always chose put her at or above eye-level with most men, but she stood several intimidating inches shorter than he did.

This close, she breathed in the scent of him. Power and the subtle scent of citrus. It was as alluring as it was potent.

Refusing to succumb to the intimidation and the raw sensation of feminine vulnerability that threatened to engulf her, she tipped back her chin. "I'll meet you in the conference room in thirty-five minutes. We should be early. Down the hall, past the elevators, on the right."

"We'll arrive together," he contradicted as he released her hand.

She'd met a number of powerful, obstinate men in her life. He was light years ahead of all of them.

With a crisp, silent nod, he returned to his office.

Once he'd shut the door, she allowed her shoulders to slump.

The man's vortex consumed her and part of her wondered how she'd survive it, and whether or not she could.

Though she no longer needed it, she took a big drink of the coffee before making the meeting arrangements.

Within two minutes, she'd received a handful of curious replies. A couple of people said they'd be late but they'd be there. The IT manager predictably sent back a message complaining about the short timeline, especially since it was so early on a Monday morning.

She heard the sound of Donovan's voice, and though she couldn't make out the words, his tone was firm and reassuring. Leadership qualities, she noted begrudgingly.

Precisely thirty minutes later, she put her card key badge around her neck and knocked on Donovan's closed door.

That was another thing that was different. Mr. Newman prided himself on accessibility to the staff. Unless he was in a rare private meeting, his office was open.

"Enter."

She turned the knob and popped her head inside the door. "Ready when you are."

Nathan stood then turned down his shirtsleeves. He grabbed silver cufflinks from his desk and threaded them through the small holes.

Despite herself, she watched, fascinated. Although she'd had a couple of fairly long-term relationships, Kelsey had never been with a man who wore cufflinks.

After adjusting his tie, he grabbed his suit coat and shrugged into it before giving a tight nod. "After you." He picked up a manila folder and a silver pen.

He followed her from the office, and the fact that he was behind her made her a little more nervous. Aware.

As they walked down the hall, he fell in step next to her.

"Anything I need to know?"

She purposefully redirected her mind to work. "We've got a couple of people who will be arriving late. Other than that, IT should have the video communication system ready when we get there."

They reached the door and she waved her card key in front of the sensor. When it didn't work, she tried again.

"Allow me," he said.

Skeptically, she stepped aside. Nathan put his hand on the pad and she heard the snick of the lock releasing.

She stared, part in shock, part in awe.

He opened the door, and she went inside and turned on the lights.

"Tell me there's a coffee pot in here," he said.

"One of those individual cup thing brewers, yes." She pointed toward the corner. "You'll find everything you need over there."

He regarded her for a moment, and she squirmed a little uncomfortably. He stood close, too close. But she refused to let him know just how badly he affected her.

Nathan put down his manila folder at the head of the table. He placed the pen atop it at a jaunty angle. "Can I make you a cup?" he asked as he walked away, giving her some much-needed space and simultaneously leaving her uncomfortable that she hadn't offered to make his.

"I've had enough, thanks." Kelsey took her customary place, first chair to his right, and she experienced an unwelcome awkwardness as she watched him try to figure out how to work the coffeemaker.

Then, just because she didn't have it in her to get any satisfaction from watching him struggle any longer, she sighed and stood. "Let me help." She joined him and pointed to the pods. "The ones on the top row are regular. We keep the decaf ones beneath them."

He plucked a pod from the top row. "Don't suppose it can hold two of them?"

"What time did you get up?"

"Three," he replied.

"Seriously?"

"It's a big day."

"For all of us." She poured water into the machine and showed him which button to press.

"We'll need to order new mugs, pens, pads," he said, as he picked up a cup emblazoned with the Newman company logo.

Kelsey nodded. "I'll see to it when I order the corporate giveaways for the party."

"These need to be gone today."

"I'll handle it. Where can I find camera-ready art?"

He tapped his watch and entered a reminder. "I'll have them to you five minutes after we're done in here."

As she started to turn away, he touched her elbow. Kelsey froze as white-hot lightning seared a jagged path through her.

"We don't have to be enemies." His voice was lower than it had been before.

Unconsciously, she moved in closer in order to hear him better. Then, realizing what she had done, she took a step back. "Sugar is in there." She pointed to a glass jar. "And creamer is in the fridge." Needing to escape, she hurried back to the table.

"Please take the chair at the far end," he said.

She blinked. "Mr. Newman preferred I sit next to him." He relied on her to jot reminders on his pad, keep the meeting moving along and to ensure he covered everything he wanted to talk about.

"And I'd prefer you do as I ask."

Her temper started to simmer.

It had been less than a minute since they'd each offered a peace token, and the very next time they spoke, they were at odds. It wasn't just his words, it was his implacable, immovable tone. The man was obviously accustomed to being obeyed. In all things.

Kelsey knew her capitulation wouldn't come easily, and it wasn't an option in the long term. She just wasn't capable of it.

"You're a bigger asset to me if you're at the far end of the table," he continued. "Divide and conquer, as it were. If there's gossip, you'll be able to stanch it. And if we're separated, we'll be able to answer twice the questions." The coffeemaker spit out the last few drips, and he grabbed the cup. "By placing you there, I'm also sending a message that I hold you in high regard. It's a good strategic move."

His logic was sound and reasonable, but no less annoying for it.

"Please," he added.

She exhaled. "Of course, Mr. Donovan."

"You have no idea how much I like hearing those words."

On the contrary. She suspected she did.

He took a drink of his coffee and closed his eyes. For a moment, she caught a glimpse of the stress that he, too, had obviously been experiencing.

Afraid that she was close to feeling a little sympathy for

him, Kelsey shoved it away. After gathering her belongings, she carried them to the far end of the table.

Moments later, Martha swept in smelling as if she'd bathed in lavender. Her long silver hair had shocking chunks of black laced through it. Her toenails were still Halloween orange, and her black T-shirt bore a picture of her oldest grandchild. If that hadn't been enough to demolish the tension between Kelsey and Nathan, her infectious smile would have. It was as if she'd personally hand delivered a ray of sunshine.

"*Ciao*." She waved a hand that was weighted down with rings bearing the birthstones of her kids and a dozen grandkids.

"Morning, Martha," Kelsey replied.

The older woman angled her head toward Nathan with a puzzled frown.

"Martha, I'd like you to meet Nathan Donovan."

"Donovan?" After pursing her lips, the woman faced him. "And what are you doing here, young man?"

Kelsey turned away to hide her smile, really happy she hadn't warned Nathan about the woman's directness.

He greeted her with a smile and a handshake before resting his hips comfortably on the edge of the table. The act made him look less intimidating, more approachable. "I've heard great things about you," he said.

The intractable tone had vanished from his voice, as if it had never existed.

Kelsey clenched her back teeth.

"I know it's a shock, but Mr. Newman is in the hospital." He held up a hand, forestalling her next question. "He's expected to make a full recovery. Ms. Lane will be sending flowers on behalf of the company."

Kelsey scowled, more than a little frustrated that it hadn't already occurred to her to do exactly that.

"As for what I'm doing here..." Conversationally, Nathan relaxed his shoulders.

It wasn't just his posture that invited trust, it was the

warmth in his tone, something she hadn't heard until now.

"Mr. Newman would never have wanted it to be announced this way, but he was in the process of selling the company. We were originally planning to close next year. Obviously the timeline has been moved up, something no one would have wanted or been able to foresee. From here forward, it will be known as Donovan Logistics. Because you've been here so long, we wanted you to be among the very first to know."

He was good. Friendly, direct, inviting trust. Not at all what she'd expected based on his reputation.

"While there will be some changes, I can assure you that there are no immediate plans to restructure. We're pleased with the way things are going, and we'll continue forward."

She noted the way Martha responded to his charm, part sympathy for Mr. Newman, part reassurance for the future. And giving her plenty of gossip to spread through the company. Kelsey was beginning to get a toothache from the way her jaw was set in response to the youngest Donovan brother.

The door opened and two VPs entered. A few seconds later, a sales manager joined them.

It was go time.

She squared her shoulders and made introductions. Within minutes, she was dealing with IT, ensuring remote logins from the docks were coming online and answering questions about Donovan's intentions and Mr. Newman's health.

At one minute until eight, Nathan took control of the room.

He raised his voice the barest hint and asked people to be seated, and he pulled back the chair next to his for Martha. The woman nodded in satisfaction.

As much as Kelsey was loath to admit it, he did a masterful job. Mr. Newman's meetings almost always started around five after, since he waited for everyone to arrive, grab a coffee and get situated.

At exactly eight o'clock, Nathan began. He took out a piece of paper and began addressing the people in attendance as well as those joining via video. He had obviously prepared and rehearsed for this. Though he waved in two latecomers, he kept going and never tripped over a word. Meticulously, he crossed items off his agenda before moving to the next topic.

At every turn, she was reluctantly impressed. She'd spent years trying to keep Mr. Newman focused, but his meetings had always meandered. In contrast, Donovan was on target.

Then he surprised her by inviting her to say a few words about the going-away party. She promised details would be forthcoming by the end of the weekend.

"Thank you," he said, taking control again. "If you have any questions, feel free to ask." He reiterated his key points—jobs were safe, Mr. Newman was appreciated and everyone's help was needed in order to make the transition smooth. "I know you'll do an excellent job of informing your people."

Next he addressed the video attendees, letting them know he intended to visit the docks before the end of the workday.

He passed out a stack of business cards. "Please send me an email by lunchtime letting me know how your meetings went."

Shockingly, he wrapped up in under fifteen minutes. He stayed around to answer a few questions and greet the late arrivals.

Kelsey realized Nathan had set a new tone. Things were more precise and better organized. He'd left no doubt there was a new boss, one who was serious.

She stood and gathered her belongings.

"I like the young man."

With a frown, she turned to look at Martha. "Mr. Donovan?"

"Seems honest. I don't think Mr. Newman would have chosen him as the new CEO if he hadn't been the right person."

Kelsey kept her mouth shut. But she had to acknowledge he'd done a good job if he'd managed to charm Martha so quickly.

After a few more words, Martha went to talk to someone else, and Kelsey took aside Lawrence, the head of HR, to notify him they'd be releasing Seward. She added that she wanted the tug captain to receive three months' severance pay.

"I'll get it calculated right away and request a check from accounting," he said.

After the man nodded and went on his way, Kelsey felt a strange tingle at the base of her neck. She glanced up and saw Nathan looking at her.

Though he was surrounded by others, he was watching her intently.

Did the man miss nothing?

She chatted with a couple of people before escaping to her office to call Sofia Donovan. The number Nathan had provided was her direct line rather than a general number for the company, and Sofia answered her phone on the first ring. Was every Donovan efficient?

Even though she had misgivings about her new boss, Kelsey instantly liked Sofia. The woman struck a balance of warmth and professionalism as she went through a list of questions. Then she added that her sister now ran the Houston branch and promised to have Zoe call Kelsey within the hour to set up a meeting.

Afterward, Kelsey telephoned the florist to arrange flowers for Mr. Newman. Then she texted Holly about the party plans.

Nathan rapped on the corner of Kelsey's desk when he entered their suite, but he didn't slow down on the way to his office.

Still, as if a whirlwind had swept through, it took her a couple of minutes to remember where she was and get back to work. She forwarded the new corporate logo to her preferred vendor and placed an order for pens, mugs and pads before going back to the conference room to clear it of everything that had Newman Inland Marine on it.

Kelsey fought back a gulp of sadness, told herself to focus on the future and show the type of leadership the Newmans had asked for. In her work life, she'd never done anything more difficult.

When she returned to her office, Lawrence was waiting for her.

She slipped into her chair, and he sat across from her. He slid a folder containing Seward's termination package across the desktop toward her.

When she went to scrawl her name on the bottom of the check, she noticed that it was drawn on a new bank. Since she'd never filled out official paperwork, she doubted Donovan had made her a signer on the account, which meant she had to take the check to him. "I'll handle this and get it back to you," she said.

"Yeah," he said. "I don't envy you your job."

Lawrence left. She stood and straightened her skirt before picking up the file folder and crossing the room to knock on her new boss's door.

He called out for her to enter. Too late, she realized he was on the phone. Regardless, he waved her in, and she took a seat and waited for him to finish.

"Second weekend of December is fine, Colonel," he said. "I'll let Connor know we'll be there." After a few more words, he hung up. "That was my grandfather," he explained, unnecessarily.

"He's a colonel?"

"No. Yes." He twisted his lips wryly. "I'll explain when we have more time. Donovan Holdings, which is essentially just family members, is planning a retreat. It's an annual gathering before the holidays. We discuss all aspects of the various businesses and make the strategic plan for the upcoming year. With the acquisition of Newman, I'm too busy to travel far, and since Cade will use any excuse to skip, the Colonel has decided we'll hold it at the ranch."

"The ranch?"

"The Running Wind. Maybe you've heard of it?"

"I think most people in Texas have," she agreed. If it wasn't the largest ranch in the state, it was certainly close. In fact, it was one of the biggest in the country. She knew the Donovans had owned it for more than a century and that only small, select parts were open to the public.

"The timing on this takeover wasn't ideal. We'd hoped to put it off until the first of the year." He shrugged. "As my assistant, I'd like you to be there."

She blinked. "Me?"

"I'll want your input, and I'll want you to be part of the strategy for the logistics business. I have financials to prepare for all the companies as well as a general overview."

"Are you still CFO of Donovan Worldwide?"

"In my spare time." He gave a tired half-smile.

Absently she wondered if his exhaustion had been there the whole time and why she hadn't noticed it.

"Think about it," he went on, bringing her back to the present. "It's more than a month from now, and you don't have to give me an immediate answer. Theoretically, we'd leave work around lunchtime on Thursday so that we'd be in time for an evening overview. We'd stay through early Sunday afternoon."

She'd had no idea that he expected his assistant to travel with him. "I typically ran the offices when Mr. Newman was gone."

"I'm sure we have VPs who are capable of stepping in. Or, preferably, Martha could sit at your desk."

"She only works part-time," Kelsey replied.

"See if she can cover. It's only a day and a half. If not her, find someone else. We'll be available in an emergency."

She nodded slowly.

"What can I do for you?" He clasped his hands on the desktop.

"About Seward..." She placed the manila folder in front of him.

He flipped it open, scanned the contents faster than should have been humanly possible then looked up. As if it had never existed, the momentary weariness etched beside his eyes had vanished, replaced by steely intensity. "Three months' severance? Do you think that's appropriate?"

"It's not atypical for someone who's been with us for so many years."

"And will potentially cost the company tens, if not hundreds, of thousands of dollars?"

"I'm thinking more about his family."

"As Seward should have done. Donovan Worldwide pays severance when it's warranted but never in cases of severe misconduct."

"*Potential* misconduct."

"Ms. Lane." He pinched the bridge of his nose. "Please."

She exhaled. While she knew Seward might eventually be cleared of responsibility, the truth was, he had violated the company's abuse policy.

"Have this amended to cover only his to-date pay and accrued vacation." He closed the folder and pushed it back to her. His action and tone left no room for argument. "We'll set you up as a signer on the bank account in the next couple of weeks."

"Yes, Mr. Donovan," she said, voice tight. She snatched back the folder and left his office.

Instead of returning to her desk, she headed to HR to request a new check. Rather than riding the elevator, she took the stairs, needing the exercise to clear her mind.

After meeting with Lawrence, she decided to grab a latte from the coffee-cart vendor in the building's lobby. She took it outside and crossed the road to the urban park with concrete seats, a large swatch of grass, oleanders that had lost most of their blooms and several small fountains.

Since she only had on a lightweight suit jacket and the sun was obscured by clouds, the breeze chilled her.

After a couple of sips, she called her friend Andi.

"What's going on, girl?" Andi asked.

"Not sure you'll believe it."

"Hold on. Let me get away for a minute."

Andi owned a massively successful salon or, in her words, a hair artistry and design studio. They'd been friends since high school. Both of them had lost their moms early, and both of them had fathers who were overbearing.

"You're calling to make an appointment, right? That's what I won't believe. You're finally ready to do something about those poor, neglected tresses. Highlights? A new cut? Oh halleluiah, tell me we're going to get rid of some of that length. We can always put in extensions to make it look longer." Andi growled deep in her throat.

"Was that supposed to be sexy? Or were you trying to sound like a cat in pain?"

"Bitch."

In the background, Kelsey heard blow dryers and a man yelling. "Lorean?" she guessed.

"Shampoo girl didn't do a proper rinse," Andi said. "Honestly, I'm not sure how much longer I'll put up with him being a bitch."

"Another ten years?"

"Probably. But only if he takes his PMS medication."

She knew Lorean had been Andi's first employee. Despite, and maybe because of, his mercurial moods, he brought in tons of clients. Pissed off plenty of them too. But all the bad reviews that former clients left online just seemed to fuel the drama and attract more interested people. He was becoming a legend in Houston.

"So if you're not going to let me do something about that mess on top of your head, why did you call?"

Andi's bluntness was her most compelling asset. Kelsey never knew what her friend would say, or show up wearing—from a designer dress and heels to cartoon-print leggings and an oversized sweater. But it was the hair and makeup that was always the best surprise. Blue. Pink. Bob. Shoulder-length blonde extensions, or even ash-gray ones which gave her purple eye shadow and false lashes the look of a movie star's.

"Come on," Andi encouraged. "I'm going to need to run to wrestle a fucking flatiron away from Lorean. Jesus H. Where's my Xanax?"

"The Donovans have" — she ran her finger around the plastic lid covering her cup and settled for — "acquired Newman Inland." She mentally patted herself for the word. It was better than her first choice, stolen.

For a moment, there was silence. "Donovan? Like Donovan, Donovan?"

"Yeah. As in Nathan Donovan is my new boss."

"Holy fuck bunnies." Andi whistled, and the noise was so high-pitched that Kelsey had to move the phone away from her ear. "That's a fine man right there."

Except for the personality that went along with the classic good looks and stunning body. "He's a hard-ass."

"Meaning he acts like a Dominant?"

"What?" Kelsey demanded.

"Just askin'," Andi said. "I forget which, but one of the brothers is part owner of that new club."

Kelsey frowned. "What new club?"

"You know, the one I was telling you about. The tie-me-up-and-beat-my-ass-hard club."

"The BDSM one? You're not talking about Deviation, are you?" Kelsey had read about it in an exposé in the alternative newspaper that could be picked up for free at the trendy places around Houston. A man who lived in Boston and was reputed to be a friend of Julien Bonds was the majority owner. But she didn't remember seeing the name Donovan. Maybe because it hadn't mattered at the time. But now... A kaleidoscope of questions turned over in her mind. Could Nathan possibly be a Dom? Could that explain her visceral reaction to his personality?

She shook her head to clear it. Even while she told herself she wouldn't think of her new boss that way, she said to Andi, "Keep talking."

"I may or may not have personal knowledge of said club."

"What? You? You went to a kink place?" Kelsey almost dropped her cup. "When?" According to the article, the place was all very secretive and exclusive. It had some amazing high-tech additions, making it unique among all the clubs in the country.

She thought back to Nathan, his watch, the unique things it did. Was it possible that he was the brother who'd invested? She discarded that thought almost as quickly as it had formed. Even in the short time she'd known him, she doubted he'd put his money into something with that kind of risk.

If Andi actually answered her question, Kelsey didn't hear her. She was so consumed with her own thoughts that she was no longer listening. "Can you get me in?"

Andi interrupted herself to demand, "What? Seriously? Shut your mouth. You want to be tied up. Or wait…"

Kelsey could imagine Andi's pseudo-frown. She'd had too many face-freezing injections to actually get wrinkles, but she managed to bring her carefully drawn eyebrows somewhat closer together when she was genuinely caught off guard.

Truthfully, Kelsey was more than a little surprised that she hadn't been able to prevent the question from tumbling out.

"Wait… Do you want to do the tying? Do you want to beat some little subbie's ass?"

Kelsey rolled her eyes. "No." But the image of *her* body, bound and naked, tantalized her.

"I had no idea you really were kinky. Girl, we gotta talk more about this. I get off early tomorrow night. Martinis and confessions?"

"I'm not sure I'd be brave enough to talk about it without fortification," she admitted. "Friscos at six?" She named the nearby downtown hotspot. They had a great happy hour, meaning she could eat dinner for almost nothing. She might have unkindly called Nathan a penny-pincher but the truth was, she, too, was a master economizer.

"Six it is, and girlfriend, I'm telling you this. Get me Sofia or Lara Donovan as a client, will you? If you do, I'll make your first cut and color half-price."

"Half-price? Your generosity knows no limits."

"You know, I want Erin. She's your boss' sister. You can get her, right? Talk to him? God above, get me Erin and I'll give you a BOGO."

"Buy one, get one? Which means I have to pay full price for the first one?" Kelsey asked. Clearly Andi was insane.

A male shriek cut across the phone line, and Andi screeched in return. Knowing the conversation was over, Kelsey hung up.

As she finished her coffee, she spent a few minutes thinking about Nathan. It made sense that he was a Dom. He seemed to have the personality. Well, as much she knew. Or guessed, really. She read a lot, chatted with a friend who enjoyed participating in scenes with men, was in a few online groups and owned the movies featuring one of her favorite actors as a Dom.

Kelsey told herself to end the fantasies right there. That's all they were.

She dated men who were considerably gentler than he was, always friends before lovers. And in bed, they were polite. Polite and mostly perfunctory.

The fact that she was curious about BDSM was a conundrum for her. Of all people, she shouldn't fantasize about being submissive to a sexy man. But she did, more often than she would dare to admit.

She took her last sip and closed her eyes.

Fuck.

Unbidden, the image of Nathan crooking his finger at her and indicating she should lower herself across his lap filled her mind. She saw him lift her skirt and all but felt a trembling in her legs as she prepared for him to lower his hand in a punishing spank.

She heard herself begging, but since she didn't know whether she would want him to continue or stop, she shoved aside the image.

What in the hell was wrong with her?

Purposefully Kelsey stood and dumped her cup in the nearby trash bin. Making a point to herself as well as the world, she brushed her hands together, as if washing away thoughts of him.

It took the entire walk back to the office to banish the lingering tingles that the images had given her.

Thankfully Nathan's door was still closed.

Not having to see him after her discussion with Andi was a blessing.

A phone call from Zoe McBride, Sofia's sister and manager of the Houston branch of Encore Events, distracted Kelsey, made her think about business rather than entertaining outrageous fantasies. They set up a meeting for the following morning.

Thankfully, the next hours passed in a flurry of phone calls and meetings. Nathan left to visit the docks, giving her some appreciated time alone.

She reached out to Holly Newman, and they discussed plans for the going-away party. The woman agreed that the end of the month or beginning of December would be fine.

Before they hung up, Kelsey arranged to visit Samuel at lunchtime the next day.

Nathan returned a few minutes later.

The office temperature seemed to increase as he swept in, full of harnessed energy. Seeing him there, big, powerful, confident, she wondered again if he was a Dom.

Kelsey hoped he'd continue past, but he stopped in front of her desk and pulled up a chair.

"Ms. Lane?"

"Sorry." She shook her head. "You were saying?"

He repeated that the meetings had gone as well as he had expected, then added, "Anything I need to know?"

She brought him up to date on preliminary plans for Mr. Newman's party. "If he's up to it, after Thanksgiving and before your retreat seems to be ideal."

"Agreed. Did you get the artwork I sent over this morning?"

"I did. I've ordered a few things that will be expedited. As for the rest, I'll get you my recommendations and pricing in a couple of days."

"Good." He stood. With a crisp nod, he returned to his office, sucking energy out of her and the room.

It took her a couple of minutes to refocus and get back to her task list.

Toward the end of the afternoon, Lawrence dropped by with a corrected check and termination letter.

"Thank you. Sorry for the confusion."

"It's not going to be easy," Lawrence said. "The changes, I mean."

"I know," she replied. Nathan's words about loyalty seemed to echo in her head. And while she stood by her statement that he had to earn it, she knew she was a crucial part of the company's future success. And for all the employees, she had to back her boss. Even if she had to bite her lip. "Mr. Newman believed this was the right course."

"Remains to be seen."

"And it's up to all of the management staff to ensure the success of Donovan Logistics," she said firmly, leaving him no room to argue. "There's a lot at stake here, beyond your personal opinions. We're counting on you to help set the tone."

"We've had a lot of questions," he said.

"No doubt." She chose her words with care. "If you need to talk to Mr. Donovan, you should. Give him a chance." She could hardly believe the words came out of her mouth.

"Honestly, Kelsey, I'm not sure."

"No one is," she agreed. "But what's another option? We can leave. And we should if we believe the company is going the wrong direction. Or we can trust that Mr. Newman knew what he was doing and help him fulfill his vision for the company."

"Seward has been with us a long time."

"And he screwed up. You know it. I know it. Better than anyone, you know about family leave. He was entitled to it, and he chose not to utilize it."

"I don't like it."

"You don't have to. Neither do I. But he was given a second chance." And both of them knew how much worse it could have been. If the barge had sprung a leak or sunk, the company would have been damaged.

"He's got a problem." Lawrence pressed his point.

"And we have help for that too. You talked to him, explained it to him, didn't you?"

He nodded.

"He was given every opportunity. You can only save people who want to save themselves. He'll be awarded unemployment benefits."

Without another word, Lawrence put the file on her desk.

"Go home," she told him. "Enjoy spending some time with your wife."

He scowled.

"She won't be pregnant forever," Kelsey said.

"If I have to go to the convenience store one more time at midnight…"

"Stock up. Hide the stuff she craves in your car. All you'll have to do is walk to the driveway."

He loosened his tie. "Not possible. I don't know if it's going to be pretzels or ice cream. Last night it was licorice. Black licorice. Who the hell ever wants black licorice?"

"Goodnight, Lawrence. Give Erika my regards."

"Go home yourself," he said.

After he left, she glanced toward Nathan's office to see the door was open. She wondered when he'd done that, and how he'd managed it without her being aware of it. With a frisson of alarm, she replayed the conversation, just to make certain she hadn't said anything he'd take exception to.

She locked the file in her cabinet for the next day before contacting Seward's field supervisor. The man explained that the tugboat captain was currently in the middle of his days off, so the termination would occur when he returned.

Though the field supervisor didn't argue, there were long, uncomfortable silences on the line. She knew it was the man's least favorite part of the job, and truthfully, it was hers too. No matter how justified, she hated it. Especially when she had a personal relationship, like she did with Seward. "If you need me or someone from HR to be there with you, let me know."

"I'll think about it overnight."

Kelsey ended the call then finished a few more tasks before uncomfortably shifting in her chair. Her lower back felt stiff, and she did a gentle stretch. In surprise, she realized it was after seven o'clock. On some level, she'd been aware it was getting dark, but she'd had no idea it was so late.

She heard Nathan's deep baritone in conversation, and she debated whether or not to let him know she was leaving. With Mr. Newman, that hadn't been a problem. Holly expected him for dinner promptly at five-thirty, so he never stayed later than five. Generally, Kelsey was still at her desk when he walked past with a wave and a cheery goodnight.

Since she didn't want to interrupt Nathan, Kelsey reviewed her upcoming calendar then made a list of her priorities for the next day. After tucking the paper beneath her keyboard, she shut down her computer.

Then came the big, internal debate. She wanted a hot bath and a glass of wine. She needed a workout. Kelsey knew that if she went straight home, the workout would never happen.

She grabbed her workout bag and purse before riding the elevator to the building's tenth-floor fitness center.

Except for one other woman who was in the shower, the locker room was empty. This late in the evening, that wasn't a surprise.

Kelsey changed into her gym clothes, pulled her hair back into a ponytail then grabbed a bottle of water and picked up her phone.

The message icon was on and she checked it. Not surprisingly it was from Andi.

Called Deviation. I think we're in for this weekend. More deets with drinks.

Kelsey's hand shook. She couldn't believe she was actually considering going to a BDSM club.

Her hands were still trembling as she selected some music then put in her earbuds and walked toward the fitness center.

Though the area wasn't large, it was well equipped with a small free weight area, a few circuit machines and plenty of cardio pieces, all of which faced windows and had views of a downtown park.

She froze when she saw Nathan on the treadmill next to the one she liked to use. It was difficult to believe she'd been in the locker room for so long that he'd managed to beat her to the fitness center.

His headset was plugged into the machine, and he was watching business news on the attached monitor.

He wore a dove-gray T-shirt and shorts that showcased his powerful, muscular legs.

Damn. How was it possible that he was more appealing out of a suit than in it? He ran with a fluid, purposeful grace, making the exertion seem effortless.

Everything in her responded to him. Her pulse thundered, her lips felt parched. On some deep, core level, she wanted to be possessed by him.

She'd never had that kind of visceral reaction to a man before, and it terrified her, made her edgy.

Kelsey had a moment of choice. Leave before he noticed she was there, or be brave and pretend it didn't matter that they'd be alone, not just in the building but in the small room.

Then the decision was made for her.

3

In the window's reflection, Nathan met her gaze and didn't let it go. He seemed focused on her in a way he hadn't been earlier.

For a wild moment, she wondered if he'd known she would head for the fitness center rather than going home. Then she shook her head to clear it. The thought was ludicrous. Even if he cared what she did, a man like Nathan Donovan wouldn't alter his plans to spend more time with her.

She rationalized that it would be ridiculous to skip her workout just because her boss was in the same room and she'd noticed how masculine and appealing he was, so she fiddled with the settings on her phone, pretending she'd been doing that all along.

As she walked behind him, he gave a curt nod.

Maybe he wasn't getting enough oxygen to actually speak to her. She hoped.

After stepping onto the belt, she selected her favorite workout music, a mix of pop tunes from various decades by different artists. Kelsey pretended to ignore him and her questions about whether or not he was a Dom and concentrated on pushing the correct buttons to program her machine for an interval workout. Satisfied, she pressed the green button to begin.

She started at a medium pace. Over the next few minutes, the belt went faster until she was at an easy jog.

Even though the music in her ear was loud and she was into her own workout, she could hear his feet pounding on the machine next to her, making every part of her aware of him. He set a punishing, grueling pace that she realized was most likely a metaphor for the way he approached life.

Did he ever slow down or relax? And would she ever be able to keep up?

Helpless to resist his magnetic draw, she glanced over at him.

Sweat dotted his brow, and his Donovan Worldwide T-shirt clung to his damp skin. Seemingly unaware of her, he continued to focus on the screen in front of him.

Or so she thought, until he suddenly turned his head and caught her looking at him. He captured her gaze, compelling her not to look away.

What was it about him?

Unnerved, she missed a step and had to grab the rail to steady herself.

"Are you okay?" he asked.

Obviously he hadn't missed a thing. His lack of attention had been an act.

With a half-smile, she nodded and found her stride again.

For the next few minutes, she played with the controls for the television monitor, looking for something to occupy her interest — anything to drown out the overwhelming man next to her.

She found a comedy show, and since it had captioning on, was able to immerse herself. Until he reprogrammed his machine and slowed to a walk.

His machine beeped and he hit the stop button.

He was barely breathing hard, which seemed really unfair.

Then he pulled off his shirt and wiped it across his face.

If she hadn't been holding on, she might have misstepped again.

She'd been very much aware of his size and breadth, but until now, she hadn't realized just how muscular and toned he was. His abs were hard and tight, and there wasn't any excess fat on him. Everything about him, from his posture to his attitude to the state of his body, screamed restraint and discipline and, damn it, sex appeal.

He went to find sanitizer and cleaned off the machine.

Finally. She'd have the place to herself and could finish her workout in solitude.

Instead, he pulled his shirt back on before walking into the free weight area.

Because he was looking in a mirror to check his form, she was free to study his reflection.

As he bench-pressed enormous plates, she noticed the flex of each of his muscles.

Her heart rate accelerated in a way that had nothing to do with the workout. She told herself she'd never hit the gym with her boss again. He was too dangerous to her physical state.

A few minutes later, he finished his weight training. He lifted a hand in acknowledgment as he passed behind her.

She waited a few minutes to make sure he was gone before ending her workout and crossing to the locker room.

Rather than changing into her regular clothes, she toweled off then reapplied some mascara.

After pulling on a lightweight jacket and slinging her bag over her shoulder, she grabbed her purse and exited into the hallway.

Nathan Donovan stood there, arms folded, leaning against the wall, waiting for her.

She stopped so quickly that her bag slipped to her forearm.

Quickly, he took two steps toward her to readjust it.

"I... That's not necessary." And because he raised an eyebrow, she added, "But thank you."

With her in tennis shoes instead of heels, he loomed even taller, broader. He'd showered, if his damp hair and the scent of the woods after a rain were anything to go by. And he looked devastating. He wore a crisp, white, long-sleeved shirt, with the top two buttons open. His slacks were gray, and his shoes had a mirror-like polish. The addition of a buttery leather bomber jacket was enough to make her weak.

More than ever, she felt as if she were at a disadvantage. The man overwhelmed her.

"I think you should let me buy you dinner."

To hide her shock, she said, "I'm sorry?"

"Today has been...unusual. I want to be sure we get off to a good start."

"It's a little late for that, Mr. Donovan."

"Which is even more reason to let me buy you dinner."

She gave him a false smile. "Really, it's not necessary."

"I insist, Ms. Lane."

"I'm hardly dressed to go out," she told him, especially with him looking so fresh and in charge. Though damn it, her traitorous pulse thundered at the idea.

She wanted to dislike him, and she certainly did on some level. But she also couldn't deny how much he physically appealed to her.

Her resolve was complicated by the sudden, wickedly hot images tumbling through her mind...of being in his arms, of him looking at her purposefully before lowering his mouth toward hers, of him skimming his fingers up her spine.

She shook her head. Thinking of her boss in that way would be a rabbit hole leading to pure, pure madness.

Damn pheromones.

"We don't have to go anywhere fancy," he persisted.

"Perhaps another time."

"You need to eat," he countered. "If I'm correct, you skipped lunch, like I did."

"Are you accustomed to always getting your way?" She tilted her head back.

"Yes."

He let the word hang between them long enough that she squirmed and looked away. How the hell did he manage to do this to her?

"And I always get it when I'm determined to have it." He paused. "When it's important."

Was he saying that she was important to him?

"We're going to be working together, Kelsey. Presumably for a very long time."

Somehow, he'd managed to read her mind. And that frightened her more than anything. "That's exactly why it's best to keep it professional," she said, though she wanted nothing more than to accept.

"I'm not implying anything otherwise."

What the hell was going on here? Of course he hadn't implied otherwise. Just because she was having reckless thoughts about him being a Dom and spanking her didn't mean it was mutual. Embarrassment clawed at her, heating her from the inside out.

"There's a sandwich and coffee shop a few doors down."

"Marvin's," she said quickly, too quickly, eager to move on from her revealing mistake.

"They have espresso drinks."

"And the best chocolate cake on the planet." And it was okay to pop in wearing workout clothes or a suit. "How do you know about it?" She frowned at him. Though Marvin's had a good reputation, it was more of a neighborhood place, or somewhere people knew about if they worked nearby.

"I've needed coffee and food over the past few weekends. The building attendant recommended it."

Which meant he *had* been spending time in this area.

"I'll even buy your dinner," he said.

"I'm pretty expensive," she warned. That ought to slow his miserly ass down.

"Some things are worth the price," he told her, a smile flirting with the corner of his mouth.

Her breath caught. Anything but that. *Anything* but him being charming.

"It's only a meal," he said with a light shrug. "What harm can there be?"

Intuitively she knew the question wasn't as harmless as it sounded, not to her, anyway. With his searing eyes and inviting words, the man demolished her resistance.

"What do you say?" he asked. "We could have a truce for

the time being."

Damn him. He'd worn her down. Truth was, she wanted to spend time with him more than she wanted to avoid him. "Half an hour," she relented.

He reached for her duffel bag.

"Thanks, but I can manage," she protested.

"I'm sure you can." Without further argument, he took it from her.

Though she'd never admit it, she appreciated him carrying the extra weight.

He led the way to the elevator and pressed the lobby button as the door closed to seal them inside.

She moved to the far side, away from him, overly conscious of her post-workout attire and the way his presence overwhelmed her. They were inside the elevator less than three seconds before she realized that agreeing to spend more time with him was a mistake.

Once they glided to a stop and the doors whooshed open, he stepped aside like a gentleman and allowed her to exit first.

"Evening, Mr. Donovan. Ms. Lane," the on-duty security guard said.

More and more, she was discovering how well known her new boss was. Even though she'd never met him until today, it was obvious he had taken the opportunity to interact with people.

He held open the oversize glass door. The early November air hung heavy with moisture, chilling her. She zipped up her jacket a little farther.

Like he had when they walked to the conference room this morning, he fell in step next to her.

"Do you always work such long hours?" she asked.

"It's not unusual," he replied. "You?"

"Mr. Newman often told me I shouldn't, but yes. I like to be organized."

"It's appreciated."

When they entered the coffee shop, she inhaled the scent

of sugar dancing on the air. It was a good thing she'd already worked out.

"Chocolate cake?" Marvin guessed when she walked to the counter after taking a peek at the pastry case.

"Come here often?" Nathan teased.

"I've been in once or twice," she replied.

"A day," Marvin added helpfully, after wiping his hands on his apron.

"There goes your tip," she told the older man. "What are you doing here so late, anyway?"

"Lydia wasn't feeling well," he replied, mentioning his daughter. "So I sent her home. Told her I would cover for her." He shrugged. "Figured I'd keep baking since I was here."

"The place smells amazing." Her mouth was already watering.

"Cappuccino to go with that?"

"Please."

He glanced at the clock. "Decaf?"

"That would be perfect. Thanks."

He started to enter the amount into the cash register but she hooked her thumb toward Nathan. "He's paying."

"About time you brought a young man in here."

Heat seared her face. "He's my boss."

"Anything you say, Kelsey." Marvin nodded, as if he didn't believe her.

She glanced over her shoulder at Nathan, frantically hoping he wasn't as mortified as she was.

Nathan quirked an eyebrow at the man and gave a conspiratorial shrug.

"What will it be, Kelsey's boss?"

"We're sharing the cake."

"What?" She spun to face him. "I don't share my cake. Not with you. Not with anyone."

He swept his gaze over her before saying, "You can't eat the whole thing."

"Watch me."

"Two forks," he said to Marvin. Ignoring her scowl, Nathan continued, "I'll have a cappuccino, as well. Regular."

"I'm serious," she warned him.

"Your *boss* must know you well if he knows you always get a to-go box," Marvin said.

Shaking her head at both of them, she went to her favorite table and watched Nathan finish placing his order then pull out enough cash to pay the bill. She unzipped her jacket and hung her purse from the chair back while still watching him. He went up a bit in her estimation when she saw him stuff a five-dollar bill in the tip jar.

After putting his wallet back into his pocket, he sought her out with his gaze.

For a wild moment, she wondered what it would be like if they were more than employer and employee. But before the thought could careen across her mind and spin out of control, she shoved it aside and took her seat.

Nathan Donovan was her boss. Nothing more. Not ever.

He sat across from her and dropped her duffel bag at his side. "You know I invited you here for ulterior motives," he said.

Kelsey frowned. "Something you want to discuss about work?" Maybe the fact she'd left without saying goodnight?

"No. That stays at the office."

She crossed her legs. "Then?"

"I'm curious about you."

"Me?" She glanced around, as if he could possibly be talking to anyone else.

"I've read your résumé. I know about your job experience, your education, your GPA and the civic organizations you volunteer at. Now I want to know about the blank lines. The stuff you left out, either because you needed to or thought you should."

She crossed her legs in the opposite direction. His cell phone was out of sight. His watch was blanked out. He was watching her so intently it was as if there were no other person on the planet and he was determined to uncover all her secrets. Some of them were so deep even she didn't want to excavate them. But she had a sudden and uncomfortable feeling that he knew something about her that she'd prefer he didn't. "And why would I tell you?" she asked. Then she realized her tone sounded sharp, defensive.

"I'll go first," he said conversationally, as if they were friends, or even more than friends. "Earlier you asked about my grandfather, the Colonel. He was really only a captain, but after he married my grandmother, he was placed in charge of one of the divisions of her family's business. That was their wedding gift from her father. He had to work his ass off to prove himself. And apparently he was gruff. So he earned the nickname."

"Must run in the family."

As if she hadn't spoken, Nathan picked up his story where he'd left off. "My dad was nothing like his father. He was supposed to marry my mother, but he fell in love with a woman named Stormy."

"After he was married?"

"No." Nathan shook his head. "He was at the Running Wind, learning about the ranch. She was a riding instructor, if I remember. She'd been hired by the ranch as a wrangler. Once he met her, Dad lost sight of the woman back home. To be fair, they weren't officially married or engaged. But the families had arranged for it, and he went along with it. He knew her and liked her. And since he hadn't dated much, she seemed like a logical choice."

"So it was an arranged marriage."

"Of sorts. More like an agreed-upon marriage."

Intrigued, she leaned forward.

"But Stormy got pregnant and ran away. She didn't want to be part of the Donovan family, and she refused to let them take her son away. Even though my dad went on to marry my mom, I think they both knew he was still attached to Stormy. All that passion versus the responsibility he had back in town and at Donovan Worldwide. He was expected to run it, when his heart was at the ranch."

"Are your parents still together?"

His eyes seemed to cloud over momentarily.

The glimpse of emotion got to her, softened her, made her understand him a bit better. She wasn't sure that was a good thing.

"No." His voice was flat. "My dad died in a car wreck."

Her heart twisted for him. She resisted the impulse to touch his hand. "That kind of loss is never easy."

"Rebuilding Donovan Worldwide has taken a lot of time and attention. I never take the responsibility lightly."

"Is that part of why you're—?"

"A penny-pinching miser?" he supplied helpfully.

She winced.

"We're all a product of our experience," he said, sounding somewhat fatalistic.

"But we get to choose what we do with that, how we use it, how it shapes us," she replied. "Do we grow? Become more determined? Get angry?"

"And you chose to become determined."

His statement cut through her defenses. Startled, she met his gaze.

He was regarding her, his green eyes deep, interested.

"How much research have you done on me?" Kelsey asked. "Do I have any secrets from you?"

He lifted a shoulder. "Only the ones you choose to keep. But those are the ones I'm especially interested in."

She waited for him to go on.

"Your reaction gave you away," he explained. "When you used the word determined, you frowned as if you were remembering something, then you brought your chin up a little bit. There's nothing in your personnel record except for your work history, so you don't have to worry that I know a lot about you. But you were in a fairly powerful position with Newman. You weren't just his assistant, you were fulfilling the role of an advisor, more like a VP. The question is, what drives you?"

The man made her squirm. By nature she was a private

person, so the fact that he so clearly saw things that others missed made her uncomfortable. Rather than answer him, she countered with, "Are you nosy with everyone who works for you?"

"No. But I don't share an office with anyone but you."

Fortunately, Marvin arrived, interrupting further conversation. "Decaf for the lady," he said. He slid her drink in front of her. As always, he'd put a sugar cane swizzle stick on the saucer next to the cup. "And a regular." He placed the second cappuccino in front of Nathan.

Marvin also put a plate of chicken tenders between them.

"What are they?" she asked suspiciously.

"We need protein." Nathan shrugged.

"I wanted cake."

"You get that, too," he reassured her.

"Let the battle begin," Marvin said. His grin was ridiculously broad as he lowered the gigantic slice toward the middle of the table.

She glared at the shop owner. He'd cut the piece significantly bigger than any she'd ever seen. Not only that, but he'd put a big fat dollop of fresh whipped cream on the side and garnished it with a mint leaf. Adding insult, he'd drizzled chocolate syrup everywhere. It would take her three days to finish something like that, and Marvin knew it.

"Can I get you anything else?" Marvin deposited a few napkins next to the plate then placed two forks on top of them.

"I'm fine," Nathan replied. "And you, employee?"

Marvin chuckled.

She scowled at both of them.

The man continued laughing as he walked away.

"Chicken first," Nathan said.

Though she scowled, she knew he was right.

Dutifully, she ate a few bites before eyeing the cake.

"After you." Nathan nudged the slice toward her. "This will be fun."

She took the first bite and closed her eyes in delight as she savored the delicate combination of sweet and a slight bitterness.

When she opened her eyes it was to see Nathan with his hands laced together, tapping his index fingers, watching her.

Undaunted, she took a second bite. Then a third. By the fourth, she'd had more than enough. With a reluctant sigh, she put down the fork and pushed the plate toward him. "Fine. You were right. I can't finish it."

On the other hand, Nathan's appetite seemed insatiable. He demolished the rest of the cake while she melted her swizzle stick in the cappuccino.

"You must have a serious sweet tooth," she said, somewhere between shock and amazement. She knew he had to work out every day in order to put away that number of calories while looking so damn trim and fit.

"I was hungry," he replied, sitting back and pulling his coffee closer.

Suddenly she wondered if they were still talking about food.

"I didn't forget that I asked you a question."

"I was hoping you had," she replied.

"Not likely." Gaze unblinking, he repeated, "What drives you?"

A small quirk of his lips was an invitation she couldn't resist. "I lost my mom when I was thirteen, about to go into high school. She was my anchor, my inspiration." Even now, talking about it cut a jagged path across her memory, as if her mother had died yesterday rather than years before. "I'm sure my dad did the best he could, what he thought was best."

"And that was...?" He trailed off and fell silent, as if he had the whole evening in front of him and nothing better to do.

"Encourage me to find a man to take care of me. He thought I should go to a top-ranked college simply because

I would meet a suitable husband there." She shrugged. "That's perfectly fine for a lot of women."

"But not you?"

"My mother didn't read us stories about princesses who were rescued. We were taught we shouldn't be damsels in distress. She told us we could be anything we wanted. Back then, my sister wanted to be a ballerina."

"And you?"

She hesitated for a moment before revealing, "Are you familiar with that one day a year that parents bring their kids along to work with them?"

He nodded, but his mouth tightened.

Someone like Nathan who breathed profit and loss had to be frustrated at the loss of productivity. "Well, my dad took me to the office because my mother insisted. I loved it. I liked the constant activity, the way he always seemed to be in demand…" She paused, trying to find the right words. "There was an energy about my dad when he was at work. It was as if he were a different person when he put on his suit and drove into downtown. Sounds silly."

"Not at all. I want to hear more."

"He had to go to a meeting that I couldn't attend, so he left me in his office. I sat behind his desk, tipped back his chair. I imagined myself there, moved stuff about, picked up the phone. I pretended I was the person that everyone came to for answers. He seemed so very important to me. I remember deciding that day that I wanted to grow up and run a company." *Damn it.* She dropped her swizzle stick. Why had she revealed that? *How* had she let that out? She should have kept quiet, guided the conversation back to Nathan and his goals. Instead, she'd given him a glimpse of things she'd never shared with another person…the real her. "It's getting late." She stood.

"Please," he said. "Wait."

Reluctantly she sat. And since she'd already given away so much anyway, she decided to finish. "My mom had dreams of her own. She loved being a mother, don't get me

72

wrong, but she was a lawyer, and she wanted to be a judge. But when she got pregnant with me, Dad wanted her to stay home. I guess it was a complicated pregnancy, so she ended up on bed rest. Then came my sister. And then... She had started to take on some pro bono cases when she got ill and was talking about working as a public defender. I remember hearing my father shout at her." Damn, she hated the way this still bothered her. "Before she died, I promised her I would stay focused on my goals." She zipped her jacket. "Dad told me she got over-exhausted from trying to do too much. He told me he wouldn't pay for my college unless I was planning to get married after graduation. So I turned down his money. And I'm helping my little sister pursue her degree. She's got her law degree, she's active in the political process, and she plans to be a judge." She slung her purse over her shoulder. "Thanks for the appetizers and cake."

"I'll walk you to your car." He stood at the same time she did.

"Thanks, but I'm on light rail today."

"And you didn't plan on staying so late."

That much was true.

"I'll give you a ride home."

"Really, Mr. Donovan—"

"Nathan," he corrected.

She exhaled. "I'm capable of seeing myself home."

"That was never a question. I'm heading out. So are you. No sense in it taking longer than it needs to."

If he'd been overbearing like her father, she would have refused. But he was being practical. And getting home, to her bath, wine and bed that much faster had a lot of appeal.

"Be reasonable, Ms. Lane," he continued, his tone light. "As I said earlier, not everything, including this relationship, has to be a battle."

"In that case, thank you."

He picked up her duffel bag then put his fingers on the small of her back as he guided her toward the exit.

She went rigid. His touch was intimate, too familiar for a superior. But for a Dom, it was exactly perfect.

Suddenly she could barely breathe.

Kelsey told herself she was making too much out of this, that he meant nothing by it. He was probably being a gentleman, the way he was raised. But her response was anything but nonchalant.

A wayward part of her wanted him to take her into his arms. She told herself she shouldn't like it, but she enjoyed the strength and power he exuded. The more rational part of her personality, the one that kept her working toward her goals — and away from overbearing men — urged her to protect herself, flee if needed.

She moved her purse to her other shoulder as a way to create a little motion to pull away and promised herself she'd put more distance between them once they were outside.

"I'll be back for more of that cake," Nathan told Marvin on the way out.

"Enjoy your evening with your *employer*, Kelsey," Marvin said.

"I'm warning you..." she replied. But she realized how it might look. Nathan had stood close to her, paid for the order and now he was touching her as few other men had.

"Shall we?" He opened the glass door for her, and his genuine, easy smile made all of her tension vanish.

Until they arrived at one of the nearby garages and walked toward the farthest car in the lot, a serviceable but nonetheless luxurious SUV. "I'm a bit surprised," she admitted when he opened the door for her and she inhaled the scent of expensive leather. "I expected you to drive something a little less...showy."

"Because I'm cheap?"

"You're making me wish I could eat those words like I did the cake."

"You've misinterpreted frugality with suffering. This vehicle has one of the best warranties on the market. It gets exceptional fuel efficiency, retains its resale value, has a five-star crash rating and features I enjoy, such as satellite radio to keep up with the stock market and local news." He put his hand on the car frame above her head. "It's Wi-Fi and Bluetooth equipped so I can talk on the phone or listen to messages and emails while I drive. It allows me to continue the business day. I consider it a mobile office. Economizing further would be a bad decision. And I don't like to make many of those."

"No. I imagine you don't."

"I understand you're interested in BDSM?"

Scorched air rushed out of her lungs. She couldn't think or breathe. "What?" she managed, but even she realized it sounded like an admission rather than an incredulous question.

"The manager of Deviation called my brother this afternoon. Seems your friend Andi sent an email inquiring about bringing a guest to this Saturday's event."

Oh my God. She allowed her shoulders to collapse against the buttery leather seat.

"Of course, all requests are vetted before a pass is approved. My brother Connor recognized your name. And I'm curious why you want to go." He grabbed the safety belt then reached over to buckle her in. "Dominance or submission? Maybe bondage, Ms. Lane? Or are you perhaps a bit of a masochist?"

His face was inches from hers and his fresh, spicy, scent was potent, further scrambling her thoughts. Something deep inside her compelled her not to look away, even though she wanted nothing more than to vanish.

"Which is it?"

"I..."

"Submission?"

Unsure how to answer, she nodded slowly.

"I will teach you whatever you want to learn."

Oh God. Yes. No. *Yes.* She was terrified, thrilled.

"Hang on, Ms. Lane." There was no smile on his face,

nothing but cold, calculated intent. "Your life is about to get interesting."

4

"Are you going to invite me in?" Nathan asked after he'd parked near her condominium building on Caroline Street.

Since he'd first set eyes on her, he'd been captivated.

When Connor had called a couple of hours ago, Nathan had been speechless. So much so that his brother had checked to be sure they were still connected.

From the little he'd known about Kelsey, Nathan would never have suspected she had an interest in BDSM and he'd asked a dozen questions, enough to ascertain that it had been a female friend who had called and not a Dom or sub calling on her behalf. Connor had said he didn't have any further information, and Nathan had been determined to discover the rest.

Only one thing was sure in his mind. If she was interested in learning about D/s, she would do it under his guidance.

He'd ended the call and searched her out, only to see that she'd left for the day. His fucking watch had shown that his heart rate was elevated. Nathan had told himself that wasn't possible. But as he'd stared and focused on regulating his breathing, the number had decreased.

Because he'd skipped his usual morning workout, he'd decided to spend some time in the fitness center while he thought through the best way to approach her.

And the moment she'd walked into the cardio area, he'd known it. All his protective senses had gone on alert, and he'd seen her in a completely new light.

He'd noticed her surreptitious glances and the way she'd turned her head the moment he'd acknowledged them. When he'd walked past her after lifting weights, he'd made his decision. Talking to her outside work was more appropriate. And he'd been honest earlier. Once he'd made a decision, he acted on it.

He'd been waiting a couple of minutes when she'd exited the ladies' dressing room. And he'd registered her reaction to seeing him.

The same attraction he felt had been reflected in her wide, hazel eyes, in the way she'd parted her lips and the way she'd paused. He'd known that getting her to go out with him might take a little persuasion, but he was determined.

Something hot had arced through him, searing him with possessiveness.

He turned off the engine and angled his body to see her better beneath the overhead streetlight. "Kelsey?"

"Uhm…" She looked at him and brought her chin up. "This is awkward."

"Is it?"

"You don't think so?"

"Tell me why you do."

"Isn't it obvious? You're my boss. My job depends on pleasing you."

"Would you like me to fire you?"

"What?" She threaded her purse strap through her fingers. "Will you be serious?"

"I am. If you working for me stops us having an honest discussion about this—"

"About what?"

"The attraction we both feel."

"I…" She let out her breath.

"Deny it," he told her. "Go ahead. But I'll know if you're lying."

"Mr. Donovan—"

"Nathan," he reminded her.

She squeezed her eyes closed for a long time.

Patiently, he waited.

She eventually looked at him again. "I'm not sure I've ever felt more uncomfortable."

"We could discuss it inside. That would enable us to have a little more distance between us. Make no mistake, though, we will talk, either tonight or in the future. I have questions, so do you. We both want and deserve honest answers."

For a few more seconds, she fiddled with her purse strap. "I'm nervous."

"Thank you for saying so. And you don't need to be. It would be more disconcerting for you to show up for work tomorrow knowing Connor had told me you were going to Deviation. You'd be wondering what he'd said, guessing at my reactions, thinking that maybe you should resign. Let's put it all on the table, have a look at it, discuss it, see where we are."

"You're making this sound very…" She let go of the thin strap of leather that she'd been playing with. "Reasonable."

"Good. It should be." *For now.*

"You can leave your car out here," she said, pointing across the street.

Which meant she was inviting him up. He was unaccountably happy about that.

"Or there's a parking garage."

"Perfect."

He followed her instructions and navigated to the guest spaces. After he'd shut off the engine, he came around to open her door then grabbed her duffel bag.

She led him up a flight of stairs then exited in her hallway.

Her building was in a vibrant area, near museums, the medical center, restaurants. By comparison, his house seemed a bit isolated. That was something he really hadn't paid attention to until now.

"Watch out." She put an arm across his chest to prevent him from taking a step forward.

A small plastic ball rolled past them. It appeared to have some sort of furry, honey-colored creature inside. "What the hell?"

"Sinbad."

"Sinbad?"

"Mr. Martinez's granddaughter left her hamster at his house about a year ago. She supposedly never came to get him, but I think the truth is that he likes the company."

Nathan shook his head. "That's a hamster?"

"Sinbad," she repeated.

He looked at her to see her smiling. Damn. He wasn't just attracted to her, he liked her. The way she'd defended Seward was admirable. Even if he didn't agree with her, he appreciated her fierceness and loyalty. The way she'd interacted with Marvin, knowing his work schedule, told him she cared about people. And now...this. Patience, even good humor, when a fuzzball prevented her from getting to her condo at the end of the day. "Okay. I'll ask the obvious. Why is there a hamster rolling down the hallway in a ball?"

"He's getting his exercise."

"Of course. I should have known."

The ball hit the far wall, and somehow the thing— Sinbad—figured out to move to the other side to get the ball moving again. Impressive. And he had no idea whether that was unusual or not.

Sinbad rolled past them again, and he heard a door open down the hallway.

"Hi, Mr. Martinez," she said.

The man was wearing a red fuzzy robe that appeared to be covered in fur that matched the color of the hamster. His feet and legs were bare, and his combover had seen better days.

"Hey, Kelsey." Mr. Martinez bent to pick up the ball as the hamster approached. "I've got some peanuts for you." Without another word, the man entered his apartment, focused only on the animal.

"That could be one of the most bizarre things I've ever seen."

"Doesn't everyone take their hamster for a walk?"

"I honestly have no idea."

"What kind of pets did you have growing up?" she asked, leading the way to her condo.

"We didn't have any. There were dogs at the ranch. Cade still has a monstrosity of something. Sheepdog, I think. I don't know how it sees."

"No pets? Ever? Not even a goldfish?"

"Nothing."

She slipped her key into the lock and jiggled the mechanism a couple of times before it released.

"Do you have building maintenance?" he asked.

"No."

"That could be dangerous. Or you could get locked out."

"It's on my to-do-when-I-have-time list. I'd need to arrange for time off from work to meet a repair person, and that never seems convenient."

"There are Saturdays," he replied.

"And I go into the office on some of those," she said. "Or I take care of other errands."

"You could ask your boss for time off."

She met his gaze. "How is he with that? He seems to be a bit of a tyrant."

"You could always make up the time." Since he knew she was still smarting from their earlier clashes, he didn't take a bite of the bait she'd tossed him. "Like on Christmas, for example."

"Grinch." But maybe because of his response, her word had no hostility.

He'd remember that in future. Backing down from an insult didn't come naturally for him, but he'd get further with this woman if he engaged only when the stakes were high.

And truthfully, he probably had earned a reputation as a tyrant, whether deserved or not.

He followed her inside, then she closed the door behind them.

"No security locks?"

"I've never had any issues," she replied as she dropped her purse on a long, granite-topped table. She met his gaze in the starburst-shaped mirror that hung on the wall above it. "Besides, we have a guard hamster on this floor."

"That's not good enough for me."

"I'll look into it."

Probably not before he did.

"You can put my gym bag anywhere. I'll take care of it later."

He dropped it on the floor and had a look around. Over the years, Houston had seen many older buildings rehabilitated and converted into apartments and condos. But this appeared to be a newer building, and her unit had an open floor plan.

A small, well-designed kitchen stood off to the right. He didn't immediately see a dining room table, but the kitchen bar had a placemat as well as a laptop computer.

Off to the left was a fireplace and mantel. An oversize television sat atop a modern stand in the corner. A cream-colored leather sectional was strewn with vibrant-colored pillows and a turquoise throw. A metal-and-glass coffee table was littered with piles of magazines, and the local business journal was folded in half and open to page three. The area was cozy, inviting.

But her condominium's most compelling feature was the set of French doors leading to a balcony. Even though it was dark, he could see distant lights from downtown skyscrapers. Every day when she woke up, her first view was of the city.

Nathan was the second owner of his house. Though he was still inside the 610 loop, his neighborhood counted as his version of suburbia. He'd opted for a commute since he could get more value for his dollar, and he'd gambled that it would be a good long-term investment.

In contrast to her view of concrete and activity, he had landscaping designed by the local gardening club, complete with a pond. The back yard was lush with oleander bushes, bougainvillea and other tropical plants, including bamboo.

Unfortunately, working in the yard didn't relax him as he'd hoped. Instead, it seemed to demand constant attention.

The bamboo was now as tall as the house and threatened to engulf it. The bougainvillea had spikes so nasty they gave him pause. Even the koi that had been so alluring during the sale were nothing more than an invitation to passing birds.

The sight of his city in the near distance filled him with its seductive energy. Now that he saw the view from the outside looking in, he understood why his brother Connor had opted to live downtown. "Nice view," he said.

"I waited for this particular floor plan and sightline of downtown to become available," she said. "It meant I spent a year longer in an apartment than I wanted, but I think it was worth it."

A number of framed photographs hung on the wall next to the doors. They all had a similar feel, as if they were taken by the same person. The play of light and form drew his attention? "Mind if I look?"

She shrugged. "Go ahead."

He crossed the hardwood floors to study them closer.

One picture he recognized as a sunrise over Pleasure Pier on Galveston Island. Another was of the lighthouse on the Bolivar Peninsula. A third was of a flock of soaring pelicans. The largest and most stunning was of a large, bright full moon rising over the Gulf of Mexico.

Nathan looked back at her.

She was standing there, silently studying him.

"Who's the photographer?" he asked.

"Me. They're mine."

"Yours?" He glanced back at them. "You've got some talent."

"Thanks. I think you're being generous. I only display them because I like the sights."

"Galveston and Bolivar in particular?"

"Not necessarily." She shook her head. "To me it's more about the ocean. Dad had a decent job, but with Mom's health issues and the fact she stayed home with us..." She trailed off then visibly refocused. "We didn't have a lot of extra money, so my dad would take us to the beach for vacations. I loved watching the boats in the ship channel. I always begged him to let us ride the Bolivar ferry, and he invariably agreed since you can walk on for free. There's a restaurant in Crystal Beach where the barges pass by — really close — and I always imagined that if I reached out I could touch them."

And maybe her love of that had also influenced her career path?

"Galveston isn't far away. Even with my schedule, I can get there several times a year for short trips," she went on. "I've been wanting to get to Corpus Christi, though, and maybe South Padre Island."

"You can do both when we go to the ranch."

"We haven't talked about that yet." She unzipped her jacket and tossed it on the back of the couch. "Can I get you something to drink? Wine? Whiskey?"

"Whiskey," he said. "Thanks. On the rocks, if you have ice."

"Make yourself comfortable."

He followed her toward the kitchen but paused near the mantel to look at her snapshots. They appeared to be mostly family photos. One was of Kelsey and a smiling woman, arms over each other's shoulders. Both were wearing huge smiles. Kelsey had much shorter hair, only to her shoulders, and her friend had icy lilac-colored tresses. The metal frame had the word *bestie*, in block letters.

She returned with a small glass for him and white wine for herself.

"Do you want to show me around?" he asked.

The ice cubes clinked in the glass as she handed it to him. "Not really," she answered.

He regarded her.

"It'll ruin your image of me as neat and organized."

And encroach on her personal space. "All the better."

"Are you serious?" She squirmed a little, and he liked that.

"I'd like to see your place, yes." He took a sip of the liquor. It wasn't as fine as the stuff Connor stashed at the Running Wind, but it was more than serviceable. "I've been clear that I want to know all about you. Especially the things you don't want me to know."

"Why?"

"The Dom in me is curious."

Color flooded her cheekbones, staining them red. She didn't answer. Instead, she stared into the wine, obviously composing herself.

After expelling a breath, she met his gaze. "Fair warning, you might change your mind after looking around."

"I'll take my chances." Little did she know this was only the first of her hesitations that he intended to destroy. "Where should I put my coat?"

"The back of the couch is fine."

Rather than putting down his glass, he extended it to her, and she held it without protest.

He shrugged out of the leather bomber jacket and tossed it on top of hers before turning back to her.

"I could have taken it for you," she said. "That was rude of me."

"Yes. It was." He looked at her, hard, uncompromising. To him, this wasn't a game, and he was going to be damn sure she knew it. "We both know it's happened more than once. Lack of civility is not something I find appealing, whether the behavior is intentional or not."

"I...er..."

"It's never acceptable, and it's something I'm likely to punish a sub for."

"I'm not a submissive," she corrected quickly, breathlessly.

"Are you sure?" He made sure his voice was soft, rather than commanding. And that took a fuckton of effort.

He watched as the twin telltale streaks of red crept back onto her cheekbones. Her reaction was perfect. Pleasing. "Are you? Or are you secretly hoping you'll push me far enough that I'll have no choice but to take you in hand?

Do you want me to make it easy for you? Shall I remove the choice so you can pretend it wasn't consensual?" He added the last sentence quietly, so quietly that she had to lean forward to hear him.

"You're my boss." Desperation made her words rushed, slamming them together. But she was still looking at him, head tipped back, her hands clenched on their drink glasses.

Nathan wondered which one of them she was trying to convince. "I am, and I can be your boss in other areas, as well." Then he clarified, "If you want it. And hear me clearly. You will have to ask. Take too long and I'll change asking to pleading."

"Nathan…"

"Do you have a safe word?"

"No." Her answer was quick. Too quick.

"Choose one," he instructed. It wasn't a suggestion, and he knew she heard that in his tone.

"I don't know. I wasn't expecting this."

"You were hoping," he countered. "You knew what you were doing when you invited me up here."

"I…"

"Be honest, Kelsey, with yourself, if not me." He reined in his impatience. "You'll never get what you want unless you are brave. Your choice."

After a few seconds of silence, she admitted, "I want to be clear that this isn't what I ultimately want for my life. I've fought for a really long time to make my own choices and decisions. I avoid men like you."

"Like me?"

She sighed. "You know. Who like to be in charge. I prefer to make my own decisions. Being independent hasn't always been easy."

"Understood."

"But there's part of me that's curious."

He continued to wait for her, letting her work through things at her own speed. Emotion played across her face before she gave an almost imperceptible nod.

"I'll use red."

"You *have* been studying."

She met his gaze. "And yellow for slow."

"Good." He smiled, and he knew she appreciated the approval by the way she exhaled. "Now that we understand one another, we can move forward. If you're uncomfortable about something, say yellow."

Her shoulders rose as she sucked in a deep breath. He was enchanted with the image of her on her knees, ankles and wrists tied to a spreader bar behind her.

"Do you punish your subs?"

"I typically scene with submissives at a club, with women who know what they want and make sure they get it." He accepted the glass back from her. Her hand trembled so badly that the ice cubes clinked together.

She took several steps toward the French doors, putting some distance between them.

"Have you ever been punished for bad behavior?"

"No. I've never been with a Dom. Everything I know, or think I know, comes from reading, from websites, online groups, renting movies."

"Do you think you might like to be?"

"Oh God... Really?" She regarded him, her hazel eyes wide, as if hoping he would relent and change the subject.

"You're planning to go to Deviation this weekend," he reminded her. "You'll see a lot, hear a lot, experience a lot of different thoughts and emotions, maybe even participate in a couple of activities. You'll want to be more comfortable with it than you seem to be right now."

She nodded, but when she spoke, her voice was low and lacking the confidence she had at the office. "I'm not sure about it. Parts of it intrigue me, but I struggle against the feeling I shouldn't want it. I'm an independent businesswoman, and I've been making my own choices since... I don't know. Probably since my mother died. I don't like being told what to do." She shrugged. "I want to be a partner with any man I'm dating. An equal."

"And yet, when you're provocative—" He waited a moment. "As you have been…what then?"

"What happens at work is different."

His reaction was swift and powerful. "Not if we have a relationship."

"Seriously? Are you considering that?"

"And so are you," he said softly.

Even from across the room, he heard her breath catch. She might not want to consider it, but she was.

"Don't you have rules about fraternization?"

"No. Not unless things are problematic for either party or for others in the department. It happens less often than you think, except for when the couple breaks up. In any case, we can arrange a transfer for one of the people, elsewhere in the company if possible, or maybe to another Donovan holding. But we recognize that workplace entanglements happen. We try to mitigate potential damages, but we're not going to fire someone for falling in love with a coworker. If we go forward, you won't lose your job, but you can request a transfer, and I'll do my best to accommodate it." Nathan had an honesty-only policy, and he knew he was violating it. Fuck if he could stop himself, though. If they got involved, he wasn't sure he'd allow her to move to another part of the company. He was already hot for this woman, and he wouldn't let her go easily. If at all. "Don't think I've forgotten the main thread of this conversation. Let's go back to discussing punishment when the subbie is being intentionally rude at home. Would you have me ignore it? Or is it better to deal with it and try to correct the behavior?"

"I don't know. I'm not sure I'm comfortable with it."

"And yet you wonder what it would be like to be over my knee with me ripping off your underwear before I spanked you."

Kelsey swirled the wine and watched the liquid run down the inside of the glass before meeting his gaze again. "Yes." Her word hung on the cool autumn night.

"Despite what you may think, I'm not mercurial. Rules would be discussed and agreed upon, and so would my range of punishments for breaking them."

Across the room, they regarded each other. Him with interest and unusual protectiveness. Her with wariness in her wide, unblinking eyes.

"So let's be clear. What happens if you're rude to me in future, like you were a few minutes ago?"

That alluring blush was back again. "Maybe a spanking?"

God, what she did to him. His erection pressed insistently against his fly.

She brought her other hand up so that she was cradling the glass between both palms.

"More effective for you than anything else, such as a timeout? Or maybe a sincere apology from your knees? Writing out a hundred times that you'll be better behaved in the future?"

Her mouth was set. "Those would probably piss me off, which probably wouldn't get you the results you desire."

"Good to know." He smiled. "So what's your most prevalent fantasy? Lying across my lap? Bending over and linking your hands behind your knees? Being secured to a spanking bench?"

Her eyes went wide, unblinking. "You have one of those?"

"I do, indeed."

Nervously she brushed stray wisps of hair back from her face.

"Happy to show it to you." *Frozen hell.* He couldn't get the image out of his mind. The gorgeous Ms. Lane, naked, that hair in long, glorious disarray, strapped down, legs spread, pussy exposed, helpless to escape his paddle.

He hadn't had many women in his playroom, but he would love to show her all of his toys, introduce them to her, give her experiences she'd only fantasized about.

Nathan gave her a moment to compose herself — and fuck, he needed one too — before reminding her, "I'm waiting for your answer."

"Over the knee seems more personal, and I want to experience that sometime. And your spanking bench seems interesting." She shifted. "Uhm, does it have to be for a punishment?"

Because her breaths were coming in fast bursts, he decided to bring down her tension before ramping it up even higher in a few minutes, the ebb and the flow. The pace. The journey. The pain and the pleasure. And the way they could never be separated. "No. I'm happy to give you what you want without your misbehaving. I'd rather it, in fact. I want to give you orgasm after orgasm, making you scream from pleasure and not pain. That, Kelsey, you will have to ask for. You were going to show me around."

She blinked, obviously reeling from his abrupt change of conversation, like he'd intended.

"Don't say I didn't warn you about the mess."

"I understand."

As he followed her out of the kitchen, she pointed out the half bathroom and adjoining area containing a stackable washer and dryer. Then she took him into her office.

It was an absolute disaster of books, papers, photographs, prints, camera equipment and a desktop computer with an oversize screen. The walls were painted white. She had photographs spotlighted by track, gallery-type lighting. He recognized one as an Ansel Adams. Another, a portrait, might be the work of Annie Leibovitz.

Shelf after shelf contained cameras, all different types, digital as well as old-fashioned ones. Some were clearly collector's items.

Most startlingly, she had several trash cans, all of which were overflowing with discarded work.

This room displayed a creative side of her that she kept carefully hidden, showing how exacting she was.

"It's messy," she said. "But I never seem to clean it up."

"It's because it's part of your work in progress."

She nodded. "I come back in here and pick up where I left off. I never start with a clean desk." She rolled the globe of her wineglass between her hands. "I've never thought of it that way before, I guess. It's as if I remember exactly where I was and what I was thinking. My photography is always unfinished. I can do something else to it, enhance one thing, blur another, change the focus, the saturation."

"Trying to make it perfect?"

She shook her head. "I don't have that kind of genius or patience. I just like to see what's there."

He wasn't sure he understood at all. But he wanted to find out more.

Then she led him toward her bedroom. This room also had French doors and a patio. She had a queen-size bed with an inspiring wrought-iron frame. Though the bed was messy and an empty coffee cup had been abandoned on a nightstand, all of her clothes were hung up. Her closet door was cracked, and a number of dresser drawers stood open. One had lingerie spilling across the top.

"The bathroom's over there..." She pointed then shrugged. "That's all there is to see."

"Except for the sex toys. Maybe some books?" He lazed against the doorjamb.

"Uhm..." Her face turned scarlet.

"Show me," he said, his tone more of a command than an invitation.

He remained where he was, wondering whether or not she would comply. This, more than anything, would tell him what he needed to know about Kelsey Lane and how strong her submissive tendencies were.

A ghost of something that might have been nervousness or excitement, he couldn't be sure which, crossed her face.

"I'm sure it's nothing exciting compared to what you're used to."

"On the contrary. There's nothing boring about you, Ms. Lane."

She opened the bottom drawer of her nightstand.

From where he stood, he noticed she had quite an assortment.

Slowly she pulled out adult novelties and began to place them on the bed. She started with a purple dildo then added a vibrator with an angled head. Maybe for G-spot stimulation.

Next she brought out a thin paddle. The leather was likely faux as it looked more like a toy than a spanking implement. It had a word cut into it that he couldn't make out, and she placed it upside down on the bed so he couldn't read it. "What does it say?"

Her grip was wobbly as she turned it back over. "I… It was a gift at one of those adult-themed home parties. You know, you answer a trivia question right and you win a prize."

"But you kept it. What does it say, Kelsey?" he repeated.

"*Slut.*" The word was barely a whisper, and she didn't look at him.

"Really?" he asked softly. "What kind of slut?"

Her chin came up. "Mr. Donovan, I am not—"

"A fuck slut?" he interrupted. "For the right man? The right Dom?"

She sucked in a deep breath.

"I want you to be," he told her. "The word can have a negative connotation, I'll grant you that. But you see beyond it, don't you? You know what it really means. A person who's unashamed. Someone who enjoys sexual relations, who's unafraid, uninhibited. Most of all, honest. I want you to be all those things with me. I want you to be proud of being *my* fuck slut. I want you to wear the word on your ass, want you to celebrate when I whisper it in your ear."

"You make it sound…"

"Dirty? It is. Be proud of it. It can be liberating to claim the word for your own. Fuck what anyone else thinks. This is about you. Me." Fuck him to kingdom come, his cock was hard. "Us."

She looked at him, and passion had turned her eyes the color of scorched whiskey. "That's hot," she said.

"Take what I'm offering."

"You scare me a little," she admitted.

If that was true, she'd never shown it to him. "A little fear keeps a sub properly in compliance."

"Was that meant to make me really scared?"

"Did it?"

"I'm probably foolish for admitting this, but no."

"So what did it do to you?" he asked.

She was quiet for so long that he wasn't sure she was going to answer.

"Be my slut," he encouraged. "Tell me what my words did to you."

"They excited me, made me want to know what would happen if I wasn't in compliance, if I tested you."

"I hope you can get what you want from me without having to do that. I hope you feel safe and secure enough with me to ask and trust instead of test." And if she wasn't, he'd be there to guide her, encourage her. "Has anyone used the paddle on you?"

"Seriously? No. Well, I mean, except for Andi."

He frowned.

"She's a girlfriend. It was her party that I attended. The salesperson passed it around and Andi smacked me. I was wearing jeans, so I didn't feel anything." Obviously trying for levity, she added, "She hits like a girl."

"Use it on your hand."

"What?"

Without repeating himself, he waited for her to do as he'd said.

"I feel ridiculous."

In her eyes, Nathan saw the reflection of her struggle. Her gaze was fixed on him and she searched his features. Maybe for reassurance?

She picked up the paddle and struck the palm of her left hand. "It didn't really hurt."

"It wasn't just that Andi hits like a girl. But I'd like to see that."

She rolled her eyes. "Do all men say things like that?"

"Of course not. We all think it, though. But you're right, this one makes a nice thud. It's got two pieces that aren't attached. It sounds sexy, but it doesn't do a lot of damage. Unlike a real paddle made of leather or wood, which is what I wanted you to know." He took another step into the room. "It sounds intimidating, though, doesn't it? And that adds to the experience, the sensuality of the whole thing."

"I'm not sure I understand."

"In a scene, all of your senses should be involved. The scent of leather, or perhaps PVC. A paddle like that will make a very satisfying sound when it lands on the fleshy part of your ass."

She continued to look at him, as if riveted by what he had to say.

"Sometimes I use a blindfold on my subs, but I do it deliberately to enhance the other senses, make the anticipation even keener. But one thing I want you to be clear about, the word on your paddle? It only has the meaning you choose. To me, it means a woman who is sexy and confident, who knows what she wants. Including her man, her Dom. I never disrespect women, and I don't ever use that term in a derogatory way. But I want my sub to be my slut, to desire me the way I crave her. There's no room for pretense, only honesty. Calling someone my fuck slut is among the highest honors there is. It means she's mine, that she appreciates and values me the way I do her."

She exhaled. "That might take some rearranging of my brain cells."

"Happy to help."

"I'm sure you are."

"What else is in there?" He folded his arms across his chest and waited.

She pulled out a pair of wooden clothespins.

"Where do you put those when you masturbate? And don't tell me you don't use them."

"Do you not allow anyone to have secrets?"

"Where do you use them, Kelsey?"

"My nipples."

"Plastic ones are better, since they don't twist. Metal clamps are better yet. But these can be used elsewhere. Like your toes."

"What?" She gasped. "Are you kidding me?"

"Certain things I don't joke about. And sex? The things I'd enjoy doing to your body? I take that very, very seriously."

"I could use a safe word, right? I mean, hypothetically, if we were going to try that?"

"Absolutely. But if you are merely uncertain or nervous about something, I'd encourage you to try it."

She flicked a glance back to the pins. "Putting them on my toes sounds painful."

"More pressure than anything." He was glad she hadn't said no. "A distraction from other sensations, and an addition to them at the same time. When I play with a sub, I like for her entire body to come alive. I find that her orgasms last longer and happen more frequently that way."

She picked up her wine and took a big gulp, as if looking for fortification. "Well, maybe for some women."

He waited.

"I can't believe we're having this conversation. Then again, I can't believe I'm showing my boss my sex toys." She shook her head.

"What is it you don't want to tell me?"

"I almost never have orgasms when I'm with a man."

"Oh? Maybe it's the fault of the person you've been with. Have you ever been with someone who made your satisfaction his sole mission? Who watched you intently, every action, reaction. Every moan, groan? A partner who drove you to the edge of your endurance? Not just once but over and over?"

She scoffed then laughed a little. "I'm sorry," she said. "That wasn't meant to be rude."

He noticed that she absently rubbed her rear. Interesting. Hot.

"Honestly, it sounds like the stuff I fantasize about. You

know…" She seemed to cast about for clarification. "You know…something that you want to have happen but never does. It seems it's over before it ever starts."

"Challenge accepted, Ms. Lane."

Her mouth parted before she pressed her lips together. "It wasn't meant that way." She shifted her weight from foot to foot. "It's probably just me."

Then, as if anxious for the conversation not to continue, she lifted a small butt plug from the drawer.

It was a thin, silicone thing. Not much fatter than one of his fingers. "Do you play with that?"

She put it down on the bed, but he realized she'd used the action to avoid eye contact.

"Do you?" he repeated.

"I have. A couple of times," she admitted.

"Do you like it?"

She turned her head so that she glanced at him for a second before going back to what she was doing, which was mostly hiding from him. "It helps me get off," she admitted.

"And do you enjoy anal sex?"

"I've never had it."

"Would you like to?"

"I've heard it hurts like hell."

"That wasn't an answer. Look at me."

Slowly, she did.

"What's the biggest thing you've had in your ass?"

"I'm hoping the floor is going to just open up and swallow me at some point."

"There's no escape from me, Ms. Lane. I will pursue you relentlessly. I will have my answers. I'll force you to think about things you never have before."

"You already have."

He nodded tightly. "So answer the question. So far, what's the biggest thing you've had up your ass?"

"Just this."

"You've never experimented with your boyfriends?" he persisted. Even if he were vanilla, if he knew his woman was interested in being fucked in that tightest hole, he'd have been all over it.

"I tried with one." She did look at the hardwood plans, as if still hoping for escape. "He couldn't...ah..."

"Maintain an erection?"

She breathed out in a huff. "Exactly."

He nodded, appreciating her honesty, then asked, "Anything else in there?"

"My wand."

Of course. Many women he knew, and a good number of Doms, owned one.

She pulled it out and put it on the bed next to her other toys.

"How often do you use it?" he asked.

"Every time I masturbate."

"Which is how often?"

"I don't know."

"Approximately?"

"You are annoyingly persistent," she said around an irritated sigh. "Twice, maybe three times a week."

"And you orgasm then?"

"Most of the time. Sometimes, I just use it to help me relax so I can go to sleep."

"If we play together, you won't be using it unless I give you express permission."

"What?"

"My submissive's orgasms belong to me."

Color drained from her face. "I'm not your sub." But her voice lacked conviction, and her words were barely above a whisper.

"You want to be."

"Oh my God." She closed the drawer.

"Isn't that why you're going to Deviation? Because you know there's more to life, a relationship, sex than what you've experienced up until now?"

"Mr. Donovan..."

"It's your call," he told her. "Nothing will happen

97

that you don't agree to. You can go to the club with me this weekend, if you want. I'll make sure you experience everything you've ever imagined. But you'll go as my submissive. And that means we'll play together before we attend. We've got several days."

"What about work?"

"There will likely be some influence on our work relationship. Hopefully you'll be a little more respectful so that you don't get your bottom spanked so hard that you can't sit comfortably."

Her scowl was fast and furious.

"What if you deserve it?" she countered.

"If I'm disrespectful to you, you're more than welcome to whip down my pants and spank me."

She put down her glass with enough force that the wine sloshed to the top of the rim. "Can you take this seriously?"

He'd given her enough space, kept his hands off her longer than he'd thought possible. Nathan devoured the distance between them and captured her shoulders, bringing her up onto her toes and only inches from him.

Fuck. She smelled amazing. Feminine… His senses blazed. "You have no idea how serious I am about all of this, Ms. Lane. The question is, what do you want to do about it? Do you want me to escort you to Deviation on Saturday night? If your answer is yes, I will expect you to let me train you, starting now."

5

With Nathan's hot breath on her face and his strong fingers on her shoulders, Kelsey couldn't think rationally. The heat of him overwhelmed her. His touch ignited something inside her that she'd never felt before. There was no way she could deny how much she wanted him, ached for him.

On all levels, this was wrong. She shouldn't be fantasizing about submitting to her boss. Even if a relationship was permitted under corporate policy, it didn't make it a smart thing to do. In fact, it was insane. How was she supposed to show up at work and pretend everything was normal if he'd spanked her the night before? Tormented her naked body? Oh God, or worse…fucked her.

Everything he'd said had fascinated her. He'd spoken of things so matter-of-factly that he'd taken away her embarrassment, given her an avenue to be honest with herself as well as him. She was finding courage to admit things aloud. In such a short time, she'd been more frank with him than any of her lovers.

Despite the risk, she wanted him to force her over his knee, make her bend over while he hiked her skirts, tied her to a spanking bench. These were the types of fantasies that helped her to orgasm when she played with herself.

He was offering her the experiences she so desperately desired. At the same time, the idea of being trained by him, spending all her time with him, scared her witless.

And there was the fact that some of it would freaking hurt. "This whole thing is exciting, but it also makes me nervous. I don't know what to do. Where to start." But she did know that the longer she stayed in his arms, the more she wanted to be there. His touch seduced her.

"Tell me you want to do this," he said, asked, demanded. "The rest we can figure out from there." His fingers bit into her skin, communicating his seriousness.

This man's power, his strength, his overwhelming personality... How could she deny him anything? For him, she was lost. "Yes. I do." Knowing that Andi would understand her decision to go with him, she repeated herself with more conviction. "I do. I'll be yours for the week." She didn't know what the hell it entailed, but she vowed to get everything out of the experience that she could, no matter the cost later, maybe in regret or recrimination. It was better than a lifetime of wondering.

"Kelsey?"

How long had he been talking? "Sorry."

"Let's pretend this is a dance. I'll lead. You follow. Nothing will happen that you don't want."

"I know. I know." Was she only imagining that his voice was less harsh than earlier? That his eyes were greener? "Stop. Please. And... And do something." She wasn't sure what. Now that she'd told him she would be his for the next few days, she was horny in a way she'd never been before. Showing him her sex toys, lining them up on the bed, had cut past her first level of embarrassment. Now she wanted him to use them on her.

He moved slowly as he released her and brought his hands up to capture her face. His grip was firm and relentless as he looked at her, refusing her quarter.

"I'm going to kiss you. Hard. Deep. And you're going to open your mouth for me and give yourself over to me as if I own you."

Her knees wobbled. Because he seemed to be demanding an answer, she whispered, "Okay."

"Yes," he corrected. "I won't accept half answers or prevarications. It's yes or no, followed by Nathan, Sir or Mr. Donovan."

"Yes, Mr. Don—" Before she could finish his name, he'd

sealed her lips with his. She opened her mouth for him and he plundered her immediately, hard and fast, making it impossible to breathe.

She wrapped her hands around his wrists, holding on to him for her sanity, her life.

His mouth was hot and demanding.

His kiss consumed and destroyed.

He commanded her surrender, and she gave it.

Kelsey allowed her body to relax, and he pressed forward, asking for more.

Nathan moved one of his hands and curved his fingers into her hair near her scalp then eased her head back as he deepened the kiss.

His teeth abraded her. She'd never experienced anything so primitive, causing her reality to splinter.

His reputation was that of a ruthless man, reserved. She'd had no idea he was this passionate.

Slowly, by measures that left her unable to draw a full breath, he eased away.

With her head still pulled back, he traced his blunt thumbnail across her upper lip. She allowed her eyes to close, aware that her responses seemed heightened, and her pulse pounded in her ears.

"Nothing connects like a kiss," he told her.

Before now, she wouldn't have agreed. But this wasn't like any she'd had. The men she'd been with had been gentle. But Nathan took. He set the mood. Demanded. The act had separated her regular world from his more intense one.

"This evening is about your orgasm," he said. "I won't tolerate shyness or hesitation."

"Or...?"

"I will use corporal punishment."

Her mouth dried. Although she was reeling from the kiss, she wondered if she'd made the right decision.

But then she recognized the truth. She *had* to find out. "I understand."

Not backing off or giving her any space, he waited.

Still breathless, she tried again. "I understand, Nathan."

"Good."

The air thickened with expectation.

"Let's start by getting you undressed."

Having him stare at her was unnerving. Reminding herself what he'd said...promised...threatened...about corporal punishment, she toed off her athletic shoes before hopping on each foot to remove her socks.

He reached out a hand to steady her, and she flashed him a smile before looking away again. She had to pretend he wasn't there in order to fully concentrate.

Her hands shaking, Kelsey lowered her workout pants. "I could use a shower," she said.

"Go ahead. I'll wait."

And by that, evidently, he meant right where he was. "You might be more comfortable in the living room."

"Get on with it." His voice lacked the harshness she expected.

"I—"

"Kelsey."

His tone told her he wouldn't compromise. "Fine." She stepped out of the pants.

He scooped them up and placed them on the bed.

She pulled off her shirt and he took that from her, as well.

"Spin around. Let me look at you."

Slowly she turned, glad that she had on a sports bra and panties rather than a thong.

When she faced him, the gleam in his eyes was appreciative, vanquishing the embarrassment that had been unfurling.

"Now the rest."

She removed her undergarments, then instinctively crossed her hands over her body, trying to preserve her modesty.

"Put your hands behind your head."

It took her several seconds to get herself into the right mindset. He wasn't a boyfriend or lover. He was a boss. A

Dom. For the next few days, she was in training.

He let her stand there long enough that she squirmed uncomfortably. And still, he made her wait.

Eventually, he said, "Into the shower."

Relieved, she escaped.

Kelsey reached into the shower unit to turn on the faucet. She turned around and took a startled step back when she saw him there, his hips propped against the granite countertop, drink in hand.

"Do I ever get any privacy?"

"Not in a D/s with me."

The flatness of his reply made her throat dry.

This wasn't going as she'd anticipated. She'd wanted a few minutes to regroup and sort through the evening's events, but her temporary Dom was clearly having none of it. "Excuse me." She maneuvered around him to grab a clip from a drawer. No other man had ever shared bathroom space with her.

"May I?"

"Yes," she replied. "But I'm not sure why you would."

"Intimacy. Little acts of service can bond two people together. You taking my coat, for example."

A bit embarrassed, she looked away from him.

"Or preparing my drink the way I like it. Turn around."

When she did, he continued, "Or me doing this for you." He scooped her hair from her shoulders and clipped it high up on her head. "And this..." He ran his thumb up the back of her neck then leaned in to kiss her nape.

A shock wave went through her.

It was soft, magical, simultaneously sexy and sensual. She was undone.

Then he slapped her ass.

She leaped and squealed.

"Into the shower."

Was this the way it would be between them, so multidimensional and complex?

Steam billowed around her in the shower stall, but it

103

didn't provide much of a curtain to shield her from his view.

"Tomorrow night, I will wash you," he said.

Her heart stopped before she remembered she had plans with Andi. "About that..." She grabbed a bar of soap and lathered it, not meeting his gaze. "I am meeting a friend for happy hour."

"No problem. Call me when you're done and I'll give you a ride home."

She turned to look at him. "I might be out late."

"All the more reason for me to see you home safely."

"Really, Mr. Donov—"

"I take care of what's mine."

"I'm not yours." She could hardly think over the roar in her head.

"This week, you are." He paused. "Stop trying to make things difficult, Kelsey. It will be easier that way."

She exhaled. What the hell had she gotten into?

"And you're stalling. Finish up. I don't like to be kept waiting."

Kelsey slid the soap back into the holder and washed her body, aware of how hard her nipples were.

"Tomorrow we'll shave your pubic hair."

She froze. "What?" She kept it trimmed and neat. "I like it as it is."

"Would you prefer a Brazilian wax?"

"Oh, hell no."

"Try again with the proper response. You do remember what that is, don't you?"

Her head spun. It was one thing to read about this kind of thing, but another entirely to have the words directed at her.

"I can't hear you," he prompted.

"Yes, Nathan, I remember."

"Would you like a Brazilian wax before we go to Deviation, sub?"

His words and uncompromising tone unfurled a ribbon

of heat in her. "No, Sir."

"Take the showerhead down to rinse off."

She did as he'd said, and she washed the lather from her shoulders, allowing the warm water to run down her back and torso.

As she was ready to turn off the faucet, he said, "Turn the setting to pulse then masturbate with it."

Kelsey didn't consider herself a prude, but she'd never had a man watch her play with herself. *Intimacy.* He hadn't spoken aloud, but the word hung there. That was what he was doing, she realized, weaving a spell between them. He would be asking things of her that no other man ever had.

She moved the dial as he'd instructed, then she spread her legs.

"Face me."

Though she exhaled, she didn't protest.

"Gorgeous. Now part your pussy lips. I want to see your clit get red and swollen."

She used two fingers to expose herself.

"Farther. Or I can go get clips and tie back your labia."

"You wouldn't!"

"Try me, sub."

She considered him. He had one eyebrow raised. Even though he seemed completely at ease, there was no doubt he was serious. Fuck if his implacability didn't make her even hotter.

He lifted his glass to her.

Trying to ignore her sense of embarrassment, she spread herself even farther before directing the spray toward her pussy.

Involuntarily she clenched her muscles.

"Better," he approved. "Much."

The nozzle forced out another burst. The feeling of heat and pressure, along with the knowledge he was watching, made her legs wobbly.

"Keep your legs wide," he said. "That's it. Move the showerhead and your hips. Make sure your clit gets plenty of attention."

Focusing on all his instructions while the spray continued to arouse her was difficult.

"I love watching my sub get horny for me."

His words magnified the sensations.

"Do you wish it were more?" he asked. "Hotter? Greater pressure? More constant?"

Her body jerked in response to the spray, and she couldn't find the words to answer him.

She tightened her buttocks as an orgasm began to build. She bit her lower lip and moaned a little.

"Stop."

The word was impossible to process.

She was so close, so aroused... Kelsey closed her eyes. *Almost. Just a few more seconds...*

The water went cold.

"I said stop."

She dropped the showerhead.

Her pulse thundering, her body shockingly chilled from the abrupt temperature change, she met his uncompromising green eyes.

"I decide when you come." He turned off the water and rehung the showerhead. "In the future, sub, when I give you a direct order, you obey immediately."

"But—"

"This is about giving you what you want."

She grabbed the towel he was holding. "I wanted an orgasm."

"And when I decide to let you have one, it will be more powerful than any you've ever experienced."

"Uh-huh." With a glare that she hoped would wither him, she dried herself.

"Do you show all your lovers this side of you?"

"So far you're the only lucky recipient of my anger and frustration."

"And fire. How does your clit feel?"

"No idea. It's frozen."

He grinned. "Is it?" He snatched the towel from around her and tossed it on the floor behind him. Then he skimmed a finger down the center of her chest, over her belly then lower, between her legs. Unexpectedly he plunged a finger inside her heated cunt. "Oh, Kelsey. When will you be honest with both of us?"

He melted her.

He drew back his dampened finger and began to torment her clit.

Suddenly she was an inferno. All the arousal that had been there returned, amplified. "Damn." She was hungry, leaning into him.

In under twenty seconds, she teetered on the edge. She gritted her teeth so as not to let him know how close she was. *Maybe, just maybe…*

He pulled away.

"Seriously?" she demanded, flabbergasted.

"Yeah, seriously. This is on my terms. Not yours."

Her chest heaved from frustration.

"Walk into the bedroom," he instructed. "And don't think about your clit or your need to come."

Curse him. The more she tried not to think about them, the more insistent the thoughts became, as she was certain he intended.

"Sit on the foot of the bed. Put your hands behind you and thrust out your chest."

If she hadn't read about Doms making these kinds of demands she would have been paralyzed. Even though his words weren't a huge surprise, her reactions were. She was so very aware of her movements, her posture, the way her pulse turned thready as she walked ahead of him.

She got into position and waited while he studied her.

Then he surprised her by picking up the vibrator and going into the bathroom to wash it. Less than a minute later, he returned and placed the toy near her.

Though she was tempted to ask what he intended to do with it, she remained silent, as did he.

Finally, when she could take no more, he took two steps toward her.

The fact that he was completely dressed while she was naked intimidated her, made her feel like the submissive she insisted she wasn't.

"How sensitive are your nipples? If you put clothespins on them, I'm guessing you like a lot of pressure." When she didn't respond, he asked, "Well?"

"I suppose," she said. "I've never had a man use too much or even..."

"Enough?" he guessed.

She realized she liked the sound of his rich, deep, hypnotizing voice. "Yes."

"Let's start finding your limits."

His words seemed to go straight to her pussy. She knew he was waiting for an answer, one she had to give, one she was terrified to give.

6

"Kelsey?" Nathan prompted.

"I want this," she admitted, shocked by how tight her voice sounded.

"Then spread your legs."

Their gazes were locked as she did what he'd said, and he moved in closer. He towered over her, smelling of spicy soap and unfettered power.

Her mouth dried.

"Tip your head back. Look at me. Keep your eyes open. I want to see all of your reactions. No hiding."

"Yes, Nathan."

"How's your clit?"

Until he'd said that, her mind had been distracted. Now all her attention was redirected toward her pussy. "Still swollen, Sir."

He grinned, rogue and careless in equal measures. "Show me."

"Sir?"

"Do it."

Kelsey reacted immediately, moving her right hand to her cunt while keeping her left hand propped behind her, her face tipped back to meet his gaze. She spread her pussy lips for him. This was so much more intimate than being in the shower with him watching.

Keeping her gaze locked with his, he said, "Open your mouth."

He put two fingers in her mouth. "Now suck."

It was so fucking erotic. Every part of her responded to him. Her breasts felt heavy, her nipples needy. She was tempted to play with her clit, but achingly aware he hadn't given permission.

He pulled out his fingers then traced one over her clit. She hissed. The denied orgasm seemed to intensify her reaction to his touch. Suddenly she was right there on the edge again.

"It is swollen," he agreed.

He gently abraded her and she whimpered.

"How long has it been since you had an orgasm?"

"I don't know." She lifted her hips, pleading in silence.

"Little liar." There was no anger in his words, more of a tease. But he didn't relent.

"Friday," she confessed. "It was after work. I couldn't fall asleep."

Nathan continued to play with her and study her reactions. "And how was it?" He tweaked her clit again and she screamed. "Tell the truth."

With him, there would be no hiding, she knew. And she appreciated it. She'd wanted something like this for years, someone so into her that he knew her thoughts, studied her reactions. "It was hot."

"It'll be nothing compared to the rest of tonight."

She already felt that way. Kelsey scooted toward him, desperate for him to get her off. It wouldn't take much — a firmer touch, or for him to put his fingers in her.

"You are shameless, aren't you?" His voice dropped by an alluring, seductive octave.

"I never was before."

"And now?"

More and more, she was beginning to understand the seduction of BDSM. The mind game. The thrill that came from giving herself over to another person.

"In the shower," he reminded her, "you were going to defy me. And now, you're trying to get me to let you come."

"I'll behave better," she promised. But her breaths were constricting her, choking her. With his achingly gentle touches, he was making it impossible for her to obey him.

"Good. Show me. Move back, away from my hand."

Even as he gave the command, the bastard continued to play with her pussy.

Fuck.

He was driving her out of her mind. The orgasm was right there, and she could take it.

"Are you going to be a good sub and do as your Dom wants?" There was no compromise in his ice-green eyes. "Or are you going to steal something I told you not to?"

Kelsey whimpered. "Please…" She'd never asked for an orgasm before. Never begged. He was right. She was shameless.

The sound of her labored breaths filled the air.

"Don't you *dare*." His words were a whiplash through the haze in her mind.

She squeezed her eyes closed and shoved herself away from him. She cried out in frustration. Her body was dotted with sweat and she wanted to wrap her arms around herself for protection.

"Keep your pussy lips spread." He continued to play with her while holding her gaze hostage.

She whimpered. There was no way she was capable of doing what he required.

Kelsey drank in deep, desperate gulps of air.

Finally, her tormentor relented and pulled away his hand. "You're good," he said.

She voraciously consumed his approval.

"That will get you out of a few of your upcoming spanks."

Spanks? He still intended to spank her? Her shoulders fell before she remembered to pull them back.

"Very, very good," he amended. "Now put both hands behind you."

Grateful for the reprieve, she did.

"Where was I?"

Kelsey's mind spun as she tried to remember. "My nipples."

"Indeed."

He moved his hands to cup her breasts. Then with feathering motions, he brushed across her nipples, making them hard, making her ache. With each stroke, he used a little more force, and she liked it.

"Is that enough for you?"

"It's good."

He rolled her nipples between his thumbs and forefingers, and she sighed.

"It's not enough, is it? Kelsey, you're going to have to ask for what you want, be truthful." A smile played around his lips, shaving years off his age, making him seem more accessible, less formidable.

Letting herself think that, she knew, was a mistake.

By degrees, he increased the pressure.

No matter how hard she fought, she couldn't keep her eyes open. She was simply too overwhelmed.

He continued to press on the hardened nubs, and she drank it in. *Finally.* A man capable of giving her what she had never dared ask for.

"What will you tell me if it's too much?" he asked.

"Something from the rainbow. For God's sake, more."

"Oh, Kelsey…my pleasure."

He pulled her nipples, out and up as he pinched.

Everything in her went weak and she reached for him, putting her hands on his forearms.

"I can smell how aroused you are. How does your clit feel now?"

She forced her eyes open. He was only inches from her, intently focused. It was as if she were seeing him for the first time, not just as her boss, but as her Dom, with the chiseled angle of his jaw, strong nose and eyebrows that were set in a rigid line. Though his lips were narrowed in concentration, she knew how powerfully he could kiss her, claim her.

This man's eyes got to her. There were numerous demands on his time, but he had no room for anything or anyone except her, he couldn't, not with the single-minded way he focused on her.

"Tell me," he bit out, pulling even harder on her nipples.

"I could come in an instant."

"You like this?"

"More than I had ever imagined." The pain was deep, exquisite.

"We'll get you some clamps. I want you to be able to experience this while I play with you in other ways."

Unable to speak, she settled for nodding.

So gently that she wasn't aware of it at first, he began to release his grip on her nipples.

Before she could complain, he leaned in and began to suck on her left nipple the moment he let her go. With his mouth, he soothed and comforted until the blood flow returned to normal.

Then he did the same thing with her right nipple before taking a step back.

Her nipples throbbed with a delicious type of pain that left her totally needy. She'd only imagined what a taste of BDSM might be like. She'd had no idea it would be so complicated, but at the same time, simple.

"Before I leave you, I'm going to give you a spanking."

"What about an orgasm?" She wondered whether or not it was possible to crawl out of her own skin.

"Demanding, aren't you?"

"I mean, please?" she hazarded, feeling her way around the new world and rules of a BDSM partnership.

"Continue to trust me."

With that roughness in his tone, how could she refuse? Slowly she nodded.

He offered his hand. She accepted it and stood in front of him. Her first impulse was to look down, but she remembered his last order had been to meet his gaze.

"You're a quick study. That pleases me very much." He didn't release her, and she didn't want to pull away. "I'm going to spank you," he said. "But tonight, it won't be for any of your transgressions. As you noted earlier, we need to

113

establish rules around what is and isn't acceptable behavior for the week that I'll be training you. After this moment, though, I'm uncompromising on lack of respect. It will be met with swift retribution."

She shuddered.

He waited.

Helpless to him, she said, "I agree, Sir."

"For now, though, tonight, I'm going to spank you because I want to, and because you're curious and because you want it as much as I do."

"I want it," she admitted.

Heat blazed in his eyes, thrilling her.

"At first, I'm going to use my hand. Implements are wonderful, but I want your first experience to be skin-on-skin. I want to feel you and see my handprint on you."

She sucked in a deep breath. Everything he said sent shock waves through her.

"When I tell you, I want you to turn away from me, bend over and link your hands behind you, just above your knees, sticking your ass out for me."

The room seemed to have chilled several degrees, even though the air conditioner hadn't cycled.

"Now."

She let go of his arms and felt unsteady as she turned.

Kelsey bent and linked her arms. It made her breathless to realize how vulnerable she was with her rear sticking out and her pussy exposed to him while she couldn't see him. But he was there, gliding his hands over her, offering reassurance that she gulped in.

When she settled, he began to rub her ass cheeks. "I don't want to leave any bruises," he told her. "Not tonight."

It stunned her to realize she wasn't sure how she felt about that. The idea of being uncomfortable and squirming in her chair as he walked past her desk on the way to his office fed a delicious fantasy.

Over the next minute, he moved faster and faster, covering her upper thighs.

The longer she stayed in position, the more blood flowed to her head, making her feel a bit disconnected from her body.

The first crack of his hand on her right ass cheek brought her immediately back. She gasped. It hurt way fucking more than she'd imagined it would.

"How's that?" he asked.

"Frigging hell," she ground out.

"Oh?" He drew a finger down her pussy then inserted it into her.

She jerked. The pain had already vanished, and she was cloaked in warmth.

Nathan pulled away then spanked her again on the other buttock.

This time — maybe because she'd been prepared — it didn't seem to hurt as badly.

He fingered her again, and she moaned. The need to orgasm returned with more force than it had earlier

As if knowing that, he withdrew from her.

She moaned. "Nathan!"

"You're doing great." He rubbed her heated skin. "Give yourself over to the experience. Don't think. Don't demand. Feel."

Did he have any idea what he was asking for?

He spanked her several times — on her rear, on the tender flesh just beneath. His smacks weren't as hard as earlier, and her entire body tingled.

"Keep your ass high and out. Concentrate on that one command if you're having difficulty focusing."

She closed her eyes.

Nathan caught her flesh with upward strokes and he alternated them with mind-bending touches to her pussy. She was getting damper and damper, aware of every part of her body.

"How many more should I give you?"

From her reading, she remembered an answer. "As many as you think I deserve, Sir."

"Ten."

Not knowing if she could take that, she bent her knees.

"Twelve."

Immediately she forced herself back into position.

"Much better. Spread your legs."

Feeling a bit like she had the grace of a penguin, she stayed bent over and kept her hands behind her as she moved her feet farther apart.

Kelsey saw his hand move, and the overhead light seemed to play with his watchband. She was distracted by the sound of something humming then she felt the press of smooth, hardened plastic against her pussy.

She pulled away.

"Stay still," he told her.

"I can't. Can't, can't, can't."

Instead of arguing, he slowly inserted the head of the vibrator into her pussy. Unerringly he angled it so that the tip pressed against her G-spot.

"Nathan! Sir!"

He slid a palm against her belly to hold her in place, and it seemed to magnify the sensation in her.

"Close your legs."

"That's going to make it more difficult."

"Yes, it will," he said agreeably.

Driven wild, so mad that she gave hardly a thought to her lack of style, she whimpered and tried to do what he said.

"I'm going to come."

"You're going to think about holding your position and making sure the vibrator doesn't fall out. If it does, we'll start over."

"No." She shook her head. "No, no." She did an inelegant little dance, jerking as the evil little wiggling vibrator relentlessly buzzed against her most sensitive spot. When she'd used it on herself, it had never been this maddening.

"How many?"

"Ten, Mr. Donovan."

"Pardon me?"

Fuck balls. He turned up the dial, making her twitch. "Twelve! You said twelve, Nathan."

He spanked her right ass cheek six times with horrible, accurate precision, landing one right above the other, searing her. She drew in breaths and pretended she were anywhere but here. A beach. On a tram tour at Space Center Houston. Hanging onto the rail on the Bolivar ferry. Heaven help her, even in a church. Though she knew nothing could help her now.

It wasn't possible for her to maintain the position.

"Not yet."

She couldn't...

With a scream, she came, harder than she ever had in her life. The force dislodged the vibrator, but she didn't hear it hit the floor.

She shuddered, squeezing her hands together tighter as she fought to make the room stop spinning.

All the while, Nathan held her, said things she could hear but didn't understand.

"I've got you," he said. He helped her stand then turned her to face him.

"That was..." She wasn't sure she had words. "Powerful."

"It gets better." He swiped strands of hair back from her face and tucked them behind her ears.

"Thank you." This, too, was odd to her. He'd been the one to drive her to the edge, but he'd been there to catch her when she'd gone over.

"You okay?"

"Yeah. I think." She noticed that her toes were curled under, a remnant from her climax.

"You're much less feisty after orgasming." He gave her a cocky grin that made her think of a movie star.

She tipped her head from side to side, working out the knots that had settled in her shoulders from holding her body tense for so long.

"On your back." He nodded toward the bed.

Kelsey blinked at him. "What?"

"Want to make it fifteen?"

"No, Sir. Twelve is fine."

He let her go, and she scrambled onto the mattress.

"Legs apart."

Unbelievably, she felt even more exposed in this position. Apprehensive.

"Cup your right breast."

She searched his face for any signs of teasing before remembering that he'd said that he didn't joke about certain things. Her motions were a bit jerky as she complied.

Kelsey's mouth dried when he returned to her holding the clothespins.

"Again, these aren't my preference, but they'll do for now. Unless you have some sort of plastic clips for laundry?"

A bit nervous, she shook her head. Her nipples were still tender from when he'd played with her earlier.

"How about some in the kitchen?"

God no.

"Which drawer?" he asked, obviously taking her silence as agreement.

He wouldn't. They were really grabby and a bit scary. "They're plain, small, for bags and such."

"I asked which drawer."

She sighed. "Bottom one. Next to the refrigerator."

"Remain in exactly that position."

Her heart thundered as she heard him moving about the condo. The position he'd left her in wasn't uncomfortable physically, but it was mentally. Part of her wanted to get up and put her clothes on. But a naughty impulse made her want to know what was next. The orgasm had been powerful, as he'd promised it would be. She thirsted for another and wondered whether or not he'd allow it. Nathan had to have known how close she was earlier and how hard she'd struggled to follow his orders.

The only thing she was certain of was the fact that she didn't want the evening to end.

His footsteps sounded confident as he returned to her.

"That's a sight, Kelsey," he said.

His warm tone of approval made her glad she'd followed his instructions.

He stood next to her, two plastic-coated, spring-loaded clips in hand. "Usually I like my subs on their knees, but this…?" He inhaled deeply. "I'll dream of this."

In her fantasies, she'd replay this moment over and over.

"These may hurt more, but they won't twist, meaning they're more predictable."

Already, she knew that about him. He didn't take unnecessary risk. "Is that supposed to make me feel better?"

He grinned, more wolfish than accessible. "I wasn't concerned about your feelings." Quickly, he moved, bending over her to suck on her right nipple, making it bead. She continued to hold her breast even as arrows streaked through her, straight to her pussy.

God, even though the suction hurt, it wasn't enough. His earlier attention had made her more sensitive, but not sore.

He lifted his head. "Pull on your nipple for me."

A day ago, having a man make such a request of her would have been unthinkable. Now it seemed natural.

She held her breast with her left hand then pinched the nipple, tugging it out and up as he'd done to her.

He placed the clip, and she hissed out a breath between clenched teeth as she dropped her hand.

"Nice, isn't it?"

"No." She shook her head. "Not even." In response to the pain, she clenched her buttocks, feeling as if her whole body were on fire.

"Do you need to use a safe word?" He slid a hand between her legs and rubbed back and forth.

The combination of his words and touch grounded her, bringing her back from the hole she'd started to fall down. She noticed the pain was no longer as significant. "I'm okay."

"Then you need to relax your muscles." He continued to strum her clit, and he stroked her left nipple.

She became aware that she actually wanted it to be clipped, as well. The difference between one aching for attention and the other burning from it confused her.

"Offer me your left nipple."

Kelsey's forearm brushed the clip that was already in place, making her wince.

"Pay attention," he told her.

She cupped her left breast and struggled to concentrate on elongating the nipple for him.

"I may have to do this for you every day," he said.

"*For* me?" she demanded incredulously.

"Can you not smell how aroused you are? Feel how slippery your hot little cunt is?"

Without her noticing, he stopped playing with her pussy and set the clip on her nipple.

Pain made her arch off the bed. She tried to sit up, but he held her down with a hand on her chest.

"Kelsey," he cautioned softly, reassuring her. "You can do this."

"You've got way more confidence in me than I do."

"It's already been thirty seconds for the first. You've endured it. Look at yourself. You're beautiful. See yourself as I do."

She lifted her head to glance at her breasts. "Nope. Don't see it."

"You will when I get you a set of metal ones." He offered his hand. "Back into position. You still have twelve spanks coming."

"What?"

"I told you if you didn't hold the vibrator in place until we were finished, we would start over."

From his expression and his tone, she knew he meant what he said. He arched an eyebrow, signaling her to move.

Reluctantly she slid her hand into his. This time, she wasn't just aware of their size difference and his strength. She was ridiculously conscious of the fact he'd touched her intimately and that he'd blazed her ass with his palm.

Once she was standing, he said, "Back into position. Legs apart."

The addition of the clips made her movements slower than usual.

She was aware of him going into the bathroom and rinsing off the vibrator, which likely meant he was going to use it on her again. With her current level of arousal, she wasn't certain she could take much more. "I'm not sure about this," she admitted when he returned and pressed the tip to her pussy.

"No?" He sounded unconcerned.

He began to slide it in and out by slow measures, going deeper with each stroke. It only took a few seconds for the toy to be completely seated inside her. Then he turned the evil little thing on.

She jerked. "Nathan!"

"Close your legs." His voice was a soothing contrast to her high-pitched protest.

His touch unbearably gentle, he stroked her spine.

The feel of him settled her, despite the persistent buzzing in her pussy.

"How many spanks?" he asked.

Already, she was having a difficult time thinking. An orgasm was building again.

"Kelsey?"

"Twelve, Sir."

He landed the first on her right ass cheek, bringing pain back to the area.

She scooted away from him, but that made the wiggling inside her seem more pronounced.

"If you drop it—"

"I won't." No matter what, she'd keep the damn thing where it was. She couldn't start over again. Couldn't.

He didn't spank her again, and she finally, impatiently said, "I'm ready."

The blasted man took his time, layering the next few barely on top of one another.

"I love the sight of my handprint on your ass," he said, voice gruff.

For a mad second, she saw herself as he might, bent over for him, exposed and waiting. Was it possible that she might look as sexy to him as the women in some of the pictures she'd seen online?

"How many more on this side?" he asked her.

"Two. Sir?" It was a guess. Her ass was on fire, and she had been so caught up in her mind that she wasn't sure.

With his thumbnail, he traced the outline of his handprint, and she wasn't sure she'd ever felt anything more sensual.

He gave her one more then took hold of the vibrator's handle and jiggled it around.

She pitched forward and managed to catch herself on the foot of the bed. The movement made her breasts sway, intensifying the searing pain in her nipples. She felt overwhelmed and more alive than she ever had.

He was there, holding her, helping her. She drank strength from him. "It's too much."

"Is it?"

Kelsey was aware of him crouched next to her, stroking her hair. There was no challenge in his voice, just calm curiosity.

He captured her chin and turned her to face him.

Damn. He radiated masculine reassurance, and she sucked it in.

"You have a safe word. If you absolutely believe you have nothing left, say it. If you need me to stop temporarily, give you a break for a few minutes, the rest of the night, say yellow."

The head of the vibrator continued to shimmy against her G-spot. "If we…" She bounced her hand off the mattress a couple of times. "Will I have to do this again?"

"Yes."

She hated him for being so implacable. Loved that he was so implacable.

He feathered a finger down her cheekbone, giving her

time to process her answer. As she lay there, her nipples throbbed, her ass burned, and there was no place she'd rather be.

Quickly she calculated how many more spanks she'd have to endure. Six? No. Seven. "You'll let me come if I get through this?"

"At least once."

"At least?"

"At least."

He offered his arm, and she held it while she pushed herself upright then bent her knees to get into position.

"Amazing stamina. So much more than I hoped for."

"Are you serious?"

"Oh, very much. Very much."

That was the encouragement she needed.

"If it helps, count. If you want me to talk to you, I will. But think about how pleasing you're being."

"Please." She realized she was indeed asking him as he'd promised she would. And not just asking, pleading. It was as if she were in a race, and the finish line had come into view. "Please, Nathan. Please, Sir, will you continue?"

"Seven more."

She closed her eyes. Rather than spanking her right buttock, he caught her on the left one, stunning her, throwing off her expectations.

After delivering three more shocking smacks, he twisted the vibrator a full circle. It took all her concentration to keep her legs together and the blasted toy in place. She'd never felt so full, to the point of delirium.

"Well done," he said.

She held on to his words through the next few, even as she twitched, not just from the spanks but also the insistent dance inside her pussy.

"How many more?"

"I have no idea," she said. Then hopefully she added, "As many as you say."

"You *have* been reading. Two. And I will enjoy it. Your ass is so red, hot to the touch."

Mixing it up again, he seared her right cheek.

She yelped, and he delivered the last spank in a blaze of pain.

Before she finished reacting, he'd taken hold of the vibrator's shaft and said, "Spread your legs."

He angled a foot between hers and nudged her right ankle to the side.

While she struggled to comply, he reached up to tug on the clamps.

She moaned through gritted teeth, then he teased her clit. The sensations collided and crashed over her.

Instinctively she thrust her hips back. He pressed against her, and she felt his erection. The realization that Nathan Donovan was hard for her did crazy things to her equilibrium. She'd never been hungrier for a man's possession.

The image of a silver spiral consumed her mind.

"Come for me." He pressed on her clit and turned up the dial on the vibrator.

The increase in speed made her cunt clench.

Her legs weakened, but he was behind her, supporting her. His strength took her weight. Desperately crying out his name, she came.

Her body convulsed, and he spoke softly against her ear in approving tones, helping her to ride the crest even longer.

Nathan turned off the vibrator and continued to hold her until her chest stopped heaving and she was aware of him cradling her body.

"Are you back?" he asked.

She slowly, slowly exhaled, her legs feeling heavy. At some point, without being aware of it, she'd unlinked her hands and she was gripping his wrists.

"I want to take off the clips. But first I'm going to remove the vibrator."

"As long as you promise to put it back at some point."

"That's the spirit," he said as he grasped it and pulled.

It slid out with a slight pop. For some reason, having him remove it seemed potently intimate.

He tossed the toy onto the bed then helped her to stand, and once he'd made sure she was steady, he said, "You won't have bruises, but this mark" — he pressed his hand into her buttock — "will be there at least until you go to bed."

She couldn't believe that by tomorrow she would have no visible signs of that painful a spanking.

Nathan turned her to face him. "It's going to hurt when the blood flows back into your nipples."

"I'm ready."

He slowly removed the first.

"Crap *balls*." She'd never experienced that kind of pain from the clothespins.

He sucked the abused nipple into his mouth and laved her with his tongue. The pain dissipated, to be replaced with something delicious, similar to the floating feeling she sometimes experienced before falling asleep.

"Now the other." He cupped her breast and lowered his head.

More prepared this time, she held her breath. But there would have been no need. He was sucking on her less than a second after he'd plucked off the clip. The blood returned while she was in his mouth, and the expected pain didn't crash through her.

"How's that?" He pulled back from her.

She exhaled a shuddery breath. "The whole thing was beyond what I expected."

His answering smile was slow and proud. "Good."

Kelsey noticed his dick was still hard, and she reached out.

He put his hand over hers, guiding it the rest of the way to his cock.

She looked up at him. "Are we going to have sex?"

"Not tonight."

Maybe because he'd said no, she desired it even more.

"Another thing for us to talk about," he said.

"Does everything have to be discussed to death?"

With his free hand, he scooped her hair from her shoulders. "I tend to be cautious."

"What shakes you up?"

"Nothing."

"Does anything make you move faster? Cut through your reserve?"

He shook his head.

Suddenly, she wanted to be the one to do it, make him as mad for her as she was for him.

She squeezed his cock and stroked it.

He captured her hand in his unrelenting grip. "After we've talked about it."

"But—"

"I want it too," he said steadily, as she'd come to expect from him. "But you need to be very clear that BDSM doesn't necessarily involve sex. I have no expectations, and I don't have to fuck you for us to enjoy the week together. Besides, you've had quite enough for one evening. I'll tell you this, though. I will be jacking off in the shower, and I will be thinking of you."

"Take a video?" She had never been all that concerned with sex. It didn't really matter to her whether or not she had it. But with him, it did. She wanted to feel him in her, filling her. "Let me see it?"

"Another time." He fisted her hair and pulled back her head. "Welcome to my world, Kelsey. Do you want more?"

7

More? What more could there possibly be?

All night, the question had consumed Kelsey, making her toss and turn.

It had been a mistake to try to sleep naked, as she had found out when she'd rolled over and the sheet had abraded her nipple. Around two, she'd finally gotten out of bed in frustration and donned a T-shirt.

This morning, she was still tender, even though they hadn't actually had sex.

She pulled on a thong. Unable to help herself, she looked in the mirror at her ass. As impossible as it seemed with the way she tingled, there wasn't a single mark or bruise on her body. She was strangely disappointed.

Her phone chimed, telling her she only had fifteen minutes until she had to leave if she wanted to be on time to catch the train.

The reminder prompted her to think about Nathan again.

He planned to let her drive his car and pick her up after happy hour.

How the hell had all this happened?

Last night's image of a spiral returned to her, and she realized it was symbolic. Since she'd arrived at work yesterday morning, everything she'd believed seemed to have been challenged, from the fact she no longer worked for Mr. Newman to having Nathan Donovan introduce her to BDSM. His world, he'd called it. And she was hooked. To the point it was a challenge to think about anything other than their upcoming evening.

She finished dressing, telling herself that she hadn't

intentionally chosen one of her tightest, shortest skirts or her highest confidence-giving heels. Her hand trembled, just a little, as she applied her makeup. Today, though, unlike others, she applied red lipstick, just in case he was already at the office when she arrived.

Kelsey gripped the counter then frowned at her reflection and sternly told herself not to be ridiculous. What happened in their personal lives was separate from work. She was going to show up and do her job with the utmost professionalism. It made no difference whether or not Nathan was in his office when she arrived.

Then she realized the more she was lecturing herself, the more she was thinking about him and the more excitement arced through her.

With a frustrated sigh, she gave up and instead concentrated on the tasks she needed to accomplish in order to leave on time.

With seconds to spare, she dropped her makeup bag into her tote and shrugged into a blazer before leaving, phone in hand.

It took two attempts to get the lock closed. With a frustrated sigh, she made a mental note to call a locksmith. Maybe she could schedule something for later in the week, drive in, take a long lunch. Or perhaps come home early one day. *As if.* She hadn't left the office before five in over a year.

She dashed to make the train. Once she reached her stop, she headed straight for Marvin's.

"Morning, Kelsey," Marvin said when it was her turn. "The regular?" he asked, pulling a paper cup from a tall stack.

"Please." She fished a ten-dollar bill from the wallet in her tote.

He marked the cup with a capital M for mocha. "Just one?"

She nodded, and a jolt went through her when she realized that she'd never again need to buy one for Mr. Newman.

And she doubted it would be a good idea to take one to the hospital.

"Whipped cream?"

She smiled. "Does the day end in the letter y?"

"Tuesday. Yep." He scrawled her name on the cup and added a smiley face beneath it.

"You should have been an artist."

"Mostly, I am. Flour is my medium. The finished goods are my canvas."

That was true. The cupcakes were decorated in different colors, and frosting swirled and dipped. Even the scallops on the petit fours were perfect. He rearranged the cases throughout the day, ensuring everything was perfectly, temptingly displayed. More than once she'd bought something because it was gorgeous.

"Anything else? I have scones if you haven't had breakfast. Maybe a slice of quiche?"

He knew her too well.

"A spinach feta scone." She thought about it for less than a second. "And a large coffee of the day."

"For your boss?"

"Marvin," she warned.

He held up a hand but didn't even attempt to hide his grin. He rang up her order, dropped the pastry in a bag then glanced over his shoulder at her. "Room for cream?"

"No." At yesterday's meeting, Nathan had taken it black.

After putting a lid on the cup, Marvin handed it to her. "He seemed like a nice young man, if you ask me."

"Don't you have other people you need to help?"

His grin got bigger. "Have a good day, Kelsey."

Nice?

She wasn't sure she'd ever use that word to describe Nathan Donovan. Focused. Intent. Relentless. Those were more accurate. And after last night, a few more could probably be thrown in. *Nice?*

She paid Marvin, dropped the change in the tip jar, picked up the scone and Nathan's coffee then walked to an empty table. Since the barista had a couple of drinks in front of her mocha, she put the pastry in her tote and pulled out her phone to check messages. There was a frantic-sounding text from Andi. She'd had a mimosa for breakfast since Lorean had called in saying he'd be late because he had cramps.

Kelsey laughed so hard that a man near her turned to stare. Sometimes she wondered how she'd survive life without Andi.

She sent back a tiara emoticon. Then she sent a message of her own.

Lots to tell you.

About your hunky-dunky-hottie boss? C'mon. Tell me more.

Unable to resist the opportunity to create some drama, she responded.

We hung out last night. Oh. Mer. Gawd.

Girlfriend, you wrecked my day worse than it was. Dish.

I will. Over martinis.

Bitch.

Love you, too.

God knew Kelsey needed someone to talk to.

When her mocha was called, she grabbed it then carried it to the table. In one of her favorite indulgences, she pried off the lid then grabbed a stir stick to scoop out some of the whipped cream. She savored it while she stirred in the rest.

She took a sip to make sure it wasn't overly hot and that it tasted good before taking a couple of much longer drinks.

The cup was half empty before she gathered everything and headed toward work.

In the building, the elevator doors closed behind her, and

her heart rate increased as she was carried up each floor. Mentally, she began preparing a strategy for dealing with Nathan.

By the time she arrived at their suite, her brain was in overdrive.

Since the door was unlocked and the lights were on, he'd obviously arrived before her. But thankfully he wasn't waiting for her.

Kelsey exhaled a breath she hadn't realized she'd been holding.

His office door was closed, and she heard the cultured tones of his voice as he spoke. She wondered whether he had a visitor or if he was on the phone. Or maybe a video call.

Until Nathan, she'd never really appreciated the sound of a man's voice. He controlled his so well, from commanding to reassuring, corporate inflexibility to encouraging. It wasn't just with her. It had been the same with Martha Leone as he'd charmed her. Then with the senior management team. The man intuitively knew how to get what he wanted.

She placed the cups on the desktop then glanced at her wire inbox. A wink of metal caught her eye. With a frown, she reached for it.

Cold lanced through her as she picked up a set of nipple clamps.

He'd remembered.

Suddenly she was careening back to the previous night. Her nipples ached anew and she was breathless, needy.

Even though their time together had been sexy and she'd come at least two or three times, she'd been left somewhat frustrated by the fact they hadn't had sex. That bothered her more than she cared to admit. She ached to feel him inside her.

His office door opened. Until then she hadn't realized he'd stopped talking.

With a guilty start, she dropped the nipple clamps.

"I'm looking forward to watching you put them on your

tits tonight."

Vertigo seized her. So much for her attempt at professionalism. She wasn't sure how to feel knowing he would be blurring the lines between work and submission.

She'd been thinking about him since he'd left her condo. How was it possible that she hadn't remembered exactly how devastating he was in a suit and power tie?

He exuded power and seduction. Though he was clean-shaven, his hair was just that little bit long, leaving him looking rakish.

Without meaning to, she glanced at his hands. She shivered as she remembered the way he'd spanked her, fingered her, squeezed her breasts.

She wanted him to do all that again. And more. So, so much more.

God. How was she supposed to survive the week? Professionalism, she reminded herself. "Good morning, Mr. Donovan."

"Kelsey," he said with a nod. "How are you doing?"

Because of the huskiness in his voice, she knew he'd been thinking of her. This wasn't the way he'd greeted her yesterday, it was more intimate.

"I'm fine, thank you."

"Sleep okay?"

"Yes."

He cocked an eyebrow and stared at her as if seeing through her.

She shifted, unable to hold the line on her lie. "I've slept better," she admitted.

"Yeah?" He waited. "Me too."

His response flabbergasted her. Had she somehow affected the dynamic Nathan Donovan? Even the possibility was enough to make her giddy. Screw professionalism.

"How does your ass feel?" he asked.

"No bruises."

"Show me."

It wasn't a question or a request, she knew. Her mouth

132

fell open.

"Lock the door and show me."

His green eyes were icy with implacability. Using a safe word was always an option. But damn it, with her libido in overdrive, she didn't want to.

Conscious of him watching her intently, she walked to the big double doors and threw the lock.

"Stop."

Her back to him, she froze.

"Face me."

A tremor passed through her. Slowly, conscious of making her movement as elegant as possible, she did so.

"Now lift your skirt to your waist."

Having him raise it was one thing. Doing it herself was dizzying.

She had on a thong, and the way he looked at her as she raised the hem made her wish she'd had the courage to go bare.

"Black lace was a good choice. You're a beautiful woman, Kelsey."

She saw in his eyes that the words weren't meaningless, and she drank in confidence from them.

"I want you to walk to the desk, drop your underwear to your ankles then bend over the top."

"Yes, Mr. Donovan." In her imagination, she sounded much more self-assured than she did in reality.

He remained in his doorway, master of the domain. And for right now, of her.

The skirt was so slim-fitting that it stayed in place without her holding it. Feeling more exposed than she had when she'd been at home naked with him, she followed his order.

When she reached her desk, she slid her thong over her hips and down her legs before bending over. She was grateful that she didn't have to look at him.

His footsteps were muffled by the carpet, but she was aware of him as he closed the distance.

He trailed his fingertips across her buttocks then between

her cheeks to tease her pussy and flirt with her anus.

"By the end of the week, I want you showing up to work wearing a butt plug."

She swung her head to look at him.

He shrugged. "If you don't, I'll put one in for you. Nothing would please me more than knowing you're sitting here, ten feet away, stuffed full for me."

The image saturated her mind, and suddenly she couldn't stop thinking of it, either.

"You're right. No bruises. Good. We've still got a lot of days to get through."

The reminder thrilled her.

"Are you hot for me already?"

Jesus. He touched her pussy. "Mr. Donovan." She was breathless.

"Oh...you are."

"This is impossible. We're at work."

"Almost an hour before business starts. I'd say that counts as personal time."

Very personal.

"You're welcome to use a safe word," he invited. "Or I can continue and slide my finger into my sub's cunt?" He moved a little, teasing. "Which will it be?"

"Your finger," she whispered.

"Please, *Sir*," he said seductively against her ear.

Kelsey repeated his words.

"Good. Now say, please, Sir, put your finger in my hot cunt."

Those words seemed lodged in her throat. She couldn't be so bold and brazen.

He stopped moving.

Damn it. "Please, Sir," she capitulated. The need for him to continue was greater than her need to avoid embarrassment. "Please, Sir, put your finger in my hot cunt."

From somewhere in the distance, she heard an elevator ding, and she realized others were starting to arrive for their workday. It heightened the danger and her response.

"Please, Sir," he said again. "Put your finger in your sub's hot cunt?"

She collapsed flat onto the desktop. He was single-minded in his determination to push her. Wildly she remembered that he'd promised exactly that. "Please, Sir," she repeated, her pussy even wetter than it had been last night. "Please put your finger in your sub's hot cunt." Her words had an air of surrender to them, and it did strange things to her insides.

"Oh, my sub, I'd love to." He entered her slowly, sliding in and out in an erotic finger-fuck.

Within seconds, she was hot with need.

The knowledge that the orgasm was his to give or withhold was excruciating.

She hoped he'd change the angle and press against her G-spot, but he didn't. Instead, he ground his thumb against her clit.

"Please, please!"

"Which would make it easier for you to make it through the day?" he asked. "An orgasm? Or the sharpness of hunger?"

"Don't deny me," she begged. "I can't take it."

"You can. Whatever I say. Whatever I ask."

"Yes," she said.

"For today, wait."

She smacked her palms against her desk.

"And with a little more patience next time, sub. My will, sub."

"Has anyone ever told you no, Mr. Donovan?"

"Of course." He kept his voice soft, near her ear. "Most regret it later."

What the hell had she gotten herself into?

He helped her to stand.

Her clit was a pulsing, throbbing, annoying bundle of need. At this moment, she wanted him as much as she hated him.

"Say, thank you, Sir."

She turned her head to the side to look at him. "Thank you?"

"Or it could be a really long time before I let you come again."

In one of the forums she'd been following online, a sub talked about a Dom withholding orgasms as a way to ensure good behavior. Another had said her Master liked to leave her horny so that she came fast later in the day. They'd all sounded slightly sexy until she was the unlucky recipient, with hormones rushing through her blood and an unsatisfied pussy. "Thank you, Sir," she said without a note of gratitude.

"Pull up your underwear." He smacked her ass, hard.

She couldn't believe he'd actually leave her this way. It would be at least thirteen hours, probably fourteen, until he took her home this evening.

After she pulled up her thong, he lowered her skirt into place.

"Thank you, Sir," he prompted.

"Thank you, Nathan." Her tone was laced with more than a little sarcasm.

"That will cost you."

"But we haven't had a discussion about punishment," she protested quickly. *Damn it.*

"But I did inform you I wouldn't tolerate disrespect and that corporal punishment is my preferred form of correction."

He waited.

"Thank you, Sir."

"Is one of those coffees for me?"

She wanted to tell him no. And now she was tempted to drink his. Instead she replied, "Drip of the day. Black."

"You remembered. Thank you." He picked up the cup without the word mocha on the side.

She flushed and looked away.

"Won't convince me to overlook the other, but this is appreciated." He took a long, appreciative drink.

"Marvin's?"

"It's one of my favorite places for morning coffee."

Flustering her, he took a seat near her desk. "What's on your agenda?"

How could he go from D/s to boss/employee so fast? She picked up her mocha and sat behind her desk then moved her mouse to wake up her computer and pull up her calendar.

"Please give me access to that," he said.

She knew she had no right to refuse, especially since he'd shared his with her. "I've got a nine o'clock with Zoe McBride. Encore Events. Do you want to sit in?"

"If I'm free, I'll say hello, but I trust you to handle it."

"I'll need a budget."

He shook his head. "I want you to bring me one, and I'll sign off on it. Make every penny count and be prepared to make a reasonable case for the expenditures."

As always, he made her shift uncomfortably. "At lunchtime, I'll be seeing Mr. Newman."

He nodded.

"Then happy hour with Andi."

"And...?"

Her pussy moistened from the way he regarded her. "Whatever pleases you."

"Specifically?" He took a drink. "What would that be?"

She uncrossed her legs then recrossed them in the opposite direction. "Putting the clamps on my nipples."

"Very, very good." He picked up the clamps and hung them from his index finger.

Kelsey took them from him and dropped them into her tote.

"Are your evening plans on the calendar?"

"Since they're private, no."

"Where are you going?"

"You don't need to pick me up," she told him again, even though she suspected he wouldn't listen to any arguments.

Silence hung between them. He let it drag until she could

no longer tolerate it.

"Friscos." She gave him the address.

"Alcohol and scenes don't mix well, so you'll want to limit yourself if you want to scene. If you just want to go have fun with your friend, that's perfectly fine."

Before she could say anything, he went on, "Either way, I'll be driving you home. What's your phone number?"

She should have realized he'd think that through as well. He'd provided his information yesterday and given her access to all his files, but she hadn't done the same.

He angled his wrist so that his watch was exposed. A large pink heart hovered above the screen.

"What's that for?"

He impatiently swiped a finger across the surface. "Heart rate monitor."

"A pulsing heart hologram? Pink is definitely your color."

From his scowl, he didn't seem nearly as amused by the sight as she was. "Your number, Ms. Lane?"

She forced away her smile, and Nathan touched the corner of the screen as she provided the number.

"Call Kelsey Lane," he instructed.

"Dialing, Mr. Donovan."

Seven seconds later, her phone rang.

"End," he told the watch.

"Ended."

"Now you'll have no excuses for not contacting me."

The man was skilled at getting his way.

Without another word, he went to unlock the door. "I'm looking forward to this evening," he said before entering his office and closing the door.

She allowed her shoulders to collapse against the chair back.

With each moment, she felt as if she were getting deeper and deeper in a swimming pool. She'd started in the shallow end, but she could no longer reach the bottom.

What the hell was it about her that made common sense pack a bag and head for parts unknown?

Yesterday Nathan had told Kelsey that he was cautious, but that was a fucking lie when it came to her. If he'd been cautious, he wouldn't have reacted when Connor had told him she wanted to go to Deviation. As long as it didn't interfere with job performance, it didn't—*shouldn't*—matter to Nathan what his employees did during their free time, but somehow it did with Kelsey.

And if he were cautious, he wouldn't have driven to his favorite kink store in South Houston after he'd left her condo last night.

The store had been a forty-five-minute drive each way, but he'd been obsessed with getting her the nipple clamps, a small plug, a leash and a collar that she could wear on Saturday night. He'd wanted the items in his possession and he'd been too impatient to wait for overnight delivery. With her, he refused to take chances.

He hadn't gotten home until nearly eleven, and he'd jacked off before going to bed, but that hadn't stopped him from waking up with a hard-on six hours later.

That one, he'd ignored. He knew he'd pissed her off this morning. What she didn't know was that he was suffering along with her. He wanted the low-grade yearning to consume him, sharpening his focus where she was concerned.

For the tenth time today, his watch vibrated. He glanced at it to see a 3-D heart image pulsing rapidly above the screen. "Out of my head, Bonds."

But the God damn heart icon beat even faster, and he detested that it was an accurate representation of what was going on in his head.

This need for her surprised him.

It had been more than two years since he'd been involved with a woman. But now that he'd had a taste of Kelsey's submission, all he could think of were things he wanted her to know, about BDSM, about herself.

He wondered if her toughness had surprised her. It had delighted him.

When he'd felt how wet she was from his spanking, he'd given her a little more than he'd originally planned to. She'd rewarded him by thrusting back into him, calling his name, orgasming harder than anyone he'd been with.

It had taken all his self-control to leave her last night, and he hadn't until after he'd reassured himself that she was fine.

While he'd told her having a relationship wasn't forbidden, it wasn't intelligent. He knew that ignoring his internal warnings might prove disastrous. And damned if he didn't intend to do exactly that.

A knock on the door brought him back from the dangerous territory his thoughts had led him into. "Enter."

Kelsey stood on the threshold, so damn appealing in her heels, borderline-too-tight skirt and white button-down shirt.

Since this morning, she'd freshened her red lipstick.

Fuck him to within an inch of his life.

"I just got off the phone with Holly Newman. She said it's a good time for me to visit the hospital."

"I'll walk you to the car. It's in the VIP lot today."

"I'm sure I can find that. Probably. Maybe."

"You don't have a spot there?"

"Is that a serious question?" Her chin came up in a move he already recognized as defensive. "And would you be asking now if we didn't have a personal relationship?"

Anger arrowed through him. "Is *that* a serious question?" he countered, pissed. "It's about safety. You get here earlier than almost anyone in the building. And from what I can see, you leave later than most. And you're my assistant."

"Being the CEO's executive assistant has never earned me privileges before." Then, as if she wanted to defuse his anger, she added, "There are a limited amount of spots and a lot of competition for them. Besides, most times I take the train." She smiled. "Besides, if you remember, you drove me home. If I can borrow your keys, I'm sure I can find the lot. It can't be that difficult."

He stood, grabbed his keys from his top desk drawer then said, "Follow me."

Lightly, she placed her fingers on his forearm. Earlier in the day, he'd removed his jacket and rolled back his sleeves, so they were skin-to-exciting-skin. He loved her touch.

"Nathan, really, there's no need. I don't want to take you away."

"Kelsey, what gave you the idea we were still discussing this?"

Her nose flared as she drew a deep breath.

"I like you better when you don't struggle."

"You like it better when you win," she countered.

He grinned, feeling feral. "Especially that."

After placing his fingers on the small of her back, he guided her from their offices. In the elevator, she moved to the far side of the car.

And because of the way she'd acted this morning and the fact he couldn't get her out of his head, he hit the stop button.

Her eyes went wide, the whiskey color banked by fire.

He advanced on her. She retreated until she couldn't move another inch.

"You feel it too."

"You frustrate me."

"You wanted that orgasm this morning."

She hesitated before admitting, "Yes. I don't like being left unfulfilled. It's annoying." She grabbed a hank of hair and moved it over her left shoulder. "I'm trying my best not to think about it and to concentrate on my job. Honestly, Nathan? This whole submission thing is more complicated than I thought it was."

He saw the struggle in her eyes, and it mirrored his angst. He fucking wanted her pleasure as much as she did. "If you want it, you'll have to take it. I won't make it easy for you."

"What?"

"Take it." He held up his hand.

Her breaths were rapid, and she dropped her tote bag to the floor.

An alarm sounded, followed by slightly disembodied words from the metal speaker. "Everything okay, Mr. Donovan?"

He recognized the voice of the head of security, a dedicated, intelligent man Nathan had met last week. "Fine, Rankowski. Give me three minutes."

There were a few seconds of silence before the man said, "Ms. Lane?"

"Fine, John." Her voice was flustered, her vocal cords strained.

"Any longer, I'll have to ask you to continue or I'll need to call the fire department."

"Thank you," Nathan replied.

"Are there cameras in here?" she asked.

"In the hallway. Not in the elevator."

"But...people will know."

"We're having a private discussion." He regarded her. "Your choice. We have three minutes. What will it be?"

"I think we've both lost our minds," she whispered.

Wondering about that himself, he captured one of her hands and moved it to his wrist. "Fuck my hand."

For a long second, he had no idea whether she'd be brave enough or whether she'd push a button to continue the descent.

He inhaled, sucking her into his senses. Honeysuckle and hesitation.

"Yes," she said.

He captured the bottom of her skirt and yanked it up, exposing that black lacy confection.

"What now?" he asked her.

"Please, Sir."

"Please, what?"

"Please put your hand in my panties, give me an orgasm."

"Now? Here? In the elevator? You want me to fuck you

with my hand?"

She looked up, then back at him. "Yes."

"Then tell me."

"I want you to fuck me with your hand, Nathan."

"Scream for me?"

"Make me."

That was why he was so captivated, he knew. It was the combination of sass and bravery, of hesitation and innocence. If he could have wrapped up a gift for himself, she would be wearing a bow. "Kelsey, my perfect little sub, I will give you anything."

She guided his hand inside her panties. Her pussy was drenched.

"Did you already come, you naughty sub?"

"No, Sir. I'm just that ready."

Without another word, she pushed on his hand and he plunged three fingers inside her.

"*Fuuuuck,*" she said, gasping. "That's too much."

"Take it. Take me. And tell me to stretch you wide, push against your G-spot, make you drown us in your pussy juices."

"You're crude, Sir."

"And you're fucking hot for me."

"Yes. Stretch me." It wasn't a request.

Right now, he didn't care. He was as consumed as she was. He and caution were no longer on speaking terms.

"Make me come," she said. Then, as if remembering herself, added, "Please. Nathan."

He crooked a finger and found her G-spot. He continued to move inside her while he flicked his thumb over her clitoris.

"I've got to come," she said.

"Wait," he told her in a rough voice, pushing her, making her call on all her mental and physical reserves, relentlessly driving her in ways he was sure no man ever would. And at this moment, he refused to think of a time when another man might think he had the right to claim her.

"Now, now, now… *Now!*"

Her fingernails bit into his skin. He leaned forward to bite her shoulder.

She screamed.

"Now," he demanded, moving a second finger against her G-spot and ruthlessly pressing her clit.

Kelsey, his woman, his sub, screamed.

He captured the sound with his mouth, devouring it and her.

Her body sagged forward, and he happily caught her. He'd hold, protect this woman for as long as she needed, probably longer than she wanted.

"Mr. Donovan?" the head of security interrupted again. "Everything okay?"

He leaned forward. "You should probably reassure him that you're okay," Nathan said, impressed with Rankowski's persistence. The man had been around a lot of years. No doubt Nathan wasn't the first to stop the elevator with a beautiful woman aboard.

"Give us another minute, please, John," she said. She cleared her throat.

"You're sure, Ms. Lane?"

Since he'd known who else was on the elevator, no doubt he'd been watching security cameras.

Nathan feathered his executive assistant's clit, and she scowled at him.

"One minute," she reiterated.

"Sixty seconds, ma'am. If the car isn't moving, I'm taking action."

Nathan slowly pulled his fingers out of her cunt and shoved them in her mouth. "Suck me dry. And pretend they're my cock."

Her eyes watered and she gagged because he was knuckles-deep in her mouth, but she wrapped her hands around his wrist and took everything, licking, cleaning.

Then, no doubt with less than three seconds left, he pulled his fingers from her mouth.

He saw satiation in her eyes, and he fucking liked it.

Nathan straightened her thong and smoothed her skirt before stepping away from her. He tucked wayward strands of hair behind her ear then wiped a smudge of lipstick from her skin. He made sure she was perfectly put back together before resuming the trip.

They exited into the parking garage, and they were met by the efficient Rankowski. "Problem with the elevator?" he asked.

"None," Kelsey assured him.

He looked at both of them intently. "I'll ride it up to be sure it's in proper working order."

Nathan nodded. They both knew the elevator was fine. Rankowski was simply excusing himself now that he was reassured that everything was okay.

"He's protective," she said. "Tends to be with all female employees. He's even offered to walk me to my car if I leave after dark."

"Good." He pointed toward the SUV. When they were about twenty feet away, he unlocked it with the remote.

After she'd slipped behind the wheel and adjusted the seat, he gave her a few instructions to familiarize herself with the dash, and he added her number to the vehicle's Bluetooth system.

She opened her mouth to protest but closed it again almost immediately.

"Drive safe." He grabbed the end of the safety belt and reached across her to fasten it before trailing a finger down the side of her face. "Feeling better now?"

"That was…" She grinned.

He smiled back at her. A shared experience neither would ever forget.

"Did we really do that?"

"You tell me."

She pressed her legs together. "My pussy is throbbing still."

"Will you make it until this evening?"

"I don't know. Maybe."

"My sub." He meant it. With a nod, he took a step back then closed the door.

Before she made the turn to exit the parking structure, she stopped. He saw her glance in the rear-view mirror, and she found him standing near the elevator, watching her.

She gave a little wave before accelerating.

With a jolt he realized the last few minutes had been more than D/s for him. They'd been primal, and he'd been a man powerfully driven to satisfy his woman, mark her as his, keep others away from her. With every thud of his heart, he heard one word echo in his head. *Mine.* Tonight, he'd be sure she knew it as much as he did.

8

"Every single detail," Andi demanded as they slid into a booth next to the window at Friscos, one of downtown's most popular eateries. Since it was Tuesday night, it was busy, but not crazy, so they'd be able to talk.

"I want all the deets," Andi went on after they'd placed their orders with the server. "The dirtier and nastier the better. Give them to me, my pretty."

Kelsey had been anxious to talk but now that they were here, she wasn't sure how much she wanted to share. She was still wobbly from what she and Nathan had done in the elevator this morning. She'd behaved in a way that was so wanton it was unheard of.

Shockingly, she knew she'd do it again.

In her office, he'd left her so horny it had been difficult to do her job. She'd never experienced anything like that. Until him, she would have said she possessed a low libido. But with the way she'd happily humped his hand and come all over him, she'd realized he'd been right when he'd suggested maybe the problem hadn't been with her, but with the men she'd been with. She'd orgasmed outrageously fast with Nathan. He'd been singularly focused on driving her to the edge, involving her mind before ever touching her body. It was as if they'd had five hours of foreplay before he'd savaged her pussy in the elevator.

The server returned with their martinis, and they clinked their glasses together.

"Don't make me wait," Andi insisted.

"You go first. You had a hell of a day if you were drinking by nine."

147

"It was eight, actually." Andi took an unladylike gulp then said, "Fucking-A, I needed this after dealing with Lorean's crap. He said he was too bloated to cancel his own clients, so we had to reschedule them. Then he floated in around eleven, said he'd had a hot bath and felt better. Told us to call back his fans and tell them to come in after all."

"Fans?"

"Most of us have customers or clients. He has *fans*." She traced a black-painted fingernail over one of her masterfully crafted winged eyebrows. "He drives me to drink."

"You mean he gives you an excuse to drink."

"Thank God for any excuse to drink!" Andi lifted a chunk of her hair, and Kelsey noted that it was light pink with stripes of baby blue.

Her friend went to New York at least three times a year to keep up on the trends. Pastel-colored hair wasn't something Kelsey had ever desired, but Andi rocked it.

Kelsey sat back then licked the rim of her glass and closed her eyes from the rush of sweetness.

"Yuck. I don't know how you can drink that." Andi shuddered so hard her whole body shook, and her dozen or so bangles sounded a bit like a wind chime.

Most people would never dip a glass in cane sugar before pouring in a chocolate martini, but to Kelsey, it just gave it that extra pizzazz she loved. The fact the bartender knew her preference was one of the main reasons she came here. "I could say the same to you."

Andi speared the olive at the bottom of her glass and popped it into her mouth. She closed her eyes and sucked on it then moaned as if she were having sex.

"Maybe I should switch to dirty martinis," Kelsey said.

"Come to the dark side. We have extra olives."

They both laughed, and after the intensity of the last couple of days, it was a welcome break. Seeing Mr. Newman at lunchtime had taken her aback. His color had been a frightening shade, more gray than pale. He seemed to have lost ten pounds and aged twenty years in less than a week.

Holly Newman had joined Kelsey in the cafeteria. The woman had said it was a good thing the Donovans had acquired the business when they did. Even though he'd tried to hide it, her husband's health had been failing for some time. Each challenge was getting progressively more difficult to manage. And she confessed she'd been after him to sell or retire for several years. On a lot of levels, she was grateful they had more time to spend together. She already had a trip planned for them to see their grandchildren in California.

But as she'd driven back to work, Kelsey had felt a little shaken.

To her, Samuel Newman had always seemed so confident, vigorous. Seeing him in the hospital gown, ashen, had made her accept the fact he wouldn't be returning.

And that meant she was truly stuck with Nathan, unless she wanted to look for another job.

Right at this moment, she wasn't certain she wanted to.

But what happened after their week was up? Or when she slept with him?

And how the hell did all thoughts lead straight back to Nathan?

Andi snapped her fingers near Kelsey's face. "Earth to Kelsey."

She shook her head. "Sorry. Thinking about Mr. Newman."

"He's going to be okay, right?"

"It appears so."

"Good. Now tell me about the new boss. You hung out last night. And is he?" She fanned herself.

"Is he what?"

Andi leaned forward. "A Dom?"

"Yeah."

She popped another olive into her mouth. "I knew it. So how did you find out?"

"I think I owe it to you."

"Me? What do I have to do with it?"

The server brought a plate of hummus, surrounded by carrot and celery sticks along with pita chips.

"Thank God," Andi said. "I didn't eat today." When they were alone again, she scooped up some dip and said, "Continue."

"He confronted me about wanting to go to Deviation."

"How did he find out? Did you tell him?"

Kelsey shook her head. "It was his brother. I'm not sure how, but evidently the manager recognized my name when you called. And Connor notified Nathan." Kelsey swirled her glass to dislodge some of the chocolate syrup clinging to the inside. She could see the teardrop-shaped piece of milk chocolate at the bottom, sitting there like a reward for consuming every delicious sip.

"I'm going to need another drink," Andi said. "This is going to be interesting. Until yesterday, I didn't know you were into kinky shit. I mean, I know you won that paddle, but you flushed about seventeen shades of red when I smacked you on the butt with it. So I was sure you were scandalized."

"Well, you haven't talked much about it, either."

"I like working over a sub or two occasionally."

Kelsey choked on a drink. "You're a Domme?"

Andi shrugged and signaled for their server to bring another round. "More of a switch. I like to bottom sometimes, just because I get sick of being in charge all the time. But mostly, I like being Queen Bitch, and I love to use a flogger on a woman. Their asses are so much hotter than a man's, rounder. Softer. Though if I could get Lorean to drop his leather pants for long enough, I'd use a carpet beater on his tight butt. That's a man who needs a serious ass-whooping."

"You're not his type."

"No?" Andi took a bite from a carrot.

"Isn't he… Wait… What?" She drained her glass. Kelsey hoped the server returned soon. She definitely needed that second drink. "You're serious? You have a thing for

Lorean?"

"Confounded drama queen."

"*Lorean?*" Kelsey repeated incredulously. Her friend had worked with the man for at least three years. Constant arguments, challenges and upsets seemed to be their norm. Kelsey had no clue there was any interest there.

"Stupid, right?"

The server arrived with their beverages, saving Kelsey from an immediate answer.

"Are you finished here?" The man reached for Kelsey's glass.

"I think she'll break your fingers if you try to take it," Andi said.

"Are you kidding me?" Kelsey pickup up her cocktail straw. "This is vodka-infused chocolate we're talking about."

"Not just your fingers," Andi said to the server, wagging her artful eyebrows. "You're in danger of losing your whole arm if you try to move it."

"I'll be back." The man grinned and made a show of stepping slowly away from the table.

Kelsey tilted the glass and used her straw to guide the little slice of heaven into her mouth.

Since her whole body seemed warmer, she decided to go a little slower on the second drink. "Does he know?" she asked when they were alone again. "Lorean, I mean."

"Oh, hell yes."

"And you two...?"

"We have."

Kelsey had known the conversation this evening was going to be wild, but she'd had no idea it would be anything like this. "So what's the problem?"

"His lack of seriousness. Try snuggling on the couch with him."

"Uhm. No. Good. Pass. Thanks." To drown the image, Kelsey took the last, long drink of her martini.

"I do everything at Mach speed, and he slows me down.

And it takes him longer to get ready to go places than it does me. Two of us in the bathroom doing makeup. And he even wore some of my earrings."

"I…" She shrugged helplessly. "I've got nothing. I don't even know what to say."

"Doesn't really matter. We're on a break now."

"Since last night," Kelsey guessed.

"Exactly."

"You okay?"

"I will be. Or I am as long as I don't think about him. So. Enough about all that. Entertain me. I want to hear about Nathan and what happened between the two of you. And, oh, wait. Have you had the opportunity to get me a referral with Erin Donovan yet?"

"In the last twenty-four hours?" Kelsey scowled at her friend. "Not everything is about your business."

"I forget that."

"I did meet Zoe McBride today. Sofia's sister."

"How's her hair?"

"I'd be surprised if she wasn't already one of your clients."

"I'll send her a coupon. You know, if you send people to me, it won't cost you much for me to add some burgundy lowlights to your hair. Normally, as long as it is, it would cost you a fortune, but—"

"I like my hair as it is. Thank you." Kelsey took the first sip of her second drink.

Andi sighed. After falling silent, she went after some more hummus and waved a chip, encouraging Kelsey to get on with the story.

"We had coffee after work, and he gave me a ride home. And when we got there…"

"Go on."

"He told me about the call from Connor, and he said that if I wanted to go to Deviation, he would escort me."

Andi's hand froze on the way to her mouth. "You're going as his sub?" She fanned herself. "There's more, isn't there?"

"He wants to train me this week." Kelsey took another

fortifying drink. "He, uh, gave me an introduction last night."

"What did he do? Tell me he spanked you."

Kelsey hesitated a couple of seconds. "He did."

"And how was it?"

This was unbelievably difficult to answer. "Amazing. Mind-blowing. Left me with about a hundred thousand questions."

"Anything I can help with?"

"I don't get why I like it."

"Why is that a question?" Andi demanded.

Kelsey made little circles on the base of the glass. "It's that I think I shouldn't."

"Because of being a badass executive assistant who's fought male oppression half her life."

"Well, when you put it that way..." She smiled and took a bite.

"And did you feel oppressed last night?"

"No." Kelsey shook her head. "It was weird. It was more liberating to be that honest about what I wanted." She remembered being bent over and the way reality had been so skewed that it felt as if she were fantasizing. "The orgasms were devastating."

"Then why not enjoy it? Suspend judgment for the week. If you decide at any point that you don't like something— Wait. Tell me you have a safe word."

"Yes."

"Then if you don't like something, don't do it. Problem solved."

Problem solved? As if it were that easy.

Andi popped the rest of the carrot in her mouth. "You could decide not to judge yourself for what you like and don't like. Think of it as new food. You didn't know you liked hummus until you tried it. Now you order it every time we come here."

Kelsey rolled her eyes. "It's a little more complicated than that."

"Doesn't have to be. BDSM isn't a one-size-fits-all thing. There's no right or wrong, and don't listen to anyone who says there is. Everyone has limits, things about it they like, things they don't. Some people are lifestylers, others practice it in the bedroom. Others mix it up, like doing it only on vacations or weekends. A bunch of us mostly keep it confined to clubs. For example…"

Now Kelsey was the one desperate to hear the dish.

Andi leaned in a bit. "I didn't really like bondage all that well. Took too damn long. I normally prefer impact play. But when I tied up Lorean one time—wait, do you want to hear all this?"

"I'm not sure." She took another sip. "Okay. I'm ready."

"That pink rope around his…well…"

"I get the picture." Not that she wanted to.

"I kind of want to see him in it all the time. It takes a long time, but surprisingly, I find it kind of Zen. Like yoga."

"You gave up yoga."

"They make you breathe. Child's pose. Downward dog. Only got time for that in the bedroom. But anyway, I digress. Sometimes my knots aren't as beautiful as he'd like them to be. He doesn't care if I spend three hours tying him, but if the knot isn't perfect, he throws a fit. That boy needs an ass-whooping," she repeated. "And I'm thinking I'm going to be the one to do it. Really soon. Oh. Oh. Incoming."

"Incoming?"

"I could be mistaken, but I'm not. Nathan Donovan is heading our direction."

"What the hell?" She swung her head to see Nathan devouring the distance with long, purposeful strides. Andi wasn't wrong. Kelsey was his intended target.

He was still dressed as he had been at the office, dark-gray suit and power tie. His shirt looked as crisp as it had this morning.

She'd been planning to freshen up before calling him, but he'd caught her off guard.

He was totally devastating.

"Ladies," he said by way of greeting when he stopped at their table. "Kelsey."

There was something mesmerizing about his eyes. Even though the restaurant wasn't brightly lit and nighttime had fallen, his eyes were fiery, and he was focused entirely on her. Her throat went dry. "Is there a problem, Mr. Donovan?"

"Not at all. If you'd like to scoot over, I'll join you."

Andi busied herself scooping the last of the hummus onto a chip.

Reluctantly, Kelsey made room for him.

"Are you going to introduce me to your friend?" he asked as soon as he was seated.

Instead of replying, she asked, "What are you doing here?"

"You didn't answer my phone calls or text messages."

"My phone's in my bag. Under the table." She gripped the base of her glass. "I told you I'd call when I was done."

"You did. And when we spoke earlier, you said you'd be an hour, hour and a half at the most."

"And?"

"It's been closer to two. You're always welcome to spend as much time with your friends as you want. I was simply concerned your phone wasn't working, so I figured I would make sure you weren't waiting on me, wondering where I was." With a smile that devastated, he said, "Am I intruding?"

"Of course you are." Kelsey was annoyed.

"It's fine," Andi said. "I'm the friend who's the bad influence, Andi Malloy."

"I've heard of you."

"You have?"

"The party. Where Kelsey won the paddle."

Of course he'd remember everything she'd told him.

"Well, now that we have that out of the way..." Andi laughed. "When I'm not corrupting my friends, I own From Hair to Eternity. It's a salon not far from here."

"Delighted to meet you. Nathan Donovan." They shook hands. "Your hair is your advertisement, I take it."

"Getting it to look like this takes magical unicorn powder, a master artist, two glasses of wine and four hours."

"I'm willing to bet my sister would be interested in that."

"Are you kidding me? I've been begging Kelse to get me a referral."

"Consider it done," he replied. "Do you have a business card?"

Andi dug in her oversize black tote emblazoned with a vibrant sugar skull and pulled out a purple card.

"Good marketing," he told her. "No one has cards like this."

"I'll give your sister her first service free."

Kelsey rolled her eyes. "What happened to half-price?"

"My kingdom to have Erin Donovan at my color bar."

"Is that what it's called?" Nathan frowned.

"At From Hair to Eternity, we have a separate area where we do color. We have magazines and some interactive tablets where we take the customer's image and show them various colors, highlights, lowlights, balayage. Sort of a 'try it before you wear it' kind of thing. And we want to keep them entertained while they process, so we have complimentary wine and mimosas."

"I'm sure that's a good idea."

Kelsey was sure he had no idea whether or not it was.

"I keep trying to get my hands on Kelsey."

He turned and looked at her. "Me too."

"Hair, Mr. Donovan. She wants to get her hands on my hair." But his softly spoken words had sent an illicit ripple through her.

"It's perfect as it is," he said.

"Copper," Andi went on as if he hadn't spoken. "Forget burgundy. We could add some copper. Highlights, maybe. Brighten it up."

"Up to Kelsey." He shrugged. "Personally, I wouldn't change a thing."

Andi glared.

He held up his hands in mock defeat. "No one asked my opinion, though."

The server walked over and asked if he could bring anything else.

Nathan ordered a Texas single malt, neat.

"Anything else? Maybe some sliders? Chicken wings? Happy hour ends in about twenty minutes."

Instead of answering for them, Nathan looked at each woman in turn. "Ladies?"

How did he manage to do that? At once, he was annoying and charming.

Even though another chocolate martini sounded like heaven, she shook her head, consciously making the choice to scene with him when they got back to her place. The simple decision made waves of anticipation roll through her stomach.

"Did you eat anything besides hummus?" he asked Kelsey.

She shook her head.

"Would you like to go somewhere else for dinner or eat something else here?"

The idea of going out to dinner with him didn't appeal to her, but she was still hungry. "Sliders," she said.

"Andi?" he asked.

"I'd eat some."

"Two orders, for the table."

"With French fries," Andi added.

The server committed the order to memory before leaving.

Over the next half hour as they ate, she was surprised by how charming Nathan was, asking Andi about her business and listening to her plans for expansion. But the whole time, with the way he touched her beneath the table and looked at her when she spoke, he made her feel extraordinarily special.

A master of conversation, the way he was with everything else, he directed the discussion toward the upcoming weekend. "I invited Kelsey to go to Deviation with me this weekend. I know you were the one to call to get her on the guest list, and I apologize most sincerely for interfering in your plans."

Kelsey knew he wasn't sorry, and she was sure Andi knew it as well. But she appreciated him for owning up to being the one to step in and alter things.

"Since it's unexpected," he said to Andi, "I'm happy to pick you up if you'd like to ride together." With his words, he made it clear he was offering transportation and nothing more.

"Thanks for the offer, but no. And honestly, I'm glad," she said. "I'd forgotten it's my dad's birthday party. I wouldn't be able to get out of it. I was going to see if you could reschedule, Kelsey."

Kelsey studied her friend, looking for signs of lies.

Andi turned up both palms as if to say she was telling the truth.

When the server brought the check, Nathan handed over his credit card.

"That's not necessary," Kelsey said.

He put his hand on her knee and caressed her. "It's an honor to have dinner with two beautiful women."

After the bill was settled, he asked, "Can I give you a lift somewhere, Andi?"

"Thanks, but I valet parked."

Outside, both of them handed over claim tickets, and he said, "Get the lady's car first."

Andi was already safely on the road before the valet brought around Nathan's SUV. He handed Kelsey into the car then gave the valet a tip that was bigger than she would have expected before getting in the vehicle.

"Is the temperature comfortable?"

"Fine. Thanks." She was still slightly annoyed with him for showing up and cutting her time with Andi short.

This evening, he didn't need directions to her house, and when her phone chimed, she pulled it out of her bag.

As he'd said, he'd sent a couple of messages and called. Because of the background noise, she obviously hadn't heard the notifications. And she could see it from his point of view. He'd been waiting to hear from her, and he hadn't contacted her until after six-thirty, the time she'd said she might want to leave. Even then, he'd given her another thirty minutes before seeking her out. He hadn't insisted she leave. And he'd paid the bill. Maybe she was overly sensitive to the overbearing male syndrome.

"I'm sorry that I didn't hear the phone."

"I enjoyed meeting your friend." Since they were at a stoplight, he looked at her. "And I can't wait to get you home."

She wiggled against her seat. He'd dropped his voice before adding the second part, and he'd wrapped her in his cloak of intimacy.

Concentrating on anything but him, she looked at the text from Andi.

Holy hotness. He's sex on a stick. I'll do him if you don't want him.

With a grin, she shook her head, turned off the screen then dropped the phone back in her bag.

At this time of evening, traffic was light.

"Have you done any thinking?" he asked. "About proper behavior."

In an instant, he'd gone from general conversation to something that only concerned them. "I was hoping we could skip that part."

"I'm sure you were."

"Don't tell me you've actually had time to think about it. Aren't you busy snapping up companies all over the city?"

"The state, actually," he replied.

"You're not joking?"

"We're looking at an electronics company. Been around a long time, was a blue chip at one point. Market has changed.

159

They're not as relevant as they were. They need an infusion of cash as well as vision and a team to manage strategy and tactics." Across the darkened interior, he shot her a grin. "You don't need to hear about it."

"On the contrary. It's fascinating." The enthusiasm in his voice was contagious and she wondered how he had the mental adeptness to switch between projects. Taking over Newman was time-consuming, and yet he was already planning another acquisition.

"I'm happy to tell you about it, when we're not focused on Donovan Logistics or personal matters. When we're in private, I want you to be sure my attention is unwaveringly on you."

She shivered a bit, even though she wasn't cold.

"Back to my question."

"I agree," she said, unable to believe they were having this conversation. But she remembered his words from last night, about detaching a bit. So she approached it as she would a work conversation. "Courtesy is a must."

"And willful disrespect? You'll submit to my corporal punishment for it?"

"Can you be more specific?"

"Of course. I'd never use anything other than my hand or a belt on your ass and upper thighs. There's no mistake, you'll know you've been rude."

"That's not the way I usually act."

"Not everyone annoys you the way I do, I suspect."

"There's some truth to that." It wasn't just because he was overbearing, overconfident, overwhelming at times. It was because the way she reacted scared her.

"Deliberate disobedience," he went on. "Like arguing when I request something of you and you have no intention of using a safe word or having a discussion about it. I want you to use safe words, to discuss things with me. But for example, last night, when I said I could shave your pussy or you could have a Brazilian wax. Do you remember your response?"

"*Hell no.*"

"And it should have been…?"

"Can we discuss this, Mr. Donovan? Or, this scares me. Or, hell no, *Sir.*"

He laughed. "You think you're safe because I'm behind the wheel with my seat belt on."

A delicious threat was woven through his words. Damn it, she was already getting damp for him.

"So in that instance, I may take you to a salon on our lunch hour. Perhaps even to Andi's place. I'm sure they have services there."

And Lorean probably specialized in them. "Shaving is fine, Sir."

"You're a perfectly reasonable, compliant sub."

"Never anything but," she agreed happily.

In only a few minutes, they'd parked. After helping her out of the vehicle, he grabbed a bag from the back seat. She'd noticed it earlier, when she'd borrowed the car, and she'd wondered what it was for, but she hadn't thought it might be for her.

She led the way inside. There was no rolling ball filled with Sinbad to slow them down. She slipped her key into the lock and wasn't surprised when it didn't function properly. At times it felt as she had to pay homage to the mechanism gods, standing on one foot, whispering to it, promising it would be taken care of one day, holding her tongue just right…

"Try this." He held a key near her face.

"What's that?"

"Your new key."

She scowled.

"It works for the deadbolt, also."

"Are you serious?"

"I met the locksmith after work."

"You…"

"It matters to me that you're safe, Kelsey."

She accepted the key. "I don't know what to say."

"You can celebrate by turning the lock several times and cheering each time it works the way it should."

The key went straight in and the tumblers worked perfectly. "I can't believe this. How did you get in?"

"Is that a real question?"

"It was really that unsecure?"

"You were working harder to lock it than it was to unlock."

"Then double thank you."

Just then, Mr. Martinez's door opened and Sinbad rolled over the threshold for his nightly walk.

The man crouched to guide the ball to the middle of the hallway.

"Let's get out of the way," Kelsey said. "Night, Mr. Martinez."

He lifted a hand in a silent goodbye.

She effortlessly opened the second lock. Within seconds, she had them both sealed inside.

No one had taken care of her since she'd left home at age eighteen. Not necessarily because they wouldn't, but rather because she didn't want to be told what to do or encouraged to find a husband. Suddenly, though, she realized it might be nice to have some help.

"Extra keys are on the table," he said, pointing. "Along with the locksmith's card in the unlikely event something goes wrong. And I promise I didn't invade your privacy. We didn't take two steps into the room. Your Mr. Martinez conveniently decided to walk his hamster the whole time. Keeping an eye on us, I'm sure."

"Did he really?" They'd hardly exchanged two dozen words in the time they'd been neighbors. It was nice to know he was looking out for her. "I'm not sure how to thank you," she said to Nathan. "What do I owe you?"

"Your undying love and devotion."

She dropped her bag on the floor. "Will you settle for a hundred dollars?"

"I was sure that's what you'd say." His grin was quick and easy.

"Were you actually teasing, Mr. Donovan?"

"I might have been, Ms. Lane. Then again, I might be deadly serious. Question is, how will you know?"

Not knowing quite what to say, she shrugged out of her jacket. He took it from her and hung it up.

"May I take yours?"

"Thank you." First he put down his bag.

It surprised her to realize how much she liked helping him with his suit coat.

"Remember to get the nipple clamps," he told her.

She bent to get them out, and he offered a hand up. Just like last night, now that he had expectations, she was nervous.

After putting the set in his outstretched hand, she asked. "Something to drink?"

"Water, if you have it."

She went into the kitchen and returned with two bottles. Then, because she couldn't tolerate not knowing, she asked, "What's in your bag?"

"Why don't you have a look?"

She didn't need to ask whether or not he meant it. "Where? Here? In the bedroom?"

"Your table is fine."

This was reminiscent of last night where she'd shown him the items in her drawer, but it was ten times more disturbing.

He carried the bag to the table then stepped back while she unzipped it.

Her hand shook as she pulled out the first item, a box of condoms. "Uhm..." She turned her head to the side. "Does this mean we're *finally* going to have sex?"

"It's not an expectation," he reminded her.

She'd never been involved in a relationship that was this direct. Generally she sort of let things happen. But she preferred it this way. There would be no misunderstandings. "It's something I want."

"I haven't thought about much else."

As she put the box down, she noted that they were size extra-large. Her fingers seemed nerveless. It shouldn't surprise her—she'd felt him though his pants. But the idea of having him in her made anticipation crawl around, making her skittish. "We could skip everything else and go to bed."

"We could." He paused. "But we're not going to."

She wasn't sure she could wait.

"See what else is in there," he encouraged.

Hardly able to concentrate, she pulled out a thick, black leather choker. It had a large metal D-ring attached to it, and a line of small, red embroidered hearts softened the austerity making it somewhat feminine.

"I'll put it on you later and every time we play. I'd like you to wear it Saturday night to the club."

She ran her finger over it. The leather was softer than it appeared, and the inside seemed to be lined with some sort of fur. The idea of wearing it outside the house alternately chilled and intrigued her.

Kelsey placed the collar on the tabletop, and he laid the nipple clamps alongside it.

The next thing she pulled out was a long leash. Her stomach plunged. Dozens of images seized her. Her on all fours, the leather strip in his hand as he held her in place and spanked her. Him leading her through a room, half-dressed, or worse, naked. She shuddered and looked at him. "This might be hell no."

"Okay." He shrugged.

Prepared for an argument, she blinked. "Okay?"

"I won't force you to do anything. As I said last night, I'd like it if you tried things you're merely uncomfortable with. If you refuse, I'm fine with it. There are plenty of other toys we can play with."

"You'd really be fine with me saying no?"

"Perfectly."

"Really?"

"I might show you the way you look in it, my reaction. But

164

the decision is yours. Aren't you in the least bit curious?"

"It's too controlling."

"How so?"

She gave him her best killer stare. "Can you be any more obtuse?"

A smile flirted with his lips in a way that made it impossible for her to be annoyed with him. "I promise you, Kelsey. I'm not. And I'd like to make a note of the fact this is the first time in my life I've been called obtuse."

"*Noted*," came a voice from his watch.

"That's creepy," she said.

"This thing may go back to Bonds." He touched the lower right hand corner of the screen. "You were telling me how it's too controlling."

"I couldn't move more than a few feet away from you," Kelsey protested.

"And?"

"Hey, watch, please note this is the second time Nathan Donovan has been called obtuse."

"*Noted.*"

This time, he scowled as he pushed and held a flashing icon on the screen.

"I'm kind of liking the thing," she said.

"I'm sure you are." He put his cuff back in place. "Where were we?"

"Me objecting to the leash." Even as she said the words, she realized he knew exactly where they were.

"Come here."

It was phrased more as a request than command, seductive and compelling. She was lost to this man. She took a couple of steps toward him and tipped her head back to look at him.

"Lift your hair for me."

Obediently, she did.

He fastened the collar around her throat.

It was thrilling and overwhelming at the same time.

He checked the fit by putting his fingers between it and

her throat. "Maybe one more notch." He tightened it then asked, "How's that?"

Hell. How would she ever have the courage to tell him the truth? She settled for, "Fine."

When he raised his eyebrows, she added, "Sir. Fine, *Sir.*"

"That respect, Kelsey. It does it for me."

Him saying he was pleased made her want to please him more.

He threaded his finger through the D-ring and gently brought her toward him.

She sucked in a hot, needy breath.

He captured her lips with his then devoured her mouth, leaving her breathless.

"Woman, you would destroy a lesser man."

"I'm only interested in one."

He grabbed her hand, moved it to his cock. She needed no encouragement to stroke him. "Tonight, I want you, Nathan. Don't make me wait any longer."

"I think it can be arranged." He released the D-ring and picked up the leash. "Trust me? We never have to do this again if you hate it. Try it?"

Almost everything in her rebelled. But there was a tiny piece that was willing to go along, simply because it mattered to him.

"If you want me to take it off, say yellow or red. I will remove it instantly. No questions."

"Because it pleases you."

"Oh, Kelsey..." He kissed her forehead.

In that moment, she wondered if she were capable of refusing him anything.

She looked up at him as he attached the clip.

Her hands fisted at her sides, she waited for the flash of panic that she expected. But there was none. Instead, desire streaked through her.

"Come with me."

Surprisingly, he didn't tug on her. He walked a fraction of a step ahead of her, as they might in public.

He stopped in front of the mirror above the entrance table. "See what I see."

Kelsey stared at a woman she barely recognized.

The leather was wrapped tautly around his hand, and he held it near her shoulder. And the sight of it with the collar... It felt erotic, but it looked ten times more so — thick, unyielding, possessive. The harshness of the collar, though, was softened by her hair, the addition of femininity. "I like it," she confessed. Her eyes were wide as she met his, whiskey-shot hazel mixing with molten green fire. His pupils flared with desire, hers tightened in response.

The way he looked at her made the world tilt. He communicated passion and possession, and both collided, claiming her.

"You understand, don't you?"

"Yes," she whispered. None of this, wearing his color or leash, meant that he controlled her. It meant he wanted to protect and keep her near.

She traced the silver metal buckle and knew she was safe with this man. She felt it in every nerve ending.

"This is only the beginning, Kelsey. Only the beginning."

9

She saw what he did, the power of her surrender, the trust, the hunger. Nathan wasn't sure he'd ever been with a woman he desired more. "Do you want me to remove it?" He tilted his head.

"No," she said softly.

His balls drew up. "So fucking hot and sexy, woman."

"For you." She said it like a vow.

Her words slayed him.

It took all his powers of self-control not to yank up her skirt and plow his throbbing dick into her. He had a plan for the evening, and he was going to stick with it no matter the cost. It was a good thing he'd masturbated before leaving for work this morning. "I want you to see what else is in the bag."

Slowly she nodded.

He held his hand with his palm up, indicating she should walk in front of him.

Looking somewhat nervous, she bit her lower lip.

He kept enough slack in the leash that she didn't strain against it, and he stayed close to her.

"If anyone had told me a week ago that I'd be leashed... Heck, fifteen minutes ago," she corrected.

"Don't think about what anyone else might think. Your opinion—and mine—are the only ones that matter. And I don't think it unusual in the least, and even if it was, it's so God damn sexy that I'd be convinced."

When they were back at the table, she pulled out a detestable small butt plug that made her scowl.

He laughed. "There's more in there."

She removed the remaining items — a razor with a package of fresh blades and a travel-size can of shaving cream.

"I was hoping you forgot."

"The thought of doing it kept me awake last night."

She sucked in a small breath.

"There's one more thing."

She shook the bag to locate it then pulled it out. "A candle? That seems a bit romantic for you, Nathan."

"We won't be having dinner by candlelight, if that's what you mean."

"No?" She frowned. "For the bedroom? Ambiance?"

He shook his head.

"Then…?"

"I'm going to drip the hot wax all over your naked body. Your nipples. Your belly. Your shaved pussy."

She shivered. "That sounds painful."

"I'll make sure it's only painful in the best possible way."

"Fuck nuts," she whispered as she rolled the bright-blue tapered candle between her palms. "I know you're serious."

"I promised you I was going to wash you and give you a shave." He plucked the candle from her hands before unfastening the leash and removing the collar.

He liked the way she ran her fingers across her throat as if missing the strip of leather. She couldn't know how sexy that was to him. "Please undress," he said.

"Here?"

Nathan raised his eyebrows.

"Now?"

"Unless you're planning to use a safe word, get on with it. Delay might earn you a few stripes of my belt."

She flicked a quick, hot glance to his waist.

Oh, yeah. He intended to lay leather to her ass. If he did it right, they would both benefit from it.

Unexpectedly, she stalled, and he was taken aback. His little sub was deliberately provoking him.

He had never wanted her more than he did in that moment.

She kicked off each shoe, making her instantly a few inches shorter, fueling his protective impulses.

Then she went into a strip-tease, moving her hips back and forth as she reached behind her to lower the zipper. She exaggerated the motions a little more as she shimmied out of the skirt.

She bent to scoop it from the floor and tossed it onto his head.

In future, he'd have to be more careful what he asked her to do.

"Twelve is my favorite number, Sir."

"As in stripes from my belt?"

Her cheeks were stained scarlet, so he knew she wasn't as comfortable with this as she seemed. He schooled his features so he didn't show how stupidly happy she made him. His Kelsey was way outside her comfort zone and seeking his reassurance. "I'll do my part," he told her. "But I may have a different number tonight."

Her blush deepened and spread.

Nathan wondered if he'd be capable of going back to a professional relationship after Saturday night.

She grabbed the hem of her shirt and pulled it up and off. This time, he held a hand to catch it.

Kelsey stood in front of him in her thong and black lacy bra.

"You couldn't be more beautiful. And I'm impatient."

She unhooked her bra then shrugged so that the straps fell. She took her time pulling it off all the way, and when she did, her nipples were already beaded.

"So fucking sexy," he said.

Within seconds, she'd discarded the thong.

Maybe it had been a mistake to have her do this. His control was being severely tested. "I'll need a bowl," he told her. "Now, please."

"What size?"

"At least a cereal bowl. Mixing bowl is fine, as well. Maybe that's even better."

She walked to the kitchen, but she was looking at the ground as she brushed past him.

"Head up, Kelsey. Flaunt it."

"I'm not all that comfortable walking around naked." She opened a cupboard. "Especially in front of you."

"I'll give you plenty of opportunity to practice."

She swung her head in his direction.

"The more you do it, the easier it will become," he said.

"I'm not sure I want it to be easier."

"And I'm sure I want you naked. And in this case, at least, what I want wins."

She returned to him and extended the bowl. "Until tonight, the only thing this has held is chocolate chip cookie batter."

"Until tonight," he agreed easily. "Carry it, along with the other items. I'll get the leash and collar."

Something, maybe the leading edge of disagreement, flashed in her eyes. But she relented and did as he said.

Her collar and leash wrapped around his hand, he followed her to the master bedroom. He placed all of the items on the nightstand. "Go and take a bath or shower," he said. "I'll be there directly."

"Is this part of my training? You telling me what to do and me doing it without arguing?"

"Well" — he couldn't help pointing out — "you're arguing."

She folded her arms.

Recognizing she needed a connection, he took hold of her shoulders. "I'm not simply issuing directives because I like to order you around. I want us to be in accord on Saturday evening. If you've proven to yourself that I'm trustworthy, that I have thought things through where you're concerned, then you'll be less apprehensive when we visit Deviation. Relying on me will help it feel less overwhelming. You'll be free to let yourself go physically and mentally. We're on an accelerated schedule to establish the kind of relationship that will help you have a relaxed experience so that you give yourself over to me when you're on the St. Andrew's cross or the Punishment Pole."

A ripple of something went through her, maybe trepidation, maybe anticipation. Perhaps a combination.

"That sounds scary."

"We can watch for a bit and then you can decide whether or not you're interested." Nathan moved his fingers soothingly. "Most of all, I mean for this to be about your pleasure and you gaining confidence in yourself as a sexual woman and as a hot little sub. If this isn't enjoyable for you, we should stop right now. You can get dressed, turn on a movie, make some popcorn and open a bottle of wine. No harm. I won't hold it against you."

She exhaled. "No. It's not that…"

"Tell me." He looked deeply into her eyes and gently massaged her.

"I'm not sure why the hell I'm struggling when this is what I want. I just didn't have any idea it would be this difficult."

"You're incredibly intelligent, Kelsey. Driven. Determined. It's not a surprise that you're conflicted. You made certain decisions about the way the world works and the way you needed to behave in order to succeed. And you've had spectacular results. There aren't many women in the kind of position you are right now. You're poised to go wherever you want. You've been strategic and focused. And maybe you think you're betraying your own principles every time you agree to do as I want. Tell me this. When you did that little strip-tease and tossed your skirt on my head, how did that feel?"

"Exhilarating."

"Until you thought that independent women don't do those kinds of things."

"There could be some truth to that."

"Here's a new truth. Independent women get to do what the hell they want. It's when there's no choice that there's a problem. Did your friend Andi judge you?"

"No."

"Then why are you?"

The words hung between them.

"Your call. Either that pussy hair is coming off and you're going to get the spanking of your life or we can watch *The Godfather*."

"Don't take sides against the family, or something like that?"

The line of dialogue wasn't exact, but it was damn fucking close. Close enough for him to want to kiss her.

"That has particular meaning to you, doesn't it?" she guessed.

"Probably applies to a lot of families."

"True. And you feel a special obligation to yours."

Nathan nodded. Kelsey had remembered what he'd told her about what drove him. Ms. Kelsey Lane went up again in his estimation. "So what will it be? *The Godfather*? We could do a marathon, go straight to number two as soon as it finishes?"

"I have uncles and more male cousins than I can count. We have boy movie marathons every holiday. I'd rather have a toothache."

He grinned. "Is that your answer? Or do you need to discuss it some more?"

"You helped me sort it out. Thank you." She put two fingers on his mouth.

Nathan kissed them. "In that case, my sub, into the bathtub." He pulled her onto her toes and he saw it…the answering spark in response to his command.

And it fed the fire growing in him.

Hungrily, he kissed her. Consumed her. He took from her, gave to her. He wanted her to know how much she meant to him, how much he appreciated her submission.

When he ended it, her lips were swollen, her eyes sleepy. "Maybe I should fuck you now."

"Maybe you should."

Despite the temptation, he held on to control, and not for his sake, but because he wanted her to know, especially so

173

early in their D/s play, that he meant what he said and that he wasn't easily dissuaded.

That didn't stop him from picturing her on her hands and knees with him pistoning into her from behind, filling her up.

Slowly he released his grip. "Go."

He swatted her ass as she scampered away.

For longer than he should, he stared after her.

Then, after shaking his head, he turned down the comforter and organized their equipment, some on the bed, other things on the nightstand. "Are there extra towels in this closet?" he asked when he entered the bathroom.

She was still standing outside the bathtub, bending over to check the water temperature, giving him a hell of a tempting view.

"Yes," she said, looking at him.

"Scissors?"

"Are you… Never mind. Of course you're serious." She sighed. "Kitchen drawer. Next to the refrigerator. And there are others in my office, smaller ones, in a mug on top of the desk."

"And matches?"

"In the kitchen."

He gave her a crisp nod.

Before he left, he grabbed a couple of towels and several washcloths. In the bedroom, he spread a towel on the mattress and placed the others nearby before opening the package containing the razor. He attached the blade then tested it for sharpness and to be sure it was properly secured.

After retrieving the things he wanted, he put the matches and scissors on the nightstand then joined her.

She was in the tub, steam rising around her, her hair piled on top of her head. He'd never given much thought to how much he enjoyed seeing a woman relaxing in the tub, and he could get accustomed to the small intimacy.

After putting down the bowl, he rolled up his sleeves and

picked up the lilac-colored pouf that was sitting on a ledge. She had about a dozen different body washes, all lined up like sentries, from shortest to tallest. "Do you want to pick one?"

She grabbed a bottle from the middle. "This one makes a nice lather." After flipping open the lid, she squirted some gel on the mesh ball.

Her tub was oversize, making it easy for her to sit with her back to him. He knelt on the tiles and started just beneath her hairline, running the pouf downward, then across her shoulders, trailing down her spine.

She gently moved her head from side to side, working out tension as he washed her.

"I could do this for you every night," he said.

"I'm really not sure why I was objecting," she replied softly. "This is pretty wonderful."

He cupped handful after handful of water and rinsed her off. The feminine scent of the cream filled his senses, tuning him even more keenly into her. "Scoot around."

After she did, he continued, washing her upper body and slightly abrading her breasts.

"I'm not sure I can tolerate that," she admitted. "I'm so sensitized. Like I'm already coming undone."

"Good. Now stand up."

He offered a hand, and she put her warm one in his.

Nathan washed her pelvis then her ass and her legs, before dipping between her thighs. She grabbed his shoulders for balance.

As he rinsed the lather from her body, he told her, "Take your time. Enjoy your bath. I'll be waiting for you in the bedroom."

He filled the bowl with warm water and carried it to the bedroom.

As he'd hoped, she didn't keep him waiting long.

She stood in the doorway. Her long hair curled damply against her shoulders. Without being instructed, she dropped the towel she was wearing and walked toward him, her gaze on him.

"Exactly right," he said approvingly.

She stopped a few inches from the bed.

"Please kneel for me."

Kelsey looked at him for long seconds. He wondered whether or not she'd argue, but then she accepted his offered hand.

She was born for this. For him.

After she knelt, he fastened his collar into place. Not *the* collar, but *his*, he realized. "I bought this for you," he told her.

"You couldn't have," she replied.

"I went to the store after I left you last night. All of these things, they're yours. No other woman has touched them. No other sub ever will."

He saw the breath catch in her throat.

"Thank you," she said.

"I want you on your back, your butt on the towel."

Nathan helped her to stand, and he held on to her for a few seconds as she looked a little wobbly. *That* he liked. He wanted her as affected as he was.

Once she was in position, he said, "Please tuck your hands underneath your bottom and keep them there until I give you permission to move."

"Yes, Nathan."

Were there any sweeter words? "You can spread your legs and hold them as far apart as possible, or I can tie them in place. Which do you prefer?"

She looked at him, squirming around. "I think I'm supposed to say whatever you prefer, Sir."

"So say it."

"Whatever…" Kelsey cleared her throat and tried again. "Whatever you prefer, Sir."

"Perfect." He smiled at her, and he was rewarded when she closed her eyes and quietly sighed. "Hold them apart."

After she'd spread her legs wide, he picked up the scissors and trimmed her pubic hair. Since she kept it neatly groomed, there wasn't much for him to do. "You know, if I were your permanent Dom, I might let you grow it out periodically just so I could do this."

He grabbed the can of shaving cream and sprayed a large dollop into his left palm before covering her mound with it.

She squeezed her eyes closed as he dipped the razor into the water.

"You'll be okay," he promised as he removed the hair from above her labia. He continually rinsed the blades and wiped her with a washcloth.

He focused intently and took his time as he shaved her outer labia. Then he folded back each lip to shave the most intimate area.

Nathan carefully removed every stray wisp before using a washcloth to wipe off the excess shaving cream then he patted her dry. He ran a finger over all the newly bared skin, reveling in its softness. "Beautiful," he approved. "Feel."

Without him having to tell her twice, she pulled a hand from beneath her and trailed her fingertips across her pussy.

"I think you'll like it once you get used to it."

"I'm not as convinced."

"You don't have to be," he said.

To reward her, he parted her labia and teased her clit with a long, sweeping lick. She arched from the bed, moaning. "Yeah," he said. "You hate it, don't you?" Without waiting for an answer, he inserted a finger in her then flicked his tongue across that swollen flesh several times, teasing her.

She began to moan.

When he suspected she was close to an orgasm, he pulled away from her. "I'll be right back."

"What?" Exasperation oozed from the word. "What is your deal with stopping me from coming?"

"Besides the fact that your orgasms are mine to give?" he reminded her. He looked down at her and compelled her to meet his gaze. "I want you to be so needy that you scream for me."

"I already am." She started to draw her legs together but he pinched the inside of her thigh.

She glared, but got back into position.

"I'll be right back. And I might be of a mind to reward good behavior."

He gathered up the bowl, razor and used washcloths. "Don't move an inch," he warned as he walked past her.

Nathan retrieved the water bottles she'd taken out of the refrigerator earlier. When he returned, he was pleased to see she'd stayed in position, waiting for him, a fabulous sub. "Impressive. Very well done, Kelsey." He uncapped a bottle and offered it to her.

She accepted a hand up before taking a long drink.

"What was your favorite number, again?"

"Uh…"

Nathan remembered her saying that over the knee was one of the things she thought about when she masturbated. He wanted to feed her fantasies for months to come. "Little sub, I'm going to light up your ass in a way you've only dreamed of before I fuck you."

"I am so ready, Sir."

After she'd downed half the bottle, he recapped it and set it aside. "Need a longer break? Anything else?"

She rubbed at the goosebumps on her arms. "I'm fine."

He carried over a chair from the far wall and positioned it in a large open space. "Now," he instructed standing to the side of the chair, "I want you over here, on your knees. Remove my belt and offer it to me."

"This seems a bit like asking a condemned man to put on his own noose."

"It does, doesn't it?"

She climbed from the bed and took a step toward him.

"Stop."

Instantly, she did.

"I need to look at you, drink you in." For a moment, he didn't know how to breathe. Kelsey, his sub, stood there, her cunt shaved bare, her body naked, wearing his thick collar. Soon, her skin would bear marks inflicted by his belt.

He was awed. She was perfect. "Thank you." His voice cracked, maybe for the first time ever as he said, "You..." He cleared his throat. "You may continue."

After she was in position, she fumbled with his buckle. From where he stood looking down, he saw that her hands were shaking. But since he wanted her to experience every moment, he didn't help her out.

Finally, concentrating hard, she managed to unfasten it and pull it free.

She hesitated, apparently thinking through the best way to present it. Finally, she folded it in half, laid it across her palms and bowed her head.

"If you had studied how to do that, you couldn't have done it better."

Kelsey looked up at him.

He wondered how few people, men, had given her praise. And he vowed to ensure she heard it often from him.

Obviously surprising her, he set the belt aside. Instead, he instructed, "Put the clamps on your nipples."

She shook her head, as if to clear it.

When he'd laid out the toys earlier, he'd placed the clamps on the nightstand, and she easily found them.

"I've only ever used the clothespins," she said.

"Make sure you place them back a bit. The closer it is to the tip, the more it will hurt. You'll figure it out."

He stood over her, watching as she held up her left breast and played with her nipple until it hardened.

The sight of her, so intent, trying to figure it out, made blood surge through him. She looked at once innocent and sultry, Madonna and sinner.

She winced when she affixed the first one.

If he hadn't been a hardened Dom, he'd have plucked it from her tender flesh. Instead he drove her, willing her to take more, experience everything she craved. "It looks sensational," he said, his voice seeming to echo in the room. "So swollen."

"It's painful," she protested.

"And it will get more so," he assured her.

Maybe because she knew what to expect, it took her considerably longer to put the second one on.

He closed his eyes temporarily to sear the image into his brain. "Beautiful," he said. "Now put your hands on your hips and thrust out your breasts."

She gasped as she did so and the chain moved, pulling on the clamps.

"Even prettier than I might have imagined." She wasn't just any sub. She was his. "Knowing that your tits are going to be so tormented will make your spanking even more difficult to endure." Nathan grabbed the belt and took a seat in the chair. "Across my lap."

"Did I say twelve was my favorite number?" She put a hand on the mattress to help her stand. "I meant two."

"Stay brave, and hurry your hot little ass up before I add extra stripes for stalling."

She walked slower than normal, as if trying to minimize the pressure on her nipples. But he could see it was a losing battle for her.

When she was close enough, he grabbed hold of her and yanked her across his lap, sending the chain swaying frantically even as she reached for the hardwood floor.

He caught her legs between his to keep her steady as well as to trap her.

"Sir!"

"Cease your thrashing, sub."

It took her several seconds to settle down and find her balance, but he didn't wait to start rubbing her skin to get it ready for the taste of his leather. "This, tonight, may leave a couple of marks."

Before he started, he played with her pussy, distracting her, and he even pressed a finger to her anal whorl.

Her sounds changed from protest to encouragement,

something she probably wasn't aware of. No doubt she had no idea how perfectly compliant she sounded. How natural.

He continued to rub her vigorously for many seconds more than necessary, then he said, "Count these for me, Kelsey."

The moment he spoke, she clenched her entire body.

"Relax." He stroked her skin. "When I talk about training, this is part of it. My words—that we are about to start—are a signal to you, and ideally I want you to exhale and let your body go soft rather than rigid."

She expelled a breath and lessened the tension in her body.

"That's it," he approved. "Keep that in mind in the future, as well."

"Yes, Nathan."

He spanked her with the belt using an upstroke on the tops of her thighs.

She groaned and wiggled on his lap.

"I didn't hear a number," he said.

"One, Nathan." The words sounded grudging and forced.

By the time he was finished with her, she'd be much more compliant. He gave her the next four in quick succession, forcing her to count nonstop.

Finally he relented, allowing her to allow her to catch her breath. "Keep your body pliable," he suggested.

He landed the sixth stripe across both of her buttocks.

"Six, Nathan." She squirmed away and flattened her hands on the floor to keep balanced.

He pulled her back up and landed the belt again, a little higher.

"Seven, Nathan."

On the eighth, she grunted and gave the count, but she stopped trying to maneuver away. "Yes," he softly. "That's it. My sub."

"Nine," she whispered after the next one.

"Your ass is getting so red for me." He paused for several

seconds to rub her skin and ease the ache he knew she must be experiencing. "Is twelve still your favorite number?"

"This hurts way more than last night, Sir."

"Lucky for you, it's less fatiguing than spanking you with my bare hand. So if you want to go to fifteen or twenty, it's not a problem."

"No!" She dug her toes into the floorboards.

"Which number is next, sub?"

"Ten?" Then a second later, she said, "Ten," with much more confidence.

Since she was expecting the stripe, he surprised her by holding off. Instead, he dipped a hand between her legs to tease her clitoris. "Your pussy is as hot as your bottom, Kelsey."

"Oh God," she said, squirming, arching back to him, silently pleading for more.

"You like a taste of leather, even when it burns."

"Sir! Nathan! I'm so ready to come."

"You can hold off." He moved his hand out of the way and delivered a stinging eleventh smack.

"Oh dear God," she said, whimpering.

He eased a finger into her cunt. "How are your nipples?"

"The clamps are maddening. They ache, but I like it. It makes absolutely no sense."

"And every time you move, they sway."

"Making me hornier," she said. "Please, may I have an orgasm?"

He'd known she'd be compliant. He just hadn't known how much he would enjoy it.

"Nathan."

She tightened her body as she fought off the orgasm, and he saw an alluring sheen of perspiration dotting her back. At some point, maybe without her being aware of it, she'd given herself over to him, obeying him completely.

To him, it didn't get any better. "Take another for me," he said.

"Yes." She drew in a breath then forced it out in a shudder.

When she was completely relaxed, he brought the belt down, landing it just above her buttocks. She screamed and bucked.

He reached beneath her and yanked on the dangling chain, making her writhe. Then he rubbed the mark left by his belt and said, "You deserve this." He plunged three fingers into her cunt. "But I'm still going to make you work for it."

Nathan kept his hand still.

At first, she whimpered, but then she began to move, evidently letting go of her hesitation and gaining confidence as she dug her fingers into the floor to gain some leverage to push herself against him. She shamelessly rotated her hips, trying to reach orgasm.

"Yes," he encouraged, moving a bit so he could squeeze one of her breasts hard, forcing flesh against the rubber-coated metal.

"Oh God. Too much, too much."

He eased off then squeezed again harder. In response, her pussy tightened.

She lifted onto her tiptoes and arched.

The moment she found the right angle, he knew. He felt her internal muscles clench his fingers and she cried out his name.

By slow measures, he released his grip. After she'd ridden out the orgasm, he pulled out his fingers then helped her to stand.

Instead of letting her go, he pulled her onto his lap and wrapped her in his arms, holding her close until her breathing returned to normal.

Eventually, she put a hand on his chest and eased away from him.

"I never suspected anything like this existed."

"Me either."

She tipped her head back. "I'm not sure I quite believe you. You've played with a lot of subs."

"None of them have been you." They'd all had much

more experience, and he'd appreciated them, but there was something unique about being her first. It sharpened him, made him carefully craft scenes in his head before he ever touched her. There were things he wanted her to know, confidence he wanted to instill before Saturday. Damn. He was already proud of her. "How does your body feel?" He looped the chain of her clamps around his index finger and lifted it a few inches, testing, watching.

She closed her eyes and tipped back her head.

"You like a lot of pressure," he observed. A lot of women would have snarled at him or used a safe word by now, but her face was slack from pleasure.

"The clothespins were never enough. But these…?"

He waited.

"You did say they're mine."

"I did. But I didn't say they would stay at your house."

"That's mean, Mr. Donovan."

"And what have I ever done or said that would make you think otherwise?" But because they'd been on there long enough, he cupped her right breast. "This may hurt. Or not." Just in case, the moment he opened the clip, he pinched her nipple and slowly, slowly let it go, massaging it the entire time.

Instead of yelping as he might have expected, she sighed.

A minute or so later, he had the other one off her, as well. "We can put them back on anytime you're ready."

"I may ask you to do that."

"Courageous sub. Or maybe you're a masochist in this area?"

"I don't think that's true. But I liked it."

"Ready for more?"

Her eyes darkened in response.

"On your back. Keep your body on the towel."

While she did as he asked, he put the chair back where it belonged and lit the candle's wick. It took a moment to catch, then it flared with a satisfying hiss. "This is meant for sensation play. It melts at a lower temperature than most wax. It won't hurt. Much."

When he looked back at her, her gaze was focused on the flickering flame.

10

No matter how hard she tried to look away, Kelsey was mesmerized.

Nathan had talked to her about trust, and everything he did tested it. Especially this.

He loomed over her with the round blue taper, and her mouth dried a little when the wax started to melt.

Nathan cupped his hand then tipped the candle sideways until a drop of wax fell onto his skin.

That it hadn't hit her surprised her, made her more interested in what he was doing.

Systematically he moved higher, testing the temperature on his wrist. Then he grabbed another of the washcloths and wiped his skin clean. "Masturbate for me, Kelsey," he told her.

She tamped down her instinctive embarrassment and the flash of fear as she worried about what to expect. Focusing on pleasing him, she moved her hands over her breasts, brushing her tender nipples.

Her whole body lit up from the brief contact. The nipple clamps had been amazing, giving her a sensation she'd never had before. If he intended to take them away from her, she would be going online to order a pair.

She closed her eyes to concentrate on what she was doing and not on the image of him standing over her with the burning candle.

Kelsey ran a palm down her ribs then over her belly to her pubis. The bare skin was a momentary shock. Though she probably wouldn't ever tell him, she enjoyed being even more sensitive.

She was distracted in her own thoughts when hot liquid danced across her right nipple.

She sucked in a breath.

Before she could decide whether or not she liked it, a second followed, then a third.

Almost instantly the wax dried and the heat dissipated. It was a tiny, enthralling lick of erotic pain.

And she liked it.

He dropped another on her left nipple.

Naughtily she lifted her chest, inviting more.

He gave it to her, trailing from right to left, then starting in the middle to work outward in the opposite direction, creating a design she couldn't see.

She stroked her pussy faster. The dozens of pinpricks breathed life into her nerve endings. Kelsey had never experienced anything like it. The more he gave her, the more she wanted.

"Watch."

Hypnotized by his voice, she opened her eyes and did as he said.

The fallen wax had hardened but didn't stick to her skin. He swiped the blue beads from one of her breasts, then he squeezed the nipple to a tight bud. Nathan held the taper close, exquisitely close to her flesh.

"Yes," she encouraged, suddenly afraid he wouldn't do it.

He didn't disappoint.

It stung and burned.

She stroked her pussy harder, delving inside, finger-fucking herself as he crowned her nipple with the wax. With sudden insight, she realized he'd instructed her to masturbate as a way to distract her from what he was doing, but also to enhance the entire experience. He was masterful with her.

Again he made a pattern she couldn't decipher, but each drop was liquid heaven.

"Do you like this?"

"Favorite thing," she said, unable to form a complete sentence.

"It might be mine too." He drizzled the wax lower, and she pumped her pussy harder in response.

"I'm going to come," she warned him.

"Not yet." He dropped wax from a great height and it landed in a cool splash just below her belly button.

Kelsey recognized that he could control the intensity based on how far away he held the flame.

He drizzled several drops on her shaven pubic area as he'd promised then he pressed his thumb deeply into it, leaving his print, temporarily marking her.

She felt dizzy and delicious.

"Put your hands at your sides."

Any urge to protest vanished when she saw the way he loomed over her, sinfully dominant.

With his cuffs rolled back, necktie tossed casually over his shoulder and eyes blazing, she saw what she did to him.

This overwhelming need wasn't one-sided. That knowledge made her feel powerful.

Lust was banked in his dark-green eyes.

She could deny him nothing.

Slowly she moved her hands from her throbbing pussy.

Keeping the candle a foot or more from her, he drew a broken line as he continued to move down, farther and farther. He wouldn't...

"Show me your clit."

She'd never been more terrorized by a command. Nervously she glanced from his face to the flame then met his gaze. Kelsey fell back through her memories, of the things he'd asked her to do, her hesitations, her triumphs.

The candle started to drip. He put his hand beneath it, capturing it, letting it harmlessly splat in his palm.

She clenched and unclenched her butt cheeks, searching for courage, wondering if she'd find it and knowing she'd regret it if she didn't.

"You're curious. You want to know. How bad will it hurt?

How much pleasure will it give?"

"More than anything."

"Then pull back that hood." Waiting, Nathan turned the candle upright, letting a reservoir of molten wax pool.

With her jaw clenched, she squeezed her eyes closed and used the index fingers on both hands to expose the tiny bit of nerves. This…this she couldn't watch.

Her breaths came so fast she almost panted, and she expected him to encourage her to relax, maybe to ask if she was ready, but a series of warm drips seared her, making her scream, writhe, beg…fuck if she wasn't begging for more.

He dropped one more, much closer, so searing she orgasmed with a shriek…the most intense thing she'd ever endured.

And then, then it was over.

She was gasping, and she inhaled the sharp scent of smoke as he blew out the candle. After wiping her body clean, he helped her to sit and pulled her against his chest. It took a couple of seconds for her to realize that he'd sat on the bed, back propped against the headboard, and that he was holding her close, saying amazing, loving, approving things against her ear. Kelsey held on to them as if they were a lifesaver, breathing with him, matching the rise and fall of his chest until the room came into focus.

Kelsey had no idea how long he cradled her against him. All she knew was that he was the one she'd turned to for comfort.

Long moments later, she became aware of the hardness of his cock beneath her.

And that was the one thing that would complete her.

The orgasms had been spectacular. He'd taken her places she had not even been capable of imagining. But the truth was, she was restless, unsated. She ached to have his cock in her. It was as if the scene wasn't real without it.

She turned and straddled him.

With unusual boldness, she began to unfasten his necktie.

His eyes were an interesting color, a mix of dark and light, focus and curiosity. It unnerved her. But she continued, pulling the knot free.

"Did you think I was done with you?" His mouth twitched in an appealing way that made him seem younger, more accessible.

Her heart melted. "I was hoping you still wanted sex," she admitted.

He reacted so fast she could never have prepared for it. Within a second, he had her pinned flat on her back, arms over her head.

"What do you want, Kelsey?" He plucked the tie from her hands.

His voice was raw with passion, giving her courage to meet him with her own truth. "You," she said. "In me."

Expertly, he threaded the tie around her wrists and looped it through in a figure eight. When she tried to pull loose, the knot tightened, effectively preventing her from moving.

Nathan climbed from the bed but stayed close where she could see him. He unfastened the first few buttons on his shirt then pulled the hem free from his waistband and undid the rest.

Finally.

God, he was sensational.

She took the opportunity to drink him in. His chest had the exact amount of hair that she preferred, arrowing down toward his honed abs, and his waist was trim. The result of his hours in the gym showed in each cut muscle, every bit of precise definition.

Nathan's biceps were even more defined than she'd remembered, though with the way he effortlessly moved her around, she should have known.

Kelsey wasn't the type to drool over hot men like some of her friends. Rather, she hadn't been until now.

He bent to remove his shoes and socks before unfastening his trousers and letting them slide down his powerful legs.

Beneath his tight navy briefs, his dick was hard. The

material barely contained his straining erection.

Restlessly she shifted, impatience making her body tingle.

Nathan took the time to drape his pants over the footboard and tuck his socks inside his shoes before slipping them under the bed. Once again, she wondered what it would take for him to lose even a little of his carefully harnessed self-control.

Finally he removed his underwear. He was every bit as big as she might have guessed. She'd never been with a man whose cock was so thick. As she watched him roll a condom on, she moved around a bit, preparing for his penetration.

He knelt on the bed between her legs and squeezed her nipples.

In response, she pushed her ass into the mattress. His touch was torturous and not nearly enough.

He stuck two fingers into his mouth then rubbed between her legs. Her heated flesh blazed. Nathan had sensitized her skin, and each touch seemed magnified. She'd never felt more alive.

With gentle strokes that were a contrast to the way he'd been with her, he slid his fingers in and out of her pussy, preparing her.

Not just from the physical way he treated her, but because he was so determined to care for her, she was starting to care for him. And that, she knew, would be disastrous.

He continued to torment her, and when she was slick, he pressed his cockhead into her opening, and she moaned. The contact was even more than she'd hoped for, intimate on an entirely different level.

"Tell me you want me."

"Mr. Donovan, I almost grabbed your dick and put it in me a couple of minutes ago."

Despite that, he moved slower than she'd hoped, entering her then pulling out before going in again a little deeper.

She placed her feet flat on the mattress, spreading her legs wider in silent invitation.

Finally, he sank in the rest of the way with a deep thrust.

Even though she'd been sure she was ready, his length and girth filled her. "Holy hell," she gasped.

"Almost deep enough."

He grabbed her right leg and lifted it, putting it on his shoulder, taking control of her and the rhythm.

Nathan pulled out almost all the way then plunged back in and she let out a screaming, shuddering sigh.

This was what submission was about for her, the fantasy of being helpless, of having rough sex with an unbelievably caring man.

Maybe because of her dreams coming to life, a climax gripped her.

"Take it."

It stunned her to realize he'd read her so accurately that he knew she was so close.

He thrust deep, shooting spasms through her as she orgasmed.

He held her, an arm under her back, supporting her, silently letting her know he had her.

The paradox between his strength and gentleness made her weak.

Slowly at first, he began to move again.

She looked at him, saw the lines of concentration, the way he willed her to keep her gaze on him.

Then he kissed her, so fucking gently that she melted.

As he pistoned faster, he kissed her deeper.

Then the answering response arced through her, and she met him tongue to tongue, feminine to masculine.

His lovemaking went on for an impossible amount of time. Then he broke the kiss and tightened his jaw.

She gave herself over to the thrill of his orgasm and brought her free leg up over him.

"Kelsey." Her name sounded part endearment, part growl.

He came deep inside her, and she felt the pulse of his ejaculation. For that moment, she felt powerful too.

Eventually, she opened her eyes, and she smiled at him.

She wondered how she could feel so tender toward him after experiencing all this.

He released the grip he had on her wrists and brushed wayward hair back from her face. "So perfect for me."

"For me as well."

He stayed there for several seconds, looking at her. His smile faded and a frown replaced it, and when he spoke, his tone was gruff. "Let's get you untied."

She wondered what thoughts had gone through his mind, but before she could ask, he'd pulled out of her and eased her leg from his shoulder.

After releasing her, he spent a few seconds rubbing her hands and wrists and studying her. "Any problems moving?"

She tested her range of motion to show him she was fine. "No. I'm fine."

He helped her sit up, then went into the bathroom to discard the condom.

Then, surprising her, he wiped her with a damp washcloth that he'd brought back. Instead of getting ready to leave, he pulled up the blankets then climbed into bed, propping a pillow against the headboard. "Come here."

Common sense urged her to refuse. After everything they'd shared, things she'd never done with anyone else, she was feeling vulnerable.

As if he knew that, he opened his arms.

Damn him.

She snuggled against his chest and he wrapped his arms around her. The sound of his pounding heart soothed her.

He smoothed her hair and curled a lock around his index finger, toying with it.

Kelsey had never felt anything more reassuring. This, she knew, was the intimacy he'd spoken of.

She wasn't sure whether or not she dozed, and for a few minutes, she drifted in the altered state between sleep and consciousness.

For a while, he seemed as content as she was to stay there and enjoy the silence.

"Tomorrow night, I want you to come to my house and stay. We can drive in to work together."

"That seems a little too personal."

"Not much more than what we've already done."

Though she wasn't looking directly at him, she heard the smile in his words. "Spending the night is different."

"I want to introduce you to my spanking bench. Since it will be late, I don't want you driving home. And if I've done a proper job, you won't be capable of it anyway."

"You could always take me home."

"I could."

She hated that he was always so agreeable. It made it difficult to argue.

"I'd prefer that you stay. We could ride in together Thursday."

"What if someone sees us?"

"We had an early meeting."

She cocked her head to look at him.

"Which would be true. I would want to bury my morning erection in your hot cunt."

Breath whooshed from her lungs. "And now it's the only thing I can think of as well."

"And when you pack a bag, be sure to include your butt plug and your slut paddle. I want to mark you as mine."

There was a reason Nathan didn't fuck his subs.

Even though he'd been home for an hour, had taken a shower, sipped some particularly fine cognac and streamed part of *The Godfather*, he hadn't been able to clear his mind.

Nathan changed into a pair of shorts and headed into his home office. The space didn't contain only a computer and desk, he'd outfitted it with a couple of pieces of cardio equipment, a television and a sound system. Outside of work, he spent more time in this room than anywhere else, including his bedroom.

He set the treadmill for eight miles an hour. When thoughts of Kelsey continued to creep in, he notched it up again.

Surely starving his brain of oxygen would help.

Even when his feet pounded the belt, he couldn't outrun the events of the night.

His attraction flirted with being a fucking fixation, and it confounded him.

Since he'd been inside her hot pussy and held her in his arms afterward, he'd opened a door to his heart that was better closed. As she'd rightly pointed out, they had a work relationship. Even though that wasn't necessarily a bad thing as far as he was concerned, the fact that he was thinking about her when he shouldn't be, planning her next experience, waiting for her to get to the office, all that weakened him, made him less able to compartmentalize each part of his life.

He notched up the speed on the treadmill one more time and looked outside at the sliver of a moon, barely visible through the quickly moving clouds.

Twenty minutes later, he wasn't any clearer, and the burn in his lungs matched the one in his legs.

He slowed to a walk, and when his annoying-as-hell watch pinged to alert him to the fact his heart rate was once again normal, he decided to channel his energy into something productive.

After wiping off with a towel, he went into the playroom. Earlier, he'd put his bag next to the counter, and now he unzipped it and placed the items he planned to use, including her nipple clamps, on a white towel.

As it had been a long time since the equipment had been used, he wiped down the spanking bench before opening the armoire that held his equipment. He pulled out his short flogger, made from supple cowhide, and flicked it several times, testing it and himself before returning it to its hook.

He grabbed a few leather cuffs and attached them to the spanking bench.

Finally he checked his supplies, ensuring he had adequate sanitary wipes, lube, condoms and bottles of water.

That done, he returned to his office and logged into his email. Most he left for the following day, but he confirmed an appointment the next week in Dallas with Connor.

Then he sent a text message to Erin suggesting she check out Andi's salon. Couldn't hurt for Kelsey's friend to be an advocate.

Proving she didn't sleep much, either, his sister responded within minutes.

On Westheimer? You know that's one of the pricier salons in the city, right? It costs money to go there. Like more than ten dollars for a haircut.

He shook his head. He paid more than ten dollars for a haircut. Most times. With a grin, he replied.

If her pink-and-blue pastel hair is any indication, she does, indeed, have access to magical unicorn powder at her color bar.

His phone lit up again almost instantly.

Who are you and what have you done with my cheapskate sibling? No, wait. Never mind. I don't want him back. Whoever has Nathan's phone, will you be my brother?

She said the first service is free just to get you into her salon.

Now I know I'm talking to my brother.

Brat.

Love you, too, cheapskate.

He tossed his phone on the desk, plugged it into the

charger then headed for another quick shower to rinse off the sweat.

Thoughts of Kelsey drifted to him, and he remembered her in the bath, on her knees, over his lap, hands secured with his necktie.

He took hold of his cock with his right hand. The left, he braced on the far wall. With his eyes closed, he stroked himself. Images of Kelsey superimposed themselves one on top of the other. He recalled her whimper, could almost hear her scream.

In a short amount of time, she'd given him a fuckton of trust, and he consumed it as if it were food.

Shaving her pussy, dropping hot wax on her tits, her belly, her pelvis, her red, throbbing clit.

He moved his hand faster.

Thoughts of her made him as horny as if she were there, looking up at him, begging him to slide into her.

With a grunt, he ejaculated, hot spurts of cum dripping from his hand.

But it didn't help.

Christ alive, he still wanted her.

11

"We will need to get you something to wear."

Nathan's words echoed in her mind, making it impossible for her to concentrate on their morning meeting.

"Ms. Lane?"

She glanced across his desk at him, mortified he'd caught her daydreaming. But since he'd left her house last night, she hadn't been able to think of anything but him. Nathan Donovan got to her in ways no one ever had. He relentlessly pushed her, even when she wasn't sure she could give him what he asked for. But each time she met the challenge, she felt as if she'd climbed a mountain. Every experience was exhilarating and try as she might, she couldn't help but focus on the next.

"Ms. Lane?"

"Sir?" Since when had that been so natural? "Sorry."

"You'll need something to wear." He frowned at her. "When we go to Deviation on Saturday night."

No wonder she couldn't concentrate. Every thought connected to him led to BDSM or sex. It seemed to consume her life.

"I was thinking we'd go shopping tomorrow after work."

She wrote the word *tomorrow* on her notebook then circled it endlessly, stuck on the idea of entering a lingerie store with him.

He walked a silver pen through his fingers and sat back, regarding her. "Are you going home with me this evening?"

Stunned, she looked up.

After he'd left last night, she'd spent an hour thinking about it, debating, listing a dozen reasons she shouldn't and only one why she should. She wanted to. That mattered more than anything. "I packed an overnight bag," she admitted. Though technically Kelsey didn't start work until eight, she'd arrived at two minutes before the hour. To her, that meant she was at least half an hour late, something unheard of. She'd spent far too long packing makeup, toiletries, hairbrushes, even sex toys. But choosing clothes had been the most difficult. Office wear was no problem, but lingerie? Bras and underwear? She'd pulled out her entire drawer as she'd dug through it, shoving aside briefs, thongs and boy shorts. She had no idea what he'd find appealing. It hadn't helped that she told herself it didn't matter. It did to her.

The most agonizing decision had been what she was going to sleep in. She'd discarded nightshirts—too lame. A silk chemise—not warm enough. A peignoir—too sexy. Thermal pajamas—not nearly sexy enough. In frustration, she'd tossed in several different things. She could figure it out this evening. "And I rode the train."

He stilled his hand, the pen seemingly frozen in air.

She met his eyes. The green color seemed richer, more inviting than ever. In that moment, she was glad she'd made the decision she had.

"Do you need to do anything after work?"

"I was planning to use the fitness center."

"No problem. I'll work a little late, and we'll plan on leaving at…six?"

She nodded.

"Anywhere specific you'd like to go for dinner?"

Kelsey shook her head.

"Pizza?"

She blinked. "Pizza?"

"There's a place near my house, owned by twin sisters from Sicily. You might like it. Decent chianti, as well."

He couldn't have said anything that would have shocked her more. She would have thought he might suggest a steak or something else upscale. Pizza didn't fit the image she had of him. Suddenly she realized she really didn't know this man. Despite the fact she'd had the hottest sex of her life with him and had studied his business practices, she had no idea who he was at the deepest level.

As much as she wanted to find out, she was scared. She was starting to care for him, and now she was in deeper danger. She might lose her heart to him. Again she warned herself about falling for an overbearing man.

"So how about it? We could call ahead so we don't have to wait long."

"If it doesn't have anchovies, I'm sure I'll enjoy it."

They agreed to meet at six o'clock, then he switched subjects back to work so fast she was baffled and scrambling to keep up.

She scrawled notes as he spoke. She needed to get out a company-wide email about Mr. Newman's going-away party, consult with Thompson, Connor's admin, on flight arrangements for the Dallas trip the next week and ensure that everything had been handled correctly for Seward's dismissal the following day when he reported for duty.

Though she tried to concentrate, she was thinking about the night ahead.

"And, Ms. Lane?"

She regarded him. This morning, he wore a charcoal-colored suit, so dark it was nearly black, with a pale yellow tie. For a moment, before she derailed the thought, she entertained the idea that he might pin her face down on the desk and join her wrists at the small of her back, confining her with deft twists of that tie. "Mr. Donovan?"

"I enjoyed fucking you last night."

Her mouth dropped open.

His cell phone rang, and he picked it up and glanced at the caller identification. "If you'll excuse me?"

"Of course." She stood and left, closing the door behind her.

Kelsey paused for a second, shoulders against the wall.

The juxtaposition between intimacy then being shut out

when his phone rang jarred her.

This, she told herself, *is a good reason not to date the boss.*

It didn't make any difference whom he talked to. He had every right to his privacy. Still…she was curious.

For the next few hours, she handled what felt like a million administrative tasks, calling Zoe McBride, working out the details for Nathan's Dallas trip, checking in with Lawrence to be sure they were on track for Seward's termination.

Then she sent an email to Thompson, Connor's assistant. The man responded immediately, also asking for their arrival dates at the family's annual meeting.

She promised to get back to him as quickly as possible then set a reminder on Nathan's calendar.

Kelsey decided to head to Marvin's for a much-needed coffee before facing the rest of the day. Last night, she'd slept worse than usual. Nathan had offered to stay, but she'd insisted she was fine. Truthfully, being in his arms would have helped. The wax play, the over-the-knee punishment from his belt, the sex… It had been a lot to process, no matter how strong she pretended to be.

Her phone vibrated, and she checked the message. She was a bit surprised that it was from Andi.

Erin-Fucking-Donovan called me. She's coming in this week. I'll buy your martini next time we get together.

Kelsey shook her head. Before she could reply, asking what happened to her BOGO service, she received a second message from Andi.

Your boss is a rock star. Have fun Saturday night. I almost wish I could be there to see him beat your ass.

Kelsey sat back. She was sure he'd be glad to know there was another member of the Nathan Donovan fan club.

The rest of the day passed in a flurry of calls, emails, discussions with Zoe and the Newmans about the upcoming party, lunch at her desk and impersonal, businesslike conversation with Nathan that left her feeling a little raw.

He was in his office with the door closed when she picked up her bag and took the elevator to the fitness center.

After twenty minutes on the elliptical machine, Kelsey hit the circuit equipment to work her legs and upper body. She used more weight than normal and forced herself to concentrate on her form, shutting out all other thoughts.

When she was on the final go-round, she noticed Nathan, his hips propped against the air-conditioning unit, arms folded across his broad chest, studying her.

She froze. Then deliberately she got back to her workout.

When she finished the final twenty-five reps on the ab board, he was standing next to her, holding a towel.

With a small smile, she accepted. "Thank you."

"Take your time," he told her. "I can wait while you shower, or you can shower at my house, either way."

"I'll do it here," she said.

"Good. I assume you have your butt plug with you?"

She felt her face drain of color.

"Please put it in. I'll check for it when we get in the elevator."

"Do you..." She struggled to find the right words. "Do you always...?"

"Think about you?" he suggested. "Plan what I'm going to do next? I suspect you know the answer."

"I was going to ask if you're always planning to raise the bar and shock me."

"You know the answer to that, as well. And the correct response is..."

"Yes, Sir. Yes, Nathan. Yes, Mr. Donovan."

"There are no more words more beautiful than those."

After wiping the back of her neck with a towel, she excused herself.

The idea of inserting the plug made her hand shake.

It was after hours, and she had the place to herself, but still...

The whole time she showered, she thought about his

request. She wasn't all that adept with the plug. But the idea of sitting on it, full up for him, as he drove her to his house and took her to dinner, appealed to her naughty side.

After wrapping a towel around herself, she clipped up her hair then grabbed her gear and went into one of the two dressing rooms, tugging the curtain closed behind her. She put her bag on the built-in shelf then unzipped it and picked up the plug.

"Kelsey?"

Hearing her name startled her, and she dropped the slender silicone plug on top of her bag. "Give me about five minutes," she shouted back.

With a quick yank, the curtain was opened and Nathan stood there, large and foreboding.

"You can't be in here!"

"Oh?" He took a step toward her and closed the curtain behind him. "I want to watch you put it in."

"You're going to get us arrested," she protested.

"Embarrassed, perhaps, but not arrested. Get on with it."

Her boss overwhelmed her. "This is outrageous."

"Would you like me to do it for you?" He stood there, crowding the space, unrelenting, smelling of power and determination. "Your choice." He pulled the towel off her.

She stared at him for several seconds before sighing. "I'll do it myself."

Her heart racing, she lubed the plug then she squatted to help with the angle.

The plug bent as she tried to slide it in, and it slipped free. "May I help?"

She knew her face had turned scarlet. "Please."

"Squirt some lube on me." He held out his index finger.

Shockingly aware of the risk they were taking, she did so.

"Hand me the plug." Once she had, he said, "Bend over and grab the bench. Spread your legs as wide as you can then get on your toes."

He placed his slick finger against her tightest hole. Instinctively she tensed. Then remembering his instructions from the past couple of days, she exhaled.

Nathan entered her slowly but determinedly, forcing her anus apart. Since it had been so long since she'd had any kind of ass play, the pressure was uncomfortable. She kept her mouth shut so that she didn't yelp and attract the attention of anyone who might be passing by.

After he moved around, stretching her, he pulled out his finger. Moments later, she felt the press of the rubbery-type material instead.

He seated it in one long stroke.

Even though she'd been determined to remain silent, she gasped. She felt full and oh-so-much-more submissive.

He kissed the side of her neck then gave her right buttock a hard spank. "Hurry up."

"Yes, Sir." She stood and turned to face him.

"Pepperoni?"

"What?"

"I'll order the pizza while you finish up."

"And extra cheese," she said.

Without another word, he left the dressing room, the curtain swaying in his wake. Unable to believe the whole thing had just happened, she reached into her bag for a pair of clean underwear.

She heard running water, and from a small crack where the curtain wasn't entirely closed, she saw his back as he stood in front of the sink.

"Oh, excuse me!"

Hearing a strange female voice, Kelsey froze.

"Am I in the wrong place?"

"Not at all," Nathan replied easily, grabbing a paper towel. "Goodnight."

He disappeared from sight, and she heard the solid soles of his shoes against the tile.

More mortified than she'd ever been, she took her time brushing her hair before dressing in an oversize T-shirt and yoga pants, hoping the other woman had already left the room. But as Kelsey walked through with her bag over her shoulder, the blonde was still there, putting her earphones in place. They exchanged quick smiles, and Kelsey strode nonstop toward the door.

Nathan was standing near the elevators, and he pushed the button when he saw her. "How does it feel?"

She was so concerned with almost being caught that she'd forgotten her discomfort. "Fine. I think."

When they were descending to the parking garage, he eased his hand inside her pants.

"These are almost as good as a skirt," he said.

He pushed on the base of the plug and she sucked in a breath and stood up a little taller. "Damn," she said.

"I'm looking forward to you wearing it all day on Friday."

Kelsey wasn't sure she could tolerate it. She also knew better than to argue.

He took her bag from her as they made their way to his vehicle then helped her into the car before reaching across to fasten her belt. She should have expected that, but she hadn't. His size, proximity and take-charge attitude made her utterly aware of her femininity. When she squirmed to get comfortable, it wasn't entirely from the effects of the silicone up her rear.

"You know, Kelsey, you're a very good sub. That won't get you out of what I have planned for you tonight, though." With that, he smiled and closed the door.

She sank against the seatback.

As they drove, she checked her phone and found that the ever-professional Thompson had gotten back to her about Nathan's Dallas trip. "You're confirmed for next Thursday. You're meeting Connor at the airport at six a.m. The meeting with OneTech is at nine. That will give you time for breakfast and account for any flight or traffic delays. You'll depart Dallas Love Field at three."

He glanced at her. "And be home in time to fuck you."

Unsaid words hung between them. They'd only agreed to spend this week together. She refused to think past that.

"Where are we on plans for the family retreat?"

"Second weekend in December," she confirmed. "Both your grandparents have said they will attend, as has Erin. Your aunt Kathryn has not agreed yet. There's some sort of dispute about the guests she wants to bring with her."

He nodded as if that wasn't a surprise.

"Connor and Lara, of course. Cade and Sofia will be there."

"Hard for them to avoid since it's at their place. I'd still like for you to attend."

"Thompson will be there to handle admin for the family," she said.

"It'd be a good opportunity for you to get away. Corpus Christi. Picture taking…"

"You know how to tempt a girl, Mr. Donovan."

"Did you ask Martha about her availability as I requested?"

"I…" She felt his steady gaze on her. "No. I did not."

He exposed his watch and touched the screen. This time, the heart that hovered above it was more red than pink, and she wondered if that meant anything.

"Memo," he said.

"Ready, Mr. Donovan."

"Contact Martha Leone to find out her availability the second week of December."

"Noted."

He drew his cuff back into place. "If you're not intending to do something I ask of you, Kelsey, please have the courtesy to say so." Despite his words, his tone was light, but direct. "Give us the opportunity to discuss it."

"It's not that," she said. It had been on her to-do list since Monday. When she'd been making arrangements with Thompson for the family gathering, she'd considered sending Martha an email or phoning her, but she'd put it off. "I hadn't decided whether or not I want to go."

"My point remains. Please let me know if you're not going to do something I asked."

She exhaled. "You're right." And he was. "I'll contact her tomorrow."

"I'll handle it." His tone said the conversation was over.

"I apologize, Nathan." She reached across the compartment to put her fingers on his wrist. "It won't happen again."

"I know." He sounded sincere, and she exhaled.

A few minutes ago, she'd been prepared for an argument, but she realized that he had the knack for making a point then moving on. It was a skill she could learn from.

He pulled into the parking lot of a small strip mall. Nonina's was at the end and took up two storefronts.

After he'd parked, he met her at the front of the vehicle and placed his fingers at the small of her back as they walked to the door.

The restaurant was small, with red-and-white checkered tablecloths. Empty chianti bottles served as candleholders, and the scent of garlic and fresh bread greeted her like an old friend. Her mouth watered. Suddenly she remembered how long it had been since lunch.

"Nathan!" A petite woman with short blonde hair beamed a smile across the distance.

"Elena, meet Kelsey."

"Delighted," the woman said.

"Elena and her sister make the best food on the planet," he said.

"I can't wait to try it," she said, noticing that he hadn't introduced her as his employee.

"Your pizza will be right out," Elena said, wiping her hands on her apron. "Wine with that?"

Nathan looked at Kelsey with a raised eyebrow, and Kelsey said, "I'd love a glass."

"Make it two," he said. "Chianti."

"Should I bring a bottle?"

Kelsey shook her head.

"Just the glasses, Elena. Thanks."

Nathan led Kelsey to a small table in the back of the dining room. The plug felt even more rigid against the wooden chair. "Is there a reason you didn't choose a booth?"

"Yes."

"You did this on purpose?"

"Knowing you're uncomfortable with the plug I put up your ass? Yeah. I did it on purpose."

She shifted her weight to one butt cheek, hoping for a little relief.

"Imagining you enduring it all day on Friday makes it even better."

Elena walked over carrying a tray with silverware, napkins, plates and their wine.

When she left, Nathan offered a toast. "To your first experience on the spanking bench."

"I don't know if I want to drink to that," Kelsey said. They clinked their glasses, then she stared into the bottom of hers to distract herself from his gaze.

They discussed business for a few minutes and were interrupted when Elena returned with an enormous pizza and placed it on a metal stand. "I'm not sure I've ever seen anything that big."

"We don't like you to go home hungry." Elena served them each a slice before telling them to let her know if they needed anything.

"This looks amazing," Kelsey said when they were alone again. She lowered her head and inhaled a whiff of the garlic and tomatoes.

Nathan picked up his slice and folded it before taking a bite.

Not nearly that adventurous, she cut hers then forked it into her mouth.

The flavors exploded on her tongue. "This could be some of the best pizza I've ever had." The crust was nicely browned, and the cheese was hot and melty. She thought she might be in heaven.

"Told you."

She managed to finish two slices, but Nathan kept going, surprising her with his appetite. "I think you could have eaten that entire piece of chocolate cake the other night."

"Easily."

"Thank you for recommending Andi to your sister." Another reminder that he followed through on the things he said he intended to do.

"No thanks needed. Erin is always looking to try something new. She wore a corset to the ranch's centennial celebration. I'm not sure the Colonel has recovered yet. And she's annoying as hell. You'll like her."

Since there were still two slices left, they had the leftovers packaged to go before promising Elena they'd return soon.

Kelsey barely had time to relax on the short drive to his house.

The neighborhood was older, well-established, with oaks, magnolias, even some palm trees. Houses were spread out for privacy. This, she'd expected. The house had to have been a solid investment, one that would retain its value and increase over time, but it wasn't in one of the pricier areas where homes were overvalued because of their zip code. It suited his fiscal personality.

He pulled up a long driveway then parked in the garage and turned off the vehicle's headlights.

She grabbed the leftovers while he got her bag. He flipped on some lights to illuminate the path and breezeway that led to the back door.

As far as she could see from the numerous solar lights, his landscaping was lush, if overgrown. With its numerous benches and chairs, the yard issued a silent invitation to sit and relax.

Their lifestyles couldn't be any more divergent, she realized.

Inside, the air conditioning hit her in a welcome break from the day's cloying humidity.

She fell in love with his house instantly.

A breakfast nook was next to a window. Before he closed the shade, she noticed that the sightline included a magnolia tree. His kitchen was a designer's dream, with under-cabinet lighting and an island at least half-again as wide as her own.

"Refrigerator's over there," he said, pointing.

She placed the box inside then put her purse on a counter and followed him when he offered a tour.

Whereas she was cramped in her space, he seemed to have miles of it—a two-story entryway, a dining room that seemed to be unused, a great room and a guest room on the main level.

"Did you decorate?" she asked, appreciating the crown molding in each room, and the way various cool colors complemented the hardwoods and tiles. Throw rugs, paintings and tapestries softened some rooms.

"No. I liked the way it was painted and modernized, and Erin and my mother bought the furnishings." He shrugged. "Some of them came from the attic in the ranch, and a couple of pieces were donated by my mother."

"Thrifty."

He glanced over his shoulder at her.

"I wouldn't have expected anything else."

Nathan opened a door to show her a guest room adjoining a bathroom.

"Is this where I'm staying?"

"No. You'll be in the master. With me."

It had been a year or more since she'd stayed with a man. Last night, after he'd left, her place had felt empty. When she'd snuggled into him, part of her had wanted him to stay.

Next he showed her the study.

"I love it. Love it. Love it." The room had three long but narrow windows, dozens of drawers, shelves and several cupboards. When she'd bought her condo, she'd been hoping to find a place with a room like this. There was more than enough space for her cameras, tripods, pictures, albums. "How does envy look on me?" she asked.

He tipped his head to the side. "A little green," he said. "Maybe Andi could give you highlights that make it look not so obvious?"

She grinned.

Before they climbed the stairs, he grabbed her bag.

"The master bedroom is to the left."

She hesitated for a moment, unsure which way to go.

"We'll go there first."

She led the way into the bedroom. The room was stunningly big, with a tray ceiling. Other than a nightstand, there was nothing in the room except for a honeyed-oak four-poster bed. It was covered with a navy blue comforter and the whole thing shouted dominance and masculinity. "I bet you picked this out."

"One of the only things I purchased, yes. And you'll be the first sub I tie to it."

Her mouth dried.

"Bathroom and closets are through here."

The space they entered was almost as large as her living room. "I'm not sure I've ever seen a chandelier in a bathroom before."

"It's gorgeous. Erin's idea. But I keep thinking I'll replace it with an overhead fan."

She looked at him, stunned.

"In summer I could use more air circulation in here."

"I think I'd rather suffer than get rid of the chandelier. The light refraction off the mirrors is stunning."

"I'd never really noticed," he admitted. "Give me a minute to change? You're welcome to get comfortable, settle in, put on a robe or get naked."

There were his-and-her closets with built-in drawers. While his was filled with suits, ties, shirts, shoes and slacks, the other was empty. He put her bag on a shelf.

Since it would be easier to find what she needed if she got organized, she hung the dress she'd selected for work, put the shoes on a rack, moved her lingerie and sleepwear into the top drawer then carried her cosmetics bag and hairbrush to the vanity. "Which sink should I use?"

He came out of his closet wearing all black, from a pair of lightweight casual slacks, to a form-fitting T-shirt to shoes. She realized it was the first time she'd seen him without his ever-present watch.

He stole her breath. Nathan looked every part a Dom, and her entire body vibrated with the need to offer what he silently demanded.

How was it possible that he was more intimidating now than he had been last night? Even his hair made him look devilish, and the evening stubble hardened his appearance.

"Ah..."

"The one on the right."

She momentarily forgot what she'd asked.

"The sink," he said. "Yours is the one on the right. The drawer next to it is empty, and there's room under the cabinet, as well."

"Thank you." She looked away, severing the impact his gaze held over her.

"Is your paddle in the bag?"

She nodded.

"Good. Get it."

She went into the closet, and he followed. Kelsey lost her grasp on the zipper pull and had to grab it a second time with him standing merely inches from her.

Kelsey reached into the bottom of the bag and pulled out the paddle. She put it in his outstretched hand, with the word *slut* facing up.

"Thank you. Are you ready?"

She shook her head. "I need a few minutes."

"Can I get you anything?"

"Maybe a brain with circuits that don't get fried when I look at you." Part of her couldn't believe she'd said that aloud.

"Maybe we can get a two-for-one deal."

In that moment, she realized she was in danger of falling for this man. Not in a small way, but in a total, complete, unrecoverable way.

She mentally shook herself.

Falling in love with Nathan Donovan wouldn't be stupid.

It would be beyond stupid. Monumentally disastrous. He was dynamic, powerful, ruthless, single-minded in his pursuit of his goals…until he achieved them. Then he moved on. Even with Donovan Logistics, he wouldn't be there forever. He was already considering taking over a company in Dallas.

He was everything she didn't want in a man, and he'd never given any indication that he was open to anything more than BDSM and sex with his assistant. Ending their intimate relationship after Saturday was going to be difficult enough. She couldn't imagine how she'd manage if she let it go on for weeks or months.

It made much more sense for her to focus on her career and her life goals. She told herself to enjoy their time together and not think beyond the moment. As if that were possible with the way he stood so close that they breathed the same air.

He left the room, and she took a few minutes to freshen up. Since he'd said she could dress as she liked, she'd hadn't changed from her post-workout outfit.

Before she was completely finished brushing her hair, he returned. He still held the paddle and tapped the thick part of it against the side of his leg.

Unsettled, she put down the brush.

"Ready?"

As she would ever be.

On the way to what she presumed was the playroom, he paused to show her his office.

Though the room was uncluttered and contained few personal effects, his college diploma hung from a wall next to the window. He had a treadmill and an exercise bike. A television was mounted from the ceiling and appeared to be on a swivel so he could move the screen.

Two notebook computers, each with the Bonds logo emblazoned on the closed top, sat in the middle of the glossy desktop. His watch and cell phone were nearby, along with a number of electronic chargers, looking a bit like long, thin snakes where they protruded from the cutout in the desk's surface.

A whiteboard took up most of the space on one wall. The words *Donovan Worldwide* were stenciled at the top. Other Donovan interests were listed, and she saw that Newman Inland Marine had a line leading up to Donovan Logistics.

Some company names she recognized, others she didn't. There were lines drawn from a few, linking them to others. A couple of others were circled. One had been crossed out. "Is this your strategy board?"

"Yeah. It helps to have it all laid out visually."

"Why are some of the names circled?" she asked, appreciating the glimpse of the man he was at home. He was consistent, she realized, no matter where he was.

"Those companies are in play, meaning our research tells us they could be vulnerable to takeover, logical acquisitions for existing Donovan businesses." He shrugged. "Or it means they've approached us and we have begun preliminary investigations."

"There are quite a few of them." She noticed that a line divided US holdings from those overseas. Until now, she hadn't considered just how vast the family's interests were. "Do you travel a lot?"

"We generally bring our C-level leaders to Texas rather than us going to them. But I do when it's unavoidable."

"This is where you spend most of your time," she guessed. It was a place he could exercise his brain and his body at the same time. It was more lived-in than the rest of the house, but that didn't mean much. The man was meticulously organized.

"Too much, my sister tells me."

"So you don't take time to enjoy the back yard?"

"Was its resemblance to a jungle your first clue?" he asked.

"I'd spend most of the day outside if I lived here." With the foliage, he was sure to have birds, dragonflies, bees, green anoles. She could snap the camera shutter for hours without leaving the premises.

He tapped the paddle against his calf. "Shall we?"

All of a sudden, she noticed how warm she was, despite the chilled air whispering over her skin. As she walked behind him, the intrusion from the butt plug seemed magnified.

At the end of the hallway, he pushed the door open and stepped aside. "Welcome to my playroom, Kelsey. Have a look around."

Feeling edgy, filled with trepidation from the unknown, she squared her shoulders and walked past him.

Not surprising her, the room was decorated sparsely. The floor was a rich, reddish hardwood. The walls were painted a contrasting gray, much like his office at Donovan Logistics. Rather than the blinds she expected, the window was covered by a blackout shade.

As promised, he had a spanking bench, and it was covered in smooth black marine vinyl. Sturdy O-rings protruded from several locations, and he'd attached cuffs to some of them. A number of mirrors hung from the walls. No matter where she looked, she saw reflections of herself and Nathan, with his forbidding countenance.

The granite countertop appeared to match those in the kitchen. He'd spread a white towel across the top, and she saw her collar and leash alongside the nipple clamps.

A violet-colored yoga mat lay on the floor, and there was a large armoire which, she figured, probably held his equipment.

He placed her paddle on the counter then faced her with the collar in his hands. "Remain in place and lift your hair."

Gaze focused on him, she did so and watched him close the distance between them.

She loved it when he stood so close that she was able to inhale his scent.

He buckled the strip of leather into place then stood there for a moment, looking at her.

"This is something I won't get tired of seeing." His voice

was hoarse.

Kelsey let her hair fall over her shoulders and down her back.

"There's a flogger hanging behind those doors." He nodded toward the piece of furniture.

"Yes, Sir," she said, unsure what to say and having no choice but to rely on intuition to guide her.

"Bring it to me. Present it to me."

She didn't know exactly what he meant. In books, the Dom sometimes expected the sub to kneel, sometimes just hand it over. "On my knees, Sir? Standing? Bowed before you?"

"Excellent," he whispered.

His approval made heat lance through her. She realized his instruction had been a test. Would she have the courage to admit what she didn't know and ask for his guidance?

"Head on the floor," he said.

She went to the masculine piece of furniture and opened the doors.

Breath chilled her lungs. He had all sorts of stuff hanging from hooks—floggers, whips and two paddles. One was carved from thick wood and had a capital D burned into it. The other was much thinner, crafted from a lighter-colored wood, and it had rows of holes marching across the surface. Either of them, she was sure, would hurt considerably more than hers. He had a couple of other implements on the shelves that she'd never seen and couldn't name.

"It's the short one on the far left," he said from across the room. "Golden colored."

He had several there. One was black, intimidatingly long with at least thirty strands. There was a red one that appeared to be made from rubber. Kelsey picked up the one she thought he meant. It was about twelve inches long, and the thick strands were soft and supple, but it was still daunting. "Is this correct, Sir?" She turned toward him.

"It is."

Schooling her mind and her racing thoughts, she took a

few steps toward him then stopped. Her pulse fluttering, she lowered herself to her knees then went lower still, until her forehead was pressed to the hardwood. Kelsey stretched her arms in out in front of her, palms together and facing up with the handle of the flogger across them.

Since her eyes were closed, she relied on her other senses. The sound of his footfall seemed to echo throughout the room and inside her head, reminding her of her submission.

Then… Nothing but the whisper from the air conditioner.

He allowed the tension to stretch and grow, and it took all her concentration to remain in position.

Eventually she felt him lift the flogger from her hands.

"Very, very nice. I couldn't have wanted anything more." He went quiet for a moment. "Look at me."

Through barely opened eyelids and with her forehead a scant few inches off the floor, she tipped back her head.

He was crouched in front of her, his legs spread.

She met his gaze. "Sir?"

"When you're ready, sub, strip. Stack your clothes in the bottom drawer of the armoire, then put on the nipple clamps I've laid out for you here…" He pointed toward the countertop. "Then position yourself over the spanking bench."

She waited, unable to respond.

"When you do, I want you to tell me how many times I should use my flogger on you."

Kelsey squeezed her legs together and felt the plug shift.

"And when we agree on that answer, I'll do exactly that."

"Yes," she whispered.

"Once we're done and you can't take any more, you're going to ask me to sear your ass with the paddle. I want you, me—both of us—to know that you're *my* slut. And I want you to be proud of that."

She shifted, already needy.

"Do you understand me, Kelsey?"

"Yes. Yes," she whispered. "Yes, Sir."

She forced her gaze up.

"And then, my obedient submissive, you're going to beg me to fuck you."

12

The reality of having Kelsey in his playroom surpassed his fantasies.

He stood near the countertop and watched her take off her clothes. Her hands didn't shake as badly as they had a couple of days ago, meaning she was gaining confidence, perhaps relying on him and his direction to guide her. Fucking heady stuff.

As he'd instructed, she placed her clothes in the bottom drawer, and she tucked her shoes out of the way.

She walked toward him, her bare feet silent on the floor. Though he loved the sight of a woman in high heels, there was something about her being completely nude that made her appear more submissive.

He continued to study her as she picked up the clamps and put them in place. She winced and moaned softly. Other than a scream, he couldn't imagine a more appealing sound. "Wait."

She stayed where she was, and he fisted the chain and tugged up, forcing her onto tiptoes.

Kelsey rewarded him with a small, satisfying yelp.

"You are so damn sexy."

"Thank you, Nathan."

After he released her, she followed his instructions and went toward the spanking bench.

"Climb up," he said. "Lie on your stomach. Your elbows and knees go on the rails."

It took her several seconds to get herself situated, and she gingerly moved her upper body a few times as she flattened her breasts and clamps against the surface. Her ass was prominently displayed, and he saw the hilt of the butt plug.

Damn. "Such a beautiful picture." He walked around her, trailing his fingers down her spine to soothe her. "Comfortable?"

"Not in the least, Sir."

"Good." He checked to ensure her position didn't put undue stress on any part of her body. Then he fastened her ankles into place. "I can't stop thinking about your world-class ass, Kelsey." He pinched the fleshy part of one of her buttocks. "And these dimples...?" He pressed a fingertip into the small indentations near the base of her spine. "Fucking hot."

She squirmed, and he put a hand between her shoulders to keep her still.

He checked her position and decided she'd be able to move too much. "Stretch out a little more," he told her. He moved the wrist cuffs down to another O-ring then secured her in place.

Kelsey tested the bonds, and they held her firm.

"Much better." And the position had the added benefit of thrusting her ass just a little higher in the air.

She cocked her head to look at him, and he brushed her hair back from her face.

"How many times should I use the flogger on you?"

"I've never felt it before, so I don't know how bad it will hurt."

"Some night, we'll do it for fifteen minutes or more, half an hour, maybe."

Her eyes went wide. "That's not possible."

"On the contrary. Depending how hard the hits are and where I place them, it's an achievable feat."

"There are certain events I'm not planning to get a medal in, Mr. Donovan. I'll settle for a participation ribbon."

Ms. Kelsey Lane sounded so prim and proper that he grinned. "Standing is a better position for a real flogging, and you'll get that at the club, either on the Punishment

Pole or St. Andrew's cross. This is going to be more sensual than anything."

She pressed her lips together.

"I'm waiting for an answer," he reminded her.

"Two dozen? Is that a lot?"

"Quadruple that."

"You've lost your mind, Sir."

In response, he trailed the leather throngs down her back, and little goosebumps danced across her arms.

He gave her a couple of sensual hits, and her body remained stiff. He did a couple more.

"I might like that." Her hips swayed from side to side.

"Give me your number?" He continued to caress her with the flogger, warming up her body.

"Four dozen."

"Six," he countered.

"Five," she said.

Brave girl. He'd been willing to settle for three, not that he'd ever tell her that.

He played with her butt plug, mostly to catch her off guard. He gave it a couple of quick twists, making her clench her buttocks.

"That thing makes me feel so full," she said.

"It will be more so when my cock is in your cunt." He rubbed her body all over until he saw her sink deeper into the upholstery. "That's it. Let it take your weight."

She rested her cheek against the vinyl.

"Excellent." He began to work the flogger back and forth over her thighs and buttocks, then with much less force over her back and shoulders.

When he got to the first dozen, he saw her unfurl a finger from her fist.

"How are you doing?"

"This feels…"

He continued to flog her.

After the second dozen, she unfurled another finger.

"Feels?" he prompted.

"Stingy." She turned her head to the other side. "I had no idea." She sighed deeply, extending a third finger and letting her body become even more pliant.

Now that she was ready, he increased the force of the flogging, landing each hit with more force, moving her body around.

"My God…" She added a fourth finger, and she moved her hips, silently seeking more.

Her body was pink, glowing, and she began to thrash her head, making a mess of her hair. Though he often separated BDSM from sex, his dick was hard, throbbing, insistent. He'd never had this kind of reaction to a woman, never wanted to spend this much time together. Being with her at work was powerful, but nowhere close to enough. "Where are we?" he asked.

"Five?" she guessed. "But I want to keep going."

The request stunned him, pleased him. "A few more," he agreed, not wanting to give her too much the first time. He landed a few between her legs on her upper thighs. And she squealed when he caught her pussy lips with the tips of a couple of strands.

The last few, he landed in the sweet spot area, hoping the sensation would radiate through her.

He looped the handle over one of the O-rings and rubbed her.

"That was incredible." She stretched her neck. "I'm relaxed and edgy at the same time."

"Good. Ready for me to use your paddle?"

She tightened her body before visibly exhaling. "Yes."

"What word is on it?"

She was quiet for so long that he wasn't sure she was going to answer. "Slut," she whispered.

"A little louder?" he encouraged.

"Do I have to?" She pulled against the restraints, but then said, "Slut."

"What kind of slut?"

She turned her head to the side, and he was there, meeting

222

her gaze, being sure she knew she was safe.

"A fuck slut, Sir," she said.

"Whose? Whose, Kelsey?"

She closed her eyes momentarily then looked at him. "Yours, Sir. Your fuck slut."

He kissed the side of her neck. "Yeah. Only mine."

"Please," she said, evidently remembering his earlier instruction. "Sear my ass with it."

He picked up the paddle and returned to her. He placed it on her flesh, exactly where he wanted it then he pulled his arm back and laid it on her with full force, marking her with the word.

The slap reverberated in the room, underplayed by her yelp.

He traced the outline of the word while he still could. It would fade in minutes, maybe sooner.

He released her wrists first and he massaged her skin and shoulders. "The minute you move, the clamps may feel worse."

"I believe you."

He unfastened her ankles. "Can I help you?" He offered an arm for stability, but she pushed herself onto her knees.

She gasped as the chain dropped.

"I'll get them right off," he said. He helped her to sit on top of the bench and she shifted her weight to avoid the plug. Nathan removed the clamps, toying with her nipples until her breathing returned to normal. "How was your first flogging?"

"Uhm…" She raked her hair back from her forehead. "We can do that any time."

"You liked it?"

"Yes."

"And the paddle?"

"Your fuck slut, Sir."

His cock throbbed. "I want to take you from behind," he said, "so I can see the word imprinted on your sexy little ass."

As he undressed, she folded his clothes and put them in the drawer alongside hers. "Put the condom on me," he instructed.

"First time," she admitted.

"You'll do fine. The box is on the counter."

She returned and ripped the package open and placed the condom on his cockhead.

"Other way," he said.

"Of course." She held his penis and rolled the latex down, grasping him firmly.

"I'll let you do that more often," he said.

"Say the word, Sir," she said saucily.

"On your stomach, sub."

She took her time climbing back onto the bench, swaying, moving her body into position with the grace of a ballerina.

"Teasing me, sub?"

She looked over her shoulder? "Me?"

He smacked her ass.

Her smile widened.

"I've created a sassy submissive."

"And what are you going to do about it, Sir?" she asked.

"Fuck you as hard as you deserve." He fingered her a few times, being sure she was wet for him.

"I'm ready," she insisted.

"You are when I say you are." Nathan teased her clit, stroking over it, pressing it, remembering the way she'd screamed when he dripped the wax on her.

Finally, when she was pushing her bottom back toward him, silently asking for more, he repositioned her, pulling her hips toward him. Her knees were near the edge, meaning she was precariously perched, dependent on him to keep her from falling.

It also led to deeper penetration, a greater feeling of possession.

The word was barely visible, but there were a few light marks from the flogger.

He began to ease into her, and she pulled away with a

224

tiny moan of protest.

"It's different with the plug," he said soothingly.

"You're telling me?"

"Give me a second," he said. "Move forward. Put your knees on the bench." Nathan left her long enough to squirt lube on his cock before going back to her. He went slowly, going in a fraction of an inch at a time then easing back out then, when he was all the way in, he pulled her hips back.

"God," she whimpered. "This is so hot. So worth it."

He fucked her hard then, deep, fast, filling her cunt, digging his fingers into her hipbones.

Kelsey responded in kind, thrusting her hips back to meet him, asking for more, telling him what she wanted.

Showing complete trust, she allowed him to take more of her weight, and he bent his knees to piston into her. He felt his orgasm build, but he wanted her to come first. "Give it to me," he encouraged.

She shook her head, and her hair spilled riotously around her. Nathan gripped her tighter, and she moved one hand to her pussy to play with her clit.

The difference in her from when they'd started to play was startling. It was as if she'd decided to embrace her sexuality, abandoning embarrassment. He couldn't be any prouder.

She began to jerk, and he ground his back teeth together to distract himself.

"Fuck me, Sir."

"Happy to accommodate." He lifted her slightly to gain greater leverage, and he pumped his hips faster.

She arched back, and he bit the tender flesh between her shoulder and neck. She screamed then, convulsing, shaking, calling his name.

Only after she'd come did he unleash his orgasm, and he ejaculated in hot, thready pumps that jolted him.

He held her for long seconds, hearing her breathless gasps, aware of the aerobic-like rise and fall of his chest. He maneuvered her back on the bench, making sure her body was supported before he withdrew his cock and pulled away.

Though it was momentarily difficult to stand, he rubbed her shoulders. "How about a shower?" he suggested.

"I can wait until after you've had one," she replied.

"We can do it together. And I want to remove that plug."

She turned over and looked at him. "Every time I think I can keep up with you, you add something new to the mix."

"No secrets between us," he said.

"But—"

"Shower." He discarded the condom then helped her up, making sure she was steady before they went to the master bedroom.

"What about our clothes?"

"I need to come back to clean up the room," he said. "I'll get them then."

He liked watching her walk naked through his house. The idea of seeing her do it every day was an idea that could fuel dozens of fantasies.

While he turned on the faucet and adjusted the temperature, she scooped up handfuls of hair and clipped it atop her head, and he noticed her looking in the mirror to see if he'd left any marks on body. "Nothing that will bruise," he said.

"From what that paddle felt like, it should have."

He checked the heat one last time before stepping into the shower stall. She joined him a few seconds later. "Put your hands on the far wall," he said. "And spread your legs."

"I…" She closed her mouth. Silently, without telling him yes, she did as instructed.

He grasped the base of the plug and pulled it out in a single movement. "Not so bad."

"All of this stuff is easy for you to say," she protested, turning back to face him with a scowl. She plucked the toy from his grasp and rinsed it.

"I could put it back in and pull it out again, repeating until you do it without complaint."

"You'd really do that?"

He captured her chin. "As many times as it took for you to get over your hesitation."

She made a show of pretending to button her mouth.

"Good call." He grabbed his bar of soap, lathered it then ran his hands over her body.

As he cupped her breasts, she closed her eyes and gripped his wrists. He lazily made circles on her flesh and gently squeezed her nipples. Her knees weakened, but he didn't stop, relentlessly soaping her until she opened her eyes. The hazel color had turned smoky and inviting. "You are one responsive woman," he said.

"For the right man, Sir."

Holy Christ. Even though he had fucked her less than twenty minutes ago, he was ready again.

He moved his hands lower to wash her abdomen and legs. Then he turned her around to wash her back. He took down the showerhead to rinse between her legs, and he used his hand to be sure he'd removed all the lube.

"You're thorough," she said.

"I may have told you that I take care of mine," he replied.

She slowly pivoted to face him again. "Should I return the favor?" Without waiting for an answer, she picked up the bar of soap that he'd slid back into the holder.

As he had with her, she took her time washing him, and she spent an extraordinary amount of time on his genitalia.

"May I?" She held out her hand for the showerhead, and he offered it to her.

With the water, she lazed her way across his front and chest then rinsed his dick and balls for far longer than necessary.

"Do you mind holding this again?"

He accepted the handle even as she lowered herself before him.

It had been a long time since a woman had given him head. When he had a lover, he focused on her, knowing he'd find his pleasure in her pussy or ass. But this? With her so eagerly sucking him into her mouth…?

Nathan dug his hand into her hair, dislodging the clip, sending the tresses spilling. He held her, guiding her.

His cock went from semi-flaccid to erect in a matter of seconds.

Before he could spill in her, he turned off the water, helped her up then left the shower. He bundled her into a white fluffy robe then shrugged into one himself, pocketing a condom.

She gasped when he scooped her into his arms and carried her into the bedroom. "We'll finish what you started," he warned in a gravelly voice.

Caveman style, he tossed her on the bed. When she laughed and scooted away, he captured her foot, then dragged her back.

"Sexy, Sir," she said.

He had their robes off and the condom on in record time. "Is this what you want?" he demanded.

"What? Your dick in me?" She reached for him.

Passion driving him, Nathan moved between her legs and smoothly lifted them to press his shoulders into the backs of her thighs. He licked her, teasing her still-swollen clit. He needn't have worried. Perhaps because she had no apprehensions, she was slick.

Nathan positioned himself, and she sucked in her breath as he slid inside her with one long, continuous stroke.

This time, he pinned her arms at her sides and took his time fucking her, making love to her.

And this time, when she came, he compelled her to keep looking at him. He watched her eyes go from light to dark. Her voice went from sigh to whimper.

Because of his angle, he was able to penetrate deeper than before.

As he got closer, she fisted her hands in the bedspread. She tilted her pelvis and he surged in, filling her completely.

He held the orgasm back longer than he could imagine, and when he came, he shuddered from the force.

So as not to crush her, he rolled to his side then pulled her against him, holding her silently. He spooned her, wrapped her up for a few minutes while he half dozed.

A few minutes later, he climbed from the bed, leaving her asleep. He disposed of the condom before handling his nighttime chores—turning off lights and ensuring the doors were locked before heading back to the playroom. He wiped down the equipment, put everything back where it belonged then gathered their clothing and returned to the bedroom.

She was asleep, curled up where he normally slept.

He grinned. Her dark hair was spread wildly across his pillow, and she only had a sheet tucked around her naked body.

It surprised him how natural it seemed to have Kelsey here, in his house. Even better, in his bed, despite the fact she was in his spot. After putting away their clothes, he shocked himself by getting into bed on the unfamiliar side.

She extended a hand, finding his chest.

It made him ridiculously happy that she'd reached for him. If she'd been awake, he knew that wouldn't have happened. He placed his hand around her wrist, silently reassuring her he'd be there.

The problem was, if she had her way, it would only be until Saturday night.

He was no longer sure that was acceptable to him.

Kelsey opened her eyes. Reality seemed distorted, and she blinked, trying to clear her vision. But she didn't recognize anything. She felt suffocated, as if something was pinning her down. She thrashed, trying to get free before waking up enough to figure out she was at Nathan Donovan's house, nude in his bed, with a sheet, blanket and comforter covering her. But he wasn't next to her.

Memories of the previous evening seeped in, and she

remembered him cuffing her to the spanking bench, flogging her, giving her one solid spank with the paddle then fucking her. Heat made her flush anew when she recalled the way he'd taken out the plug.

But he was so matter-of-fact about things that he didn't tolerate embarrassment. And because of the courage she'd gathered, she'd been the one to initiate sex after the shower. Until him, she hadn't been capable of that kind of behavior.

And afterward... She didn't remember anything after he'd fucked her in his bed.

She often slept badly, sometimes struggling with insomnia. She always woke up at least twice, but last night, she'd slept through, so soundly she didn't know whether or not he'd even come to bed.

Except... He had. She knew it. Somewhere in the deepest recesses of her mind, she recalled him wrapping himself around her, protecting her, giving her the comfort to rest peacefully.

The scent of coffee teased her. The room was dark from the heavy shades, and she had no idea what time it was. She looked around for a clock but didn't find one, and she'd left her purse on the kitchen counter.

Curious, she climbed from the bed.

Nathan had hung the white fluffy robe from the footboard on her side of the bed, and she put it on, tying the belt around her as she left the room.

A light was on in his office, and she knocked on the doorframe before entering.

The television was on, the volume low, and he was on the exercise bike, slowly pedaling. He wore shorts and no shirt. Perspiration dampened his hair and he looked devilishly handsome.

"Come in," he said, smile wide, inviting.

A cup of coffee sat on his desk, abandoned.

"You can have it." He obviously noted her forlorn expression. "But there's a fresh pot downstairs that may appeal to you more."

It seemed bizarre, waking up in her boss's house, talking about coffee in her robe.

"How did you sleep?"

"I woke up nude."

"That's unusual, I take it?" He grinned. The bike beeped, and he pedaled even slower, obviously cooling down. "Can't say that I'm sorry you slept so well."

"Are you taking credit for it?"

"Total and complete," he said shamelessly.

She picked up his cup and sat in his chair. The coffee was tepid, but strong and rich. "What time is it?"

"A little after five," he said.

The machine beeped again, and he pushed a button to stop it before dismounting. "I need to do a couple of things before I shower," he said, coming closer to her.

She nodded and stood. "I'll grab a fresh cup then get ready to go."

"Bring me a cup back?"

"So you'll give me a crappy cup of coffee but you won't drink it?"

He touched her nose and emotion cascaded through her. Damn, she liked his gentle teasing almost as much as she appreciated the fact he'd gotten up early enough to make coffee, which was something she rarely managed.

Downstairs, she fished her phone from her purse and dropped it in the deep robe pocket. He'd he set out a cup for her. She liked the way he always seemed to be thinking about her, but she told herself not to get too accustomed to it.

After rinsing his cup, she filled both. She found an unopened container of cream in the refrigerator. She knew he didn't drink it, which meant he'd taken time to pick it up for her.

Cups ready, she climbed the stairs and heard music coming from his office.

He was sitting at his desk, and he had his wrist cocked as he looked at it.

"What are you watching?"

"Nothing yet. It's the way the watch starts up when you turn it on."

"It sounds like the score from a movie or something."

"It's Julien Bonds' theme music."

"I had no idea." It probably shouldn't surprise her, but it did.

She extended Nathan's cup to him, and he accepted with a smile.

"I found the cream in the fridge," she said.

"I suspected you were resourceful enough to do that."

The words *"Good morning, Nathan!"* blasted from the watch as the theme music faded.

She watched, stunned, as a small image of Julien Bonds floated above the screen. "Hologram?"

Nathan nodded and sipped.

"Is it real time? I mean, are you interacting with it?"

"No. You might as well enjoy it. There's no way to make him shut up once he starts."

"Your software update is complete. Do I look better? Sound better? Tell the watch what you think about the new voice synthesizer. It will relay it to me. Don't worry about hurting my feelings. I want to be perfect more than I want you to stroke my ego."

"I wonder about that," Nathan said.

"You may want to amp up the workout a bit today, Nathan." Bonds flexed his arm. *"It doesn't appear you walked your suggested ten thousand steps yesterday."*

Nathan pulled her into his lap and she had to readjust quickly to avoid spilling her coffee.

"And we're unsure whether or not you got enough sleep."

"Who's we?" she asked. "Does he mean the royal we?"

"It could mean his engineers or the program. Or you could be right. It might be the royal we."

"As a reminder, for this to be as effective as we want, please wear your watch in the evenings, even when you sleep. In fact... you took it off around eight-thirty last night. Were you doing

something you don't want us knowing about? At any rate, as for business... Press reports for Donovan Logistics have been mostly complimentary. I've attached all relevant search results from the past twenty-four hours to an email and they're flagged in suggested-read order. I've included a rumor from an online source that states OneTech is being acquired. They quoted an anonymous source. And Donovan Worldwide was not named in the piece. Be sure to eat right today. Pizza is not a sustainable choice. At least order a vegetarian one." The image gave a little wave before vanishing. Then screen went blank.

"Impressive and intrusive," she said.

"Isn't that the conundrum? It's so fucking useful, though, that I leave it on most of the time. His search filters are beyond anything we've seen so far, as if he's applied artificial intelligence to it. The news updates are cross-referenced. Info on all of our companies and those we're interested in, as well as relevant market updates, show up twice a day, generally around noon after the European workday is done and then again at the end of business in Houston. I didn't access it last night, so it was waiting for me this morning."

Her phone chimed, and she scooped it out of her pocket.

"More intrusive technology?" he asked.

"The worst." She swiped the screen to silence the reminder. "This is an alarm that tells me to get moving so I'm not late to work. I don't want to piss off my new boss."

"See that you don't."

She scooted off his lap and he snagged her wrist to prevent her from escaping. Before she knew what was happening, he'd plucked her coffee from her, slid it on the desk then turned her over his knee.

Kelsey yelped as she put down her hands to prevent herself from falling.

He exposed her rear, and before she was ready, he brought his hand down on her buttocks, setting her skin on fire.

When he did it a second time, she screamed. Even as she protested, heat seeped into her pussy.

"For the record, Ms. Lane, a scream is not a safe word."

He gave her a few more spanks, leaving her desperate and needy.

"Don't be late," he told her, helping her to stand. He straightened her robe and handed her the coffee.

"What was that for?"

"Kelsey, if you think you can sit your squirmy little ass in my lap without me noticing, you're wrong. Tease the wolf, you're going to get eaten."

"Is that supposed to scare me?"

"I don't know. Do you want to get eaten?"

She pressed her legs together, trying to ignore the heat in her pussy.

"Half an hour, Kelsey. Be ready to go. Or else."

13

Kelsey flirted with his words while she dressed. The *or else* part of his order was making it impossible to think about anything other than him taking her back to bed.

And the look in his eyes when she came out of the closet wearing a form-fitting black dress almost made her melt.

Today he wore a blue pinstriped suit with an equally dark necktie. As always, he was scrumptious. Right now, she didn't care whether they went to work or not.

"You managed to get ready in twenty-six minutes," he said after glancing at his watch.

"Could we pretend it was thirty-one?" She licked her lower lip.

"Get on the counter."

An unholy thrill zinged through her.

He removed his suit coat and hung it from the doorknob. While she was still trying to figure out the best way to climb onto the chilly granite, he grabbed her by the waist and lifted her from the floor.

She did some fancy moves to get the dress up past her hips. But her underwear was still in the way. Obviously impatient, he grabbed a pair of scissors from a drawer and snipped her thong from her. "Nathan!"

"You were warned."

"I didn't know *or else* meant you were going to destroy my underwear." Even though she was protesting, she was breathless from the forbidden thrill.

"You took the risk."

He spread her thighs with his large hands. She was caught a little off balance, and she arched back, putting her hands behind her, both of which gave him greater access to her already-damp pussy.

"You're wet and ready for me, aren't you?" he asked, pressing a finger into her.

She cried out from the pleasure.

He removed his finger and placed it against her lip. "Lick it."

Gaze locked with his, she did as he instructed, tasting her juices, knowing he'd aroused her.

"Tell me to eat you."

"Please," she begged, wishing she could grab hold of his face and drag it toward her pussy.

He took his time lowering his head. Then he flicked his tongue rapidly across her engorged clit. She tilted her pelvis toward him, asking for more.

Nathan parted her labia and pulled back the hood as he'd made her do the night he'd dripped hot wax on her. Maybe it was her imagination, but she still felt sensitized from that, and it took less time than usual for her to teeter on the precipice of an orgasm.

"Nathan!" She tightened her muscles, suddenly worried he wouldn't let her come.

Instead, he used juices from her pussy to insert a finger into her ass.

She groaned and scooted even closer to him.

"I'll give you thirty seconds," he said against her cunt. "Or you'll wait until I'm feeling generous again."

The ticking time element sharpened her response, and Kelsey pressed weight onto her hands and lifted her hips from the counter, shamelessly grinding her shaved pussy against his face. She was certain the sensations were more heightened than ever.

He jiggled the finger that was in her ass and plunged his tongue into her heated depths before returning to suck her clit. Him changing what he was doing, coupled with the pressure on her clit, made an orgasm knife through her.

Pumping her hips, humping his face, she cried out.

He continued to lave his attentions on her until the last ripple shook her.

Then, only then, did he move away from her and draw out his finger.

She liked his version of *or else*.

He washed his hands and face then helped her from the countertop, holding her waist while she slipped back into a shoe she hadn't realized she'd lost.

"I need another couple of minutes to put myself back together. Well, and find a new pair of panties." Which she'd already packed in her bag.

"We're late. Skip them."

"I don't go without underwear, Mr. Donovan," she protested.

"You do now. Part of the *or else*."

"Hold on," she said, looking up at him. "How many things am I going to have to do?"

"As many as I say."

His hands were still on her, imprisoning her and simultaneously making her feel cherished. Since his tie was askew from their early-morning face-fuck, she straightened it for him.

Slowly he released her then scooped up her ruined thong and dumped the remnants in the trash.

He carried her bag downstairs, and she hurried through smoothing her hair and adjusting her dress.

She felt awkward without underwear. Though she knew it was ridiculous, she was sure every person she saw would know.

"Ready?" he asked when she stepped off the bottom stair.

For a moment, she wondered what the hell she was doing.

Nathan Donovan wasn't her lover. He was her boss. The lines were blurring for her, and she couldn't allow that to happen.

Surely she could manage for another couple of days.

But as he opened the back door and she breezed past him, inhaling the subtle scent of his spicy soap and remembering the taste of his dick, she suddenly doubted her own determination.

"I'm planning to take you shopping after work," he said once they were on the road.

"To replace my underwear?"

"That, as well as getting you an outfit that will look great when I have you strapped to the Punishment Pole."

Kelsey glanced across the vehicle's interior at Nathan. Since it was still before sunrise, his face was in shadows, making it difficult to read his expression.

"For the outfit you'll wear on Saturday," he reminded her. "We discussed it earlier in the week."

She remembered scribbling notes as he'd been talking, and she recalled circling the word Thursday.

"If we don't find anything tonight, we'll have tomorrow as a backup. Unless you have something in mind already?"

"I have some shoes that might work, and I was thinking of wearing a skirt and a long-sleeved shirt."

"We can swing by your house before we go, have a look at your closet." He glanced across at her. "I have an idea of what I'd like to see you in."

"And I'm thinking it's not something I might wear to the office."

The background music cut out and the screen in front of them showed an incoming call from Lawrence.

"That's your call," he told her.

She'd forgotten Nathan had added her number into the Bluetooth system when she'd borrowed his car.

It was well before the time she would have expected to hear from the HR department.

"Push the green phone icon," Nathan told her. "Unless you want to take it in private."

She answered the call, and Lawrence got straight to the point. "Seward's boss called in sick."

Understanding dawned. "It's Seward's first duty day," she said. The day they'd been intending to terminate his employment. "Where are you?"

"Home."

And since he lived in Kingwood, which was north of the city, Lawrence wouldn't be able to drive to the docks in time to be there before Seward climbed aboard his tug. "Let me figure it out." Since she didn't want anyone knowing she was with Nathan at this time of the morning, she added, "I'll call you back in five minutes."

She ended the call.

"What do you recommend?" Nathan asked.

"We have a couple of options." She tapped her fingers on the armrest. "We can ask another field supervisor to send him home for the day." She raced through pros and cons. "That's not my preference. He'd suspect something was up, and we don't know how he'll react."

"Or?"

"Let him work today as normal. But I think you'd find that unconscionable."

"I would." After signaling, he changed lanes to pass a slow-moving vehicle.

"We've customarily had a specific way of handling terminations. We want to give the employee time to process the whole thing, ask questions, come to terms with it and let them keep their dignity. And we want to ensure no damage is done to company property, not that I'm particularly concerned about Seward. But..." The man had a family to support. "Since he's receiving no severance, the situation is potentially more volatile. And we have the question of what to do with the rest of the crew, calling someone in, moving people around, figuring out how to deal with the work that won't get done."

He nodded.

"You should fire him," she said.

"Oh?" Eyebrows raised, he glanced at her.

Kelsey glanced at the clock. "We have enough time to get to the docks if traffic flows well and we turn around immediately."

His jaw was set and he was silent.

"That's the best option," she said. "We don't have time to get anyone else from HR out here. But I can ensure we have a security guard in place. While you're handling it, I can update the field supervisors and get schedulers working on the logistics. Honestly, I don't see a more workable plan."

He nodded.

"You don't mind?"

"It's part of the job."

She searched his features and found nothing except determination.

He turned the vehicle around and headed for the highway.

"Do you need me to program the GPS?"

"I've been to the docks a couple of times," he reminded her.

He took a ramp that gave her a view of the sun bursting brilliantly over the horizon, showing how vast and endless the city seemed. Because of where she lived and worked, it was sometimes easy to forget that.

Kelsey phoned Lawrence and updated him, and she asked for instructions on where to find the final paycheck and termination letter.

"They're in Jameson's top right desk drawer. The schedulers have a key to the office. The desk is unlocked."

Nathan was greeted cordially by the crews onsite, and she figured it was a good thing he'd already been out here to meet them. The security guard ambled over, lifted a hand in acknowledgment then continued his rounds.

Barb, one of the schedulers, looked up when they entered the small office located about two hundred feet from where the tugs were moored.

"We'll need access to Jameson's office," Kelsey said after exchanging pleasantries.

Though the woman gave a puzzled frown, she went to a locked cabinet and returned with a key.

She and Nathan went into the man's office.

Kelsey moved aside a half-empty cup of old coffee and wiped crumbs off the chair before sitting behind the desk and pulling out the paycheck and termination letter. After double-checking that everything was in order, she stood and offered the papers to Nathan. "I'll send Seward in when he arrives."

He nodded and took the seat she'd vacated.

Her heart pounded when Seward walked in. Kelsey hated every part of this. It was easy to be distracted with the planning. It was another to be face to face with a man whose future was going to be devastated. "Seward," she greeted.

Around them, people had fallen quiet, except for one of the schedulers who was talking on the phone.

"Hey, Kelsey. What are you doing here?"

"Mr. Donovan would like to see you. In Jameson's office."

The man glanced toward the office, then he looked back at her. "What's going on?"

She noticed Nathan standing in the doorway. "Come on in," he said. His voice was both calm and firm.

Seward's eyes widened. He obviously knew what was happening.

"Captain Seward," Nathan said. "This way."

Kelsey gave Barb a pointed glance, and the woman got back to work. Others took their cue from her.

Seward walked slowly into the office, and once he was seated, Nathan closed the door.

"He's getting fired, isn't he?" Barb asked Kelsey when the security guard walked in.

"Mr. Donovan has had to make a difficult decision. We've got work to do. We have a tug with no skipper. Presumably we now also have an idle crew?"

The office fell silent again.

"Barb? Show me the schedule and give me some suggestions on what we need to do." She had no intention of making the decisions, but she needed people to get back to work, and she didn't want anyone overhearing the conversation in the office. The more dignity Seward could maintain, the better.

Barb sighed. "I hate this."

"Me too," Kelsey agreed. But she owed it to the company and Nathan not to let this turn melancholy. Everyone in the room was aware of Seward's accident and the circumstances. "The schedule?"

With a nod, Barb turned her computer screen for Kelsey to see.

Because she wasn't fully concentrating, the words appeared jumbled. She shook her head to focus her attention. To her, logistics were a complicated chess game and the key to success was looking toward the end of the day and working backward.

One of the other field supervisors joined them and within a minute or so, suggestions began to flow.

The meeting between Nathan and Seward lasted considerably longer than she'd anticipated. Numerous times she flicked her gaze toward the office, her tension growing.

But she schooled her features so that she projected confidence.

The tugboat crew was reassigned, timing was sorted out, extra loads were assigned and everyone returned to their jobs.

She jumped when the door opened.

Nathan walked with Seward while he collected his personal belongings then he escorted him to the front door.

From there, the security guard followed Seward out.

She exhaled.

The office would have a pall over it for at least a couple of hours, maybe more, she knew. Seward was liked by most people, but she was sure there had been some who'd wanted him fired from the beginning. She doubted anyone would think that Donovan was randomly firing people just because he was the new boss. Still, any time an employee was let go, it seemed to take time for balance to be restored.

It would take some time for her to recover, as well.

Nathan spent a few minutes visiting with the staff and

she went back into Jameson's office to call Lawrence and let him know that things had been handled.

When she joined Nathan, he asked, "Ready?"

She nodded.

"How did it go?" she asked when they were on the road.

"As expected."

Because of the way he gripped the steering wheel, his watch was exposed. She saw a 3D pulsing red heart floating just above the screen. She'd only seen pink previously, and she wondered if the thing was reacting to his mood.

"Coffee?" he asked. "I figured we could stop at Marvin's."

She nodded.

While he drove, she responded to email. He was quieter than usual, and that struck her as odd. Maybe the whole thing had bothered him and he wasn't as big of a heartless hard-ass as she'd labeled him.

He dropped her off in front of the shop and told her he'd go and park then join her.

She ordered them each a slice of quiche, and she had his coffee and her mocha on the table when he walked through the door.

The man who entered the restaurant with a cheery hello to Marvin was different than the man she'd ridden with. Nathan's face was more relaxed, his movements less rigid.

"You did well this morning," he said as he slid into a seat across from her.

"So did you."

He took a sip of the coffee then nodded appreciatively before saying, "Coming from you, that's a compliment."

Kelsey sighed.

"I know you disagree with my decision, but you put that aside. As I suspected, others in the company have taken their cue from your behavior. Loyalty is the hardest when you disagree with a course of action, and you showed impressive leadership ability. I appreciate your support of Donovan Logistics."

"I like Seward and his family," she said. "I spent some

time with the Newmans on Tuesday, and Mrs. Newman let me know that the company really would have been in trouble if it hadn't been for Donovan's flexibility in moving up timelines. She told me you'd pulled off something close to a miracle."

He shrugged. For the first time since she'd known him, he looked a bit uncomfortable.

"I'd prefer that we could have kept Seward." The next bit, she had a difficult time admitting to herself, much less him. "I was thinking on a micro level, a personal one. But I understand you're looking at the company as a whole."

"Sometimes, Kelsey, it's easier to come in from the outside. I wasn't burdened by an existing relationship with Captain Seward," he said. "Making difficult decisions, some that you wish you didn't have to, is what separates success from failure in business. It's about the bottom line. You don't have to like a particular course of action, but you have to be willing to commit to it. A good CEO can't risk the entire company for one individual."

"Career advice?"

"Probably worth every penny you paid for it."

"It was free."

"My point exactly."

Marvin's daughter brought over the quiche, complemented by fresh-cut fruit.

Since it was already late, they ate quickly then took their beverages back to the office.

A new blossom had opened on the hibiscus, the yellow a bright, welcome sight. "I've been meaning to ask," she said. "Where did this come from?"

"Aunt Kathryn. She has them everywhere. Something about the color and having them indoors is soothing. As if that's not enough, she makes the blossoms — or whatever you call them — into tea."

She smiled. "Nice of you to indulge her."

"I didn't." He shook his head. "If it died, I'd never hear the end of it. I figured the thing had a better chance of survival if you were taking care of it."

"Thanks. I think."

"We've got a lot to do," he said. "Be ready to leave at five."

Though she was still sad about Seward and her heart wasn't in either her job or the evening ahead, she knew better than to argue.

Nathan went into his office and closed the door.

She sat back and exhaled then leaned forward when her office phone rang. "Nathan Donovan's office," she answered.

"Is this Kelsey Lane?"

She glanced at the caller identification screen. It read BHI. "Yes."

"This is Lara Donovan. Nathan's sister-in-law."

"Good morning, Mrs. Donovan. Let me see if —"

"Please, call me Lara," the woman interrupted.

Kelsey heard a hint of a soft Cajun drawl in the woman's voice.

"I called for you, actually. Not Nathan."

"For me?" She frowned. "What can I do for you?"

"I know this is a little unusual. Your name was on a list that crossed my desk." Lara paused. "We're hiring for the CEO position for one of BHI's oil and gas holdings."

Momentarily, Kelsey's heart stopped, and she was certain she had misinterpreted Lara's meaning. Feeling as if she were doing something she shouldn't, Kelsey looked at Nathan's still-closed door. "I'm afraid you've caught me off guard."

"You're certainly someone I'm interested in talking with," Lara went on. "We'd have to make sure we're a match. And of course, we are considering other candidates."

She couldn't begin to understand the ethical ramifications of this conversation. Nathan's sister-in-law was reaching out to his executive assistant, someone he'd identified as key personnel, and yet...

Lara was talking about a C-level position, something that had been on Kelsey's goal list since she'd started college, the motivation that got her through. The first time she'd spoken with Nathan, she'd told him her long-term plan was to run a company. If she left, he wouldn't be entirely surprised. Annoyed, perhaps, but not surprised.

"Ms. Lane?"

"I'm here." Her first instinct was to ask Lara if she was sure she'd called the right person. Her second was to show cool interest and give herself some time to think. "Is the job in the Houston area?"

"It is."

"And pay range?"

"Commensurate with experience," they said simultaneously.

Lara laughed. "I see why Nathan likes you."

It jolted her to realize Lara had heard positive things about her. "Does he know we're talking?"

"No. And it's up to you whether or not you say anything. In fact, unless you make the shortlist — in this case, top three candidates — I won't be mentioning this conversation to my husband."

"I'll admit to being a little uncomfortable."

"I can understand that," Lara agreed. "Donovan Worldwide, and now BHI, believes each division should be run by the best possible person. We don't intentionally poach from each other's companies. But it happens."

"So if I went to work for you?"

"Under the organizational structure, you'd be accountable to BHI's board of directors."

The entire conversation was so unexpected that she was having a difficult time processing it. "When do you need an answer?"

"Take the weekend," Lara suggested. "How about you call me on Monday and let me know if you're interested in being considered as a candidate?"

Still stunned, she agreed, then wrote down Lara's office and cell phone numbers before ending the call.

Her mind going a million different directions, she sat back to let the conversation sink in.

Had she received this call on Monday morning, the decision would have been easy. She would have immediately accepted Lara's invitation and set up an appointment.

But now… Kelsey had seen other sides of Nathan. She might not agree with him on everything, but this morning she'd thought they'd made a good team, every bit as good as she'd been with Mr. Newman.

Then she wondered if the fact she'd slept with Nathan, submitted to him, had affected her rational-thinking skills. She shifted, highly aware she had no underwear on. This wasn't a typical boss and employee relationship.

Getting away, establishing herself as a leader in her own right, could give her much-needed distance from Nathan.

He wouldn't be running Donovan Logistics indefinitely. There was no guarantee she'd be considered for the job. If she stayed, she could potentially be stuck in her current position for a very long time.

She wondered if she should discuss the call with Nathan. Then she reminded herself they weren't in a committed relationship. How much did she owe him? He'd asked for her loyalty, but did that extend to telling him about her potential career moves?

Kelsey gave herself a mental shake. Lara hadn't extended a job offer. She'd only suggested they discuss it. It was very likely Kelsey was worrying about things that would never happen.

The phone rang again, and she leaned forward to answer it.

After she hung up, she glanced across the room to see Nathan watching her.

"Five o'clock," he reminded her.

Every thought, every question, every hesitation fled from her mind, and she was filled with exquisite anticipation.

The end of the day couldn't happen soon enough.

"It's too short," Kelsey protested, pulling down on the hem of the leather skirt he'd selected.

Nathan sat in an upholstered wing-backed armchair, legs stretched in front of him. "Put your hands behind your neck."

"Then it will be even shorter."

Over steepled fingers, he regarded her implacably.

Nathan had brought her to a small boutique in the Heights, a fun, trendy area that she loved hanging out in. Though the high-end shop normally closed at six, it had stayed open for him, which meant they were alone with the owner, Gwyneth.

The store was elegant with its polished wood floors accented by thick black rugs. Gwyneth had installed custom lighting to create pizazz and ambiance and the music she played reverberated through Kelsey, making her feel sensuous.

When they'd arrived, Nathan had selected a number of items from the racks, all of which shocked her.

Her protests hadn't stopped him from insisting she go in the dressing room and try them all on.

"Hands behind your neck," he repeated, the words clipped. "Don't think you won't get a spanking right here, right now."

Believing him, she shivered and did what he said.

"Now turn around."

She slowly pivoted until her back was to him.

"Touch your toes."

Since he'd ruined her underwear this morning, she knew he was going to get a scandalous view.

"I think it's exactly the right length. Look at it again in the mirror," he said. "Less critically. And put your shoes on."

The skirt was an A-line, and she preferred something more tailored. But she understood his point. And truthfully, it wasn't much shorter than the skirt she would have selected. It just seemed that way because of the cut.

It was made from a high-grade supple leather that could

have been designed for her.

"Gwyneth, will you fetch us some shoes. Or better yet, over-the-knee suede boots? Size eight."

Kelsey blinked. "How did you know that?"

"I pay attention to you, Kelsey. Now go try the skirt with the halter top."

She went back into the dressing room but didn't bother closing the drape because he'd already instructed her to leave it open.

After pulling off the form-fitting shirt she'd tried first, she shrugged into the leather halter top. She laced up the front through the dozen eyelets.

"Leave them somewhat loose."

The top was the perfect combination of edgy and conservative. The straps were thick, offering plenty of support. It covered enough flesh that she felt comfortable, but offered tantalizing glimpses that she found sexy.

Gwyneth carried a couple of boxes to them, and said, "Yeah. Freaking hot."

"I tend to agree," Nathan said.

Kelsey sat on a bench while Gwyneth pulled out the first pair of shoes.

"No," Nathan said. "Something classier."

Gwyneth opened the next box and removed a pair of boots. Until that moment, Kelsey had not been a shoe addict. But now... She would never have selected suede, but they looked perfect. The heels were outrageously high, yet since they had a platform, they would be wearable, at least for a few hours. There was a sexy, unexpected cuff at the knee.

She slipped into the boots and zipped them up before standing for Nathan.

"That's it," he said.

When she faced the mirror, she was stunned. She'd never worn anything like this, and she loved it.

"Own it," Gwyneth said. "You're hot as fuck. *Own* the outfit."

Then, with remarkable good sense, she left them alone.

"What do you think?" Nathan asked, leaning forward to tap a finger against his mouth.

Kelsey met his gaze in the mirror and she knew the shop owner was right. She should own it. That in mind, she pulled back her shoulders and finger-combed her hair.

"Imagine it with my collar on you," he said.

She sucked in a breath.

He stood and took a few steps before curving his hands onto her shoulders. "See yourself through my eyes."

Just like the other night at her house, she did.

She was transformed from businesswoman to his slut. Warmth threaded through her.

In that instant, she knew she'd do almost anything to please Nathan Donovan.

On so many levels, the realization concerned her.

She'd survived her upbringing by making promises to herself, and the most important was that she would make her own goals and pursue them passionately. Putting Nathan's wants above her own betrayed everything she'd struggled for.

"We'll take it," he said over his shoulder to Gwyneth.

"Wait," Kelsey protested. "Do you have any idea how much this will cost?"

"Approximately as much as my mortgage payment?"

"I can't afford this." She pulled free of his grip and faced him.

"It's going on my card."

"I can't let you pay for all this," she protested.

"Yeah. You can."

She exhaled. He could be as confounding, as bossy, as overbearing as her father. "Stop. Please."

"Kelsey. We're not arguing. I want you to feel confident when you're on that pole Saturday night. I want you dressed appropriately so that I can touch you. I want to flog you hard, and the leather will absorb some of the force."

"What happened to you being a cheapskate?" she tried.

"Kelsey, Kelsey." He grinned. "I think I've told you, certain things are an investment. This outfit will look just as sexy in five years. It's quality material and craftsmanship." He lowered his voice and spoke with a tone that made her weak. "Let me give you this as a gift."

"I…"

"Can't think of a reason to say no?" he suggested. "Then say thank you."

When she didn't immediately answer, he firmly held her, this time by the upper arms, and eased her back around. "Have another look. We can spend less money, but will you walk into the club and feel like you will wearing this?"

He was right. His selections suited her and she loved the way they felt on her skin.

Finally she relented. "Thank you," she said.

Nathan smiled and gave her a small nod. "I'll be proud to clip your collar to my leash."

She shuddered as the vision consumed her mind.

After he released her, she sat on the bench and removed the boots, aware that he never took his smoky gaze from her. She tucked the sex-kitten footwear inside the box before returning to the fitting room.

"All set?" Gwyneth asked when Kelsey came back out.

She nodded.

"And the boots?"

Honestly, even if Nathan hadn't wanted to buy them for her, she might have indulged in them anyway. Despite the high three-figure price tag and the fact she didn't have many places to wear them, she'd never worn anything that made her feel more vibrant.

"Let me take those for you."

"Thank you." She handed over the skirt and halter top before joining Nathan at a glass case near the counter. "I'm ready," Kelsey told him, putting her fingers on his arm. Then she dug her grip into him when she saw he was looking at butt plugs.

There were all sorts, made from wood, steel, glass. All

were elegant, befitting the store.

"Which would you prefer?" he asked.

"You already bought me one."

"It's a starter plug, and it's certainly not as beautiful as this. Which will it be?"

She wanted to say, "None," but doubted that response would be acceptable.

"And to be clear, I will want you to wear it to work tomorrow and to Deviation on Saturday night," he continued.

She looked over at him and scowled. "You didn't say anything about me having to wear one to the club."

"Didn't I?" he asked unconcernedly.

She tried to sound reasonable as she said, "Really, Nathan. The one I already have is fine." It was much thinner than most of these, and it had to be more comfortable since it was flexible.

"Any of these will look better with your new outfit."

"May I show you something?" Gwyneth enquired, coming over after she'd wrapped the clothing in tissue paper.

"The medium glass one with hot pink crystals," he said.

Kelsey tightened her fingers into his arm again, but he barely glanced at her.

Gwyneth pulled out the too-thick-looking plug and placed it in Nathan's palm.

The thing was beautiful, no doubt, with the radiant crystals refracting the overhead light. But its circumference was so much bigger than she was accustomed to, and the material concerned her. "Won't it break?" Kelsey asked.

"No," Gwyneth replied. "Completely safe, made from borosilicate glass, which makes it really durable. If you drop it, you'll just want to check that you haven't chipped it. And it can be chilled or warmed before it's inserted."

"That's a benefit," Kelsey said dryly.

Nathan turned it over, looked at the crystals, ran his thumb across the base.

"How about that one?" Kelsey suggested, releasing his

arm so she could point out a smaller one.

"Gwyneth, show us the one with the purple base," he said.

The woman pulled it out. It was at least half as big again as the one he was holding.

Kelsey shivered and quickly said, "Uhm…the hot pink one is great. I like it. A lot."

"I figured you'd see it my way." He gave her a quick smile, indicating he'd outmaneuvered her. "We'll take it."

Not even trying to hide her smile, Gwyneth returned the larger one to the case and slid the other into a black velveteen bag. "Anything else?" she inquired.

"A thong," he replied.

"I have underwear," Kelsey protested.

He ignored her as if she'd never spoken. "The skimpiest, laciest, indecentest."

Kelsey scowled at him. "That's not a word."

"She knows what I mean."

"I do," Gwyneth said, coming out from behind the counter again.

"Why do I need another thong?" she asked him when they were alone.

"Club rules. Your pussy needs to be covered."

"Are you pushing the limits, Mr. Donovan?"

"Perhaps," he said.

Gwyneth returned with a pair and showed them to him.

"I've seen bandages are bigger than that," Kelsey protested.

"I think that's what he was going for." Gwyneth smiled.

"Did you see the price tag on them?" Kelsey demanded, scowling at him.

"No."

Since he seemed unconcerned, she shut up. If he wanted to spend his money on her lingerie, why should she stop him?

Within five minutes, he'd paid the bill and they had left the shop.

By agreement, they walked down the street until they found a small bar that specialized in pub foods. They each ordered a hamburger and shared a basket of French fries.

"Not too concerned with what Julien Bonds might have to say about your food choices?" she asked.

"I intend to get plenty of exercise when we're back at your condo. And I want to put that plug up your ass."

14

Inside her condo, Nathan placed her overnight bag on the bed next to the large, decorative one from Gwyneth's shop then pulled out the butt plug.

"I'm still having doubts," she said, her gaze riveted on the glass rather than him.

"I'll make sure we get it properly placed," he assured her.

"How did I know that would be your response?"

Every minute he was with her, Nathan was more and more enthralled. Despite her numerous hesitations, she'd always opted to trust him. Seeing her at the store, pulling back her shoulders, rocking a hipbone forward, fucking owning the outfit as Gwyneth had suggested, had made him stupidly proud. She wore her submission well.

And she was affecting him in deeper ways, too. Today, with the way she'd walked into the offices at the docks, by his side, presenting a united front, had meant a great deal to him, both as CEO and as her Dom. She couldn't have handled herself any better. She'd been assertive, focused — everything he'd never realized he wanted in a woman.

"Please get undressed," he said. "I put your collar and my flogger in your bag this morning before we left the house. I'm going to wash the plug. When I get back, I want you wearing the collar, and I will expect you to have your chest on the mattress with your hands behind you, pulling your ass cheeks apart. Questions?"

"No, Sir," she said.

Her voice had a seductive purr to it. He wondered whether she knew her tone was different when they were in a BDSM scene. He adored it. And her.

removing his suit coat, he carried the plug into the bathroom. He rolled up his sleeves then washed the glass with hot water, suspecting it would retain heat for some time.

When he returned to the bedroom with a couple of hand towels, one of them wet, he saw her, perfectly in position, her asshole exposed to his mercy. He paused for a second to compose himself. Her submission thrilled him.

Nathan picked up the lube from her nightstand and spread some of the viscous liquid on his fingers before approaching her.

She moved about for a few seconds before settling.

He gently slipped a finger into her ass, sliding in and out several times before adding a second finger alongside it.

Kelsey gasped, and for a moment she let go of her ass cheeks.

He waited to see whether or not she'd correct herself, and after a small whimper she did so. "Well done," he said.

As he entered again, he stretched his fingers farther apart. "Damn."

"This will make the plug fit easier."

She nodded against the mattress.

When he was sure her anus had been stretched wide enough, he wiped his fingers then picked up the glass by the base.

He drizzled lube on it and waited a few seconds for it to seep downward. Then he added a couple of extra dollops just above the fattest part of the stem.

"Ready? Keep your buttocks apart." He knew that would be difficult for her to accomplish, but she took a breath and spread them even farther.

Rather than fuck her with the thing, he went straight in.

She sucked in a deep breath when he breached her with the widest part of the flare, pressing forward in a single motion.

"Damn." She exhaled and did a little dance as it settled.

"How does it feel?"

"Warm. Massive. Like my stomach has to be sticking out."

"It looks even better than I imagined."

"Really?"

"That hot pink next to your skin? And knowing it will be beneath that black skirt at the club? The bright flash of color? Sensational."

She craned her head, obviously trying to see in the mirror behind her.

"Let me take a picture."

"I... No."

"We can do it with your phone. You'll have complete control of it, and you can delete it immediately."

She slowly nodded. "It's in my purse still. On the table near the front door."

"You can relax while I get it. And by relax, I mean stay where you are. You can bring your legs together a little more and put your hands on the bed. I'll be right back."

He found her phone exactly where she'd said, and he returned to her before taking a few seconds to figure out how the camera app worked. "Show me the plug, sub."

She parted her cheeks for him, and he snapped several shots from various distances and angles. Then he reached forward to show her the photos.

Kelsey studied the picture. "It doesn't look all that big."

"The part holding your anus apart is fairly slender. And the base is less than two inches," he agreed. "What do you think of it?"

"That you could have been right."

"Again," he added.

"As usual." She gave him a slight eye-roll.

"That'll cost you, sub."

"Sorry, not sorry, Sir," she replied.

His little submissive had taken to spankings better than he might have expected. "I'm going to give you a flogging." He put down her phone.

"Yes, Sir."

As she stood, he pulled off his necktie. Though cuffs

would work just as well, better in fact, he loved using his clothing to bind her. "I want you against the wall, your arms held above your head. It could take some focus, but I want you to keep them there. I'm going to give you a taste of what to expect from the Punishment Pole."

"I looked it up online, and I didn't find much."

"It's a design from a Dom in Colorado. Essentially, it's a tall, thick pole covered in vinyl. It has hooks at the top so that the Dom can attach cuffs or straps, forcing the sub to hang on, rather than let herself go. There's an adjustable spreader bar at the bottom. Those of us who've used it enjoy the versatility." He shrugged. "And it's a change from the St. Andrew's cross." He'd let her find out for herself that she'd be able to grind her needy little cunt against it while he was flogging her. "Because you'll be wearing leather, I'll hit you harder than I will this evening."

She nodded.

"We'll take tomorrow off from sceneing," he said. "I'll want your body relaxed. I've scheduled you for a massage Saturday afternoon."

"I'm starting to feel a little pampered, Sir."

"You'll need it."

Without further prompting, she pressed herself against the far wall and stretched her hands above her head.

He tied her wrists together before grabbing the flogger from her bag.

Nathan tested it several times, noticing her wince each time the throngs rent the air. "Tell me you're ready."

"Sir. Yes."

He returned to her and warmed her up with a few gentle leather kisses. Then he pressed his body against hers, hard, pushing her into the wall.

Her breaths came in labored little bursts.

"Do you feel my cock?" He tilted his pelvis so his erection was near her plug, putting force on it.

She groaned and let her arms drop before she caught herself.

"That's it. That's my good sub."

"The fucking plug makes me feel so full."

"Wait until I have my dick up there Saturday night."

"Oh, God. *Oh God.*"

Before he ended up ejaculating, he pulled back and shook his head to clear it. He drew a couple of breaths, being sure his focus was on her before beginning the flogging.

A few minutes in, he stopped to play with her pussy and was rewarded by her wetness. "You're a sexy woman." He put his face near hers.

She turned toward him and he kissed her, capturing her hair, holding her prisoner while he plundered her mouth and made sure she knew how much he desired her.

She rubbed the wall shamelessly as he continued to tease her.

"A few more," he said, moving away and resuming the flogging, leaving her breathless.

He flogged her harder than he had the other night, moving his hand in a figure eight to catch her with both a back and front stroke.

Since she was standing, he knew the flogger would impact her differently. He was able to wrap the strands around her more fully. And he had a more complete swing when he landed strokes on her inner thighs and shoulders.

She began to moan, a soft, pleased sound. And that was its own reward.

He untied her and rubbed her shoulders. "I want you on top of me tonight," he said. "You'll be able to control the depth and speed." Which he was certain she would prefer since she had in a much bigger plug than she was accustomed to.

Within a minute, he was undressed and had donned a condom, not wanting to wait long enough to have her do it for him. When he was lying down, she straddled him.

She used her hand to guide his cockhead to her entrance, and she winced.

"Use lube if you need it," he encouraged.

"I'm wet enough. It's just…"

"Just?" he prompted.

"You're so freaking big, and this plug thing has already filled up all the space."

It was all he could do not to grab her and pull her down. It was sweet, sweet torture for her to take him a bit at a time.

She shifted her weight to her knees, allowing him to penetrate a little deeper.

A moment later, he grasped her nipples and squeezed.

With a yelp, she moved. He took advantage of it and surged up, filling her completely. "How's that?" He backed off the pressure.

"I'll let you know when I'm not seeing stars." A few seconds later, she looked down at him. "This is pretty… amazing."

For him too. Her channel was tight, and the feel of the glass heightened the sensation against his cock.

He wanted her to set the pace as much as she could, because if he did it, he'd come in under thirty seconds.

She began to rock, creating friction.

Determined to heighten her sensations, he tightened his grip on her nipples, and her internal muscles squeezed his cock.

Kelsey lifted herself up and repositioned her arms so that she leaned slightly forward.

Matching her seductive movements, he pumped into her. He released one of her nipples and twisted the other. At the same time he found her clit and rubbed it.

She screamed out as she clenched him hard with her cunt, with her knees.

The force of her orgasm spurred his. His hamstrings contracted as he surged up into her, ejaculating his hot cum.

Afterward, he held her for a long time, snuggled up to her back, his dick between her ass cheeks.

She relaxed into him, and he wrapped her up, wondering how she was going to react when he told her he never intended to let her go.

The outer office door opened, and Kelsey jumped, sloshing some mocha out of the cup.

Nathan closed the door behind him then turned to lock it. "Show me," he said.

Her hand trembled as she put down her drink. She knew what he meant. Even if his tone hadn't been so direct, the color of his eyes — green, spiked with intent — would have clarified things for her. If she'd still been confused, the decisive click of the tumbler falling home would have made his words clear.

He crossed the room and moved aside the chair, clearing a space for her to rest her palms.

"Good morning, Mr. Donovan."

"Ms. Lane." He folded his arms across his chest.

Following orders, Kelsey stood and walked around to his side of the desk.

He'd positioned himself so that she had to work her way in front of him, close enough that her bottom brushed him.

Mouth dry, she placed her palms on the desk and bent over, legs spread. She remembered last night, the way he'd pressed himself against her, making the plug feel as if it were seated even deeper.

This man had an endless number of ways to make her needy.

He leaned forward, pushing her against the desk.

God, he smelled good. Fresh, like spring.

His fingers caressed her thighs as he captured the hem of her skirt and drew it up past the flare of her hips, tucking it into her waistband.

He stroked her skin, and she instinctively tightened her pussy.

Nathan put his left hand on her left hipbone and trailed his right over her butt cheek, before touching the base of the ridiculously large plug.

He found, tugged on it, twisted it, making it move and

her writhe.

"You please me," he said softly, into her ear, sending shock waves of arousal through her. "Very, very much."

Her pussy all but dripped, and she was hungry for him.

Feeling like the fuck slut he called her, she gyrated her hips, trying to get him to touch her.

"I want you desperate by tomorrow."

"I'm desperate now, Sir." Her clit ached, and her whole body seemed on fire.

"Tomorrow, sub," he returned, removing his hand and sliding her skirt back into place.

Her breath and pulse both out of control, she looked at him.

His features were unreadable, but his tone had been serious.

"What?"

"No orgasm until tomorrow. And that includes masturbating."

Kelsey couldn't believe he'd left her unfulfilled, crawling out of her mind. Through his shirtsleeve, she noticed a glow from his watch. "What's that?"

He followed her gaze.

With very precise movements, he angled his wrist then swiped away the thundering heart icon that hovered above the screen.

"Looks as if the software upgrade worked," she said. "The color is more vibrant than it was a couple of days ago."

"More glitchy."

"Look, Mr. Donovan..." She lifted onto the balls of her feet then scooted back to sit on the edge of the desk. Then, more daring than she'd ever been, she reached for his cock. He was fully erect.

She stroked him.

"You're playing a dangerous game," he warned, putting his hand over hers.

"I want you just as ready," she countered. Though he'd managed to prevent her hand from moving, she was still able to squeeze him. "Just as needy."

Heat banked in his gorgeous green eyes. And the heart icon flared to life.

He leaned toward her, and she gently bit his lower lip before licking away the hurt.

"Ms. Lane—"

In her entire life, she'd never initiated a kiss, but she did now.

Within moments, he seized control, devouring her. She realized that it hadn't been a smart move. His dominant instincts were powerful and he possessed her so completely that she was hungrier for him than she had been a few minutes ago.

Knowing she couldn't take much more, she pulled away.

"Be assured," he informed her, "the only thought in my brain right now is putting my dick in you. I will make sure the wait is worth it. For both of us." He released his grip on her hand and took a step back.

She crossed her arms and rested her fingers on her shoulders.

"Tell me one of those cups is for me?" He used his thumbs to tuck her hair behind her ears.

"You know it is." Kelsey realized how quickly they'd fallen into a routine, and they were starting to know each other's habits.

She unfolded her arms and turned slightly to pick up his cup.

He accepted it then raised an eyebrow when he saw the writing beneath the lid. "Boss?"

"Marvin did that."

"What's on the list for discussion?"

Lara's phone call flitted through her mind. Again she wondered whether or not she should mention it to him.

Instead, she moved away from him and went to unlock the door while he took a seat in front of her desk like he did every time they updated each other on events.

"The going-away party for Mr. Newman is scheduled for

263

November thirtieth," she said when she was seated behind her desk. "I'm planning to send a company-wide memo about it this afternoon. I went ahead and ordered him an award for Best Boss Ever."

He winced.

"We'll be holding the party at an events center not far from here. I've got a budget from Zoe McBride for the event. And she said to take it up with Sofia if you have a stick up your ass."

"She said that?"

"I'm paraphrasing."

He smiled, as if he knew she was trying to get to him.

"I'm about done with the budget for giveaways and drawings. As we discussed on Monday, I do want to send everyone home with something that has the Donovan Logistics logo on it."

"Koozies," he said.

"Koozies?"

"Koozies. Like for beer bottles, soda cans. You know, Koozies."

It seemed like an odd directive, but she agreed. "Okay. Koozies."

"Everyone likes them." He shrugged. "Or so Cade tells me."

"Cade?"

"He sells them at the ranch gift shop. We can get you one in December."

The reminder that she might have taken a new job by then jolted her, and she focused on immediate business. "Is this in addition to other giveaways or do you want everyone to take them home?"

"How many people are we talking?"

"A thousand, maybe."

"A couple for everyone."

Her jaw almost dropped. "What happened to you being a cheapskate?"

"No one wants pens. Everyone drinks something."

"By the way, I'm not sure whether or not you realized, but I've removed all the Newman Inland Marine logoed items from the conference rooms and all public areas. New office supplies and cups arrived yesterday afternoon and I made sure they were made available."

"I appreciate you, Kelsey."

"You're welcome, Mr. Donovan."

"By the way, how does that plug feel?"

"Thanks for the reminder." But it wasn't as if she were likely to forget about it.

"I don't suppose you brought nipple clamps?"

"No!"

"I was teasing."

He turned her into a mass of shock and anticipation. "Don't you have billions to earn today? Or save? Whatever?"

"Have a nice day, Ms. Lane. Dinner?"

Confused, she scowled. "I thought we weren't seeing each other?"

"No sex, no flogging, no masturbating, no spanks, no matter how badly behaved you might be. But I didn't say I couldn't feed you."

After spending so much time together, she hadn't been looking forward to spending the evening alone. Last night he'd gone home. As much as she would have hated to admit it, she'd missed sleeping with him.

She was getting far too emotionally attached to him, and that wasn't a good thing. "How about we get some takeout and watch something on TV?"

"No."

"No?"

"If you think I could keep my hands off you while we were on a couch together, you'd be wrong."

In response to his words and the way he regarded her, she twitched, making the plug shift inside her. It was unbelievably erotic.

His cell phone rang, and he checked the screen. "It's Connor. I'll take it in my office." He answered the call as he walked to his office and closed the door.

She stared after him, sure of only one thing. There was no way she was going to make it that long without an orgasm.

15

For the rest of the day, he drove her mad.

Even though they shared an office suite, he texted repeatedly, reminding her not to masturbate. The more she tried not to think about it, the more consuming the idea became.

After work, he took her to a Vietnamese restaurant. When she excused herself to go to the ladies' room, he told her to behave. It hadn't occurred to her to play with herself until he'd forbidden the action.

Despite what he'd said earlier in the day, he'd selected a movie theater where the armrests could be lifted so that he could wrap his arm around her and absently stroke the side of her breast.

When he dropped her off, she expected passion. Instead, he gave her a chaste peck that left her even more frustrated. He reminded her to shave her pussy and be ready to go at seven-thirty the next evening. After soliciting a promise that she would obey all of his orders, he wished her sweet dreams then left her.

She tossed and turned that night in bed then woke up exhausted and set out to find a coffee shop with the largest cup available.

Because she'd gotten up so early, Saturday morning and the afternoon crawled past, no matter how busy she tried to keep herself.

Thankfully, the massage he'd booked for her was magical, and she all but melted into the bathtub when she arrived back home. She soaked for at least thirty delicious moments and took her time shaving her pussy. Her fingers brushed her clit, though, reigniting her.

When she was done, she still had almost two hours before he arrived, so she poured a glass of wine and sipped it while blow-drying and styling her hair then applying makeup.

At seven, she lubed the plug and inserted it before dressing then checking her appearance in the mirror. The boots made the outfit and everything fit fine, but hot nerves still assailed her, so she swiped on a coat of confidence-giving red lipstick.

She paced the floor, from window to the kitchen and back again, burning off energy and killing time.

At seven-twenty-five, a few minutes early, there was a knock on the door.

Her heart stuttered.

Remembering Gwyneth's advice to own the outfit, Kelsey forced down the impulse to adjust her halter top and instead straightened her spine.

The second knock was more forceful.

She opened the door, and the sight of him standing there in black leather pants, boots, a form-fitting T-shirt and his bomber jacket stole her breath. Tonight, he had a sexy shadow on his face, one she knew was deliberate and manicured.

He was every bit the Dom she'd spent months fantasizing about.

Then she noticed he was holding a yellow rose. The man undid her.

"You look even more perfect than I'd imagined," Nathan said. "And I've been imagining plenty."

Air whooshed from her lungs at his approval. "I… Come in. Thank you." She took a step back and he entered, closing the door behind him.

The room seemed to shrink and spin, and she wondered if he would always have this kind of vertigo-inducing effect on her.

"For you." He extended the blossom.

She'd only received flowers a couple of times in her life, and then, only on her birthday. His thoughtfulness touched her. "It's beautiful." She accepted the tight bud and inhaled the fragrance. "Let me put this in some water." She walked toward the kitchen, and he propped his hips on the back of the couch, waiting for her.

"Come here," he said, when she turned back around.

Her boots echoing off the floor, she went to him.

He captured her face between his hands and kissed her hard, ruining her lipstick and making her feel utterly desired. His skilled touch calmed her. How was it that he always seemed to know what she needed?

When she was limp and breathless, he released her.

"Ready?"

She nodded.

"Something you'd like to show me first?"

"Sir?" By measures, understanding dawned. "Of course."

"I want your legs as far apart as you can make them," he said. "Are you physically able to grab your ankles?"

"Yes."

"Then let me inspect you."

Slowly she turned away from him and assumed the correct position.

He flipped up her skirt, moved aside the wisp of fabric that he'd considered underwear then ran his fingers over her pussy and between her labia. His thorough touch made her jerk, and she had to struggle to keep her legs spread.

"Nice job," he told her. "In the future, though, I may want to do it for you."

She wasn't sure she could bear it. "Yes, Sir."

He gave the base of the plug several quick pulls, and she tensed in reaction.

Then he spanked each ass cheek hard. She bit back a scream as she fought for balance. Her anus and her pussy both felt inflamed.

"Now you're ready. You may stand."

She gulped some air as she stood. "That's cruel and

unusual, Sir," she protested.

"I could make you travel with the purple vibrator inside you if you'd like, make you fight off your orgasm," he suggested.

Horrified, she shook her head.

"Then let's go."

He helped her into a lightweight jacket, then she grabbed her purse before they stepped out into the hallway.

Mr. Martinez, in his red robe, froze at the sight of her in her boots and short skirt.

"Good evening," she said to him.

With a huff, he scooped up Sinbad and the ball, mid-roll.

"Good thing I had a jacket over part of it," she said as her neighbor slammed the door.

"It's the boots," Nathan said. "They make mincemeat out of a man's brain. I know how he feels."

"You chose them," she reminded him as they walked down the stairs.

"Did I?"

"You rejected the shoes." Then she relented. "Okay, maybe I fell in love with them."

He helped her into the car then headed for the loop.

The drive through town then south to exurban Houston took forty-five minutes, and her heart rate seemed to increase with each minute.

After exiting the highway, he drove for miles. Homes got farther apart, the land less manicured.

He turned onto another road, heading farther west, and she saw a wrought-iron fence with a decorative but wicked spiked top. Behind it was a row of oleanders.

She was surprised when he was stopped by a security guard at a checkpoint.

After the man verified their IDs, they were waved through.

The driveway seemed to meander forever, flanked by huge hedges.

Eventually what appeared to be a mansion came into view. It wasn't anything she imagined a BDSM club might look like.

He pulled up into a long driveway, and valets opened their doors.

Nathan came around to her side. His bag was slung over his left shoulder. He cupped his right hand beneath her elbow and guided her up the stairs.

Instead of going inside, he drew her to the far side of the wraparound porch where they'd have some privacy. "Before we go in." He put down the bag and lifted out her collar. "I didn't ask you to wear it before now. It's probably a good thing. We scared Mr. Martinez plenty."

She gave a laugh that she knew revealed her skittishness.

"Please lift your hair."

Within thirty seconds, he had her collared.

"Damn. You're even more appealing now." He looped his finger into the D-ring and pulled her close enough for a tender kiss. "You're going to be fine," he told her.

"I trust you."

"That's my perfect sub."

Inside, they were met by a hostess wearing a dark suit and friendly smile.

"Mr. Donovan," the woman said. "And Ms. Lane. Welcome to Deviation."

Kelsey realized then that the security guard had probably radioed ahead. Classy.

She'd expected something dark and maybe shadowy, but this more closely resembled a fine restaurant or boutique hotel. The entryway had a stunning, geometric pattern in the wood flooring, and the club's logo was inlaid. A couch-height table was made from cherrywood, and it was flanked by two elegant Queen Anne chairs. Potted palms provided the area with privacy. An unusual waterfall seemed to run perpendicular to a wall, and lights danced off the splashing drops.

She heard music and voices, but both were surprisingly muted.

"Have a seat, and we'll get the details taken care of."

While the woman took her place behind the desk, Kelsey and Nathan sat in the chairs that were angled toward each other.

"Ms. Lane, I need you to sign the disclaimer and agree to club rules." A pen and the appropriate paperwork were already waiting.

Kelsey scanned the agreement that included the standard legalese but also indicated that Nathan had sponsored her, and since she was a guest, she agreed to remain with him for the rest of the evening. People drinking at the bar were unable to scene afterward. It also indicated that the club's safe word was red. Club Monitors wore black blazers and watched all the happenings and had the authority to stop scenes. Members and guests were encouraged to talk to a CM before intruding on someone else's scene.

The final rules for the common areas were underlined. No sex. No bare genitalia. And women were not allowed to have exposed nipples.

Feeling as if she'd entered a foreign country, she signed her name.

"May I take your jackets?" the hostess asked.

The perfect gentleman, Nathan helped Kelsey before shrugging out of his and turning both over for a claim check.

Nathan placed his hand just above her buttocks and guided her past the plants. As she approached the waterfall, the angle shifted. She stopped to look at it. Then she realized she could see through it as if it weren't there.

"It's a hologram," he explained.

"Wow."

He put his palm on a pad on the wall in front of them.

Like something out of a sci-fi movie, an opening appeared.

They walked through, and her senses were assailed.

Music thumped in a primal beat.

Women danced sensually in cages seemingly suspended in air. She had to look twice, unsure whether or not they were real. They appeared lifelike, but...

The area was open, with only a few benches scattered around. She didn't see any windows, and the back wall changed colors while she watched, from purple to green to red, seething in time to the music.

Floors were crafted from rich wood, so dark they appeared black. The room had stunning architectural features—chandeliers and elegant, Grecian-looking pillars that should have been incongruent with the stark equipment, but somehow it worked.

From her online research, she recognized the St. Andrew's crosses, but they looked bigger, more structurally sound than the ones she'd seen. In a couple of places, people were being bound with colorful ropes. There were a number of sturdy suspension hooks hanging from the ceiling. In the middle of it all was a round pole that had to be at least eight or nine feet tall. Most of it was covered in black vinyl, but the top was glossy wood.

Courage fled, and she stood rooted in place, staring.

Obviously sensing her distress, he guided her to the right, toward a large, private area with chairs, a couple of couches and rows of small, elegant lockers. The top ones had brass nameplates, the others appeared to be available to anyone. Right now, they were the only people in the alcove.

"It can be overwhelming," he said.

She was glad for the reprieve.

While he dropped his bag onto a chair, she studied the surroundings, seeing a cozy, elegant bar off to the left, with waitresses clad in flowing goth-looking dresses.

"We'll have a walk around. Let you get comfortable."

Over here, the music was somewhat muted, and she was able to talk to him conversationally. "I'm not sure whether I can go through with that pole thing."

"There are a couple of others in more private spaces."

"That's not reassuring."

"You don't have to do anything you don't want to do. You have a safe word, and I'll be watching you."

She knew that was true.

Pulling out her leash, he asked, "Are you brave enough for this?"

Ice dripped down her spine.

She forced herself to remain calm so she could think. A part of her found it to be a humiliating idea, but she realized she'd be close to him. Then she remembered the way it had looked the other day. "Yes, Sir," she whispered.

"*Fuck.* Kelsey. Kelsey, my Kelsey." He clipped it onto the D-ring, and she curled her fingers around it. "You okay?"

"I think so." Slowly she dropped her hand. "Yes."

"We'll move at whatever speed you're comfortable with."

She drew a steadying breath.

"I'm going to leave the flogger here. We can come back for it later."

Knowing he didn't expect her to scene immediately reassured her.

"Ready? We can have a soft drink at the bar, if you want. Or we can walk around. Your choice."

"Walk around," she said, curiosity overcoming apprehension, at least temporarily.

He looped the leash around his hand a couple of times, ensuring she was close.

"So fucking proud to be with you, Kelsey."

He made her heart soar.

When they entered the main area, she was surprised that no one seemed to notice them.

She thought, with the way she was on display and a leash, everyone would look at her, but most people were occupied with their own scenes and conversations.

A short woman walked past, followed by a tall blond man, wearing tight shorts and a top that was nothing more than a leather X. There was a leash attached. Another man, wearing only a pouch of sorts, crawled behind his Dom.

What she might have thought was unusual seemed to be the norm.

They walked past a Dom who was flogging a sub attached to a St. Andrew's cross, while a female stood in front of her, a vibrator pressed hard against her pussy. The woman was screaming, her head tossed back.

A Club Monitor strolled over and offered a scarf, presumably to stuff in the poor sub's mouth.

No one stared at any of the scenes. If they were watching, it was from a distance, and there was nothing overt about it. In a strange way, it was like being at any other club.

They passed one of the women dancing in a cage. Kelsey couldn't help but reach up. Her hand went through the image.

"It looks real," he said.

"Eerily so."

"Bonds is part owner," he said against her ear. "He's got a division dedicated to perfecting holograms, believes they'll change the world. Not just prerecorded projections, but real-time ones, meaning he could appear to be in a London meeting, sitting in a chair, or holding court, while he's holed up in California."

While he'd been talking to her, his intimate tone and the heat from his breath made her feel undeniably feminine. "I had no idea," she said. "Having seen your watch, it makes sense."

Nathan led her from the main part of the club and down a hallway to another small, more private space.

Music here was much different, more solemn, a chant of some kind. There were fewer people. There was a pole and a spanking bench. One was occupied by a gray-haired woman in a plaid miniskirt, tight white top, bobby socks and saddle shoes being spanked by a man wielding a wooden ruler.

While they stood there, separated by the scant foot or so of slack that Nathan allowed in the leash, they watched a male Dom approach the pole with his male sub walking in front of him. The sub cleaned the post then moved toward it with no hesitation.

In that instant, she was humbled.

The man got into position and his Dom secured him, as

if they'd done it a dozen times. And maybe they had, she realized.

Nathan drew her to a nearby bench where they could watch without disturbing the scene.

The two were in tune with each other, evidently unconcerned with anyone else.

The Dom's stunning black flogger fell again and again, and his sub appeared to absorb the blows rather than fighting them. The Dom spoke, even though she couldn't make out the words, not that it mattered because it seemed the couple had their own form of communication.

Viewing a flogging was like seeing poetry come to life. She was captivated.

"What's it like for you?" she asked, leaning close to him. The guy on the pole looked relaxed, and the Dom's motions were rhythmically effortless. He occasionally touched the sub to check on him.

"There's not much I enjoy more than sceneing with you. Whether with my hand or belt, and definitely the flogger. I'm watching you, anticipating what you want, what you can need. I'm feeling your reactions. Your pleasure, your pain, your willingness to take it for me... There's an emotional component that's hard to convey, but it's there. An intimacy no one else can share."

She nodded, not sure she understood him exactly.

"Tell me," he said in return. "What's it like for you?"

She glanced back at the man on the Punishment Pole. "I haven't really thought about it much." To her, it was all wrapped up in her feelings for Nathan. Their personal and work relationships were so intertwined that they had become impossible to separate. And the sex... She'd told him early on that she had trouble orgasming with a man. With him, that had never been the case. In fact, she was almost constantly on the edge, something she'd never experienced until the last few days.

The floggings, spankings and the mind fuck that came from them had transformed her.

She realized she had needed a man who understood her, who was as passionate as Nathan and willing to give her what she hadn't known she'd needed.

Knowing he was still waiting for an answer, she came up with, "Empowering."

"How so?"

"You've given me a way to let myself go, to surrender in the moment." She turned toward him and saw that he was intently regarding her. "Having a safe word has given me a way to try new things." She shrugged. "Like getting a spanking with your belt. Being cuffed to your bench. Because of that..."

"Go on."

"I've never been this sexual. And the mixture of pain and pleasure? I like it."

"I'm pleased to be part of it."

They watched the Dom work over his sub for a while longer. Then eventually the pair moved on.

"Are you ready to try?" Nathan asked.

Bravery seemed to be a concept that lived somewhere other than within her. "I'm not sure."

"Since my bag's up front, I won't be beating you. I want you to know what you might expect." He stood and put a small amount of pressure on her leash. "Come with me."

He led her to the Punishment Pole. Even though they'd watched the sub clean the pole, Nathan grabbed a sanitizing wipe and went over it again.

Despite her intimidation, she went up to it and pressed her body against it.

"Raise your arms. Leave them there. Consider yourself tied by my order."

A week ago, that might have sounded ridiculous. Now she understood completely. He wanted her desire to please him to be stronger than any binding.

Nathan bent to extend the spreader bar and tapped her ankles until her feet were where he wanted them.

He hadn't attached her, but the sensation was every bit as

strong as if he had.

"You've come so far, Kelsey. I am so damn proud."

She forgot they were in public and instead remembered them being alone, pressed against the wall. This was no different, she knew. They might be in a public setting that heightened her awareness, but he was still the Dom, and she was his willing sub.

With one hand still holding her leash, he stroked her upper thighs with his free hand then trailed higher, beneath her skirt.

She wanted to accept everything he offered.

He gave her a few teasing spanks. She'd been aroused for over thirty-six hours. And she realized he'd been right to deny her. Her response was immediate, and it wouldn't take much to flame into need.

"What do you think?"

"I'm not."

"Exactly what I'd hoped for," he approved.

Nathan slipped his fingers inside her thong and toyed with her, bringing her to the point she had to fight off an orgasm.

Then, annoyingly, he moved his hand aside.

Frustration seeping through her, she rested her head against the cool vinyl.

"Yeah, you're about ready. Come with me, beautiful sub."

She moved back about a foot and waited while he wiped down the vinyl.

As promised, they went to retrieve his bag, and she was grateful for the reprieve. When they returned to the Punishment Pole where they'd observed the scene, she was much more confident and at ease than she had been.

Nathan removed her leash then asked, "Do you mind taking off your boots?"

She did so while he pulled out cuffs and attached them to rings above her head.

"I want your feet flat on the ground tonight," he explained as he crouched to wrap a set of soft, Velcro cuffs around her ankles. "You're free to use your safe words. And I want you to get everything possible that you can out of this experience."

Goosebumps rose on her arms, and the air conditioning felt extra cold.

"Come here, Kelsey."

Grabbing a burst of confidence, she went to the pole.

He secured her ankles to the spreader bar that he'd already adjusted. "Now reach up your hands."

Nathan stood and tugged her into place then tightened the cuffs one more notch. "Let me know if your shoulders or arms feel numb."

She was stretched almost uncomfortably far, which meant her motions were restricted. There wouldn't be any escaping his lash.

"Do you need anything? A blindfold? Gag? Your nipple clamps?"

The thought of the distraction they would provide made her warm a little. "I thought my nipples couldn't be exposed."

"I can put them on under your top."

"Then yes."

He moved in front of her and reached inside her clothing to tease her nipples until they beaded. Then he clamped each, a little closer to the tip than she ever had. "That freaking hurts, Sir."

"Give it a couple of minutes," he encouraged. "Once we get going, you'll be glad. Otherwise, you wouldn't feel them."

"I'm not sure I believe you."

She turned her head to look when he reached inside the bag again. Her eyes widened when she saw him pull out clothespins. "What are they for?"

"Your toes."

In reaction, she arched her feet, but he'd fastened her so tightly it was difficult to get away.

"Uncurl them immediately."

"I'm scared to."

He raised his eyebrows.

"Do I have to?" She squeezed her eyes closed while she followed his order.

He placed the first one. It didn't hurt as bad as she'd feared, and her confidence rose to heroic proportions. Then he placed another on her other foot.

She rocked her ankles as much as she was able, but the pins wouldn't dislodge.

"Are they painful?"

"No." That wasn't the right word. "It's more annoying than anything."

As he grabbed his flogger, she noticed that the clothespins were becoming uncomfortable and the nipple clamps were starting to bite. Then she became aware that her brain was receiving so much sensory information she couldn't pick out which thing hurt the worst.

"Go with it," he suggested. "If you struggle, it will seem magnified."

She gritted her teeth and rested against the pole.

He skimmed his fingers up her legs and she instantly relaxed. But the funniest thing was that she was unconcerned whether anyone was watching or not. This was about her and Nathan. Self-consciousness vanished.

He tucked her hem into her waistband and rubbed her buttocks. She let the pole take even more of her weight.

"Yes," he said.

As he had done before, he pressed his body against hers. The position was familiar and reassuring, and the weight of him made her feel more secure. But it wasn't just that. His spicy, masculine scene and the dominant way he handled her allowed her to give herself over.

She felt his erection against her. The knowledge he wanted her as badly as she craved him equaled the power balance.

"Do you know what I'm going to do to you, sub?"

"Yes, Sir," she whispered.

"Tell me." He spoke directly into her ear.

No one but her would ever hear him. He was masterful at that, creating a cocoon where she was free to be who she wanted.

"Tell me, Kelsey," he repeated.

"You're going to flog me, Sir."

"Are you going to like it?"

"*Yes.*"

He pulled back far enough to warm her up with gentle spanks, then harsh rubs.

Near her, she saw a woman being led to the St. Andrew's cross. And she heard a gasp as a man was hoisted from the ground.

The volume of the music increased and the wall in front of her was a swirling, soothing pink. Deviation provided an erogenous feast that seeped through her.

Nathan began flogging her.

With a soft mewl, she exhaled.

The leather felt like soft caresses on her buttocks, between her thighs. Because of the outfit, some of the hits licked her skin, others fell mostly unnoticed on the leather halter top.

She was aware of pressure from the clamps and the clothespins and the way he stroked her right forearm. Pain and pleasure merged to become the same sensation.

"You're doing well."

Suddenly he increased the ferocity of the flogging. The strands were no longer gentle, but hard and biting, slicing into her bare skin.

She was aroused and drenched, desperate for the orgasm he'd denied her for so long.

Her body swayed in response to the flogger, and she ground her pelvis against the now-slick vinyl.

"You've earned it," he said softly to her.

He stuck her more often, harder, driving her. She gyrated shamelessly. He continued flicking his wrists, making the strands lick her flesh, and he moved so that he could pull on her clamps.

She screamed as she came, the orgasm lighting her up.

He continued the beating and the pressure on her clamps until she'd completely ridden it out.

She thought he might release her, and she blinked in shock when he kept going with gentle strokes.

But with what she'd already endured, this wasn't enough. "I want more."

"You're amazing, sub." There was pride and approval in his voice.

He gave it to her, cutting back and forth across her body.

The clamps swayed, aggravating her nipples.

He landed half a dozen stripes on her lower legs, and she tried to curl her toes. Stunning pain overwhelmed her. She wanted to protest, but an image of the restrained sub floated through her mind. The man had been serene.

After a breath, she closed her eyes and embraced the flogger.

Her body warmed and tension drained from her. At some point, she became aware of the symphony of the sensations, each unique. On their own they'd be discordant, but together, they helped her to detach from everything.

It was as if she were somewhere warm, floating, her face turned to the sun.

Blissed out.

Her body went slack.

Nothing existed. It was as if she were simultaneously disconnected yet more connected than she'd ever been.

"Kelsey?"

Nathan was stroking the side of her neck and he kissed her forehead.

He plucked off the clothespins from her toes and removed the nipple clamps. She gave a sleepy wince and was aware that it should have hurt more than it did.

"I've got you."

With deft motions, he released her from the spreader bar before unfastening her wrists. He slowly lowered her arms, rubbing her the entire time.

Then he scooped her up and carried her back to the bench.

He sat with her in his lap, and she curled against him, half dozing.

"You were even more magnificent than I could have imagined," he said.

When she finally pushed away from him, she yawned a little.

"I'll be with you in a second," he told her.

Nathan jostled her off his lap and onto the bench then removed the cuffs from her ankles.

He paused for a moment to place his palm alongside her face. Unhesitatingly she turned toward him. The fact he was capable of such profound gentleness astounded her.

As she watched him repack his bag and wipe down the pole, she began to feel more like herself, but chilled, aware that her nipples ached and her toes felt cramped. "I think the sub's supposed to do the cleaning," she said when he returned to her.

"If I've left you with enough energy to clean the pole, I haven't done my job. Let's get some energy into you."

Cupping her arm, he guided her toward the bar. He selected a private corner where they could sit next to each other.

Keeping his arm around her, he ordered her a soft drink and requested a bottle of water for himself.

She was quiet for a while, taking in the ambience, the flickering candle on the table and the pulsing music. The women in the cages were wearing different outfits now, resembling go-go girls of the 1960s. The walls were psychedelic colors, appearing as if they'd been tie-dyed.

The waitress returned with their beverages and left them almost immediately.

"How was it for you?"

"Astounding. Nothing like I expected." She stirred her straw in her drink. "I'm not sure I can put it into words, really."

"The orgasm?"

She glanced at him. "You were right."

"Tell me again."

"It was worth the wait."

"Well, I'm about done waiting."

He went to claim their jackets and have the valet bring the car around. Kelsey was taking the last sip of her beverage when he returned.

"You meant it," she said.

"Yeah. I did."

Within minutes they were in his car, and he surprised her by stopping at a local hotel. "What are you doing?"

"Fucking you senseless," he said.

She laughed. "We could go home."

"We could," he agreed. "But we're not."

He got them a room, grabbed the bag and hustled her into the elevator.

Not shocking her, he had up against the back of the elevator, her arms above her head and his hand in her panties the moment the door closed.

Even though they'd scened and she'd had an orgasm, she was hot and ready.

The bell dinged, and he stepped away as the door opened.

The moment they carded into the room, she tore at his clothes, and he yanked open the laces on the front of her top.

"Leave your boots on," he told her.

"That's unusual."

"I have a sudden fetish for them."

He finished undressing then fumbled with a condom and dropped it on the floor before managing to get it open.

She sat on the edge of the bed and rolled it down him, squeezing and pumping his cock.

"Enough."

He pinned her arms behind her then laid her back, trapped.

Kelsey opened her legs without being told.

He entered her, fucking her hard. Every bit as desperate for him, she returned with thrusts of her own.

"I'm going to take you up the ass."

Her mouth dried.

"You're ready."

"I'm not as certain."

His cock hard and jutting, he helped her to stand then bend over the bed face down.

"I hate this part," she protested, tightening her ass cheeks.

He gave her two hard spanks, and while she was busy squealing, he grasped the base of the plug and pulled it out.

She groaned, relieved to have it out.

"Stay where you are," he told her. "Be right back."

Nathan went into the bathroom, and she heard water running. She was alone long enough for nerves to cool her passion.

The moment he returned, he lubed up his cock then fisted her hair, pulling her head back. "Ask me to do it."

His command, his touch, the way his cock probed her already-tormented ass brought all the intensity back in an instant. "Yes." Her words sounded more encouraging than she actually felt. "Do it."

She soon learned she hadn't needed to be apprehensive at all.

Nathan proved exactly how much he knew her by pressing his thumb against her clit and making slow circles as he worked his massive dick into her ass.

"I can't…"

He slid out, brought her to a heightened pitch of excitement before easing forward again. "You can. You've already taken most of me. The plug was difficult at this point a few days ago."

She gripped the comforter.

He spread her ass cheeks farther apart before playing with her pussy some more. Feeling as if he were breaking her in two, she said, "Fill me."

"Bear down," he coached before thrusting all the way in.

She didn't get the relief she'd hoped for. A plug narrowed near the base, but he was thick, turgid.

After giving her a moment to accommodate him, he began to move.

It was as if shards of reality shattered.

He slid an arm beneath her ribs and lifted her torso from the mattress, allowing him even deeper penetration. She yelped.

She was aware of him bending his knees and thrusting up.

"I'm going to come," he warned with a grunt.

That he was so affected thrilled her. She wanted him to need this as much as she did.

Kelsey squeezed her eyes as he pounded her, filled her.

Being in a hotel room made it even dirtier.

She wanted this. "Come in me, Sir," she demanded.

He managed to grab one of her nipples and squeeze it hard. An orgasm ripped through her, and she involuntarily tightened all her pelvic muscles.

"Oh fuck, yes," he said, his fingers bruising her.

He spurted in her. She felt his pulsing ejaculation more keenly than she ever had when he was in her pussy.

She loved it.

He gripped her as he pumped into her then he dropped his forehead onto her shoulder.

Nathan continued to hold on to her for a long time before going into the bathroom. When he returned, he cleaned her up with a washcloth before climbing into bed and pulling her against him.

"You've got the hottest ass in Texas," he said.

"I do," she agreed. "From the flogging, the plug and the fucking, there's no doubt."

He ran his spread fingers into her hair and turned her to face him. "Tomorrow, we need to have a discussion."

She went cold. "Sir?" What the hell was he saying? He didn't want to see her again? He wanted more? The negative, unwanted images roared in her head, making her thoughts tumble. "I'm not sure what you mean."

"It can wait. Tonight, I'm going to make love to you."

"You can't possibly be ready to have sex again," she protested.

In seconds, he had her beneath him. "I beg to differ."

16

Kelsey was weak for him. Rather than thrilling her, the idea scared the hell out of her.

They'd spent the night at the hotel and this morning, she felt as if she were struggling to keep the inevitable reality away for as long as possible.

"Breakfast?" he asked, coming out of the bathroom smelling like soap and looking like sin.

"Not dressed like this," she said, straightening from having put her boots on.

"We can drive through a Starbucks. Mocha and a scone?"

"You know my vices too well," she said, pretending her world didn't feel as if it were coming undone.

"I'm hoping to add a few more to the list."

She smiled, but it was halfhearted.

"Ready?" He glanced around to be sure they had everything in the bag before zipping it shut.

They left the room, checked out of the hotel then headed for the car. Fog hung low and the day was unseasonably cool. The clouds matched her restless mood. His promised discussion loomed, making her uncomfortable.

"There's a seat warmer if you need to turn it on," he said.

The leather was cool on the backs of her thighs, but she replied, "I'm fine."

He shot her a glance, but she made a show of looking at her cell phone for the coffee shop's address.

After giving him directions, she sat back.

Kelsey told herself that she should be euphoric this morning—they'd had amazing sex, a mind-blowing scene at the club. But all of that contributed to her discontent.

She was in danger of falling in love with him.

There was a good possibility he was preparing to discuss how they would resume a normal work relationship beginning on Monday. A worse option was that he'd want to continue as they were, with him dominating her every evening.

They had only been intimate for a short amount of time, and despite her best intentions, she'd allowed herself to become emotionally attached to him.

There was no way she could go back to a normal boss and employee relationship. Saying goodnight at the end of the day and going home alone, or maybe watching him move on and start dating someone else, would slowly eat at her.

And if he wanted to continue as they were, she'd lose what was left of her heart. There was no way she could stay with Nathan without falling the rest of the way in love. When things eventually ended, it would take a piece of her soul with it.

Too late, she realized she should have never given in to the temptation to find out what she'd been missing.

The drive-through lane had several cars waiting, and the lobby looked empty. "I could go in," he said. "Faster that way."

Her phone chimed with an incoming message. "Sounds good."

"What kind of scone?"

"Maple. And fair warning, I'm not sharing. This is not like chocolate cake. I can and will eat the whole thing."

"After last night, I need something with more protein." He parked then, after turning up his collar, jogged through the gentle drizzle that had started falling from the fat clouds.

The effort to behave normally cost her, and she allowed her spine to relax against the seatback as she checked her phone. She grinned when a picture of Andi showed up.

Wish I got to see Mr. Hottie Boss beat your ass. Was it good?

She typed in a quick reply.

Amazing.

Knew it! Ha! Happy for you.

Andi had added half a dozen smileys, hearts and fist bumps.

At a loss, Kelsey didn't reply. She wasn't sure what to say…share her doubts? Revel in how astounding the night had been? Her emotions were so conflicted that she didn't know how to unravel them.

He returned to the car and offered the drink.

"And the pastry, mister."

"Not sure which one is yours."

She pulled both bags from his hand.

"Never get between a woman and her scone," he said. "Lesson learned."

After she had broken off the end of the scone and popped it in her mouth, she gave him the other bag.

He took a few bites from his egg-and-something-that-smelled-delicious sandwich before indulging in long gulps of coffee. "I may survive until I get you home," he said.

Freeway traffic was still light, and they made it back to her house faster than she'd expected.

"Would you like to come up?" She was only half hoping he'd accept the invitation.

He nodded.

Fortunately Mr. Martinez and the shocked hamster were nowhere in sight.

Once they were in her condo, she wasn't certain how to act. Did he want to spend the day together as if they were a couple? And what would that mean? Running errands, doing laundry, cooking?

She removed her jacket. Then remembering his directive from the first time he'd visited, she offered to take his.

"Thanks."

Because she was chilled, she turned on the fireplace. She

290

was surprised when she turned back around and he was right there.

He captured her bare shoulders in his hands. "It's time we had that talk."

Her tummy twisted into a dozen knots.

"I want you to move in with me."

"You..." Her mouth went slack. She couldn't have possibly heard him. "Move in with you?" she repeated stupidly.

"It makes sense. I want you in my bed at night. I don't like letting you go home late at night, and if I'm here, I prefer to stay. My place is bigger than yours, and there's plenty of room for your photography equipment—for you to have your own space. You can rent out this place or sell it, it's up to you."

He'd clearly been considering this for a while.

"This was supposed to be a short-term thing," she protested. She'd been so prepared for their discussion to go a different direction that she was scrambling to keep up.

"You've had my collar on you, Kelsey. I like it there, knowing you're mine, under my thumb, subject to my whims and discipline."

Suddenly she felt suffocated.

His words were a stark reminder of the person he was and his expectations.

She'd spent most of her life making her own decisions, avoiding men who thought they knew best.

Her sexual attraction to him made his power over her all the more complete. She wanted to please him. But she couldn't do it at the expense of her own goals and dreams.

He tightened his grip slightly. "Say yes," he encouraged.

"I'm sorry." She shook her head.

"Your place is a little small, but we can make it work at least temporarily." He glanced around. "Unless there's a different place you'd like us to consider?"

"Nathan, no. You're not listening to me. I wasn't looking for a long-term relationship. This was only about going to the club, about exploring." *Fuck it all.* He scowled, as if perplexed, and more, hurt. Anything but that. "Living with you won't work for me. I can't be with someone who tells me what to do all the time."

"And you think that's what this is about?"

"You don't?" She pulled away from him and went to stand closer to the fireplace. "You're my boss at work, and if I said yes, you'd be the boss at home, too."

"How is this a problem?"

"Could you be any more obtuse?" Frustration collided with regret. "You want me as a submissive, you just said that, something about whims and disciplines and a collar."

"Of course." He frowned, obviously confounded by her statement.

"That's not what I want." She forced the words past the lump lodged in her throat.

"Is that true?" He folded his arms, making him look all the more powerful and appealing. "You don't like it when I pull you over my lap? Make you bend over? Tie you to the spanking bench?" He took a step toward her. "Or when I tie your hands above your head?"

She loved it. They both knew it.

"Or when I pull off my belt and double it over and you know what's coming? How about when I fuck you? How about then, Kelsey?"

Her mouth dried. "I need some separation," she insisted.

"And you don't want to be with a man who has a constant hard-on for you?"

"Nathan…"

"You have a safe word, Kelsey. You're free to stop any scene. You're the one in charge."

That was the bigger problem. She hadn't wanted to stop any of them. The more she got, the more she wanted.

"How about someone who will protect you, care for you?"

"I've been honest with you from the beginning," she said, her voice cracking. "About my background, about the importance of me making my own decisions. I can't let someone else decide what's best for me. I spent years fighting to get where I am."

"So this…this week has been nothing but a fun little experiment for you?" Jaw set, he crossed to her then brutally dug his fingers into her shoulders, forcing her to meet his gaze. "What we did, what we shared, the fact you submitted to me, wore my collar, fucking or making love meant nothing?"

"You're an excellent Dom." She felt as if she were navigating a minefield. "And it was an experience I'll never forget."

"An experience." His eyes were darkened by daggers.

Clearly he hadn't been prepared for her to tell him no. And likely most people didn't refuse him.

"I want to be clear. You're saying our personal relationship is over. You don't want any further after-hours contact?"

"Unless it's business-related, no." She remained resolute, knowing the exterior was a façade in danger of crumbling.

"Nothing?"

She gave a half-smile, but it faded before it could fully form. "I'll see you at work on Monday."

Tension grew, stretched, dragging her resistance to its limits.

He gave a tight nod.

She exhaled.

He released her, and she rubbed at the marks his fingers had left on her skin.

"No need to show me out."

Nathan stalked to the couch and snatched up his jacket but didn't wait to put it on. She realized that was the most uncontrolled emotion she'd ever seen from him. Under all circumstances, he was cool, collected.

With a decisive click, he closed the door behind him. The precision reverberated with a more pointed statement than it would have if he'd slammed it.

Numb, heartbroken, she sank into the couch and stared at the flickering flames, unable to chase away the cold…and the stunning, shocking hollowness.

"You did *what*?" Andi demanded. "What in the ever-living, Christ-giving, Satan-sucking balls are you thinking?"

That wasn't the type of support Kelsey had thought she'd get from her best friend. But she should have known better. "You're not helping."

"Oh. Sorry." Andi made a show of cleaning out one of her ears. "Okay. Start over. I clearly didn't hear you right."

Kelsey exhaled and reached for her wineglass.

After Nathan had left, she'd sat on the couch for a full hour before she'd forced herself to get up and shower and dress in something other than club wear.

She'd spent the next two hours moving about the condo listlessly, shifting papers, looking at photographs only to put them back down without even really seeing them.

Two days ago her life had been filled with excitement and adventure. And now the adrenaline had seeped away, she'd been left raw.

Unable to stand her own company and her tumultuous thoughts any longer, she'd put on a pair of sheepskin-lined boots, jeans, a jacket and a scarf and headed out of the door.

Mr. Martinez had been in the hallway, and he'd flattened himself against the wall, clutching the lapels of his robe. "Oh. You have clothes on. I was preparing for another heart attack."

She'd shaken her head.

"Twenty years ago, I could have taken that. But now? *Ay, mami.*"

She'd grinned, but she'd remained in place until after Sinbad had rolled past, cheeks twitching.

The man had scooped up the rodent, hurried inside and slammed the door.

Wanting to keep herself busy, she'd headed out for a long walk then ended up in the museum district. Not finding anything to entertain her, she'd wandered around aimlessly. Eventually, feeling sorry for herself and realizing she hadn't eaten anything other than a scone all day, she'd entered a small, trendy restaurant. It was generally the type of place that would energize her. But late on a gloomy, alone, broken-up Sunday afternoon, it had made her even more depressed.

She'd picked up her phone and sent a message to Andi saying she needed company, ASAP.

Andi, true friend that she was, had responded with two questions— *Where are you? Have you ordered wine?*

When the waiter had come over to take her order, Kelsey had ordered a bottle of the restaurant's finest merlot.

Andi had breezed in less than thirty minutes later, sporting a raven-colored bob.

"It's a wig," she'd explained as she'd sat down and filled a glass. "Didn't have time to do my hair. Now. Talk while I drink."

Kelsey had given her a thirty-second update, starting with the fact they'd gone to Deviation and ending with the announcement that she'd ended their personal relationship.

"Give it up, girlfriend," Andi said. "I need more details. Start at the beginning and let me absorb it this time. He got you to Deviation, and then what?"

Kelsey swirled her glass and let the wine dribble back down. "He gave me a flogging on the Punishment Pole. Then we went into the bar while I remembered what day of the week it was."

"Then he ripped your clothes off you in the hotel room? Don't you think it's fucking hot that he couldn't even wait to get you home?"

Especially since he was so conscious of every expenditure. "It was."

"Everything went okay? I mean, you didn't fight or anything?"

"No." She glanced down, remembering the way he'd done her up the ass.

"You're blushing! It must have been good."

"Yeah. It was. We grabbed a Starbucks before heading home. And then he asked me to move in with him."

"You're telling me that Nathan Donovan took you to a club, flogged you hard, got you a nice hotel room, asked you to move in with him, and you rewarded him by dumping him on his hunky-dunky-hottie ass? Have you lost your gray matter?"

"A week ago I didn't even know him."

"The man moves fast, I'll give you that. Is that the problem? Is it too soon for you?"

"No. It's more than that. I don't want to live with any man. Especially one who is so overbearing. Being with him twenty-four-seven all day, every day? I'm afraid I'll lose my sense of independence, who I am, what I've strived for all my life. I've worked too fucking hard to give it up now."

They each took a drink of wine.

"Are you going to be able to keep working with him? When Lorean and I break up…" She rolled her eyes. "Some mornings I just want to stay in bed and sob in my pajamas. One time I did. Ate an entire pint of ice cream for breakfast. And shit… The amount of mimosas I have when things suck just doesn't bear thinking about. Maybe I'll open a liquor store. At least I can make money from myself. Wait. Did that make sense?"

"Yeah. In a strange way." Even though the glasses didn't need to be refilled, Kelsey did so anyway. "Lara Donovan called me the other day."

"Did you tell her I'd give her a free service?"

Kelsey glared at her friend in a way that should have left Andi six feet under.

"Oh. Sorry. We'll get back to that. I'm going to do Erin, thanks to you. Well, Mr. Hottie Boss. Oops. Sorry again. You were saying?"

"She's hiring for a CEO position."

"Who? Lara?"

Kelsey nodded.

"And she called you?"

Again, Kelsey nodded.

"Wait, that's his sister-in-law, right?" Andi whistled. "That's messed up."

"It doesn't mean I would get the job. But she'd like to talk to me about it. Nothing formal, just a talk."

"Are you going to meet with her?"

She exhaled. Until this moment, she hadn't made a decision. "Yeah. I think I am."

"Wow." Andi took a long gulp. "Wow, wow, wow. You'd quit Newman Inland over this or, rather, quit Donovan Logistics?"

"I can't watch him date someone else, move on." And she knew it wasn't possible for her to see him every day and not yearn for him. Worst of all, she was afraid that if she spent time with him, she'd end up begging him to dominate her. The D/s was already part of their relationship, something she liked. Because of that, she was incredibly vulnerable to him. A clean break was better for them all.

"Aww, crap, Kelsey. Did you fall in love with him?"

"It's a good career move," she said. But she wasn't sure which one of them she was trying to convince.

"You did, didn't you? Damn it. Damn you. You fell in love with him. Now what are you going to do?"

"Gotta keep moving forward." Kelsey gave a false, brittle smile. "Companies to run. Dreams to chase."

They ordered a second bottle of wine and a plate of French fries smothered in cheese.

"Anything else?" the waiter asked.

"Ice cream," Andi said. "And chocolate cake."

"Do you want me to bring them out with the French fries?" he asked, sounding incredulous.

Andi glared.

"Got it."

Kelsey's attempt to hold back the pain was failing. Her eyes were full of tears she refused to shed, and she offered a toast. "To the man who has ruined me for all others." And then, damn it, despite the fact she was a strong woman who needed no one, the tears fell.

17

"She's been fucking shortlisted?" Nathan dug his hand into his hair and stared at Connor across the small bar table.

More than an hour before, Connor had called to ask if they could meet for a drink. The request had been so unusual, and he'd been so fucked up since he'd walked out of the door of Kelsey's condo yesterday, that he'd grabbed his jacket and told her he was leaving for the day, offering a brief nod and nothing else as he'd passed her desk. He'd driven to the hotel that housed one of Lara and Connor's favorite restaurants, ridden the elevator to the nineteenth floor, secured a window table and downed one of their finest scotches before his brother had arrived.

Connor had discussed overall business strategy for a few minutes before Nathan had told him to get to the point.

After Connor's drink had arrived and he'd downed it in a single swallow, he'd looked at Nathan straight and delivered the news that Kelsey was among the top candidates being considered for a position at BHI.

"What the fuck do you mean, she's been shortlisted?" he repeated. Through his shirtsleeve, he saw that annoying heart frantically pulsing. But this time it wasn't pink. It was red. Blood-drippy red.

"If you remember, you're the one who said it was okay for Lara to pursue Kelsey as a candidate at BHI."

"I don't give a shit what I said. That was before we acquired Newman Inland Marine. Our research on her was correct. She was more than Newman's executive assistant, she was operating in the capacity of a VP. She knows every bit of the business and is considered a key employee. I want her removed from consideration."

"Think about what you just said," Connor encouraged, sitting back and stretching his legs in front of him.

"You can't have her."

"I'm telling you as a courtesy as your brother, but the loyalty stops there. If Lara wants to hire her, there's nothing you can do to prevent it."

Every muscle in Nathan's neck froze.

"I debated whether or not I should tell you. Seems I made an error."

"I want her name removed."

The waitress had been heading their direction, but obviously sensing tension, she walked away.

Connor leaned forward. "Not going to happen. Donovan has no right to influence hiring at BHI."

"You sit on their board, for Christ's sake."

"And I rarely have input on hiring."

"At the C-level? That's bullshit, and you know it." Nathan narrowed his skeptical gaze at his older brother. Though they'd been at odds several times over the years about business decisions, things had never gotten physical the way they did between Cade and Connor. Nathan respected Connor, both as his older, wiser brother and as a man who'd become CEO of the entire company at far too young an age.

Likewise, Connor had extended his respect to Nathan. Nathan's cool, calculating appraisal of numbers had been a valuable asset to Donovan Worldwide.

They settled their disagreements amicably, with each of them presenting a solid argument until they agreed upon a strategy.

Today was the first time in his life that he'd been tempted to haul off and hit his older brother with a right uppercut to his jaw.

"This seems a little personal." Connor waved the waitress over to order another round.

"It's business," Nathan insisted.

"Is it?"

"What else could it be?"

"You tell me. I understand you took her to Deviation."

"What the hell?"

"Anything you want to tell me?"

"No." Nathan never discussed his relationships with other people. He preferred to work it through on his own. Of course, no one else had ever mattered to him like she did. He'd never invited a woman to move in with him. He'd never wanted it.

Her refusal had stunned him.

For the first time in his life, Nathan had been humbled. He was accustomed to breaking up, not being turned away.

Yesterday, he'd driven around for hours, trying to make sense of the senseless.

What in the fuck had gone wrong?

He'd had her on the Punishment Pole. He'd been attentive, taken care of her afterward. The sex at the hotel had been some of the hottest of his life.

And after breakfast, she'd blown him out of the water.

Finally, he'd gone home, changed clothes, attached his mountain bike to the bicycle rack on top of his vehicle and headed to Memorial Park for several grueling hours.

When he was done, he'd been no closer to an answer.

Though he'd been exhausted, he'd showered then worked for several hours in his home office.

"That's the reason I'm telling you. If she's been shortlisted, it means she interviewed with Lara. I don't know whether or not Kelsey is actively seeking another job, but she's at least willing to consider the idea of leaving Donovan Logistics. As CEO of Donovan Worldwide, I find that information interesting."

The idea that she wanted to leave him had been devastating. The idea that she wanted to leave the company she'd helped grow perplexed him. Unless it was all about him. What the hell had he done so wrong that she wanted to leave his life completely?

Fuck.

"And I'm saying you may want to put in a call to Ted Ramirez at North Star as a precaution."

"I need some time to think."

"It's what you do best. Strategy. Focus on that. We'll talk more in Dallas."

Dallas. He'd forgotten. This might have been the first time in his life that his obsession for a woman had taken priority over business.

"It's this week," Connor reminded him.

"I know. Dallas. I'm on it," he lied.

The waitress brought their drinks.

"Do you want to talk about it?" Connor picked up his drink and regarded Nathan.

"About?" He played stupid. Then memories of his trip to the Running Wind collided in his mind. He remembered driving to the ranch to pull Cade's head out of his ass when he'd fallen so hard for Sofia that he didn't know what day of the week it was.

Nathan told himself he wasn't the same.

Relationships were important, but they were like dessert. Wonderful, luscious, but not necessary. They could be compartmentalized, like everything else. The right amount of attention at the right time, and things were perfect.

Except it didn't seem to work that way with Kelsey.

What the hell had he done wrong?

"You okay?" Connor asked.

"Why wouldn't I be?"

"I don't know," Connor replied carefully. Then he shrugged. "Maybe because your key employee, your personal assistant who you took to Deviation, is considering leaving. It would make most of us pause for reflection."

"Not me." He picked up his glass to take a drink then slammed it down, untouched.

Without a word, he stood.

On any other occasion, the stunning view of the city beneath him would capture his interest. Tonight he hardly noticed.

The waitress moved toward him. "Put my drinks on my brother's tab."

In the elevator, his watch lit up, and the image of Julien Bonds hovered above the screen. "You may want to get a little exercise to burn off some of your energy. I recommend a kale and protein smoothie and more than three hours' sleep so that you can be more effective in your personal—"

Nathan powered down the watch. Bonds' image slowly scattered into thousands of pieces of shimmering dust.

Something more explosive would have suited his mood.

Nathan drove home, pissed.

In his office, he tossed the watch and phone on his desk.

When he'd walked out of Kelsey's house, he'd invited her to contact him when she changed her mind.

Obviously she hadn't.

He stripped off his clothes in the master bath. Damn if he didn't remember her being in there with him too. His entire house seemed to reflect her. Or worse, yearn for her. The study would be perfect for her camera equipment. This place was somewhere she could grow and flourish.

How the hell could she miss what he so easily saw?

Naked, Nathan entered the shower. And thoughts of Kelsey again returned to consume him.

What was it about her?

Yesterday, his ego had stung. He'd been so certain that she'd move in with him that he hadn't considered any other possibility.

When she'd refused, he'd been stunned to the point he hadn't known how to react.

To him, it had been the next logical step.

They worked together well. And outside of work? It was even better. She'd responded to him perfectly, they were in sync. The scene at Deviation had been everything he'd hoped it would be. Yes, she'd initially been apprehensive, but she'd pivoted on that, turning fear into trust. He'd taken her trust and turned it into the most profound pleasure she'd experienced. He'd never been with a sub who suited him so well, whom he had been so in tune with.

Anything he offered, she accepted. And she met it with one perfect word. *More.*

He stroked his turgid dick, forehead pressed against the tiles, picturing her, thinking, remembering.

He was hard, ready.

And he couldn't fucking get there.

His balls were full, and no matter how hard or soft he stroked, he couldn't ejaculate.

Then it occurred to him.

He was missing something.

Something big.

Frustrated, he turned off the faucet. His dick was still erect.

After drying off, he dressed in a pair of shorts before heading back to his office, where he turned on the television. His hair was still damp as he started pedaling his exercise bike, forgetting reality, not watching the news, just allowing his thoughts to tumble over each other.

As he rode, memories flashed by, from his first meeting with Kelsey and her initial distrust, to the chocolate cake they'd shared at Marvin's.

That evening, even before she'd known he was into BDSM, she'd opened up to him. And he recalled her talking about her mother's death and the way her father had behaved.

He took his feet off the pedals and allowed the machine to slowly spin to a stop.

Shit.

That evening, she'd been honest with him, about her dreams, her determination to run a company, her need to prove herself, not just to herself but to her father, for her mother, for her sister.

He'd heard her. But not as completely as he should have. Not as deeply as she needed. As *he* needed to.

Protection didn't matter to her. And she'd proven that she could take care of not only herself, but her sister as well, without anyone's help.

She'd spent most of her life fighting for her independence. In him, she'd clearly seen a man who wanted to take that from her.

But that was the last thing he wanted.

In so many different ways, she'd told him she wanted to be with a man who nurtured her.

How could he have been so sublimely stupid?

He'd been so focused on dominating her and assuming what she wanted that he hadn't taken the time to truly hear what she was asking for.

Independence, and even more, love. Real love. Not a love with expectations and limits, but something that empowered her to express every bit of her personality, to reach for every one of her dreams.

All of it could coexist in a D/s relationship, but he had acted too quickly without taking everything into consideration and thinking it through. After what they'd shared on Saturday night, he'd been hungry for the whole package. He'd wanted her in his bed, in his collar, in his life. And he'd moved too quickly to get it. He hadn't appealed to her heart as well as her brain. Selfishly, probably.

He'd done a hell of a job of screwing things up. He hadn't needed any help for that. But now how the hell did he fix it?

For the second time in his life, Nathan Donovan was at a loss.

"Yeah, sorry, Kelsey. We're out of the chocolate syrup for the mocha."

"What?" She blinked back her disappointment. In all the years that she'd stopped at Marvin's for her morning mix, this was the first time she hadn't been able to get what she wanted. And she'd been counting on it. She hadn't slept well for the last couple of nights, and she'd needed the pick-me-up.

"It's on order," Marvin went on. "Should have it in about

an hour. I can get you a regular coffee, and you can come back for it?" he suggested.

"An hour?"

"Maybe a little less."

"Do you have any spinach and feta scones?"

"Sold out a few minutes ago."

"Before eight in the morning?"

"Been raining," he said, as if that explained everything. "Lot of customers. Tell you what. You come back later, your mocha's on the house. Hate to disappoint my favorite customer."

"No problem." But it was. Now she was tired, heartbroken, thirsty *and* hungry.

She popped up her umbrella the moment she stepped outside and made a dash through the wind and rain.

Under the portico of the building that housed Donovan Logistics, she closed the umbrella, shook it off then headed for the elevators.

Rankowski lifted a hand in greeting as she walked by.

After pushing the button for the fortieth floor, she closed her eyes and exhaled. Until this week, she had never dreaded going to work.

Then again, she'd never stupidly had an affair with the boss.

Yesterday, tension had radiated from Nathan. They had treated each other cordially but had only interacted to talk about business matters. They were back to Mr. Donovan and Ms. Lane, but not in a friendly, teasing way.

She'd sent Lara Donovan a text message around nine a.m. By ten, they'd set up a lunchtime meeting. The meeting had gone well, and she and Lara had instantly related to each another. At the end of the meeting, Kelsey had told Lara she'd like to be considered for the job.

Because of the way she felt about Nathan, she was confident in that decision.

She fucking loved the man. Working with him threatened to destroy her a day at a time.

It had been hard to watch him come and go without remembering the way he'd touched her, the way he'd said dirty things to her that no one else ever had, the way he'd seared the word slut into her ass cheeks.

She couldn't pretend it hadn't happened.

Worse, she couldn't pretend she didn't want it to happen again.

This morning she'd woken up needy. She'd tossed and turned. Finally, with thoughts of him rolling over each other in her brain, she'd turned onto her belly and worked a hand between her pelvis and the mattress until she'd found her pussy.

Since he wasn't there to tell her she couldn't, she'd played with her pussy, thinking about the Punishment Pole, and the way he'd fucked her ass.

Memories of the last look he'd given her before walking out of the door had crashed into her, and the chance at an orgasm had vanished.

In frustration, she'd gotten out of bed far too early and heading to her office to do some work. She'd found herself looking at photographs, though, of Galveston and the Bolivar Peninsula. And she'd recalled his invitation to attend the family meeting at the ranch. The opportunity to take pictures in Corpus Christi had excited her. She also knew that the ranch was home to some unusual birds, including the stunning green jay, something she'd never seen.

She sighed. If she'd been able to accept Nathan's offer to move in, she would have had access to the amazing habitat on a daily basis.

The elevator slid to a stop. She exited before walking down the corridor to the office suite.

As it had been the day she'd met Nathan, the office light was on.

A feeling of déjà vu swept over her, and she paused to check the nameplate on the wall before opening the door and walking in.

Nathan stood there, near her desk, looking like...

He shocked her.

His suit was immaculate, but he hadn't shaved. His hair was unkempt, a lock falling over his forehead, green eyes dark, tortured, looking so ragged that she hardly recognized him as her boss and former Dominant.

She hesitated before adjusting her bag on her shoulder and heading toward her desk. "Good morning, Mr. Donovan."

He pulled up a chair, sat across from her then slid across a gigantic cup that had the word *employee* written on it.

"Your mocha," he said.

She frowned. But recognizing the logo and Marvin's handwriting, she accepted it before putting her purse in a desk drawer and taking a seat. "I'm confused."

"I stopped in. I asked Marvin to tell you they were out of mocha."

"He did." She took a big drink, and the hot, creamy chocolate and coffee taste went a long way toward her forgiving both of them. "I don't understand."

He slid a bag toward her.

"He wasn't out of scones, either?"

"I had a drink with Connor yesterday," he said instead of responding.

She froze, her hand midway to her mouth. "Oh?" She pretended to be uninterested.

"You've been shortlisted for the position at BHI."

Her hand trembling, she put down the cup. She hadn't heard. But he shouldn't have been informed before she was.

"I asked Connor to remove you from the list."

She stood. "Wait a minute! You can't do that. You shouldn't even know I applied, let alone be able to—"

"Stop. Please."

If he'd used a sharp tone or held up a hand, she would have gathered her belongings and left or snapped back, but there was a tone in his voice that she'd never heard before.

"Please, Kelsey. I don't deserve to have you hear me out. But I'm asking. Five minutes of your time. That's all. If you want to be angry, rage, fine. You'll get all the time you want and need to ask me questions and have your say. Please give me the chance to talk. Five minutes. Please."

She sat back down.

"I screwed up. I've had plenty of time to think over the last couple of days. I'm a bit ashamed of how long it took me to figure it out. And unless I'd had that drink with Connor, I still might not have. Let me start over, pretend it's Sunday morning at your condo."

She took a sip, listening.

Obviously filled with nervous energy, he stood.

"I should have asked what you wanted to do with the rest of the day. I should have asked what you wanted out of a relationship, what mattered to you. And I should have listened." He raked both hands in his hair then he propped his palms on his hips, holding back his suit coat. "I'm an idiot. I want you."

Unable to pretend disinterest, she put down her cup again.

"And I want to know from you how that can happen. If you want to move in, I'd love it. If you want to stay at your house a few nights a week, fine. If you want to firebomb my place and build a castle with a turret, fine."

Don't do this to me. This Nathan was impossible to resist.

"I talked about what I wanted from you, but not what I was willing to offer you in return. I want you to chase your dreams and choose whatever life you want. I will not stand in the way of anything you hope to achieve."

"BHI?"

"Even that."

Kelsey reached for a pen and tapped it on her blotter, thinking through what his words meant. She needed to leave him as badly as she wanted to stay.

"And I started thinking about the fact Lara has you on her shortlist. And it occurred to me you should run Donovan Logistics."

She dropped the pen. "What?"

"There's no one better. Even me. You have the trust of the employees, of me. You've got the qualifications and the experience. I think you're suited for it, and I think you'd look good in the executive office. I talked to Newman. He agrees it's an excellent idea."

"And Connor?"

"Agrees with me. Freeing up more of my time for the Dallas deal would be a good thing."

"Are you moving there?"

"No. Even if the deal closes, we'll insert one of our own CEOs. But I would be vacating this office." He jerked his finger toward the open door.

"I'm not quite sure what to say."

"My five minutes are almost up."

"You have more?"

"Yeah. The hard part."

"That was the easy part?"

"I want to marry you."

In stunned silence, she looked at him. This was everything. And every bit as impossible as her moving into his house as his sub. "I—"

"I'm not your father. I want what you want for your life, not what I want you to have. There's a difference."

"It's…huge. My dad only wanted the best for my mom. What *he* thought was the best. And for me."

"We can go as slow or as fast as you want. You can say yes now, tomorrow or in ten years. But I'm in. There is no other woman for me. No one I'd rather have as a sub. No one I'd rather have in charge of this company. No one I'd rather marry. It's you, Kelsey. You. You complete my heart, challenge my brain, satisfy me physically. I love you."

"You…"

"Yeah. The *L* word. I love you. Even if you have nothing to offer in return, even if you don't want to submit to my spankings or have me fuck you hard…"

Everything in her turned molten.

"I still want you to become the CEO. And if that's not

310

what you want, and you want to pursue a position in oil and gas, you have my support. I love you so much that your happiness is the most important thing to me. And you can say you'll marry me. Or not. But it won't change the fact I'd be honored to have you as my wife. As Mrs. Donovan." He scowled. "Or Ms. Lane, if you don't want to change your name. I'm not perfect. I'm going to screw up. You're going to wish I were way more attentive, or less attentive. And I may slip back into my old ways, but I want you to be strong enough to remind me where I failed, and I will do my utmost to make it right. Your terms, Kelsey." As if all of his energy had drained, he sat. "Please put me out of my God damn misery. One way or the other."

It took another full thirty seconds for everything he'd said to filter through her disbelief and shock. "This is a lot."

He gave a half-smile. "That's why I brought you the mocha."

"As a bribe?"

"No. I didn't want you thinking sharply. I was hoping to catch you off guard before you were awake enough to say no."

"Oh, Nathan…"

"God, woman, you wreck me. My heart, my soul. I can't be without you." His voice sounded raw, his words blazed with honesty. And his watch beeped a warning. Impatiently he swiped away the heart and the noise. "Damn thing doesn't let me act as calm as I pretend to be."

This. This was what she'd wanted. Happiness, and someone to share it with. A man who wasn't just ordinary, but one who would demand a lot from her in return for what he offered. "The marriage thing is a little sudden."

"You can take your time, as much as you need. Are you done yet?"

She shook her head. "Do you ever change?"

"It's not going to be easy." He shrugged. "*I'm* not going to be easy. But both are worthwhile. Please save my soul by saying you love me."

"I do. I've been halfway in love with you for a while. And I knew it for sure on Sunday."

"You have an odd way of showing it." He shook his head.

"I couldn't go back to a regular work relationship, maybe watch you date. But I knew if I continued to be your sub after hours and moved in with you, I might lose track of my goals. Getting a little distance for both of us could be a good thing."

"As long as you give me everything when we're together. The rest we'll figure out." He spread his legs.

Overcome, hardly able to think, she stood. One thing she did know. More than anything, she wanted to obey his command.

Kelsey went to him, collapsed against his chest and allowed him to wrap her in his arms.

He rubbed her, stroked her then he put his hand in her hair and pulled back her head to give a kiss that ignited her senses and left no doubt of his feelings or commitment. "You're mine, Kelsey. I'm going to spend the rest of my life proving it."

With This Collar

Excerpt

Chapter One

"And now, friends, Lana will offer her submission to her new husband," Damien Lowell said.

Julia scowled. Submission?

Lana and Julia had chatted on the phone earlier in the week to discuss the final wedding plans. Lana had warned that the union would be a bit untraditional. She'd been vague about the details, but she'd made Julia promise to say nothing during the ceremony.

They'd been friends since they were ten, and there was no way Julia would miss the festivities, even if they were a bit odd.

Until now, everything had been what she'd expected.

Lana and Ben were being married at their friend Damien's mountain home. Damien was also performing the ceremony.

About two dozen of the couple's closest friends had gathered in the great room and, at dusk, Lana had descended the stairs of Damien's picturesque home, carrying a single, beautiful, white rose to match her full-length gown.

The only gift requested had been a candle. In a romantic gesture, the pair had said they wanted all their friends to light their way into their future.

As Ben and Lana had joined hands and faced Damien, fat snowflakes had fallen from the cloudy sky. The vows had included the word obey, which was somewhat unusual among their circle of friends. But everything else had been normal. Lana had placed her rose on the mantel behind Damien before she and Ben had exchanged rings.

"Lana?" Damien prompted.

"Yes, Sir," Lana said.

'Sir'? Until tonight, Julia hadn't met Damien. She knew he was a friend of the groom's, and he was drop-dead, movie star handsome. The man had rakishly long, dark hair that curled at his nape, and he wore an indefinable air of command as easily as he filled out his charcoal grey suit. But still, for her friend to call him 'Sir'…?

Lana cast her gaze at the floor and gracefully turned her back to her new husband.

Ben undid the row of tiny buttons that held her gown closed.

What the hell?

Ben drew the material from Lana's shoulders and let the dress fall to the floor.

Lana, wearing stacked heels, a merry widow and stockings, stepped out of the dress, and another man scooped it up and laid it across a chair.

Like Damien, this man was also ridiculously tall. That was where the resemblance ended. This man had an olive complexion that hinted at a Mediterranean background. His head was shaved. He wore black jeans and a black T-shirt that revealed a number of tattoos. A thick, knotted silver bracelet adorned his left wrist, and a silver stud pierced his right earlobe. He could have been a pirate in a former life.

Suddenly *unconventional* took on a whole new meaning. Julia had never been more distressed. Part of her wanted to make an escape, and a bigger part of her wanted to shake some sense into her friend. But she was riveted in place by her promise to remain silent.

With a grace that spoke of practice, Lana knelt.

Jesus. All through college, they'd each vowed to keep their independence. They'd pushed against the glass ceiling, and they'd fought for their positions in corporate America. And now her friend was kneeling in front of her husband, almost naked, for their guests to see?

Julia wondered if she was the only one who was frozen in shock.

Lana spread her legs a bit farther apart, and she leant forward to kiss one of Ben's shoes.

Julia gasped.

From the front of the room, Damien looked over his shoulder at her, his eyebrows raised.

Firm, relentless hands landed on her shoulders. Her heart rate increased with her panic.

"Be quiet," a man whispered harshly into her ear.

"I—"

"I said be quiet."

She gritted her teeth. The man's tone was commanding.

He pulled her back a bit, and she inhaled the unmistakable—and sexy—scent of leather.

In that same rich and rough, for-her-ears-only voice, he added, "Or else I'll haul your sweet ass out of here and turn you over my knee."

For the first time in her life, she was rendered speechless.

"Lana's doing this of her own choice," he continued.

She struggled against his grip, but he dug his fingers deeper into her flesh.

"Surely she told you to expect some unconventional things."

"But—"

"Trust her," he urged. "Like she trusted you."

When Julia had given her promise, she'd had no idea what that had meant or how difficult it would be to keep her word. Julia spent her entire life in control, and she hung out with women like herself. And now a powerful man had her imprisoned while her friend was on her knees in front of a roomful of people. The experience was surreal.

With unshakable force, the man pulled her back a few steps so they were several feet away from the rest of the guests. He held her firmly against his body.

She still hadn't caught a glimpse of her assailant.

"Do you really want to make a scene and embarrass yourself as well as your friend?" he asked softly. "Nothing you do or say will stop tonight's proceedings. So I recommend you behave yourself."

"Damn you."

"Last warning," he said.

His tone rang with an authority she didn't dare question. He was speaking quietly, but that made his words all the more terrifying. He'd threatened to turn her over his knee, and in that instant she believed he'd do it. She stopped fighting. "Who the hell are you?" she demanded in a whisper.

"Marcus Cavendish. A Dominant, and friend of the groom's. I met Lana about six months ago. She's come a long way in the lifestyle. Ben's a lucky man to have earned the submission of such a lovely woman."

Julia felt as if Marcus were speaking a foreign language.

"If you promise to behave yourself, I'll explain what's happening."

She nodded.

At the front of the room, Lana stood and faced Ben.

"Would you like to offer your submission?" Ben asked.

Lana tipped back her head. "Yes, Sir, I would."

Damien picked up something from the mantel and offered it to Ben. Julia stood on her toes, trying to get a better look.

"To the vanilla world it looks like a silver necklace with

316

a lock on it," Marcus said. "But those of us in the lifestyle recognise it for what it is. A collar."

"Collar?" Julia repeated. The word startled her so much that she didn't think to ask what he meant by lifestyle.

"Some people use dog collars from the pet store," he said.

"You can't be serious."

"Deadly."

She wrapped her arms around her middle. "In this case, it appears to be an ordinary piece of jewellery, but it likely has a hex screw so that she can't remove it."

Ben accepted the necklace from Damien and passed the chain through the flame of an enormous candle.

"He's purifying the metal," Marcus explained. "And then he'll ask her again if her submission is given of her own free will."

Ben looked down at Lana and captured her chin before saying, "I offer you this collar as a symbol of my love, and as a promise to be a kind, consistent and honourable Master. In return, I will demand your servitude. I will enforce the rules we have agreed to, and I will never touch you in anger."

Lana linked her hands at the small of her back, while she continued to meet her new husband's gaze. Firmly she said, "I accept your gift. In return, I offer my humble devotion and a promise of my servitude."

To Julia, the words sounded just as practised as their traditional vows had.

"We're here in front of our friends and mentors, and I want everyone to hear your assurance that you are willingly agreeing to be my slave."

The blood chilled in Julia's veins. As if Marcus sensed it, he tightened his grip on her. Oddly, the touch reassured and grounded her rather than annoyed her.

"I am joyfully agreeing to be your slave, Sir."

Even from the distance and in the dim lighting, Julia saw Lana's smile.

"In fact, I'm begging for the honour. Sir, please collar me."

"Lift your hair," Ben told Lana.

Lana did. As Ben secured the lock in place, Lana looked up at her husband with an expression of surrendered bliss. Julia wondered what had happened to the woman she used to know. The two of them had sat on their dorm room couch eating popcorn, drinking wine, and making fun of old 1950s television shows where the wife cooked dinner in high heels and a dress. And now a man was placing a collar around Lana's neck, and she'd asked him to do so.

Without being instructed, Lana knelt again. She cast her gaze at the floor. Then Ben gently placed his hand in her hair and eased her head back. Lana looked up. "Thank you, Master."

"Master?" Julia whispered, more disturbed than she ever remembered being.

"Not all couples use that term, but they have elected to do so."

"Ladies and gentlemen," Damien said, "May I present Master Ben and his slave wife, Lana."

"Slave?"

Marcus again tightened his grip on Julia's shoulders, silently warning her to be quiet.

Ben pulled Lana to her feet and kissed her deeply. It wasn't a friendly peck, it was a hot French kiss. He had one hand on Lana's bare bottom, and the fingers of his other hand were spread wide across the middle of her back.

Lana shamelessly rose onto her tiptoes and pressed herself against Ben. Julia had never seen anything so sexy at any other wedding. Her friend was showing pure, unadulterated happiness, and no one seemed to notice she was only half dressed.

Some people applauded, others hollered and gave catcalls, but Julia kept her hands wrapped tightly around her middle.

"A toast!" the man who'd picked up Lana's discarded gown called out.

On his cue, several servers moved into the room, bearing

trays filled with glasses of sparkling wine. Their attire shocked her. Men wore bow ties around their necks, but no shirts. One had on a tight-fitting pair of shorts, the others wore slacks at least one size too small. The women wore aprons with thongs, stockings and garters.

"What the hell is this?" She turned to face her nemesis.

"A toast," Marcus said drily. He snagged two flutes from a passing server and offered one to her. "And you're going to continue to behave."

A sense of self-preservation didn't allow her to challenge him. Truthfully, looking at him had sucked the oxygen from her lungs. Rugged and broad, he looked at ease against the Rocky Mountain backdrop. His hair was dark, cropped short to emphasise his bright green eyes. He wore black boots and slacks, a crisp, white shirt and a soft, black leather blazer. His scent spoke of raw masculinity.

"They're half undressed," she said.

"Are they?"

Was she the only one who had noticed how bizarre the event was? No one else even blinked. She accepted the offered glass and wished it wouldn't be unladylike to gulp its contents.

"Face the happy couple," Marcus instructed.

When she opened her mouth, he raised his eyebrows. Having had a look at the size of his hands and their assorted nicks and abrasions, she wouldn't put it past him to follow through on his earlier threat to turn her over his knee.

His air of authority annoyed her as much as her instinctive response to him. She was a modern woman who ran an entire department at work. Julia didn't have a problem with a man being in charge. She had definite problems, however, with domineering men — like the one she was looking at.

"Do it now," he told her. "I will not tolerate your rudeness."

Rude? Her manners were impeccable. Or, rather, they had been until this evening.

Bristling, ready to make her escape as soon as possible,

Julia faced the front of the room, the impossible Marcus Cavendish standing next to her. She couldn't help but inhale the sexy scent of his leather blazer and, this close, she noticed other subtle undertones. He smelt crisp, like the Rocky Mountain air. There was a layer of something spicy as well, maybe from his soap.

He was all man, with a capital M.

She tried not to let him overwhelm her. But something elemental in her responded to him.

"To a long future filled with happiness," Damien said. He was standing next to the duo, and all of them were facing their guests.

Damien raised his glass and everyone, including her, followed suit.

The bride and groom clinked their glasses together then sipped.

After she'd taken one drink, Ben took Lana's glass and placed it on the hearth.

Julia clenched her teeth.

But no matter how much she might want to deny it, the truth was, she'd never seen Lana look more radiant. She didn't appear concerned by her lack of clothing, and she'd barely taken her adoring gaze from Ben's face.

For a moment, Julia stared before shaking her head. She'd never have suspected Lana would be such a doormat for any man. When the three of them had met for dinner two weeks ago, Julia would never have suspected Ben would be capable of this kind of behaviour. He'd been solicitous of Lana. Sure, Julia had found it a bit odd that he'd ordered Lana's meal for her, but he'd consulted her first, and the two had touched constantly. Julia had found their relationship endearing. She'd never suspected what went on when others weren't around.

She couldn't make Lana's choices for her, but Julia was sure of a few things—she'd never allow someone to determine when she'd had enough to drink. She would never kneel for any man. And she would certainly never let anyone put a collar on her.

"Refreshments are available in the dining room," Damien said. "The bride and groom will join you shortly. In the meantime, please, make full use of the house." He flicked a glance, she was sure, in Marcus' direction before adding, "The dungeon is available should anyone need it."

The crowd began to move away, some people towards the dining room and others towards the stairs, obviously accepting Damien's offer.

She intended to speak to her friend then make her excuses and leave. Marcus placed a hand on her shoulder, holding her in place. She was reeling from shock. "This house has a dungeon?"

"It does. In BDSM circles, his house is known as the Devil's Den."

"Seriously?"

"He didn't choose it. But since his name is Damien..." He trailed off.

She rolled her eyes.

"But it was easier to agree to meet out at the Den—outside of Denver—than to keep saying Damien's place. Then somewhere along the line someone added Devil—the press, I believe during an exposé—and it stuck. Some of us long-term guests still call it the Den. The dungeon has a punishment horse, a St Andrew's cross, stocks..."

"Thumb screws?"

"You could call it fully equipped."

She was so stunned she was unable to speak.

"Would you like to see it?"

"Good God, *no*."

"Pity. I'd love to see you on the cross."

"That, Mr Cavendish, will not happen."

"We'll see." He regarded her, and she did her best not to squirm. It was as if he saw through her words and into her darkest fantasies. "As Damien said, Ben and Lana will be back later." He nodded towards the couple. "They'll be performing a rose ceremony in private."

Lana and Ben picked up the roses they'd placed on the mantel. Even from across the room, Julia noticed both roses still had thorns. Ben's was red, in full bloom. Lana's was white, and barely beginning to open.

Damien led the two from the room. Lana followed her husband, a couple of feet behind him.

Julia finished the rest of her drink, then placed the empty glass on a server's tray.

"Another, ma'am?"

"No, thanks." She needed to get out of there. The entire evening had been too much. From Lana removing her gown and kneeling, to Ben locking a metal contraption around her neck, to servers who were dressed in little to nothing. And the house had a dungeon?

"Be grateful you were invited," Marcus told her. "Most times collaring ceremonies are closed to the outside world."

"Are you telling me I'm the only one here who feels as if she's fallen down a rabbit hole?"

"Probably, yes."

Behind him, a woman in spiky heels and a short, short skirt put a hand on her companion's shoulder. Julia stared, wide-eyed, as the tall, broad man knelt. The woman then pulled something from her pocket and affixed it to a collar around the man's neck.

"Is that..." She trailed off, unable to complete her sentence.

"A leash," Marcus supplied, looking at the pair. He took another drink and looked at her over the rim of his glass.

The woman walked from the room and the man trailed, on all fours, keeping some slack in his lead.

"I need to go," Julia said, shocked that she could find her tongue to speak. She'd never imagined something like this was possible.

"Aren't you in the least bit curious?"

"About what? People behaving this way? I'm more disturbed than anything. Appalled, even."

"Those are some harsh words."

"I would never allow myself to be treated like that!"

"Like what? Someone who is deeply cared for?"

"If that's how someone is treated when they're being deeply cared for, count me out."

"Just a moment before you go issuing uneducated proclamations," Marcus said, his tone unrelenting.

This was a man accustomed to issuing orders and having them followed. She bristled, but she was also feeling seduced by his authority. The insinuation that she was judgemental rankled.

"Did you see him protesting?" he asked. "Do you see anyone here being forced to do anything against their will?"

"Did you see what just happened?" she countered. "That man was just put on a leash."

"He's a big man. Do you suppose the woman with him, at least a hundred pounds lighter and six inches shorter, could have done that to him if he didn't want to be leashed?"

Julia scowled.

"And, furthermore, you'd look beautiful leashed."

"I'm not ever—"

"Don't say things you may have to take back," he interrupted smoothly.

"That's a pretty arrogant statement."

"Tell me your name," he said, sidestepping her comment and defusing her indignation.

They were having this kind of conversation, and they'd never been introduced. Could this event be any more surreal? "Julia Lyle," she said finally.

"Ms Lyle, the pleasure is mine." He placed his drink on a nearby end table and extended his hand in greeting.

Mindful of what he'd said about rudeness, she accepted. Shaking hands seemed so...normal, a polite societal construct that she could embrace and understand. It momentarily grounded her.

He held her too long, though, and when she would have pulled away, he raised her hand and kissed it. He looked at her, imprisoning her gaze.

Electricity lit up her nerve endings. Despite her

reservations, she was attracted to this man. She'd dated her fair share of men, and she'd been in a couple of long-term relationships. Unfortunately, the last man she'd been involved with—Jason—had been rather domineering. At first, he'd been charming and wonderful. Over time, after she'd allowed him to move in, he'd tried to control her, choose her friends, isolate her from her family.

The experience had left her determined not to let any man make decisions for her ever again.

So why was she so attracted to Marcus Cavendish? Untamed energy beat in her when he touched her. Power exuded from him, and it was slightly intoxicating. He was dark and dangerous. In short, he was everything she shouldn't want, everything she'd vowed to avoid. Yet she wanted to continue talking, despite the fact that her instinct urged her to run.

"I've been a friend of Ben's since college," he said.

"Has he always been this way?"

"A Dominant? I suppose, yes. He was a natural leader, even in school. So that he would behave that way in a relationship makes perfect sense."

She extricated her hand. "I'm not sure what you mean by that."

"Has Lana told you nothing about her lifestyle?"

Julia shook her head. "I knew she and Ben were doing things she labelled as kinky, but I think she probably should have told me more, or else not invited me this evening."

"Everyone has heard about BDSM."

She nodded. "Of course. But it's a bit different seeing it in person. I thought it was all about toy handcuffs, maybe a paddle."

"Let's go somewhere a bit quieter."

She thought about it for a moment. If she were as smart as she liked to think she was, she'd go outside and get in her car, drive back to her normal life and normal job as a statistician in Denver, forget this event had ever happened, pretend she had never met the overwhelming Marcus

Cavendish, and ignore the adrenaline urging her to follow wherever he led.

But she wasn't sure what had happened to the logical and linear part of her brain that made her such a good statistician. She was behaving like a female to his larger, commanding male. Biology. Her attraction was nothing more than basic biology.

Without waiting for her response, Marcus took hold of her elbow and guided her into the sunroom. She knew she should have protested, but she didn't — couldn't.

There were no other people in the room, and he continued to hold on to her until they stood in front of a floor-to-ceiling window. Since it was dark, she could only make out vague shadows. Being here, with him, felt intimate.

Because she needed to for her sanity, she pulled away from him. She turned to face him, arms folded.

He propped one foot on a window sill, obviously unconcerned by her hostile body language.

"Some people do use handcuffs in the bedroom, like you said. Maybe a scarf as a blindfold. All that is well and good, if it works for the couple. Some of us prefer something more complex, something that's as emotional as it is physical. To many people here, BDSM is a much more serious construct, not just an occasional playtime in the bedroom. Some of us indulge twenty-four seven."

"I'm not sure I understand."

"Every relationship between a Dominant and submissive has an agreed-upon power exchange. You heard Ben ask Lana if she willingly offered her submission. He didn't demand her servitude. He didn't threaten or compel her response. She gave it."

Julia waited.

"In return, you heard Ben promise to care for her. They negotiated their agreement over time, then they asked trusted friends to witness their public vows. Lana gave him power. He didn't take it."

"And I'm sure she can revoke it at any time," she said, her

tone tinged with sarcasm.

"Actually, she can. Most subs and Doms have a safe word, or even a series of them. A sub will use an agreed-upon word or term if she or he is feeling scared or if something is too much to handle, either physically or emotionally. The most important thing is communication. Most relationships could benefit from having that kind of arrangement, something that's discussed ahead of time. No person can be a Dominant without the other agreeing to be the submissive."

"It sounds like abuse to me."

"Does it?" He raised his eyebrows, and she squirmed beneath his scrutiny. "You've been friends with Lana for a long time, I assume. Since she met Ben, has she looked like an abused woman to you?"

Actually, she'd been giddy. Julia, Lana and a few friends had been at a martini bar on Larimer Square celebrating Lana's last days as a single woman when talk had turned to sex. Lana had been grinning and giggling as she had told stories about Ben spanking her and binding her wrists to their headboard.

A couple of the other girls had admitted they'd done similar things, and that, scandalously, they'd enjoyed it. They'd encouraged Julia to loosen up and be a bit more adventurous. Honestly, she had been intrigued by the ideas. She just hadn't been with a man she had wanted to try it with. That night, though, with her supercharged vibrator, she'd had a few wicked fantasies...

"Julia?" he prompted.

"I thought they just had an occasional wild evening. I didn't know they did this..."

He waited. "This?"

"You know, doing everything he tells her."

"Despite what you may be thinking, he doesn't just tell her what to do and have her jump to his bidding. Everything between them, everything, including punishment, is consensual. Ben will not beat Lana without her agreeing to

326

it."

Julia shivered. "That's horrible."

"Is it? I'd be willing to bet your friend has more orgasms in one night than you've likely had in the last six months."

"Excuse me?" Suddenly, she was pissed off. "You don't know anything about me."

"Lucky guess," he said. "But with your reactions tonight, you seem like a woman who has repressed sexual needs. You jump when I touch you. And when I use this tone..." He dropped his voice an octave or two. The sound sent little skitters of awareness up her spine. "You need the right man to set you free."

"Could you be any more insulting?" She tilted her chin, hoping to project a confidence and disinterest she was nowhere close to feeling. "Are you always such an overconfident jerk? Let me guess, that's why you're here alone."

He didn't react, other than to smile. That infuriated her.

"Come on, Julia. Admit it. You might be protesting, but only because you think you should. Deep down, you're intrigued."

She curled her hands into fists at her side, more to keep him from seeing the way she was trembling than anything else. Damn him—he had snared her interest.

"You're wondering what it might be like to surrender to a man. More specifically, you're wondering what it might be like to submit to me."

"Not in this lifetime."

"When Lana was talking about the things she and Ben do, you listened, maybe even fantasised about being spanked, feeling an unyielding palm on your ass cheeks, perhaps being tied up helplessly while you wondered what would happen next. And tonight, you pictured yourself in Lana's place, kneeling in front of a roomful of people."

She coolly met his gaze and pretended her heart wasn't racing. "You're out of your mind. That will never happen."

"You want to be taken in hand. You want to have someone

enforce the limits so that you can release your fear and freely experience everything."

She knew she should leave. Now. But she was fascinated, even as she was repelled.

"How would you react if I dug my hand into your hair, dislodging those carefully placed pins, then tugged hard, forcing your head back and holding you tight for my kiss?"

"You'll never know, Mr Cavendish." And if she persisted in her protests, neither would she.

"No?"

He dropped his foot from the window ledge and took a purposeful step towards her. Apparently unconcerned by her forceful words, or totally disbelieving them, he took her by the shoulders and turned her to face him.

She stood her ground even though there were only inches separating them. The breadth of him filled her vision. His proximity overwhelmed her. If there had ever been a man to tempt her, it was this one.

Gently he traced the column of her throat. "Your mouth says one thing," he commented, "but your pulse betrays you. The way you bit your lower lip betrays you. The way you're trembling betrays you."

"Maybe I don't want you touching me."

"Maybe," he agreed. "So tell me to stop."

It wasn't just the scent of him that made her oh so aware of being a woman. It was also the seduction in his voice. He was speaking softly, so no one but her could hear him, and the rough gentleness made shivers dance down her spine.

He moved his hand so he could stroke her cheekbone. Julia stood there, mesmerised.

He captured her gaze, as if she were the only woman on the face of the planet. Despite her best intentions to prove him wrong, she dropped her hands to her sides.

"Shall I keep going, Julia?" He imprisoned her chin. "Or have I offended your feminist sensibilities with my boldness?"

None of the men she'd been with had evoked this kind

of response from her. She'd had sex before—plenty of it—but she'd never been this aroused from something so simple. They'd been focused on their pleasure, rather than hers. Most of her boyfriends had performed the requisite foreplay, including eating her out, but none had taken this much time talking, looking, exploring.

"You're beautiful, Julia. I'd love to see you naked, helpless, supplicant, on your knees with your mouth open to receive my cock."

"I've told you that will never happen." But... *God.* Her protests sounded hollow, even to herself. In truth, his words overwhelmed her, made her tremble. He wasn't really saying these things to her, was he? She'd never enjoyed giving head, so she'd avoided it whenever possible. But heaven help her, she was so turned on.

"I'm not insulting you. I'm encouraging you to embrace all of who you are. There's no shame in being a submissive. In fact, it's very powerful. You're always in the driver's seat. You always have the control."

Her heart beat madly. He couldn't possibly be right.

"You want it, too. Admit it."

"No..."

His touch, commanding and compelling, felt as if it were everywhere at once. He ran his fingers across her nape, then pressed his palms against her back to draw her closer. He followed through on his earlier promise and dug his hand into her hair. She heard a series of soft *clinks* as pins dropped to the hardwood floor. Since her hair was such a riotous mess, she generally kept it pinned back or in a ponytail. But now, unconfined, it fell over her shoulders.

Being unconstrained this way made her feel slightly wanton, and she leaned closer to him.

"This will be consensual. Tomorrow, there will be no doubt you were a full participant in whatever happens tonight. Do you understand?"

Excitement drugged her. She felt his forceful grip on her hair. Shockingly, the pain only added to the bombardment on her senses. She wanted *more*.

"Ask me, Julia. Ask me to kiss you, to squeeze your nipples, to bring you off right here in the sunroom where anyone can see you surrender to me."

His words stunned her. She blinked, then stared at him.

"Ask me," he repeated. "Or tell me to release you."

More books from
Sierra Cartwright

Book two in the best-selling Mastered series

It was business only… Chelsea Barton is terrible at the whole submission thing, and she wants to snare the Dom of her dreams.

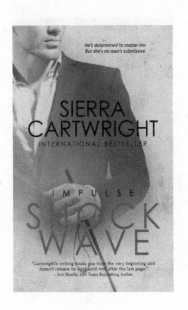

Book one in the Impulse series

There can only be one victor…

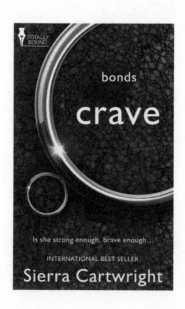

Book one in the best-selling Bonds series

*She still craved him… The sight of a collar in her
boyfriend's drawer had stunned Sarah. Panicking, she had
fled. But no other man has ever been his equal.*

INTERNATIONAL BEST SELLER!

BOUND AND DETERMINED

SIERRA CARTWRIGHT

He will have her…

About the Author

NO 1 INTERNATIONAL BESTSELLER & USA TODAY
BESTSELLING AUTHOR

Sierra Cartwright was born in Manchester, England and
raised in Colorado. Moving to the United States was
nothing like her young imagination had concocted. She
expected to see cowboys everywhere, and a covered wagon
or two would have been really nice!

Now she writes novels as untamed as the Rockies, while
spending a fair amount of time in Texas…where, it turns
out, the Texas Rangers law officers don't ride horses to
roundup the bad guys, or have six-shooters strapped to
their sexy thighs as she expected. And she's yet to see a
poster that says Wanted: Dead or Alive. (Can you tell she
has a vivid imagination?)

Sierra wrote her first book at age nine, a fanfic episode of
Star Trek when she was fifteen, and she completed her first
romance novel at nineteen. She actually kissed William
Shatner (Captain Kirk) on the cheek once, and she says
that's her biggest claim to fame. Her adventure through the
turmoil of trust has taught her that love is the greatest gift.
Like her image of the Old West, her writing is untamed,
and nothing is off-limits.

She invites you to take a walk on the wild side…but only if
you dare.

Sierra Cartwright loves to hear from readers. You can find
contact information, website details and an author profile
page at https://www.totallybound.com/

TOTALLY BOUND

Home of Erotic Romance